Jack Dumont

D1470349

The Hands of Fate

By Jack Dumont

Vol. One – The Legacy

Without forgiveness, there is only death.

Anonymous

<u>DEDICATION</u>

To my mom and dad,

Bill and Rita

As they continue to be impressed by

my antics

and for the value that I get from their amazement.

Also…

To Shanna and Cody.

To Farrah, Thaddeus and Deanaira.

To Marie and Kelly.

…And to the band, Talking Heads.

Thank You All.

Table of Contents

Act Two

Jack Dumont

ACT THREE

Jack Dumont

THE HANDS OF FATE

Vol. One - The Legacy

Act One

Introductions - Xenons

No living life-form knows, for sure, the origin of its own creation. Humans have philosophised their species' beginnings since they had their first rational thought. The Bible tells us that humans started with Adam and Eve in The Garden of Eden, while many scientists believe our beginnings were dependent upon our evolution from ocean life or Darwinian apes…or something else, entirely. David Byrne said it best: "Well…how did I get here?"

Only the ones who were created by artificial intelligence have had their history well-documented and the advantage of knowing their beginnings as computer programmers and hardware engineers, their own personal deities, recorded it all.

With that, it was only guesses and assumptions where this particular lot of demi-humans first appeared. Many names described them, but the one that many stuck with was the name "Xenon."

"Xeno"-Meaning "alien" and the "On" portion came to mean "anonymous" as fear of their discovery necessitated their hiding among the rest of the humans.

Their existence began from the alien addition to their DNA which added what they could accomplish in random bouts of superiority. They were called "Abilities," "Talents" or even "Powers" if one were to get too dramatic about it. Some of these abilities were so powerful that it led to many people thinking that they were gods. Whether they were good, or evil depended on whose side you were on.

Politics and religion have certainly brought in their definition of good and evil and how the masses were supposed to live. These monikers were not placed on Xenons at first as they descended through history with the rest of humankind.

As time grew more modern, however, they were all declared threats to humanity and left to go into hiding in plain sight while only revealing their true abilities to a chosen few or bear the scorn of those jealous and threatened souls who didn't carry incredible abilities like theirs.

This scorn led to Xenons fighting back against this prejudice with retaliation being considered a threat to humans. If driven to the point of pushing back the mob with their abilities, they would be besieged by similar individuals until their numbers were too great to fight.

Times in history like these appeared in The Witch Trials of Europe and Early America, The Spanish Inquisition, the rise of the 3rd Reich of Germany and the Killing Fields of Saigon.

The Paragon force was formed in the early part of the twentieth century and charged with defending the general human populace. Their tactics were varied for any occasion. An electric Xenon required rubber and water for a defence/offence combination along with ice versus fire, for example. Modern inventions made the capture of these renegade Xenons less stressful but not perfect. There were newer and better products developed over the years to fight the war when guns and blades just weren't enough.

There were also attempts to bring balance to this universe like the industrial revolution, the rise of modern medicine and the invention of electricity for the household of the everyday human.

Today, modern media have brought depictions of Xenons as superheroes and put a positive spin on this lot while also creating stories of super-villains to match against them on an even level. It is in more cases than not that Xenons wanted to live like normal humans, gain acceptance for what they were and improve the lives of all.

As any newsperson will tell you, however, it's the bad news that sells copy, and happy people don't make history.

Chapter 1 - From the beginning…

Birth and death never really occur on well-timed occasions. Death fell to Paula Gibraltar, the wife of Dr Unger Gibraltar at the end of 1968 A.D. late on the day after Christmas. She was 68 years old.

Her husband was not there to stop the aneurysm that suddenly developed in her brain. A sad thing as he was a doctor and quite adept at handling such events. He was on his shift at Gilderbrund Hospital, and her death occurred quite suddenly.

Their thirty-year-old son, Helmut Gibraltar, also a physician, flew in from London along with his wife, Jean, to Bern, Switzerland for the funeral. The trip was ill-advised as she was late in her 3rd trimester and about to deliver their first baby at any time. She felt the utmost need to give her respects and attend the funeral no matter what.

There was a brief moment of uneasiness when her father-in-law patted the belly of the mother-to-be with his hand with a quick "'Allo, you! I can't vait to meet you!" Jean just let go what she considered to be a social faux-paux at this place and time. No need to show anger nor embarrass anyone here on this solemn occasion.

They sat in the funeral service in black attire and Jean wearing black, round sunglasses and a black pillbox hat over her ironed-straight blonde hair which reached her shoulders. Her pregnancy hid her usually lean build that made her look like a Miss Britain contestant.

Helmut said little to his father, other to shake his hand and take his seat. The hard hours at Saville Hospital started to mat his face under his black hair with a slight curl. One would think Helmut was on starvation levels as he ate only a little. A trait shared with his wife that suggested a lean diet. The junior doctor kept up a long schedule, and a fast meal was often all he could grab while at work.

It was in the middle of the priest leading the mourning audience of Paula's family and friends to sing "Nearer my God to Thee" when Jean hit an unexpectedly high note. That was the time when her water broke, and they were too late to get her to the closest obstetrician. They piled in the hearse as it was most-suited to give her room to lay in the back.

The birth was rather brutal with no drugs and her pain all too apparent. Her husband then delivered their new-born son in the hearse while being driven to hospital. The driver ignored the bright light emerging from the rear area.

The young boy came into the world like anyone else —crying for his mother as he emerged in the middle of this foreign country on 28 December 1968. His father looked at his infant son after he delivered him and wondered, for only a flash, where the world would take him. His mother already had his life worked out for him. He would go to school, marry and become a renowned gentleman like his father, a neurosurgeon in London's Saville Hospital.

When the medical centre staff opened the rear of the modified Austin, she was holding the couple's new-born son in her arms. They took the family for a bit into Gilderbrund Hospital where everything checked out fine, and they were on their way back to Chelsea two days later chauffeured by Dr Julius Guitaeu, who was Helmut's good friend and medical partner, in his BMW.

The boy was christened with the name Harris Unger Nickolas Gibraltar. The parents couldn't be prouder of their young boy. He would grow up a solid, stand-up Catholic gentleman, attend the best schools London could offer and live the high social life. His mother called him "Growing up from good stock." He grew up a handsome young boy who had light brown hair, very white skin and "Eyes as blue as a London sky…" As said by his Aunt Jane. He would be a knockout when he grew up. They were sure of it.

As he grew, however, he seemed to deviate from the path of success. His test scores were not the best, and his interest was not in his studies…His attention was no place to be found at all. Helmut, his Da, said not to worry and that his boy would soon find his way. The young boy called his dad "Da" for all the time he knew him.

Harris grew up in a bubble of his creation and was not socially active with the rest of his peers. He attended the prestigious St. Joseph's Academy, where he did not score well in his classes which became a continuing concern for his parents. Again, the senior Gibraltar did not deter his son, but he did stress to him several times that his success was paramount to the family image.

Years went by, and he got into scrapes with the other boys in the school. They would beat him senseless, but he never carried any scars to prove their abuse.

There were a couple of times when he fought back, and that led to himself getting detention as he bore no signs of injury. The other boys snaked their way out of trouble with no marks against their records.

When Headmistress Fyre accused Harris of being the bully, he just shot back that they were her golden children and it made him wonder why they got preferential treatment. There were many occasions that he wanted to take a cricket bat to their heads but knew he would get the brunt of the punishment. He avoided getting into further trouble with the nuns and teachers by staying withdrawn and introverted.

They would go on vacation every year, and Da would have time to unwind. He seemed to need it. He was at hospital for long hours daily. Every year they stayed on the coast like Brighton or Skegness.

They even went to Spain in the middle of his 8th school year. The timing was odd, but the country was fascinating to young Harris, especially the topless beaches. Harris loved this part of Europe even though English was a second language to the locals...or not at all. The perfect place to be left alone. He was quite curious why they went on holiday in the middle of April but hated school enough to not worry over it.

When Harris turned 15, he wandered the streets of London in a daze of teen angst while the age of punk and new wave hit the music scene. Bands like The Clash and The Sex Pistols fuelled his fire. He was too young to go to pubs or clubs which furthered his anger. This music ramped the spirit of the boy in the sense of rebellion that he savoured. He just managed to eke out a passing grade to advance his education as time went on.

There were a couple of times that he would take his anger out on the sots that gave him such a horrible time during the day by ambushing them coming out of a gaming hall. He would attack and throw punches while hitting his opponents with anything handy he could find. He won his fights with a struggle, although never coming out with any signs of being pounded himself. He figured he was stronger and had a more solid exterior than anyone else, never really questioning how he didn't bruise more.

The Bobbies were the ones that dragged him home to his parents in his new wave suits and skinny ties. Mostly, to his disappointed mother.

"No, Mum!" He once shouted during her lecture on civility. "The way they treat me every day…"

As he made his case, "They got what they deserved, and you can't tell me otherwise!"

"Son, when will you ever grow up?" She said and stormed off to her room with no response. He knew he was a cock-up but didn't feel he knew better.

Between the Bobbies and the nuns, he would have taken the police as they had seen it all before and didn't lecture him about civility and what God thought about him. The nuns never mentioned the bully's actions in school. The problem was all Harris's, and he needed to change or fail. This line just drove him further from everyone and fed his depression and anxiety, especially of crowded places. His Da, God love him, did his best to be patient as he had lived all this himself in his youth. They never discussed it, though. He just let him be.

The turning point came when he was about 15 years on and walking home alone from his faith school to his residence near the end of Essex street. The blue Reliant Robin 3-wheeler came barrelling down the road with an obnoxious roar of a bust exhaust silencer. He hated these cars as they were the ugliest things on the street.

He especially hated this one as it targeted and then took out the black cat with white patches crossing the street and kept on rolling with no concern. The cat flew into the air with a loud thud and cry as it landed in a bloody lump in the centre of Essex Street.

"You wanker!!!" He shouted as the car drove on unconcerned. If he had something to throw in its direction, besides his two fingers, he would have. Harris went over to look at the cat, and it was still not dead but was in fragile shape as it uttered a painful, guttural sound.

"Poor thing." He thought. "It's just an innocent creature! It never hurt anyone!"

The extraordinary thing was when he got near the cat, his hands felt like they vibrated a little. He gave his hand a shake, but it was still tingling. He held his palm up and found it gave off a glow of white light on both sides. He then backed away from the kitty, and the vibration faded while the light dimmed, slightly. Both the humming and the glowing increased again when he stepped closer to the cat.

When he held his hand over the wounded animal, a bright torch-like beam shot out of his hand like a laser and into the feline. He fell back on to the pavement with shock. "Whoa! Whoa!" He shouted out. What was this?

His hand continued to vibrate and glow while he got up and approached again. The light gave him no pain as he held his palm over the animal and once again, the white torch-like light shot out of his extremity when he held his hand over the head of the injured cat. That remained the only part undamaged from its assassination attempt.

When he withdrew his hand, the beam stopped and then came back with a quickly repeated holding of his hand over the cat another 2 or 3 times. The light was flashing along with this manoeuvre…

Finally, with a quick look to make sure no one else was watching, he just let the light flow and watched in amazement as the body of the cat became good as new after being flattened by that sickening 3-wheeler. The cat seemed to re-inflate like a balloon the longer he held the beam until the light and vibration faded out and stopped and the feline was apparently, fine. He observed that his hand had returned to its normal state.

The cat jumped up with a squeal and started drinking from a nearby water-puddle on the ground for all it was worth. It then came back to Harris when it had its fill of fluids and curled up in his lap as he sat on the pavement's edge. Harris's dark trousers hid the blood that the purring cat had spilt a moment ago. As he petted the feline, he wondered to himself, "What just happened here?"

The healing session went unnoticed by the tabby's owner, Gina Ravalli, but the affection it gave to Harris was apparent. Gina came up the street also from their same faith school and introduced herself. She recognised Harris from class but never bothered to speak to him until now.

"Hello...I see you're a cat person" She said to the confused, yet kind Harris.

The light framed her head perfectly as she watched him pet the cat. He had seen Gina for many years in classes and struck how lovely she was as she stood over him in her school uniform. She was of Italian descent with long, curled black hair, beautiful dark brown eyes, olive skin and had blossomed early and well for a young girl, especially in her blouse! He always thought she was above his station- Way too beautiful for him.

"Yeah, I love all animals," He said, hoping he would say the right thing to this cute girl.

"Me too." She said. "Would you like a glass of lemonade?"

"Um, sure." He replied as she went into her flat and brought out two glasses of lemonade with not quite enough sugar. Harris just overlooked that.

He was never approached like this as he was socially awkward and was taller and thinner than most of his classmates. He was also rooted in thought about something else, of course. How did a cat that was near death become healthy again, and what did he do to help it?

Harris did his best to hold a normal conversation with this young girl and was at-ease and polite with her. They talked about school and how his performance was less than what he should have been. Besides the fights, he was getting too many low grades, and his parents were told many times over that Harris might be sent packing to make the school look better.

"I wouldn't mind helping you if you wanted." She said. "It gets lonely here sometimes. Even though my mum and Dad are there, they tend just to read the paper and watch the telly all night.

"OK, sure," Harris said. "Can we meet at 4:30?"

"Sure" she replied. "Bring your books over, and we'll see what we can do for you."

"OK then," Harris said and gently pushed the young cat off his lap, and it curled around Gina's ankles.

"See you soon, then." He said with a wave as he picked up his book bag and headed, happily down the street.

Gina picked up her cat, Darby and found that he had blood in his fur. The feline had no signs of any injury, so she pegged it as the cat got into something messy.

"Darby, what you get into, then?" She said as she carried the tabby inside for a quick wash.

Harris went home and changed out of his school uniform, still unaware of the vital fluids that had messed his black pants, white shirt and tie. He put on a grey casual top and jeans after he had a quick rinse at the sink and threw on some deodorant not even taking notice of the blood that stained his hands from petting Darby as the evidence went down the drain with a bit of soap. He then bounded downstairs happier than usual with his pack of books on his back.

"Mum!" He said. "Listen, I'm going to miss dinner. I have a study date with a friend...well, not a date. Just a study session, rather."

Jean Gibraltar was washing dishes as her son was on his way out the door. "Ok, son," she replied. If he was indeed going to study, then she wasn't going to interfere. "Do try to come home before your Da goes to bed. I know he'll want to see you."

"Right..." He said. "Oh yeah...weird thing today. I saw a car hit a cat on my way home."

"Oh, how horrible!" Jean said with concern. "Was it killed?"

"No, that's the weird thing...it seemed to be on the verge of death, and then it just popped up like nothing happened when I got near it. I'll tell you more about it later... Bye, then!" and closed the door behind him. He didn't want to say more as there was an appointment for him to keep, after all.

Harris wasn't sure, but he could have sworn he heard glass shatter behind him. He just ignored it and made his way down Essex Street. He then knocked on the door and was met by Gina in a white T-shirt with an Irish Wolfhound puppy on it. "Hi Harris, come on in." She said with a smile.

They entered, and he followed her to the room just off to the left, which was her father's library. The room contained a large table along with several file cabinets and shelves of books on tax law and accounting. Harris looked over the titles that sounded like a lot of boring selections. Did people really read this stuff?

"My Dad's reading choices are pretty dry." She said. "He's a crown accountant."

"Well, he must know something about mathematics, then," Harris said. "Are you versed in it as well?"

"I'm pretty good at some things." She replied. "Let me show you..." and they took a seat at the large table and got straight to work. They worked for a solid two hours in Grade 11 Maths and history until her mum called her for dinner.

"Would your friend like to stay?" Gina's mother asked with her lovely accent.

She was an attractive Italian woman with similar black hair and enchanting eyes with a few extra pounds that she carried well on her short frame. If her looks were what Gina would favour in the future, then the young girl had nothing to worry over.

He looked to Gina, who nodded with approval.

"I guess I could," Harris said, and they all took their places at a dining room table which struck Harris as odd as the only time he ate at the dining room table at home was during holidays with his family. Here, it seemed a regular thing.

A short, overweight Italian gentleman in a 3-piece suit, black-framed glasses and a red tie emerged from the loo as he dried his hands on his shirt front. He was well-groomed but had a shadow of hair on his face. As he joined his family and guest at the table, he took his jacket, tie and waistcoat off and hung them on the back of the chair and swept back his full black head of hair.

Gina made the introductions. "Harris, this is Magdalena and Vincent Ravalli."

Vincent gave Harris a gripping handshake that felt like a vice grip while he just waved at his wife who held a casserole in both hands. They all sat and blessed themselves with Gina saying grace in Latin, which was another thing which Harris found interesting. They helped themselves to something incredibly cheesy with pasta and sauce. It was, possibly, the best thing Harris ever ate.

Between bites, Vincent inquired in a similar accent to his wife about Harris's family. He told them how his Da was now a lead neurosurgeon and spent much of his time in hospital. Vincent relayed how much of his time was spent at his office sorting tax returns. He also told Harris that as a teenager, it was time to think of his future. Harris held back the fact that his Da said the same thing to him nearly every night.

Gina talked about how she wanted to pursue veterinary medicine. It was apparent that her mother thought she should stay home and raise children. A comment that did not sit well with Gina. That was obvious.

Magdalena also talked about her sons. They were all grown and living elsewhere. Eduardo had a wife and three children (a girl and two boys) and owned a restaurant in their home city of Milan, Italy. Another son, Victor, was a priest in Turin, but her son, Giuseppe, had died three years ago of pneumonia. "God rest him," Magdalena said as she blessed herself at the mention of the lost family member.

As the dinner and conversation progressed, Harris noticed Vincent was sweating. He was also complaining of his chest and arm having pains. "My apologies." He said in an Italian accent as he held his left arm as if he had banged it against the table.

"Dad, are you ok?" Gina asked.

"Vinny, honey...I tell you to take it easy." Magdalena said with deep concern.

Vincent took a sip of red wine from his glass. "Excuse me, please," Vincent said with deep breaths as he wiped his mouth with a cloth napkin. "I think I need to lay down a moment on the couch."

He got up and took two steps, maybe three and collapsed hard on the carpet. As he did, he slid the table cloth off the mahogany table, and several dishes followed on the floor saved from cracking by the plush carpeting.

Panic ensued as Magdalena ran to her husband and Gina also rushing to his side. Magdalena held her unconscious husband's head up in her arms while Gina gently slapped his face trying to wake him up. Harris went over and said to lay him out on the carpet to try to give him CPR as his Da taught him. While she was getting Vincent in position, Gina got on the phone to call 999.

As he was about to press down the first time on the man's chest, that same bright beam of light poured from both of his hands as it did that afternoon with the cat.

Harris, too amazed to stop, just let the light soak into the man, while the two ladies looked on in utter amazement.

A few moments later, Vincent woke with a start and a gasp. "What happened?" He asked in a state of confusion but appeared fine, otherwise.

Harris just looked terrified at his hands and the shocked faces of the ladies. Gina dropped the phone receiver, and with the sound of it hitting the floor, Harris then ran out the front door and up the street. He didn't stop until he got home.

He didn't go into his house, though. Instead, his panic drove him into the dog house of the family mastiff, Napoleon.

The big dog crawled into the dog house and growled until he saw Harris sobbing to himself. He laid his big head on Harris's leg in the sympathy that only dogs give. Half of the dog's body stuck out the shelter as it was only built for the large canine.

"I did it now, Nappy." He cried. "They'll be sending those Paragon-types over any minute now." The dog produced a small cry as it laid his head on his master's son's lap.

Harris never gave a second thought to Paragons until now. They were always someone else's problem. Harris could see it all unfold. Gina and her parents would either call the police directly or, worse yet, call his parents to have them do it.

11

Were there even Paragons in this country? Harris didn't know if there were or not as most news reports about Paragons and Xenons came from the states or other countries. Xenons were running about blowing things up, setting items on fire while causing more death and destruction than the IRA, Arabs or the drunken and homeless sots from downtown. Even the Xenons who didn't do anything nasty came under constant scrutiny. Would he be sent to jail for being a freak? Would they look the other way because he did something great?

He stayed hidden in there for a good 20 minutes muffling his cries while rocking back and forth in small movements as he anxiously contemplated his fate. Napoleon stayed faithfully by his side as Harris rubbed the back of his neck. He got a bit of comfort petting the dog.

Footsteps approached, and Harris was terrified. Here it comes... what was going to happen? The steps stopped at the entrance of the doghouse, and a face came into view with Harris gasping in response...

"Hello, son" Helmut said, grinning.

"Oh...Hi Da." Harris replied nervously.

Helmut continued..." When you decide to come in, I'm sure you'll have a bunch of questions you'll want to be answered."

Chapter 2 - The Legacy

Harris was still fearful as his Father walked away, calmly. His Da's outward appearance was of well-meaning and ease but figured that could be a ruse. He slowly entered the house with his mother running over and hugging him with tears in her eyes looking at him, joyfully like he had just returned from war.

"All right, then son?" she asked as she held his face.

"I…I don't know, mum. I'm not sure how I feel right now." He said. "Hang on…how did you lot know what was going on?" He then inquired.

"Well, we just had the most interesting conversation with your friend." His mum then said. Harris then looked into the dining room, and there was Gina. Her eyes revealing that she had a long cry. Harris was dumbstruck. His parent's knowledge was terrible enough, and now he would have to take whatever abuse she was about to dole out? "Fine!" he thought. "Just take it like a man!"

Gina slowly walked over to him, and Harris could only blurt out apologies. "Gina," he said with the tears in his eyes coming again. "I'm so sorry. I had no idea that would hap…"

Gina threw her arms tight around him with tears in her eyes as well in a huge hug.

"Thank you so much for what you did." She whispered between sobs. "My Dad had no clue what happened. Mum said she would keep it a secret as well... You are welcome back anytime you like."

Harris was humble. "Thank you, Gina." He said, now with his arms around her.

"Ahem…" Helmut said interrupting this moment. "My dear, I am afraid that my son is going to have to have a good talking to about all this, so if you would…"

"Yes, of course," Gina said as her eyes, still with tears of joy, looked in his. She then said to Harris "I'll see you in school, tomorrow." Then she turned to Helmut. "I will, won't I?"

"Of course, you will, my dear," Helmut said. "And do remember what I told you. The word is CPR if anyone asks you." She nodded to Helmut and waved goodbye to Harris as she walked out the door.

"That's a nice girl," Jean said. "You should give her every respect in the world for holding your secrets like this." Harris didn't need to be told twice that. He just nodded in agreement.

In the kitchen, the kettle started whistling. "I'm going to pour you both a cuppa and then step out of your way. All this is your father's area of expertise." With that, she poured two cups of tea on the table and quickly set out the sugar bowl.

Afterwards, she went upstairs and sat on the side of the bed. She then cried, silently into a handkerchief. Now her boy would have to deal with the world in ways few others did.

Helmut and Harris sat with their cups in front of them, and both shoved them to their respective left sides. "OK, son," Helmut said. "What do you want to know first?"

Harris took the easy way out to start as he wasn't sure how to begin. "How did you know I was in the doghouse?"

Helmut was surprised at this rather lacklustre question but answered. "Well, Napoleon's backside was half out the door with his tail wagging. It seemed a safe bet that you were there. Gina then came to the door looking for you and explained what happened." And he pivoted the question back to the subject at hand.

"So how did it feel to save a life, son?" Helmut asked.

"I was more terrified than anything," Harris responded. "That was, actually, the second life I saved…" Which raised the eyebrows of the elder Gibraltar.

"I kind of told mum of a cat I saved after being hit by a car earlier today," Harris said.

"I see…all right, then," Helmut said as he nodded.

Harris, finally, cut to the chase.

"Da, what is this? What's going on with me?" He asked, anxiously.

Helmut filled him in with everything:

"Son, you are now part of our family's legacy," He began.

"Legacy?" Harris asked. "What you mean by that?"

Helmut continued…

"For generations, we, that is our bloodline, have served as physicians for the most powerful of men, staying in the background for the kings and emperors to live and serve their offices. There have been many times that our kind let evil flourish, but the good leaders were served by us as well."

With that, Helmut pulled out a large book with artwork and old photographs of past family members along with similar artwork depicting royalty, archbishops and even a pope. The cover was labelled "Gibraltar Family History." Harris turned the pages of the old book that had his father as the last entry. "These, son, are what have built on over the past millennia or so," Helmut said.

His Da looked like Frank Sinatra in his younger days, A look he kept as his father aged very well. His blue eyes carried on in Harris's genetics as he continued to grow with his father's height and build, which were nothing to sneeze over. The only thing he didn't get was his voice. His father sounded a lot like Churchill while Harris had a higher pitch. No doubt his mother's contribution as they could also both carry a tune without a lot of jeers.

While Harris continued to scan the images of his past relatives in the dated book, Helmut slipped a straight razor out of his pocket and opened the dangerously sharp blade. "Of course, son..." Helmut continued "There are other benefits as well..."

With that, Helmut took the straight razor and cut his son's arm quickly with a large gash. Harris was in a mode of utter panic as the blood spilt from his arm.

"Da! What are you playing at?" Harris yelled at his father.

After Harris yelled his words, he looked again to find the wound was gone. Only the blood on his sleeve showed that any knife play took place. He looked at his arm, astonished at the lack of wounding.

"You see that, son?" Helmut said. "You realise that you have never needed a plaster for anything. No broken limbs, no bruises that lasted more than a moment...not even an illness. We had to travel to Spain in the middle of one of your school terms because of your lack of sicknesses, except in summertime...As far as they knew."

With that, Harris thought back to his first thought to now, at age 15. No mending needed on either of his parent's part, no bruising from getting beaten up, no sicknesses nor any hospital visit, not to mention the impromptu holiday in the south of Europe. This explained a lot!

15

Harris again looked incredulously at the bloodstain on his arm after his Da's rather brash demonstration. "Sorry, son," Helmut said consolingly as he put aside the razor after folding it. "I had to get the point made, even if it meant dramatically. Don't be angry. Your grandfather did the same to me."

Harris thought back to the description of his grandfather, Unger Gibraltar. He never met him but heard that he was a rather demanding figure as the head of surgery in a Bern, Switzerland hospital. Hence the reason for his birth taking place there. The funeral for Helmut's mother was at the same time as his delivery, and the trip was not easy for his wife, Jean. That, she mentioned in passing a couple of times, although they always seemed to leave out the part about being born in a hearse.

"Da…" Harris asked, "Are there others like us?"

Helmut scratched his brow a moment before speaking again. "Not that I know of, son. Certainly, there are blessed souls like us, but this particular ability is special and exclusive to our bloodline."

"Hang on!" Harris said excitingly. "What about your patients?"

"What do you mean?" Helmut asked.

"You have to cut into their skulls, don't you? Harris asked.

"Son, that brings up the point of having to do our deals in the light of day," Helmut answered with a sigh. "All my patients are healed before they even receive surgery. I agree it's a revolting fact, but we have to go through the motions of looking like the work was done, or we will receive a visit from those who oppose us. Only Dr Guiteau is in on this fact as well."

Dr Guiteau was Helmut's partner and closest confidante at Saville Hospital. When a surgery took place, Julius Guiteau was there assisting and covering any inquiries that Helmut could not. Helmut continued…

"I don't mind telling you that I was gravely concerned when your young friend was present to your healing session. I impressed upon her that our kind, no matter what level of good we do for the world, is under scrutiny. It's a sad part of our existence, but it must be acknowledged and adhered to do our part for everyone's sake." Harris became angry with this thought. All this ability to serve man, and yet in constant danger of being thrown to the wolves.

"Then why should we bother, Da?" Harris asked, honestly.

With that, Helmut pulled out his rosary with a crucifix attached. "This is why Harris." He said, "Without forgiveness, there is only death." He then put his rosary back into his pocket and sipped his tea which was just tepid in temperature as he liked it. Harris dropped a sugar cube into his cup and sipped it as well. He drank it, but always preferred his cold.

"Now then, son," Helmut spoke seriously. "Now that you know what is going on, you will have to improve your grades and behaviour. Chances are what you are studying may not come up later, but your destiny is now in your hands. You can be something else and take your chances or follow your path and be the absolute best... So, it's time to get cracking."

With that, Helmut got up and took his teacup, then put it in the kitchen sink. He then patted his son on the shoulder without saying a word and went upstairs. He left young Harris Gibraltar with his destiny laid before him and the choice whether to follow or be just another face in the crowd.

"Without forgiveness, there is only death." These words would continue to resonate with Harris for the rest of his days.

Chapter 3 – "Faire" Thee Well

Harris now had a new direction. He continued to see Gina for help with his math homework and just because he wanted to be near her. Her father bought bicycles for himself and his ladies, and they rode on Sundays to the park. Harris would have loved to join them, but his nose was now buried in medical literature every hour of the day.

He was also tutored a couple of days a week by Dr Julius Guiteau. He, who was his father's partner and equal in age. He was also a tall man who wore a sports coat most of the time and had thinning brown hair. If you told to point to who you thought was a doctor in a typical group on the street, you would pick him as his whole demeanour projected professionalism and class. He was also the only other person who knew his father was more than human.

Harris found it very easy to study with Dr Guiteau. He was easy-going and presented things in a way he understood better than St. Joseph's did. They spent most of their time going through the most relevant portions of the medical manuals. Harris would not only need to pass grade 13 but take the MCAT entrance exam for medical college. Julius also taught him some mnemonics he used to get through his studies, like "P-eanut B-utter W-ith B-read: Phlegm, Blood, Water and Bile. The four vital fluids in the human body. By the end of the first month, he had a notebook filled with these and proceeded to share them with Gina, believing that most animals shared these same traits.

After two months of non-stop Latin words for various medical maladies, Harris hit a wall. Julius saw that he was approaching burnout and said: "Take a day or two, Harris." He said. "We'll pick it up on Sunday afternoon."

That Friday, Harris was in biology class and was a bit nervous. There, lying before him in a tin tray was a frog for dissection fresh out of formaldehyde. Gina was next to him as his lab partner, and they were both wondering if a light show was about to take place? Gina whispered to follow her lead and knocked the glass jar the frog arrived in off the wooden counter, and it shattered on the floor to the shock of the class and the dismay of Mr Ramsey, the instructor.

While Gina cried and apologised profusely, Harris, secretly put his hand close to the frog. No lights emitted from his hands. He even touched it with his finger while Gina was instructed to get the broom out of the cupboard. Nothing happened.

"Lesson learnt, Harris...Dead is dead." He thought to himself.

He helped Gina by holding the dustpan while she swept. An errant piece of glass cut his finger, but the evidence quickly vanished from view.

They left class and Harris told her what had happened after purposefully breaking school property. "OK, then. I'm glad we found that out. All we need is a bunch of frogs jumping in jars off the shelves." She joked. They both laughed at that as they walked down Essex street while surrounded by other students who paid them no heed. Their numbers decreased as their homes were down different avenues, leaving only the two of them.

Gina was unique in that she didn't hang out with the other lovelies at the school that took delight in keeping the teen boys eying them as a dog would salivate over a steak. She could easily play that game but found it uninteresting and spent a lot of time alone as she was lumped in with the beauties that would turn their nose up to the so-called unworthy boys that dared to approach. Harris felt himself one of the lucky ones as his anxiety drifted away in her presence.

"Harris, you know there is going to be a fair tomorrow at Rickett's Gate, right?"

"Oh yeah..." Harris had forgotten this. He was going to invite Gina to go, but he had seen only foreign words for fungus all week. "Gina, would you like to go with me there?"

"I thought you'd never ask!" she said — her smile a yard wide.

Julius signed off on Harris getting away for the Saturday and said he would let his father know he deserved this break in routine. Julius pushed Harris to work but also gave him the pride that went along with it. The nuns never seemed to bother with that aspect.

He put on a thin black jacket, blue jeans and a black crew-neck shirt. He then went and picked her up at her place after his parents said to have a good time and not stay out too late. His father even gave him a £10 note and told him to have fun.

They walked down Essex Street and passed St. Joseph's Academy to the bus shelter where the red double-decker took them to Rickett's Gate, a park located a few miles from their homes that held a variety of games and rides this day.

They played around for an hour visiting the different stalls, got a bag of chips to share, rode the carousel and Gina even won a ring toss game with a pound note attached to one of the bottles.

Harris took things slow after realising he was getting anxious. It was very crowded here in the park and began growing panicky. Gina saw this and just led him over to a less crowded part of the park where they kept ponies for the children to ride. "Thank you, dear. I don't know what just came over me." Harris said.

Gina became distracted for a moment as she took a look at a small horse lying on its side. Its eyes were a bit glazed over, and it wasn't moving. An older white-haired woman in a dirty work shirt under a khaki mack came over and looked at the beast. "Poor devil." She said with an Irish Brough. "He's not been right as of late."

"You want me to take a look?" Gina asked. "My friend and I are looking into the medical field."

"Could not harm, I guess." She said. With that, Gina felt the creature's belly, and it was bothered by the touch. Harris witnessed the level of caring Gina displayed to the equine lying in the straw.

They also noticed the pony's stall was clean of any dung. "When did you last clean here?" Gina asked.

"Yesterday." She said. "There wasn't much to clean of his, then."

Harris knew that he could clear this up in seconds, but he was content to let Gina have her opportunity.

"My guess would be colic. The straw here is very dry, and he doesn't have enough water. He may even need a good cleaning out."

"Alright then," she said. "I'll get me boots and the hose…my husband is lazy about things like this." She then pointed over to the man in overalls leading the horses around in circles with very young riders on the backs of the beasts.

"Maybe he should do it," Gina said. "If this horse is backed up…"

The woman gave a sly smile. "Oh yeah!" She then turned to her husband. "Oy, Jimmy…!"

Gina and Harris took their leave of the stable area. "Nice turn, love," Harris said.

"I'm surprised you didn't say something," Gina said.

"Well, you said you wanted to be a vet," Harris said. "It wouldn't be proper for me to interfere."

Harris then spotted the Ferris wheel. "Hey, let's go on the wheel." He said.

"Um-OK," Gina said. It looked pretty high to her, but she didn't want to disappoint her friend, though.

The Ferris wheel was not too crowded as people were watching some music group over at the stage playing Rainbow songs, amongst others. They went in the usual vertical circles, and Gina seemed a bit tense and squeezed Harris's wrist at the apex each time. She was even more fearful when they got stuck at the summit while other riders got off and on. It seemed like it was taking a longer time than usual for the load/unload process to take place. Gina became even more panicked than what Harris felt near the crowds.

"Why don't they hurry? "She asked. She then took hold of Harris in a hug as big as after when he saved her father.

"Don't worry, honey. I got you. Everything is fine." They looked in each other's eyes, and they fell into a deep kiss. Nothing else mattered then — just this minute in time.

The next thing they knew, they were being told by the young carny with a pointed nose and oil-covered shirt to "Quit snoggin' and sot off!" They got off the ride and ran behind the pony stable. They kissed and embraced again and just enjoyed the moment.

"Oy!" A voice shouted from behind them. "Get over yourselves, you two!" The shout was from the scowling older man who ran the pony ride. He was unshaven and dirty, wearing grubby clothes and a brown coat. At this time, he was slapping the ponies with a crop leading them into their corral for the night. Gina looked in the one stall and saw the pony with colic was just as they left it.

"That little horse is going to die without help!" Gina shouted.

"Shove off, tart! He looks fine to me, so mind your place!" The farmer said grumpily. He then turned and started watering the trough from a hose.

Gina was boiling mad. "Well…" Harris said to her. "We can't leave him like that."

He reached his hand through the corral fence while the farmer continued to fill the water trough paying no mind to the two kids. Harris could barely reach the poor beast but got enough light to generate to bring the creature to his feet. The pony then let loose the contents of its bowels right behind the farmer.

"There, I guess he feels better," Harris said to Gina a bit disgusted by the air of manure.

The pony then ploughed his way past the farmer to get to the water trough in a huge hurry. The farmer then stepped in the pony's leftovers which caused him to slip and land on his back with a sickening splat on the pile. Gina and Harris walked away quickly from the stables with a silly grin on both their faces.

"I feel better, too," Gina said with a satisfied smile.

They headed out of the park hand in hand. Harris felt on top of the world with this beautiful girl next to him, walking down the street. He treasured this time and stopped to kiss her at a bus shelter. He brushed back her lengthy, black hair with his hand and just looked in her beautiful eyes.

They got on the bus and went upstairs to an uninhabited space to have some more kissing time. It was a new feeling for these two young people. The bus arrived at Essex Street way too soon. Gina's house was the first on the way. "I had a great time, hon. Gina said. "I guess I'll see you in class on Monday."

"I'm going to be thinking about you all night now." He said.

They shared one more kiss before she went into her flat. It was the best day that Harris ever had and one he would long remember. The sad part was real life would kick back up tomorrow after church.

Chapter 4 - Revision for A Levels

Gina and Harris would snatch the quick kiss here and there while they worked on their studies together. Things were finally coming along for the boy who was progressing to becoming a man and her, a woman. Julius also stepped in with his assistance, making sure above all else that Harris would be prepared to enter medical school when the time came.

It would be too easy to become lazy with Harris's shortcut, so both Julius and his Da worked into the boy's mind that not only should he cure but understand why and how he "treated" his patient because everyone would be demanding an explanation. The Government would be wanting to know how for billing purposes. If funded privately, the ones footing the chit would wish to understand the course of treatment and indeed, the patient would want explanations. All this was a pain that both Helmut and Julius knew all too well as they worked the system for many years.

If the paperwork was no longer a factor and Xenon prejudice was gone, there would be a shop in the market offering to cure anything for £20, and everyone would go away joyous.

Harris continued to see Gina through these next two years. He still studied hard in the summer, though they had more time together. They would catch the occasional film, go for a swim or go out for a meal. They had make-out sessions but nothing too far over the line. They didn't lose feelings for each other. They did what they could to keep things interesting, including going to tourist-type trips to the sights of London. Some of them were interesting, some were not, but all were worth conversing over. Being together was what mattered, not the destination.

Harris knew that there would be no future for himself if he didn't attain that A-level and get out of St. Joseph's. The teachers were now happy, probably guessing that he wanted to impress Gina. To a large degree, it was one of his ultimate goals.

Harris now got up in the morning to check the letterbox before school. "Good morning, Harris!" Said Mr Ravalli, who took up jogging in the morning. He exercised regularly and was slimmer by four stone since Harris brought him back from the edge of death. Harris returned the good morning from the letterbox and went inside with a few large envelopes. His college brochures had been coming in all week. His grades and station in life weren't quite good enough for Oxford or Cambridge, but he did have a large volume of other exceptional schools to choose.

Gina had her series of post-secondary education to choose from as well. Her Mum was still intent on her being a housewife, but Gina was head-up on making her fate her own. They also both knew that they would have to part ways for a while if their college choices did that to them. It was a sad thought but knew that they had to be pragmatic about their futures.

Helmut suggested his son should go to Zurich Medical Academy in Switzerland. After all, it was his Alma Mater. The boy didn't feel that attending half the classes in German would do him well in the long run. His mother saw a brochure on The Royal College of Medical Arts in Surrey, and if he remained in London, he would be close to them and all. Harris loved his parents but knew he needed to get away to become his own man. Julius even suggested Manchester and St. Archibald's Medical College, which was brand new. Harris figured that he would be, literally, in a class by himself. Not exactly what he was, after no matter how tempting the solitude. Finally, Harris chose his target: The Royal College of Medicine in Cork, Ireland. Just close enough to his parents and far enough away to keep to himself.

His final A-Level exam was at the ready, and he would take his MCAT medical placement a month later. He and Gina studied for A-Levels together as this test was nearly the same for both of them. He would take it on Wednesday, hers on Thursday as their last names were A-M and N-Z, respectfully. They had one session of snogging that lasted 15 minutes and then cut themselves off…They studied in her father's library, unarguably, the most non-romantic place on earth. They worked until late on Monday and Tuesday night with both hoping that their learned information didn't slip out of their heads while they slept.

Before the test, Harris woke at 6 am to get a few remaining moments in of information cramming and even tried in vain to get his healing light to appear out of his hands on to his head. Maybe that would give him some advantage. Try as he might, that didn't occur. His father peeked in on his way to breakfast as Harris sat at his desk with his notebook open attempting this manoeuvre.

"Son" Helmut said and surprised Harris at his desk. "We can only heal the physical, not the mental." With that, Harris looked down, dejectedly.

"Not to worry, my boy." His Da said. "I'm sure you'll do fine today. You have studied more this year than you have your whole life. Julius says you are coming along nicely and that girl of yours always has her nose in a book along with you."

His father then put his hand on his shoulder. "I'm proud of you, son…good luck today." Harris just smiled at the words of encouragement. He then gathered the few items he was allowed to take with him and walked to St. Joseph's for the final time that would require his brain to be at max levels.

He entered the massive testing room with over 80 other students. He brought with him six pencils, just in case. The proctor, Sister Roslyn, stood in front of the dead silent room with all eyes on the lovely woman in full habit and dress. She was one of the few good-looking nuns here, so it was hard to understand what drove her to exclusivity to God. Nonetheless, she made her final declaration...

"Students, I will wish you all luck and Godspeed as you take this final test. The grades will be posted next Monday outside the headmistress's office after 9 am. You have all done your revision, no doubt. All this will come up in the outside world in one way or another. If you remember even a farthing's worth, you'll come out ahead in your lives. Remember, the road is long, and the path is narrow." A favourite saying of hers. She then took a seat at the desk at the front of the hall and made the call…

"Right...You have two hours, thirty minutes…Start!" She said as she clicked her stopwatch. Just for luck, Harris blessed himself and said a quick "Hail Mary" just before he opened the first page. Many others did the same.

It was remarkable how unremarkable all this information was. Maths, History, Science, Physics…Ugh!!! The only good thing was that this was the light at the end of the tunnel. If he forgot everything tomorrow, it wouldn't matter a bunch of beans unless he failed.

He left the test centre after 2 hours with a sigh of relief and listening to the other students all ask each other the usual "What you think?" "How was it?" No one asked him as he walked down to get a drink at a small shop on the corner and home for a rest. No more books today! Just a nap and The Smiths on the radio.

Gina was done ½ an hour sooner than Harris as she called his phone the next day so that they could go out afterwards. For both, it was one down, one to go.

They compared notes about the test over at Korrect Kebabs and discussed their college plans. She mentioned going to Queen Anne's Veterinary College in Bristol for her veterinary science degree, and he told her about medical school and Cork.

"The scary thing is being on my own there," Harris said. "No help from you for all my studies. I hope I can keep this up on me own."

"Don't worry about that, dear." She said, touching his hand. "I have every bit of faith in you. No matter what, you are going to come out of this successfully."

"I just wish I had your level of confidence." He responded. "I was never outgoing enough. I don't even really know anyone in my class, aside from you."

"Yeah, I don't see why, either." She said. "You're a great guy. Anyone would be lucky to have you as a friend."

"I think it's my social ineptness." He responded. "You know how I am. I don't do well in crowds or social situations. I've been like this for as long as I can remember."

"Here's what you should do…" she said. "You have a chance to start again. You should find some social club when you get there and work with them. Just something with a few members and a small goal. You can get used to working with people that way."

"I guess." He said. "There is going to be a lot of time there. I'm just wondering how much of it will be actual work…How long is your programme?"

"5 years, same as yours." She answered.

"Between the two of us, we should be able to cure anything." He said to which she just smiled and held and squeezed his hand."

It then led to the elephant in the dining room. What to do while away from each other? They both knew that they had to have this discussion though neither wanted to face it.

"I know you'll find guys to date there." He said, sadly. "It's only a matter of course."

"…and you will find girls to date there." She said. "You'll come out of your shell, I know it…and you owe that to yourself."

Just then, a couple of uniformed Paragons entered the restaurant. Neither had ever seen a real Paragon before, but already had anger over the sight of them.

Not only for what their bigotry stood for but because this was all facilitating him having to part ways with the best thing that ever happened to him. They said nothing as they entered and just presented a £10 note to the cashier.

They both wore dark sunglasses, and their uniforms were black with a few orange stripes that ran up the sleeves and front of their leather jackets, and they both had a large baton attached to their belts that said Exodon. Harris and Gina just sat quietly while the officers got their orders in takeaway boxes and left in a Transit van that was known to carry a myriad of different items that were used to fight the so-called "threat" of Xenons. They both looked stoic and gave the air that one should not annoy them. Harris's thoughts turned from the fearful possibility of his discovery to relief when the officers left and then back to the one person he cared about the most.

"You realise that I would gladly give up these glowing hands if it meant spending the rest of my existence with you." He whispered to Gina. It was hard to see if she were blushing as her skin colour was darker than his own.

"Thank you, hon…" She said. "But this is a calling for you. By keeping it away from you and denying every one of your abilities would be too much to bear."

They just sat quietly over the other half of their lamb and lettuce kebab. Neither felt like finishing it. They walked down the avenue to Essex street still hand-in-hand to her house and the usual sweet sorrow of parting over a kiss. They would have the rest of July to enjoy together before the world forced their separation.

Chapter 5 - Dance to Forget

Two A's and a B! Harris couldn't be happier. Even if he missed the questions that would have improved his maths grade, he was now the possessor of enough grade score that assured his placement for medical school. That part was over. Gina stood next to Harris and looked at her test score and became angry.

"How could I only get 95%?" She said. "I studied all night and day for that!"

"Gina, C'mon! That's stellar" Harris said, comfortingly. "We'll both leave here with honours."

"What you get, then?" She asked.

"93% all around. Harris responded. "Enough to get into Cork."

They made their way out of the crowd of students all gathered around the poster boards with grades listed for them as well with sounds of both happy and sad students behind them. They also overheard the word "Paragons" while walking toward the exit from a couple of students talking, and Harris stopped Gina, and they just listened for a bit.

"Yeah, I guess he could make things melt with his bare hands." One student said.

"I heard of a guy like that. He could cause earthquakes to come out of nowhere...no wonder they collared him." The other boy said.

"Glad they did...they should all be shot!" Yet another said.

Gina pulled Harris along down the hallway. "Come on, dear." She said. "You don't need to bother with that."

Harris always felt on the outside anyway, and their comments didn't help. He also knew that he needed to get more social with this new step in his life. He had to start thinking about medical school, and that would take up much of his time with his revision, and it would be hard to see Gina for what little time they had left.

On the exit door, there was a poster that said "Last Hurrah! Graduation Dance and Disco at the Wooden Propeller Pub on 10 July at 7:00 pm. She couldn't believe what he said then:

"Gina, let's go to that dance!" He said.

Gina looked surprised. "Really?" She said. "You sure you can handle that crowd?"

"I have to do this." He said. "You said yourself that I needed to get more social, so I might as well give it a shot and see if I can do it."

"OK, then Hon." She said. "I'll get a nice dress for it."

The poster said it was a casual affair which was great as they spent enough time in a school uniform. Da always said he hated wearing a tuxedo when he went to formal affairs...it made him feel like a stuffed penguin! Harris wondered what people wore to these things...

His parents weren't going to be much help here besides being able to pass him the money for it. He went to Carvin's on the High Street and wanted to pick out something that looked good for the occasion. Rock stars and media may set the fashion, but he didn't want to go in for a shirt that was the colour of blooming flowers. Nor did he want to wear a weirdly coloured blazer like the stars of a particular American television show were wearing. He chose a silk cover shirt with royal blue stripes and a red cotton shirt with a pair of black slacks. He put on the ensemble in the shop dressing room. "I look good!" He said as he looked at himself in the mirror.

His studies were all medical from here out, so he and Julius went over the books and Harris was thinking about what interested him the most.

"I'm wondering what I should specialise in when I'm out on my own." He said to Julius.

"Well, I remember your father said that he wanted to be a neurosurgeon since he could easily hide his work. No one can see where your bleeding without a lot of effort." Julius responded.

"I do remember my father once saying he thought the human brain was the most amazing part of the human body," Harris said. "But I then told him "Look at what's telling you that!" They shared a small chuckle over that and went on with, as it happened, brain maladies."

The dance was on Saturday night. Harris went top drawer on this occasion thanks to his father who gave him £20 and said take a cab from her house tonight. He knocked up the door, and Mrs Ravalli answered.

She greeted him with a hug as she always did now when he came over. "My, don't you look smart?" She said while Vincent was using a rowing machine in the back of his library.

"Good Evening, Sir!" He shouted over to Mr Ravalli. Vincent just nodded as he was finishing his set.

"Poppa!" Magdalena shouted to her husband. "Your daughter's leaving soon. Make yourself presentable!"

"Yeah, all right." He responded in his Italian accent which meant just throwing a cover shirt over his sleeveless T-shirt.

Gina came down the stairs in a turquoise dress with red stripes. Harris was surprised in that he didn't think she could look better. "I am speechless." He said.

She kissed him and said, "That look on your face said it all."

The cab showed up and honked at the front door.

"Who's that for then?" Magdalena asked.

"That's for us," Harris answered.

"Bye, Mum…Bye, Dad!" She kissed them both, and they sprinted for the cab.

The Wooden Propeller was a good size pub on Byron Lane with a common room in the back. When they arrived, there was already a fast bit of dancing going on with a DJ in the corner. Harris was staying to the wall hoping that he could get through tonight without panic. They went over to the bar, and they both had a pint. Harris never bothered with beer as he didn't fancy the taste before but felt maybe the alcohol would do him some good in the crowd.

Gina and Harris slow danced a couple of times and fast danced as well. After an hour, a troop of dancers came in carrying a roll of lino and radio the size of Portsmouth. They announced that they wanted to show them all something new.

With that, they told the DJ to take a break and unrolled the old lino on the floor. There were about 6 of them in tracksuits and they were in the middle of about 50 or so watchers surrounding them. The music emerged from the giant cassette player that sounded like a team of robots put it together. What came next was a strange mix of gravity-defying gymnastics, back-spins, head-spins and robotic movements that were something no one here had seen before.

"What is this?" Harris asked Tom Haines, who was in his physics class.

"It's called breakdancing." He said in his heavy Welsh accent. "I saw these guys in Nottingham do it. I guess it's all the rage in the states.

Harris watched mesmerised at this demonstration and was fascinated by something called a "Moonwalk." Gina went over to get another pint for the both of them and spotted Headmistress, Sister Josephine Fyre in street clothes and a habit watching the performance, hypnotically, like Harris was. Gina went over and offered her some kind words.

"Hello Headmistress!" she said to the 60-year-old woman looking on to the performance. She said nothing and just stared forward through her bifocal lenses.

"Amazing, isn't it?" She again attempted conversation. Josephine said nothing.

"You all right then, ma'am?" she asked. Again, no reaction came over the headmistress. Gina put down the pints on a tall table and studied the face of the elder sister.

Gina looked carefully at her eyes as she stared forward with no semblance of any thought-process going on. Her face also seemed drooped a bit on the one side.

"Sister Josephine?" Gina tried to get her attention, even going as far as snapping her fingers in front of her eyes, but she was mumbling incoherently and quietly. She then ran over to Harris, who was watching the dancers do windmills and backflips. She whispered in his ear about the senior sister. They both ran to the headmistress.

"Sister?" Harris tried to get her reaction, but she continued to mummer. He recognised the symptoms from the tons of books he was cramming through for the medical school revision.

"Let's get her in that loo." He said to Gina. They led her to the ladies' washroom unseen by the other patrons fixed on the dancers. Her feet dragged as they put her arms over their shoulders. She wasn't fat, but they could feel the burden of what weight she possessed.

"Harris, what's wrong with her?" Gina asked.

"She's having a stroke." He responded as they entered. "Right, guard the door, then."

Harris stood behind her and put his beam of light from his glowing hand over the shoulder of the sister for 10 seconds while Gina observed, calmly. She then snapped-to with a yelp as if she had woken from a nightmare. Gina stood before her with a look of concern.

"Huh? What is this?" The sister asked Gina harshly like she was being talked down to in her office and didn't notice Harris standing behind her.

"Sister, you just came over queer," Gina responded.

"What do you mean I…" The headmistress began until she felt more desperate for liquids than in her entire life. The sister then grabbed her mouth and ran over to the sink and drank from the tap like no tomorrow. Harris then signalled to Gina that he would slip quietly and unseen out of the lady's loo as he was not supposed to be there.

When he came out, the dancers were taking a break and having a pint surrounded by a large group of adoring fans. Harris sat alone at the end of the bar and hoped no one would notice that he just emerged from "No Man's Land." The two females came out of the washroom with the Headmistress walking quickly out the door of the pub without stopping. Gina joined Harris and took control of the pints she set down, earlier.

"Sorry I left you like that." He said to Gina. "I wasn't supposed to be there."

"It's alright, dear." She said. "I got it sorted with her. I just said she was looking off, so I led her in the loo. I'm not sure what she thought, but she couldn't figure out how she got so thirsty all of a sudden."

"Yeah… odd that" Harris said.

Gina thought for a moment and came to a revelation.

"Harris," she said. "Your healing causes desperate thirst."

"Eh? What you mean?" Harris asked as he looked puzzled at her.

She looked around to make sure their conversation was just between them. The barkeep was still doling out pints to the dancers and their fans.

"What? You not notice that?" She asked. He just shook his head no.

"Well, when you healed my Dad and ran out the door, the first thing he did was take the water pitcher off the table and drank from that. He was fine then, but we wondered why he did that." Harris pondered this new aspect.

"The pony at the fair a couple of years ago..." He said, excitedly and quieted his voice a bit. "The water trough was the first place he went to." She nodded.

"Well, all right then," he said. "Now I'll know to keep a drink nearby when I'm healing patients."

The DJ took his place back behind his turntable and played a slow song.

"Come on, let's dance." She said, and they took to the dance floor with a few other couples. Atlantic Starr was playing "Always" as he followed her lead and they slow danced to the music and held each other tight as they fell into another kiss under the darkness illuminated with flashing coloured lights.

Chapter 6 - Trial by Fyre

Harris and Gina didn't stop studying, even after the dance. Harris still had to get ready for medical college even after he made stellar marks in the MCAT testing a fortnight later. Gina kept herself close to Harris when he took a break. They kept up the habit of kissing and snuggling and then back to studying. She went over what she needed for veterinary school, so it helped keep the information sharp in her head.

Two days after the dance, Harris was home alone and sweating over an extensive anatomy guide and a bag of crisps when he got an odd phone call from his Da's office:

"Hello?" Harris said.

"Harris, son…I hate to bother you while you are studying, but could you please come to my office at 3 pm? I need to get some information from you." Helmut said.

"OK, Da," Harris said. "What's up?" Helmut didn't give him any further details other than to be on time.

Harris took the bus downtown to Saville Hospital and went to his Da's office on the 4th floor. The hospital was a maze of rooms and offices, and Harris caught sight of a dozen people through the doors of their recovery rooms He thought of what he and his Da could do here if given a free hand.

He came to the door of his father's office with a sign on the door that said "Dr Helmut W. Gibraltar, Chief of Neurosurgery along with a few various initials of organisations unknown to him. He knocked on the door and heard the voice say "Enter." and found his father sitting behind a large oak desk. Sitting in a chair across from him was the wrinkled face of Headmistress, Sister Josephine Fyre." Her face showed no emotion toward either Gibraltar family member from her black habit and simple brass wire-frame glasses.

"Hello, son." Dr Gibraltar said. "Have a seat."

Harris took a seat next to Sister Josephine. Now what? Here was the one woman that Harris did not need to see again.

"Son…Harris…" His father said. "Sister Josephine Fyre here told me about how she had an incident happen to her the other night at an after-class party at a pub.

She said that she was watching some odd dancing going on and then she couldn't think right, and her mind went blank. The next thing she knew, your friend, Gina, was speaking to her in the woman's loo."

"Yeah, that's right," Harris said. "Gina…mentioned that to me, and I saw that you left straight away afterwards, Headmistress." Harris was puzzled as to what was going on here. "So, what do you need from me, then?"

"Well, son" Dr Gibraltar continued. "We were hoping you might have had an idea of why the sister here was missing some time from her memory."

"I don't drink!" The headmistress said defiantly as her proper English elocution reverted to light cockney. "I have a reputation to keep, and if anyone says that I may have engaged in conduct unbecoming, it will ruin me!"

"Now, sister…" Helmut said consolingly, "No one is accusing you of anything. I just wanted my son here to give us an idea of what may have caused your lapse of memory. After all, he was there."

Helmut then turned his gaze to his son. "Well, Harris, you are pre-med so you should be able to give us, at least, an acceptable hypothesis." Harris took a second to think. Not only of a believable alternative diagnosis for Sister Fyre's stroke, but why his Da was having him produce this theory. His father probably knew what happened, and this was a test. OK, then…a test it is as his fertile brain reached back to all the books that he read for the past two years and formulate something believable…

"OK, here is my theory…" Harris pronounced. "Sister Fyre was standing in an unresponsive state, staring at the dancers. I observed her having no response to any outside stimuli that neither Gina nor I, attempted."

"OK, go on…" Helmut said.

"I feared that she was having a stroke as the symptoms that I read about matched hers," Harris said. "However, she was responsive enough to enter the lady's loo, and when I saw her enter is when she came back to normal, I would guess. It seemed she had no motor skill problems and seemed coherent afterwards."

"Right…and what do you think caused that?" Helmut asked his son.

Harris continued: "I have two possibilities in mind. First, the symptoms of stroke without any damage would lead me to think Trans-Ischemic Attack, which can produce stroke symptoms without any permanent after-effects."

Helmut seemed deep in thought at this possibility. "…and the other?" Helmut asked.

"There were many flashing lights on the dance floor…Strobes and flashes everywhere leading me to believe it could have been a light-induced epileptic seizure." Harris said. "The former would be my diagnosis only if the sister's blood pressure is at hypertension levels. The latter, if not." Dr Gibraltar then took a look at her medical chart, which was laying on his desk.

"Sister, your blood pressure is quite alright. Helmut said. "I will concur with my son in that the flashing lights were most likely responsible for your absence of mind."

The headmistress seemed relieved at the mention of this. "So, what should I do about this?" She asked.

Helmut answered the same way Harris would have… "Well, the simple solution is to avoid areas with flashing lights such as those at the pub. Otherwise, there are surgeries to correct this."

"Surgeries?" She inquired.

"Yes, brain operations like this are new and experimental, but a possibility." He answered.

The latter answer didn't seem to sit well with the sister.

"I'll just avoid the lights, if it's all the same to you, Doctor." She said

"Of course, sister," Helmut answered with a slight smile. "Any other concerns?"

"No, I'm just glad I wasn't going mental." She answered. She then turned her attention to Harris. "It looks like you have a future, after all, child." She said. "I was worried about you in the past, but you seemed to have righted yourself.

She grabbed her purse and stood up to go. "Thank you, Doctor." She said with Helmut nodding in response with a faint grin.

"…And good luck to you, young Gibraltar…you go and do everyone proud." She said with a faint smile of relief and left the office. Harris grinned as she left.

Helmut then motioned to Harris to pull his chair closer to his desk. Harris was a bit nervous about what was to come out of his mouth next.

"All right, son," Helmut said. "Stroke was it?"

"Aye...perhaps even a brain aneurysm," Harris said. "I was surprised she didn't end ten toes up. It's like her body didn't know enough to fall."

"I see," Helmut said. "Well, thank God, you recognised what to do...I suppose you can guess why I brought you in?"

"To make sure my storytelling ability checks out?" Harris said with a cheeky smirk.

Helmut gave it back "That's right, Mother Goose!" They both had a smirk over that.

"Anyhow..." Helmut continued. "You have proven yourself well today, son. Just be sure that you have your diagnosis always at the ready if needed. As you've seen today, there may be inquiries, and you want to be sure to be on top of them at all times."

"Yes, Da," Harris said. "I see that now. I suppose I could keep a catalogue of them at the ready?"

"You could," Helmut said. "But use them in general, though. You are going to encounter some gentle nuances that may make one different from another, so you'll have to be ready for that as well." Harris nodded. The intercom then went off with the enticing voice of Helmut's secretary, Anna.

"Dr Gibraltar, your 4:00 is here."

"Just a moment." He responded. "OK, son, I'll see you at home. You did me proud today." He said as he smiled subtly as he always did.

Harris walked out of his Da's office with both a feeling of pride and a sigh of relief. He thought of what happened as he took the bus back to Chelsea. He did his best to remember to have a diagnosis ready at all times.

Chapter 7 - Moving right along...

Harris stood looking at himself in the mirror wearing his black graduation robe. He looked at himself and was just glad to get to this point where he could be his own man. At the same time, feeling a bit down in that the path already chosen for him. Being a doctor wasn't the only thing he could do, but at the same time, it was the best option out there. It was like being drafted into service. He took a long look in the mirror and thought what his next move was.

"Son..." His Mum said as she walked behind up behind him looking in the mirror. "You look so handsome." She said as they both looked in the mirror at his cap and gown wardrobe.

"Thanks, mum," Harris said. "I wonder what's next, though. I haven't been outside of London except on vacation, and that was always with you two."

"I know you'll do well, son." She said. "You have a path in front of you all laid out. A lot of people don't know what they want to do even in this part of their lives..."

"That's the thing, mum." Harris jumped in. "I never even thought of the medical field until I got conscripted into it. I had no clue that this..."

"Yes, son, I know," Jean said. "From what your father said, it sometimes skips a generation. We didn't know for sure if you were going to be given this mantle or not."

Harris didn't know that part of it. He didn't look at the timeline in the family history book that he reviewed, quickly, a couple of times during his studies. The visages of past family members and their stories of whom they served had passed before his field of vision. He had all the sympathy in the world for those who may have been passed over for this vestige who had wanted it. Harris turned back to the mirror and removed his mortarboard for a moment. He breathed a sigh looking at himself in his graduation robe.

"It's a lot to live up to, Mum," Harris said. "I told Gina I'd give it all up for her if I had that option. She wouldn't have accepted it, though."

"I would figure she would say that," Jean said. "Harris, you do realise that you both may part ways over your times away from each other?" She said a bit nervous over what reaction she would get.

"Yes, Mum," Harris said to her relief. "We were over that several times. She'll probably date others…so will I. We know we have to be pragmatic about it."

Helmut then entered his son's room and saw the two of them together.

"All right then, son?" Helmut asked

Harris gave the nod and said "OK, let's move on then…Life is on the other side of London."

"Right," Helmut said, "But let me get a snap of you both, first…" as Helmut readied his camera for a picture.

Several snaps were taken of him alone and with both his parents before they left for Rickett's Gate where the graduation ceremony was to take place.

Harris wanted to see one more person before he accepted his diploma.

They arrived at the park by cab and Harris was to join his class in front of the stage. He looked around for Gina until he finally saw her and her parents getting out of a car. Harris just stood and looked at the girl dressed similarly to him in a black graduation robe, there was the one adored her but would have to let go of in another couple of weeks. He then ran over to her with his mortarboard in hand. He just gave her a quick peck on the cheek as they were in public.

"You look great, Hon." He said to her.

"You do too, dear!" She said and surprised him with a big kiss, not caring who was around. Harris was taken aback but couldn't be happier.

After they regained their composure, Harris went and shook hands with Vincent who had a vice grip handshake before now had an even more monstrous grip after all these years. Magdalena gave Harris a big hug and congratulated him on his success. Harris noticed his mum and Da had followed him up to the Ravalli family. He also saw his father wincing as he gave Helmut the same gripping handshake that he gave Harris a bit ago.

"Doctor…" Vincent said. "I guess I owe you my gratitude as well as your teaching your son that CPU thing…If it weren't for that, I wouldn't be here today."

"Well, thank you, sir," Helmut said as he shook off the pain in his hand unnoticed by anyone. "Let's hope he does it a lot more." The Ravalli's also introduced their sons to The Gibraltar family.

The only daughter in their family was graduating, and the boys were in to support their sister. The brothers went and took their seats after the introduction. Father Victor Ravalli was the oldest son and wore his collar to the ceremony as was custom. A very tall, thin gentleman with very black and stringy hair wearing glasses with thick black frames. He walked behind his Mum and Da limping on a bum leg, a walking cane at his side. Harris smiled and shook the hands of the priest along with his brother, Eduardo, a handsome gent was wearing a white suit that looked like it cost more than the entire school.

His beautiful wife and children were there as well looking like they fell off a fashion magazine cover. She remained quiet as her husband did all the talking. Francine then took the kids to their seats while speaking in Italian to them all. The children were also not saying anything.

Magdalena was also heaping praise on Jean for raising such a good boy. "He has been a true delight to have around…" She said and looked around for him, but he wasn't there…Gina was gone missing as well.

"Where'd they go?" Jean asked

Harris and Gina ran behind a brick building and were kissing as if their lives depended on it.

"I was hoping to see you the other night, but you weren't home," Harris said between kisses.

"My lot took me out to dinner. My brothers are in town." She said with another kiss.

The band started playing a hymn, so it was time to take their seats. Harris ran one way, and she ran another to the two sides of the audience watching the stage. Harris found Jonas Gibbs standing and singing "One Sweet Day" so he went to stand next to him as his name was alphabetically next to his for as long as he could remember. They listened to the Headmistress, Sister Josephine Fyre, give a long, meandering speech about this and that which went on for way too long.

He walked up after sweating in his polyester graduation robe and got his diploma along with his 80 or so classmates, one at a time. After Sister Fyre's congratulations to the Grade 13 class and the mortarboards went flying in the air, Harris re-joined his family among the crowd of other families doing the same.

Jean took several pictures of Harris as she did at home. Gina came over and hugged Harris. Helmut took a couple of snaps of the two of them together.

"Harris," Gina said. "Let's get together later tonight. My folks and I are going out with my brothers. "OK, Hon," Harris said. With a kiss between them, she went back to her lot.

Meanwhile, Helmut has something special planned for his son and wife. That evening, they took a 15-minute taxi ride and found themselves at the Kensington Steak House. Harris knew that this place was one of the best restaurants in London and his father had gone there once after the invitation of a high hospital administrator hoping to retain (i.e. beg) for Dr Gibraltar's continued services. The smell of cooked cattle was terrific in this place. Harris was so glad his parents didn't raise him vegetarian. When they stepped in, who should be there but Gina and her lot? "Surprise, hon!" His mum shouted.

Gina and Harris hugged while there was a round of gentle applause. "Son…" Helmut said. "We wanted to give you both a big celebration, and we knew Gina was a big part of your life this past couple of years."

"I'm afraid my brother, Eduardo had to leave town," Gina said. "He has a lot going on at that restaurant of his."

"Oh, sorry to hear that," Harris said. "I would have liked to have talked to him."

"It's OK." She said. "He's a busy guy, and his wife would have been bored, what with her not able to speak English and all."

They sat down to an excellent couple of cuts. Da told him to order anything he liked, but Harris settled for a middle of the road porterhouse. He didn't eat a lot as his thin build exemplified. They all pretty much ordered the same size steak except for Father Victor who ordered a slightly larger steak.

"My order doesn't give me a chance at a meal like this." He said in his Italian accent.

"No problem at all, Father," Helmut said. "You just enjoy the celebration."

They blessed themselves and Father Victor said grace in Latin as it seemed to be their family tradition.

"You should hear my mum," Gina said. "She's saying how you and I should get married and have a big family…I kept telling her I have other ideas."

"Hon…" Harris said. "You got to live the life you want. No one else will do it for you."

Gina smiled as he said that. He understood her and what she wanted. They both also knew that this time wouldn't last, and they had to hang on to these good times. The meal was excellent, and Harris turned his ear to hear the conversations going on. Father Victor was speaking to Helmut and Vincent in his Italian accent about how things were at the cathedral in Turin. He even met the Pope last year.

"The Council of Cardinals are about to make some new pronouncements, many are to reiterate what has been said many times before you know…abortion, birth control, homosexuals…" Father Victor went on, and Harris was about to tune him out…

"Now they are talking about Xenon rights."

Harris and Helmut both turned their attention as subtly as possible to him.

"Really?" Helmut said quietly. Harris just let him work. He was always diplomatic when Harris got in trouble in school with bullies and the occasions he would have to go and sort it out…Not always in Harris's favour, though.

"So far, the Pontiff has stayed away from the issue," Victor said. "We don't know what we're going to be told yet, so it's up to our judgement how to proceed."

"I see," Helmut said. "Well, forgive me for saying this, but that is a decision I'm glad is not on my shoulders." Father Victor cocked his head to one side over that while Helmut continued. "I mean, it's one thing to be in charge of a person's body to their best good, but a soul…that lasts forever."

Harris thought what a skilful way to speak. His Da talked in public in the same way a great artist paints a masterpiece.

"I appreciate that, Doctor. Thank you." Father Victor said.

They left with Father Victor saying he had to get up in the morning. He was going to hear confessions at The Church of St. Peter's, which was Harris's family's church. They all made their way to a cab, Father Ravalli slowly hobbling behind, to take The Ravalli's home, except for Gina. She rode back with the Gibraltar family to their house. Gina came over sometimes when she and Harris studied together. Their parents said goodnight and left them in the living room.

They knew that they were pretty well free to do anything now, but they chose to talk, for now. Harris had a fortnight to go before he had to leave for Cork. It now felt a bit strange to be so close to someone who would not be there for long. Harris loved Gina but followed the adage "If you love someone, set them free."

"I'm so conflicted right now," Gina said. "I know I want to go to college, but I'm afraid of it, as well. Do you feel that way, too?"

"Oh yes," Harris said. "It's just so weird what has happened and now having to take this step...I can't tell you how I feel about you, Gina...it would make it hurt even more since we're going to have to part ways." With that, he kissed her again.

"You don't have to say anything, dear," Gina said. "We'll just go and see what happens."

Gina and Harris walked back to her place. It was late, and her old house was dark. They hugged and kissed on her porch until they finally found a moment to let go. Harris walked home down a deserted Essex Street. His head was still full of thoughts of how cruel the world was in that he had to leave her side soon.

Chapter 8 - The Confessional

Harris made his final preparations before he left for medical college. He and his parents took an aeroplane and then the bus to The Royal University of Medicine. The flat that he chose would be off campus at #8 Savage Street which was far better a neighbourhood than the name made it sound. It was close to the library, which would encourage his reading and studying. The on-campus cafes and restaurants along with the pubs off-site would keep him fuelled. He also stopped at the Book Shoppe and got his revision list ready. All he had to do was give them the paper, and they would give him what he needed.

Harris also made a promise to himself that he would only use his extraordinary healing abilities only when necessary and not in hospital when learning as it was of utmost importance to assure that he was getting the most out of his education. It would be cheating if he were healing on the slight.

He and Gina would spend what few days they had left, together. They would go to the shops together and pick out some suitable clothes for his time away. He realised that picking out something for her to wear would be insulting as his sense of fashion was lacking was a real understatement. She helped him by picking something out that was professional and yet understated. The last thing he wanted to do was dress better than the professors. He ended up not having some funds come into the bank in time, which led to a cheque overdraw. Ugh!

Harris went the day before he was to leave home to go to confession and leave with a clean slate. He walked into St. Peters Cathedral and took a seat in a pew and took out his rosary. The priest stepped into the confessional while Harris finished his "Our Father," so he didn't notice who the priest was when he entered the other side of the small booth. Harris then entered the confessional and took a seat inside the dark space. He blessed himself as the small window opened.

"Bless me, father, for I have sinned. It's been two months since my last confession."

"What sins have you to confess, my son?" The voice was unmistakable…Father Victor must have stayed for a bit longer.

"4 times I have had impure thoughts about my girlfriend; Twice, I took the Lord's name in vain…Oh, and I bounced a cheque at Carvin's on the High Street, but that was an accident," Harris said.

"…Then it's not a sin." The voice of Father Victor said.

"Father…" Harris interrupted. "May I ask you a question?"

"You may." Father Victor said.

"I understand that the church's view of Xenons is to be the individual priests…" Harris said.

"That is correct…" Father Victor said. "So why do you ask?"

Harris knew that in the confessional, everything was confidential between him and the priest…and God, of course.

"I just needed to know where my place in the world is…as a Xenon." Harris said.

With that, Father Victor slammed the confessional window shut. Well, he now knew his opinion.

"Father?" Harris said. "What about my penance?"

No response came from the priest.

"Father???" Harris said and knocked on the sliding window. Father Victor opened it with force.

"Look, I will not speak of you here…that is my sacred duty, but I cannot in good conscience give penance to an abomination of God! Now please leave!" Father Victor said as he slammed the window shut again.

"Abomination?" Harris was fuming. How dare he say that to him! Harris was ready to lash out at the Vicar but held himself back. He thought of his father and how he handled things, diplomatically. Harris came up with a solution that seemed just right for the situation. He then drew the curtain back and left the confessional with Father Victor sighing with relief upon hearing his exit.

However, in a full breach of protocol, Harris roughly opened the solid wooden door with Father Victor sitting there shocked and stuck his open hand over the priest's face with the full glow of light shining into his eyes. He spoke his peace after the light dissipated:

"I wonder who else you would call an abomination?" Harris yelled and slammed the confessional door as he turned and then left the cathedral by kicking the door open on his way out.

Father Victor just sat stunned in the confessional for a few seconds until the thirst overtook him. He then ran out of the confessional while grabbing his throat and, in a breach of protocol, pulled the silver bowl full of holy water out of the marble basin that parishioners blessed themselves with when walking in. Father Victor's thirst was so out of control that he thought nothing about drinking the contents which left him gasping heavily afterwards. The impact of what he did then hit him, which let him glad no human eyes saw what just happened. Disgusted with his behaviour, He then blessed himself and asked forgiveness for what he just did while leaning with his head on the cold marble pedestal.

As Harris took the bus home to Essex Street, he wondered how long it was going to take Father Ravalli to realise that he would now be walking on two perfectly good legs? He seethed with anger at this prejudice and tried to take his mind off the whole occurrence by distracting himself with anything else. He then saw a strange sight out the window of the double-decker bus. A man parked in his car sat behind the wheel while talking on some futuristic telephone. He had only heard of such a strange device on the telly.

"Well, maybe someday I'll have one if I'm ever a millionaire." He thought as his bus dropped him off at Essex Street.

He walked down the street past his old faith school and saw Gina's house was dark. Maybe they were all out to dinner. He knew he had to get used to the feeling of not being here anymore. To take his mind off things, he then went into his living room and watched a show about motoring. He even considered getting a licence to drive. Harris spent his time also wondering if he should tell his Da about the whole affair that just occurred but decided against it as he knew a long lecture about secrecy would follow. Too many long class lectures would be filling his head when the college studies began.

Chapter 9 - The New Beginnings

Father Victor Ravalli sat on the bed in his guest room after finishing his ablutions the next morning. It was time for one other procedure. Victor took a hypodermic needle out of his valise and injected himself with a dose of his "special" medicine. A couple of minutes later, he was walking down the hall of the church when his head became dizzy, and he collapsed on his way to breakfast. Several other concerned priests and church-workers called for an ambulance to take him to London City hospital. He was alive and conscious when they took him from the rectory.

Meanwhile, Harris thought "How did this day arrive so fast?" As he sat on the bench at Heathrow Airport sitting and waiting for his flight. It would be a short flight but would carry him far away from his home in less than an hour. He would also be totally on his own when he got there. Gina and Harris promised to meet up on the Christmas holiday when they came home.

Gina rode with The Gibraltar Family to the airport. Harris just held Gina's hand, which was the opposite of the behaviour they demonstrated to each other the night previous. He "kept her respectable" as her parents would surely call it. If it had gone further, only they would know, but chose not to go there as being separated would be hard enough. Harris felt like he was going to war. To not be with the girl he loved or his family who always kept him safe, he didn't know if he was ready for this new part of his life as the appreciation for what he had and was about to be without finally entered his mind.

Until he had his healing path, he was getting into fights, breaking windows and suffering the indignance of being bullied along with being hauled into the headmistress's office for daring to fight back. Now here he was having to leave the young woman who made everything all right along with his mother for keeping him on the straight and narrow and his father giving him guidance for his new set of skills that he would be forced to use sparingly.

The call for his aeroplane came over the loudspeaker. One more kiss from his love and she practically had to push him to the gangway to board up. His carry-on was on his shoulder, one large piece of luggage was stowed away in the belly of this aluminium beast. He took his seat while other people were making their way up the aisle and storing their bags in the overhead bins.

Harris opened a package that his Da gave him before he boarded. It was from Dr Guiteau, so Harris expected it to be yet another medical book. Instead, it was a copy of The Hitchhiker's Guide to the Galaxy. A note inside stated "Don't forget to have some fun as well. Signed, J.G." He sat and waited for the flight to take off with trepidation. This was uncharted territory for him. What was next?

Back on the ground at Heathrow, the taxi pulled up for the three to head back to Essex Street. Gina, however, had a favour to ask on their way back again...

"Dr Gibraltar, I...I have to go to hospital, but it's on the way if you could leave me there?" Gina asked with her tears, finally beginning to dry...

"Of course, dear," Helmut said with kindness. "Let's go." And they all piled into the cab.

"So why hospital, then? Jean asked, just realising what was said. "Not your father again?"

"No, my brother this time," Gina responded. "He's all right. He just overdosed on his insulin this morning. "He's been taking it since age 7...You would think he'd have it down by now."

Harris's aeroplane touched down on the emerald isle as he landed in another world. He was going to hire a taxi, but the busses seemed to make regular runs to the college. So here he was, alone and not knowing anyone here in a city he saw only once. He dragged his rolling luggage to the old house on Savage Street that belonged to a mid-aged couple called Emmitt and Jane MacDougall, a husband and wife that were new to the housing game. He was home for the next five years.

He dragged his bag into his flat and didn't bother to unpack. He just wanted to fall on the squeaky bedsprings with no linens and nap for 10 minutes. He woke up, and it was already late afternoon out. The only reason he woke up was the arrival of his dorm mate.

"Allo, there." He said. "I guess I'm your flatmate, then...I'm Roland Fitzsimmons." He was the same height as Roland, his brown hair was uncombed and a bit on the heavier side. Not as handsome, but, seemingly full of confidence...among other things. Harris sat up on the noisy mattress and springs and shook his head. He was still in a bit of a fog as he just awoke to the darkening sky.

"Sorry, to wake you, mate," Roland said. "Did you just get in?"

"No, I've been asleep all day…glad you woke me, actually," Harris said. "Oh, I'm Harris Gibraltar." He put out his hand and Roland shook it in greeting.

"Mate, you must have been exhausted. No sheet on the bed and your packs are still untouched" Roland noticed.

"Oh yeah…I didn't mean to sack out for so long." Harris said. "I guess I better put things in order…what time it is?" He asked.

"About 6:30," Roland answered.

"I didn't eat all day. Any place open for a bite at this hour?" Harris asked.

"I thought I'd hit the pub," Roland said. "They might have something there."

"Oh, bloody Hell!" Harris said. "I got to call my lot and tell them I got here!"

"Relax, man," Roland said. "We'll find a phone. I'll bet they think you were too busy anyway."

Harris took a breath. "Yeah, maybe…ok, let's get."

The two of them went to a pub called The Draughtsman, where a bunch of other students gathered. He started swapping life stories with Roland and a bunch of other freshmen. A few second and third years were there as well mixing it up. He and Roland got to talking about their lives. Roland lived on a farm from up north who got in on brains and luck. He followed the same path as Harris, it seemed except for the Xenon part…well, if he had any ability, he certainly wasn't talking about it.

They sat down and joined a bunch of other hopefuls. Becky McGill was a blonde, Scottish lass with a deep voice who pounded three beers in succession. Martha was a heavy-set and nervous girl from Lester that Harris sympathised with completely. Morgan was the red-headed son of a doctor from Durham. He and Harris both agreed that being the son of a physician was not easy as their fathers insisted carrying on the family name in the practice of medicine.

Then there was Julia who had dark hair and too much make-up. She looked great but probably had an even better face under all that foundation. There was Sarah Pine, a punk-rocker with purple hair and a rough attitude. Also, there was Ai Tamaki, a Japanese student with a thick accent and an Akira shirt who was happy to get along with everyone.

Last, but not final was Todd Hunter, who seemed to be the only American in the pub…maybe the University, who wanted a change of locale, so he came here from his home in Philadelphia, PA. He spoke with an accent like Harris's Uncle Thomas who lived in New York City.

This place was not like St. Joseph's. No one was throwing their weight around or playing the bully. They were all gathered there for a common goal; To come out with a degree and a future. He did sneak off to the phone box on the corner to make two calls. One call went to Gina to say how he missed her. She said to enjoy this time and to stay in touch when he could. She mentioned her brother, Victor in passing and that he had to go to hospital, but it was no big deal. Harris had an idea of why he had to go there.

The other was to call his parents, who didn't expect him to call this soon. They were, of course, glad to hear from him and glad to also understand how he was not hiding in his room like he used to. "This was what the path to growing up was." His mum said. "Just call us when you can, son," Helmut said. "When you get rolling, you are going to be up to your eyebrows in research and studies." They wished him well and let him get back to socialising.

Harris went back to the crowd that seemed even more prominent now. After a bit, the guys were chatting up the birds and leaving him on the outside as he didn't want to play that game right now. He kept his anxiety in check until he was alone for a few minutes with no one to speak to, so he decided to slip out and head back to his flat.

The silence and solitude were blissful to him. He was a bit proud of himself now as he didn't want to run out but leave calmly. Now it was on to making his room, this bit of Ireland, his new home for the time being. He took an hour to put everything in its place. There were ceiling lights overhead and a small table lamp, but that's all, and it wasn't enough. He would have to remind himself to buy a floor lamp later. There was a dresser for his clothes and a tallboy bureau with a few extra hangers for the good stuff. He also had a framed picture of Gina that she sat for before graduation that he set beside his night table so that he would be able to see her smiling at him first and last thing from his bed. He also had an alarm clock that he wound and set for the next morning.

His orientation would be sharp at 9 am, so he set it for 7 am to get ready and to get something more substantial to eat than the plate of chips and the jar of ale he had at the pub.

His small travel bag that held his ablutions for the morning was near the loo door that he would share with Roland. He would have to knock before going in or see the light coming from the bottom of the door.

Harris began reading the book Julius gave him and enjoyed reading for just the fun of it when he heard a rustle of two voices next door. One was Roland, and the other was definitely female. The two of them carried on for a bit with the sound of the bedsprings as noisy as Harris's. The session didn't last too long, however, which was a relief for Harris, but not for the female, whomever it was. Roland was told so in a tirade that seemed to last longer than their time of grunting and moaning. A loud door slam was followed soon by the shower going and then no sound at all. "Better luck next time, friend." Harris thought as he marked his book and took one more look at Gina, smiling at him from the small photo before he turned the light out.

Harris awoke at the alarm's ringing and went to breakfast at O'Deer's Cafe on the corner smirking at the jokey name. After cleaning up, he walked with Roland over to the lecture hall, where they would have their introduction to the programme. It was a long stroll as well, so they talked about life in general, such as Gina and how his family was there for him. Roland had no girlfriend to speak of before coming to the school as he didn't want to leave anyone behind before coming to Cork.

"I didn't wake you last night, did I? Roland asked.

"I was pretty dead to the world when I got in," Harris said. "All I did was set up and crash."

Harris could have said something else cheeky right then but decided Roland was feeling bad enough about himself, so he let it go as they entered the large lecture hall. They were about to sit down when Roland saw a girl in their aisle with black hair and a bit too much make-up.

"Let's sit over here, instead," Roland said. The girl took no notice of either one of them switching seats. Harris could only guess at the reason for the change of the sitting pattern.

Another thing that Harris took notice of was how many men and women here seemed to be of Indian and Arabic descent. With that, they took up the entire right side of the room rather than blend in with the left and centre rows of seats. He guessed they just enjoyed the familiarity of their own lot.

They all sat at seats with small flat desks attached to their sides and got out writing pads with pencils and pens at the ready. An older man with white hair, tweed grey jacket and thick black-framed glasses came out and tapped the microphone with a small sound of feedback to address the two hundred or so that were before him and cleared his throat.

"Let the games begin," Harris said with Roland giving the nod as they began to scribble on their notepads.

"Good morning, Freshmen…" He said with an Irish brogue. "My name is Dr Ian Rosewood, and I am Chancellor here at The Royal College of Medicine in Cork. I'll ask you to take a good look at the lot around you. The chances are that for the next five years, you will see them more than your own family…

Chapter 10 - Far from Home...

The days were nothing compared to St. Joseph's Academy in terms of the brutal scope of work that needed to be studied for and delivered in a timely fashion with time being subjective. Harris started to wonder how anyone could keep their sanity and work at this pace? His Da did, and so did Dr Guiteau. He knew that they would be counting on him to accomplish all this. They did it, after all.

All he wanted to do was make sure all his assignments were ready to turn in and done up well to go back to London for Christmas. The possibility of seeing Gina was all he wanted. Gina said she was having a time herself of getting everything together. She even told Harris that he would have the advantage of having his patients telling him what the problem was. They also knew that there would be a problem keeping in touch by phone as their schedules didn't line up, so they wrote letters to stay in touch. He managed some time away from studies for one hour every day just for himself. It was then he would write his letters to Gina, or he would call his parents as they had a regular schedule.

The first letter she sent was a godsend over all the homework they had to go over;

Dear Harris,

Life here in Bristol is nutty. I am rooming with two other girls, both from Kent, whom I believe never stepped off the farm in their lives! I had to teach them how to use a washer and a vending machine. How do you not know that by now?

We spend much of our time over books and dissecting animals to learn of all their functions. I decided to switch to vegetarian after what I have seen.

Dissecting and examining vegetables seems less of a strain as everything I eat, I am now tracking back to the source and from where it came.

By the way, when my brother Victor went to hospital the morning I saw you off, He said good luck and that he apologises for what he said to you. He also said he couldn't tell me any further about it, but that you would understand. I hope it wasn't too horrid.

Talking of family, my Dad is in next week's London marathon. He wishes we were there but understands what we need to do.

Hoping this letter finds you well with all my heart and respect.

Gina

The letters between them became fewer and further apart, though as the medical training continued to intrude. There were mountains of papers to write on every aspect of the human body and what could happen to it if you had X introduced in virus form and Y if you didn't allow for some disease to build up an immunity.

There was very little lab work in the first semester — just a bunch of notes to take and general anatomy terms to acquaint one's self. Harris was feeling good as he went over nearly all of this with Dr Guiteau.

Studying was a breeze because of this knowledge going in. He lent his expertise to Roland and let him in on his mnemonics and the mind tricks that Julius taught him for the past two years.

Harris liked Roland. He was a good guy and seemed a reliable friend. They got along well together after classes and studied with the other doctors in training. Roland cautioned that they should not get too attached to the students fresh from Pakistan and New Delhi as they would be devoting themselves so entirely to their studies that they might disappear altogether after the first year. It was nothing personal…Just that their culture dictated exclusivity to their work.

Harris spent most of his time alone in studying and knew that he had to break out and share his studies with more of the students there. It seemed, though that everyone else was keeping to themselves as well. The only other people he heard were in the library, and they had their noses in books and not speaking to anyone.

Roland's dates on the weekends were the only ones that came to the flat they shared. From the grunting and heavy breathing sounds next door, they were doing anything but studying.

The first year involved Humanities and Evolution of medicine, along with Human form and life evolution. All three of these courses felt about the same over time, although each required a mass of time and reading. He knew it was unnecessary on the outside but kept his promise to himself that he needed to stay on the regular path and at least look like he knew what he was doing. Sister Fyre gave him the lesson that he needed to provide explanations for how he treated someone.

Finally, Christmas arrived, and classes went on hiatus. Harris felt he had to get something nice for the most important people in his life. The local stores didn't carry a lot that was distinctive for the area. He chose a quilt for his mother and a silk tie for his father. For Gina, he chose a gold rose necklace. He just hoped to be able to give it to her in person.

There was just a light snowfall this year, but the temperatures were well below zero Celsius. He had no problem getting home to Chelsea where his Mum and Da awaited him and had everything in shape after the four months he left. Napoleon was the first to greet him as he was indoors due to the frigid weather that gripped London. Napoleon was his father's dog. However, he became closer to Harris as he grew into a man.

The family of Harris's mum visited for the usual festivities along with Christmas dinner, Aunt Minnie and cousins Jane and Wendy visiting from Leicester and her Uncle Thomas visiting from New York City where he was doing land acquisition work in the states.

His favourite gift though came from his Da who gave him a stethoscope, but not just any heart minder as it belonged to his Grandfather. Helmut told Harris to keep it as an heirloom if he didn't use it as it was in the family for a couple of generations, even before Grandfather Unger brought it with him to Bern, Switzerland just after World War II.

But the one he wanted to visit was his Gina. He walked down Essex Street to her house in the snow that picked up to an inch or so. Aldo, one of Eduardo's boys, answered the door in a white sweater and chinos.

"Hello," Harris said. "Merry Christmas." Hoping he knew what that meant.

"Oh, hi." The boy said in English with an Italian accent. "You're that guy-friend of Gina, right?"

"Yeah, is she in?" Harris asked and surprised and relieved he had a full grip on the language.

Just then, Gina came to the door and gave a small shove to Aldo.

"There you are stranger!" She said and kissed him full on the mouth.

Harris was longing for this moment for several months. Gina seemed so dominant every time they got together. Not that Harris had any issue with it.

"One would think you missed me." He said, joking.

"You know I did…come on in!" She said.

He first passed the library with a couple of exercise machines and a trophy on a shelf. To think that this was the same man who was overweight and prone to heart disease when he met him and now was running races and powerlifting.

He walked in and saw The Ravalli family enjoying Christmas dinner. "Hi everyone!" Harris said. "I'm sorry, I didn't mean to interrupt your lunch."

"Harris, Dear!" Magdalena said as she hugged the young man. "You don't give that a second thought…come, I fix you something."

Harris was going to tell her that he already ate, but she was serving up something in front of him, and it looked too good to pass up.

"Harris, boy…well, I should say man, now!" Vincent said as he shook Harris's hand, although his grip was not as tight. Someone must have told him about it. Also, at the table was Eduardo and his wife just smiled while toying with the manicotti in front of him. Francine was enjoying it more than her husband.

"It good to see you again, sir," Eduardo said. "I see you graduated with me sister. Where you now?"

"I'm going to medical school in Ireland. Harris said, "It's exhausting."

Eduardo translated all this to his Francine. She was, apparently the only one not able to speak the language. She was impressed with his position as a med student. That look came through her face, even without a translation

Just then, Father Victor entered the room, apparently returning from the loo.

"Ah, Harris." The father said. "Good to see you again." He presented his hand to shake, which Harris did.

Harris also noticed that Father Victor was walking straight and happily, which was in opposition to how he was stumbling about before.

"Honey, we got to go take a stroll later. Gina said. "It's beautiful out." Harris nodded while toying with his manicotti.

"Hey, watch this!" Said Eduardo's daughter, Connie, who was about seven while Aldo was ten and Sergio, who sat quietly was about 13. She had a puzzle cube that was thoroughly mixed up and solved it in less than one minute.

"That's extraordinary!" Harris said and meant it. He could never make heads or tails of those things, and this young girl could solve it in seconds.

"She's been able to do that since last year," Gina said. "I bought her one for Easter, and she could do it right out of the box!"

Harris was flummoxed. Such a young age and able to do this so easily…

"My dear, how do you do that? I could never figure that out!" He asked.

"I just look at it, and it makes sense," Connie said. Harris wished many times he had that ability.

A half-hour of discussion went by of politics and the state of the world kept Harris talking to Vincent while Gina was off chatting with Eduardo for a while. Father Victor was out of sight for a bit as well. Sergio, for a young lad, had a lot to say about the current condition and the Pope's upcoming decision about Xenon rights. He was in full favour of their being able to live like other people, and their behaviour should depend on what crimes were part of the discussion…and entrapment for unleashing what abilities they had was to be measured as well. Harris couldn't argue with any of it.

Gina came back and was not smiling. Harris figured she could use some time away from everyone else and motioned for them to go for a walk. He got on his old anorak, and the two walked out in a steady snowfall. There was no destination. They just a strolled through this part of London with decorations in the windows of the people celebrating the holy birth. He didn't notice that she seemed to have something on her mind.

"My dear…Merry Christmas." Harris said as he gave her the wrapped box with the necklace.

Gina opened the box and started crying. Harris knew it was an excellent gift but didn't expect such a reaction.

"Uh, I didn't think it was that bad," Harris said in a confused state.

"It's beautiful," Gina said through her tears. A long pause went by until she talked again.

"I…I can't see you again. I'm sorry." Gina said and just ran back to her house, crying.

Harris was perplexed as he just stood dumbfounded in the falling snow. What just happened here? He went back to his house and just spent the rest of his time with his family. They could tell something was up but didn't press it. Harris went up to his old room, now devoid of his influence. The punk posters were gone and now replaced with pictures of scenery with a movie poster framed and hung on the wall. He sat there on his desk chair, trying to make sense of what happened. What should he have done? What didn't he do?

Chapter 11 – Let's have a drink!!!

Being without Gina in his life was a devastating blow for Harris. Of course, they talked about it would probably have to be that they would take a break after intermediates, but not like this. Trying to reach her by telephone would be difficult, but he continued to write letters even though there was no response. He wrote of his shock of being sent off so fast and not understanding why. He also wrote of how angry he was that she wouldn't tell him why. He even offered to change his attitude, whatever that meant and whatever she wanted him to be, he would be. Finally, he just gave up in frustration. He didn't write it but believed Victor must have been the culprit. What better way to get back at him then to take a slash at his heart? Vicious move for anyone to undertake, less a man of God!

He called his mum on occasion to let her know he was alive along with his Da if it were in the evening. They both wished him well and just told him to focus on what is important now rather than the past. The words may not have helped, but just hearing familiar voices was a relief.

Harris did the only thing he could do after that and threw himself entirely into his studies. He had a massive distrust of people in the very few off-hours he had. Roland got an earful right after the holidays when Harris found shaving scum in the sink and another time when his roommate didn't pick up a towel after a shower. In class, he would bark at his lab mates if they dropped something by accident or were slow in practice. Many times, working alone and without apology. He held himself in check when a professor gave him grief, but it was an effort.

It came to a head on a Friday in February when Harris was about to call the landlord early in the morning when the hot water went out and wanted to give his opinion on that and everything else wrong with the flat. "Cop on, Mate!" Roland said. "Wind your neck in!" as he calmed Harris down and made the call himself. He then suggested that what they needed was a night out. "We can go to the pub. Maybe throwing some darts at the wall will relieve ya." Roland said. Harris couldn't deny he was a total nit. He had a cold-water sponge-off and went to class. They would go to the pub later that evening.

The two mates entered the pub and took seats at an open-ended booth. Roland was looking to score now that he had himself under control and could now buy prophylactics freely in Ireland since AIDS became the talk of a new plague underway.

But Harris found out something else about himself a while ago. Alcohol did not affect him. He could drink beer after beer and even tried a shot of vodka. He would feel the effects for about a half-minute or so, but they would go away and leave him stone sober. He would have loved to drink Gina off his mind, but his body would not have it.

They sat in the middle of the pub, and Harris talked Roland's ear off for an hour about how Gina was a huge help in helping him get into medical school and how she was his first squeeze, but not his first conquest as that didn't happen yet.

"Well, why didn't you say so, eh?" Roland piped up. "That's what you need! A little action to get her off your radar."

"I don't know, mate," Harris said. "That kind of thing isn't all that to me. I've always been awkward in that area."

Suddenly, a loud noise came in from the front door. A group of loudmouth rugby players marched in and took seats at the bar. They had won and were about to raise a pint each in celebration.

"Wish I played sport," Roland said. "They get the best birds."

"I sense a theme with you, friend…" Harris responded. "Are you sure you came here to become a doctor?"

"Oy, this is just wild oat time, eh?" Roland said. "As soon as I graduate, it's going to be some bird who'll spend me into oblivion and take care of the dogs and kids."

Harris held that image with Gina again for a moment.

"C' mon, mate!" Roland jumped in. "You're young and should be doing everything you'll regret now, so you don't have to later. He then spotted two girls at a booth across from them.

"Oy! Jasmine! Carol!" Roland shouted over the din of the ballers. "Hey, come here, then! I want you to meet someone!"

Harris was feeling his embarrassment level skyrocket as the girls slowly made their way over to the boy's table.

"Girls, this is Harris…Harris that's Jazzy, and that's Carol."

"Ya, we're in anatomy with you." Carol, a thin, blond girl from Yorkshire said.

"Well, C'mon…" Roland said. "Have a sit-down, then." With that, Carol sat next to Harris and Jasmine, an Estonian chick fresh from this new time of Glasnost sat next to Roland. He was into the foreign birds as they were easier to talk into anything.

They talked of classes and life outside of college for a while, but Harris only mentioned the break-up in passing as he didn't want to bring this party down. It was nice encountering new faces and pleasant ones at that. They ordered another round and kept up the discussion about how tough classes were. Jasmine talked about her schooling and her relief to get away from the iron hand of Eastern European rule at least for a while.

Carol had a similar background to Harris as she had to deal with the vicious nuns of her Yorkshire town. She seemed to have it as bad as him with the old days hazing punishment for not writing right-handed. "That all ended five years ago in 1983 with a change of diocese, thank God!" She said. "I probably would have lost all feeling in my digits if that kept up!"

They kept the conversation going even though it was getting louder in the pub as the rugby blokes were getting their drink on. Roland was getting on with his usual pick-up skills. Harris wondered for a while if Roland was a Xenon with the ability to secure birds. He knew it didn't always end with conquest. Tonight, it seemed promising. Harris was about to suggest to Carol about giving these other two some space when a hulking rugby player approached their table.

"Hey bird, how about a minute with a real man?" The player said.

"Thanks, I'm good," Jaz replied in her foreign accent.

"Yeah?" He shouted as the massive tool grabbed Roland by his collar and dragged him out of the booth. He held him up by his lapels a full foot off the floor. Roland could smell the mouldy stench of ale emanating from the beast yelling at him.

"Piss off, slag! Let the real men in!" He shouted into his face as the two girls ran out of the booth with the Rugby bawler hanging on to Harris's friend. Roland had fear in his eyes while the big lummox staring down at him. If there was one thing that Harris hated more than anything in the world, it was a bully. He knew how it was to be on the receiving end of some total bastard and refused to have it any longer. That was when he took the glass beer mug and slammed it on the table, and it smashed into a thousand pieces.

"Enough, already!" Harris shouted loud enough to be heard across the room as silence filled the pub. "Enough! If there's anything I can't stand, it's some tiny boy who can't hold his drink!"

The bawler slowly turned in disbelief to look at Harris and dropped Roland, who went right to the floor without warning. Harris didn't run. He just stood there and seethed as the player did as well. The big oaf couldn't believe anyone would have the marbles to challenge him like that. The entire pub was watching this scene intently with Tom, the barman, ready to defend himself with a cricket bat.

"Who you think you are, boy?" The player scowled and pointed.

"You heard me...I know a bully like you could hammer me into oblivion with one hit, but at least I can handle my drink rather than end up a doormat like you!" Harris shouted back with the "ooohs and gasps" of the other customers surprised he would stand up to this mass of muscle in his face.

"Right!" The player said. "Let's see what you got, scrubber!" He then ordered the barman to set up a table and a bottle of peppermint flavoured vodka along with two shot glasses.

Roland came up from the floor and tried to talk sense into Harris. "Mate hang on! That's Dermot O'Reardon! He never loses!"

Harris responded. "Yeah, he looks like a sore loser."

"What you gonna do then?" Roland asked.

Harris only responded, "Let's find out..." leaving Roland with a deep concern for his friend's reputation...and health!

He then walked over to the table, looking stone-faced while Dermot took a seat with all the confidence that he already won.

"Benny..." He called over to one of his fellow players. "Serve 'em up!"

They slammed the first glasses together after Dermot's teammate poured the liquor. The vodka did have a burn that took Harris by surprise. At least the taste was all right. He would feel the effects of the strong liquor for than a minute and then his sobriety broke through the fog. "Minty!" Harris said with a smile. "At least I'll have fresh breath after this…"

"Don't count on it, bogger!" Dermot responded with a look of evil in his eye.

After the 3rd shot, they took their drinks in turn. Shot after shot, the pair imbibed, and Dermot's arm got shakier with each. Harris remained still as stone with the crowd in admiration and disgust at the same time. At the 20th shot, after Harris took his drink, Dermot lifted his trembling arm with his body making it clear that he was ossified to the limit. With that, he lurched forward with his body falling on the table along with the past 19 shots and everything else he had that night and day spilling out of his stomach and on to the tabletop and floor. The crowd gave a cheer and applause on Harris's side along with the sickening realisation of what just happened. Harris pulled out a £20 note and gave it to the barman apologising for the mess. He didn't want Tom angry with him as well.

Roland ran up to Harris. "You all right, then?"

Harris then realised that just as he had to cover up his healing ability, he had better cover this as well.

"Fine m-mate." He said with a fake mild stammer and giggle. "I get the effets slowy." As he piled on the act that he was well-tossed by pretending to stumble and laugh when he stood upright. "I better git hom to bid or I met en up seeping on the steet." They made their way through the pub with cheers as they waved and left the rugby team with the mess to clean up. "Nita all!" He shouted as they exited.

Roland got a cab and helped Harris in. Harris just played along, and they returned home. He had his arm over Roland's shoulder, and Harris just tumbled on his bed with the noisy springs. He was just about to leave when Harris spoke…

"Roland, mate…" Harris said still in the drunken voice disguise. "Thanks for a greet nought ot, man! I needs-did it. I won't fergit it!"

"Thanks, mate," Roland said with a smile. "But I doubt tomorrow you'll remember anything." He then took his leave to his room.

Later that night, Harris recalled the night in perfect clarity along with his crass behaviour to his new friends and lab mates for the past month. He would apologise for his bad attitude in the next classes. When he was sure that Roland was asleep next door, he sat up in bed and took the occasion to pen one more letter to his Gina:

Dear Gina

I'm not sure why you left that Christmas night so unceremoniously, but I finally realised that I must accept it and respect your reasoning. It was just a shock that we parted so suddenly and without warning.

For whatever your reasoning, I will stand aside and let you have your life without my ties restraining you. I will only say that while I'm sad that our time together ended, I am also happy that it happened.

I also want to thank you for making me a better person. Without you and your help, there is no way I would have got here. Maybe we will cross paths again. I hope so. For now, I hope all goes well for you no matter where the road takes you.

All my love to you,

Harris

He then put the letter in an envelope and sealed it. He would post it in the morning. He was just about to put the framed picture in the drawer of the nightstand out of eyesight when a sad thought occurred to him:

"I never told her that I loved her…"

Chapter 12 – The Sore Loser!

It was a day after the entire pub incident that Harris found himself in bed and no motivation to get up. It was Saturday, and he slept late that morning. When he kicked his leg out of bed, he noticed a bucket next to it. Roland probably put it there for Harris's sake during the night. He got a shower and shaved being careful to not leave behind anything in the sink or on the floor to be labelled a hypocrite. He then took things slow this afternoon by reading some more of his book and to make a note to call Julius as he had not spoken to him in a while. It would be back to the hard stuff tomorrow, but a stroll to the post-box was also on his agenda.

He took notice that it was uncannily light out through the edge of the hanging curtain. He pulled the cloth back to reveal the snow piled halfway up the dustbins in the back and the white bits were still falling in mass. He would also have to buy a new anorak today as his old one was getting shabby. It was about 2 o'clock, and he was just on the way out when Roland came in and knocked a pile of snow off his boots in the hall. If it were yesterday, he would have given Roland holy hell for that, but he felt worlds better today.

"Hey, Morning, mate!" He said, smiling, even though it was late in the day. "I would have thought you would still be asleep."

"Na, I slept enough," Harris responded. "I got things to do."

"…and you're not hung-over?" Roland said inquisitively. "If I were in your shoes, I'd be asleep for a week!"

"Alcohol just doesn't affect me like that," Harris responded. "Anyway, I got to get myself something new to wear for the season."

"Hang on, I'll go with," Roland said. "I've been at the library all day to let you sleep, right? Didn't want to disturb ya." Harris appreciated the thoughtfulness and agreed to the company.

There was just enough time to get to the menswear store called Man-Z and get his new winter wear. The good-looking redhead brought over to him a beautiful coat lined with a thick white fleece interior and leather panels on the outside of the material that felt like it was made from a firehose. She said it would last longer than he would live. "For £400, it better had!" he thought. Roland gave her the glad eye the entire time as if he were going to call her later. It wouldn't surprise Harris if he did as she seemed to reciprocate his vibe.

The two then went to The Red Tent Chipper, and Harris bought a hamburger and chips in a takeaway box to have back at the flat. He felt he better get back to his books and stay busy rather than think of Gina again. With that, He posted the letter he wrote the previous night and felt what one would call "closure." It was now time to look ahead with no interference.

They continued the walk home down the footpath and quizzed each other on the way:

"OK…Fatigue, frequent bowel movements and bulging eyes…" Roland asked.

"Graves' disease!" Harris answered excitedly.

"Correct," Roland said.

"Ok, how about blood in diarrhoea with fever and stomach cramps? Roland asked.

"Um, E. Coli?" Harris responded.

"…with reactive arthritis? Roland included.

"Oh! Shigella!" Harris answered.

"Correct," Roland said. "Well done!"

…and continued the back and forward Q &A of symptoms and anatomical references as they made their way back to the flat.

The peace of the day was then disturbed when a yell came up from behind them. It was Dermot O'Reardon, and he was running up at full speed. Harris didn't run from his full charge at him.

"No one makes a fool of me, brock!!! NOBODY!!!" He shouted as he plunged a huge dagger into the takeaway box Harris was holding. The knife didn't stop there as it plunged through his new anorak right into his midsection. Harris fell backwards with his white jersey becoming soaked red in blood. He could feel the cold steel of the blade plunge painfully into his body.

"BASTARD!" Roland yelled and found a rock from the cleared street and bowled it at Dermot's head with a perfect throw. It hit Dermot square in the eye, and he barely recovered when another hit him in the head. Dermot ran while Roland gave chase and tossed more of the rocks until either he ran out or Dermot out-ran him.

Harris wasn't sure how that melee played out as he recovered from the stab wound. The wound closed, leaving only his red bodily fluid behind.

"Sore loser!" He thought. The pain had dissipated with no scars or injuries. Just his blood-covered shirt and his new parka left evidence of the attack. He then thought "How can I cover this up?"

With that, he took the hamburger out of the takeaway box that was topped with lots of catsup, the way he liked it and smeared it on his blood-covered shirt. "Close enough." He thought.

The sandwich was back in the box and Harris was back on his feet. Roland returned and was amazed to see him vertical. "Mate, you... all right?" Roland asked, not believing what he was seeing.

"Oh yeah," Harris said, breathing heavy. "He got me right in the lunch." And with that, opened the takeaway box to reveal the stabbed burger.

"Jammy! You are the luckiest bastard I have ever met...seriously!" Roland said

"My new anorak would argue that," Harris thought to himself as he looked down at the large knife hole in the new coat not more than an hour old. "Four-hundred quid just blown to hell! Damn, my luck!" he thought.

It was then an older woman, a resident of the block came up to the two of them in the street. "Ere! I saw what that hooligan did to you! You all right, lad?" She asked with grave concern.

"I am, thank you," Harris said. Meanwhile, Roland was standing dumbfounded with Harris in solid shape after the attack.

"Well, I called 999 after that eejit bully attacked you. The Gardai will be here soon, then." She said in a thick Brough. The boys just nodded and waited for the lawmen, who appeared five minutes later. After the police made their inquiries, Harris and Roland made their way back to their gaff. They stopped at a small market for a bag of crisps, and a candy bar as the officer confiscated Harris's supper for evidence. He then called his parents to let them know what happened and to tell his Da how he kept things hushed.

"Good God, son!" Helmut said. "I'm glad you kept your head through all that. You all right, otherwise?" In referring to his breakup and his mental state.

"I'm OK, Da," Harris said with a heavy heart. "I even wrote a letter to Gina saying I accept what happened...not that I like it, but I have to deal with it."

"That's a good lad, son," Helmut said. "You keep that attitude up. There are millions of girls who will want to be your misses. It will all come in due time."

"I know, Da," Harris said. "Thanks for that."

Harris went up to his room to study and finish the crisps he bought earlier. It was not easy keeping his focus after what he went through today, so he decided to listen to his Walkman for a bit, always turning up the volume when Roland had a lady friend over to cover up the sounds of bedsprings and moans. Tonight, he turned on the radio and tried to listen to something tolerable to get his mind back in operation.

It was on a break that he heard the news that he had hoped for a long while now was announced. The Vatican had declared Xenons were "people" and removed the stigma that they were demonic monsters. Harris stuck his hand up in a V-shape to himself. At least this lot was going to be on his side. Now Parliament and the rest of the world would need to play catch-up along with their law-bodies. The general populace would be a bit harder to convince.

Just then the phone rang in the flat hall. Harris didn't hear it with the headphones on.

"I'll get it!" Roland said.

"Hello?" It was Officer Brennan from the local Gardai...

"Yes, sir...OK, Great..."

"Yeah, he's having a lie-down then. He's all right, though..."

"Sure, whatever you need, then..."

"Right, ok...Bye."

It was then that Roland had a look at Harris's damaged anorak hanging on the wall hook by the phone. He examined the knife hole created through the new winter coat and, out of curiosity, examined the inner lining where there was an enormous, brown stain on the white fleece that did not smell at all like tomatoes.

The dried blood looked like some of the samples that they saw in classes earlier in the year. What was this? Roland went to Harris's room and entered without waiting for an invite in as the volume was loud from the Walkman pumping out a song banned from the radio, so he listened to it from cassette.

Roland startled Harris as he tapped him gently on the arm. Harris stopped the music as his friend spoke:

"Sorry to disturb you, mate…You just got a call from the Gardai. They got Dermot in the neck for what he done to ya. They might also need to talk to us more if'n he tries to fight it in court. Not sure why he would as it's clear what he tried to pull on ya."

Roland kept on…

"Turns out he's had an old day's hatred of the Brits. You'd think that spanner would've evolved like any other chimpanzee by now."

"OK, mate…thanks for that," Harris said with a grin.

"But if you got a minute…" Roland geared up with a long pause… "I did want to ask you about something…"

Chapter 13 - Explanation, please.

There was no hiding it from Roland, now. The blood all over the inside of his new anorak. How could he explain that away? Harris thought he could talk to Father Victor, and that didn't turn out well. There was no choice but to come clean of it.

"I got a few extra tricks up my sleeve that I was born with, mate," Harris said. "You got to understand that I'm not looked upon with a lot of favour in the grand scheme of things...what with being a Xenon and all." He looked down at the floor after saying that to his flatmate.

Roland just stood silent for a moment and took in the meaning of this. "You don't look like a monster." He said with all seriousness.

"Thanks," Harris said without thinking about it. "...I mean, no! Of course not! I'm just like anyone else. It's just that I have some extra wiring in my DNA that allows me to do more."

Roland was still trying to sort it all out. Here was a guy he was sharing quarters with whom the world was ready to condemn...for some reason, him as well.

"Is that how you won the pub challenge?" He asked.

"It is..." Harris answered. "Before and after with Dermot. Alcohol is considered a type of poison by my body that's fought off. I feel it for a bit, and then I'm back to normal. Kind of a drag, really"

"Well...I guess it can come in handy." Roland said.

There was a long pause between the two of them...

"So how are we to leave it then?" Harris asked.

Roland just gathered his thoughts...

"I guess there's nothing else to say." As he stood up and left his room. Harris found no comfort in the opinion.

The next couple of weeks found Roland distancing himself from Harris. He was always polite, but colder than he used to be. Meanwhile, Harris was getting along better with his lab mates now that he put Gina behind him and had gained a reputation of demanding respect onward from the whole pub and stabbing incident.

Harris would now spend more time in the library with the likes of Taylor Carpenter. A bookworm-type from Leeds who was a nervous wreck much of the time but was impressive at memorising chemistry symbols. In trade, Harris helped him with the basics of microbiology and swapping mnemonics. There was also Caroline Patterson, the Yorkshire blonde who was the one that Harris met at the pub before the rugby oaf interrupted them. They did anatomy homework together, and it was clear she was trying to get closer to him. Harris wasn't sure he was ready to go that direction, yet. He talked to Todd Hunter about colleges in America and how expensive it was to attend. Harris felt it was unfair to have to pay for schooling, as all he had to do was keep a good grade to assure his tuition.

The Chancellor had words with him as well in that he wanted to make sure Harris was mentally fit to continue, what with the attack on his life and all. Harris insisted he was and that all he wanted to do was to keep on. Anything else would be a sign of surrender.

The thing that bothered Harris more than anything, though was how Roland changed his attitude toward him. He preferred his old fun-loving flatmate to this stodgy version of his room neighbour. Harris sat in his room studying but heard very little from next door aside from bedsprings creaking with two people doing anything but sleeping. Roland's attitude went on until the last month when studying for year-end finals were about to start.

Harris was just about to wake up to another Thursday morning when he heard a loud screech from next door along with a loud "BLOODY HELL!!! NO!!!" and a bit of sobbing to follow.

Harris put on a dressing gown and knocked on the door and then entering without a response. Roland had his legs over the bedside and his head in his hands looking majorly despondent.

"Uh…Problem?" Harris asked.

"PISS OFF!!! Nothing you need to know of, wanker!" Roland shouted. He was always polite, albeit cold to Harris, so this was something else.

"Drop the attitude, slag!" Harris said crossly. "I can help more than you think."

"No, you can't!" Roland shouted. "I'm totally knackered!"

"OK, it's medical." Harris came back with Roland mystified in how he knew that.

"Just waking up, it couldn't be anything else…Now, C'mon! Where's it hurt?"

"FINE!" Roland shouted and then laid on the bed and lowered his pyjamas. His willy was covered with blisters and looked like a diseased piece of meat. Harris recoiled in disgust at the herpes-covered member of his flatmate.

"Satisfied…Doctor?" Roland said, sarcastically in a state of pain and anger.

"Well, mate…" Harris shot back. "You don't know how lucky you are to be getting this house call."

And with that, Harris held his glowing hand over Roland's leg as he didn't need to be near the diseased piece of flesh…or wanted to be. Roland just looked on in shock and too afraid to move. In a matter of seconds, his male member returned to a state of normalcy with no indication of any problems. Roland looked down upon his now fixed flesh in a state of disbelief.

"Right, you're fine now," Harris said with an exacerbated bend.

Roland just sat there and uttered some sounds with no definition, still being too shocked to move. He then suddenly, grabbed his mouth and ran to the loo and stuck his head under the tub spout drinking like he just spent a week in the desert.

"Oops! I forgot about that part…. oh, dear!" Harris said, sarcastically, to himself as Roland drank his fill. He then came out of the water closet with his manhood proudly on display outside his bedclothes.

"I can't believe it! Roland said ecstatically. "I'm cured" as he looked down at his exposed willy to the chagrin of Harris.

"Yeah, yeah…OK, mate." Harris said as he averted his eyes. "You want to put that thing away before you knock the table lamp over?"

Roland packed his manhood away and just stared Harris's way as his smile turned to shame. He then sat on his bed and thought what a twit he had been to Harris for the past few months and looked down at the floor.

"I've been a real arse, haven't I?" Roland asked.

"Oh yeah…without a doubt!" Harris replied. After a moment, he held out his hand to shake.

"Friends again? Harris asked. Roland didn't say anything but just shook Harris's hand. "Right," Harris said grinning and was about to leave when Roland wanted to talk more.

"So, you can cure diseases?" He asked.

"…Diseases, heart attacks, strokes…These are what I have done so far. I'm not sure yet what all I'm capable of, though." Harris responded as he stood at the door.

"So, what are you doing here, then?" Roland asked.

Harris just looked at him as if to say, "How can you not figure that out?"

"Your attitude," Harris said sadly. "It's the norm toward Xenons, unfortunately. I have to educate myself as a doctor to pass myself off as one, or it's the knacker's yard for me."

Roland just thought of his past behaviour for the past couple of months. He gave the cold shoulder to Harris without knowing what he could do for everyone. "What a fool I am!" He thought to himself. "What fools we all are!"

Harris then got a view of Roland's alarm clock. It read 8:45.

"Oh, man! Look at the time!" Harris said in a panic. "We got to hit the streets!"

Roland agreed, and the two got dressed for their fundamentals of medicine class. They would both have to skip the loo this morning.

Chapter 14 – The Hunt Is On!

Everything was theory and written down in terms of studying for the end of the year. They would start seeing simulated situations next year with dummies and real people simulating patients. Harris was adamant about not healing in his strange way, lest being led away by his oppressors. Roland tried his best to understand this unfair paradigm, although it made him angry to think Harris's skills were going to waste. He ended up asking a bunch of questions about how it felt to be a Xenon along with how long he was healing people in his way. Harris told him about the cat, Gina's Dad and Father Victor. He finally slowed Roland down by asking how he got herpes in the first place.

They finally agreed to accept the answers given to each other and put it to rest. "The carrier of this disease could have been one of three girls," Roland said. "That is Isla O'Keefe, Rhona Haberl or Jill Johns…Those are the ones that I remember from 3 weeks ago. It couldn't have been Ai Tamaki, that was just last Friday…too soon." This left Harris in awe and a bit jealous that Roland found it so easy to chat up the birds and get them in his bed with so little effort.

"OK, we're going to have to keep eyes out," Harris said. "I just hope it's something where they don't know they're carrying it. Most women don't."

"What? You mean she might be infecting guys on purpose?" Roland asked in disbelief.

"Probably not…" Harris said, "But it's possible…remember Typhoid Mary?"

Roland just nodded as he remembered her mentioned in class.

"Whether the girl in question is doing it on purpose or not, she had to be stopped from spreading the disease. Anyways, I thought you were so careful with yourself not to get in tatters."

"Well, you get in a rush when you're on the lash, then your reasoning is out the door," Roland said. "Anyways, they say they're on rhythm or the pill when I ask, and that's all I hear. I never asked before if they are bolloxed before we get down to it."

"Yeah, it's something I've not done yet," Harris said a bit down. "No point trying with exams on the rise."

"You should, mate," Roland said. "Even to get it out of your system."

Harris and Roland then spent most of their day at the library. Exams were coming, and they had to get prepared. Caroline and Taylor joined them for a study session that consisted of everything they learned in the last nine months. Caroline took a seat next to Harris but kept a demure exterior as they were focused on the work ahead of them. "Jazzy" Jasmine Rubajinski then came over. She was the other girl from the pub and was impressed that Harris was not dead from alcohol poisoning, nor the stabbing.

Finally, Jill Johns came over and asked to join in the study session. "Yes, of course, Jill," Harris said. "Jump in." Jill had long, straight hair and was from Bangor, Wales. Harris had to applaud Roland's taste in girls. She was a great looking bird, as were the rest of them, with model looks in face and body. She then went and took a seat that was between Harris and Roland. A move that seemed a bit forward to the other ladies in the group.

Roland made moves to the point that she was one of the 3 in the contention that may have been a carrier. Harris pondered over his plasma and platelets section how to get his hand on Jill in a way that would be quiet and unnoticed. She then mentioned how she left her jacket on the back of the chair while standing to fetch it. Roland stuck his foot out, and she fell right to the floor.

"Oh, sorry, Jill! Roland said. "I guess my feet are bigger than I thought!"

Harris helped her up, but no light emitted from his hands. That was a relief, though, as he didn't need to be putting on a light show to this whole lot...

"Roland! Did you do that on purpose?" Jill asked.

"Of course not!" Roland said. "Why would I do that?"

"It's not his fault, Jill," Harris said covering for Roland's antics. "His foot was there before you got up. I saw it was at a weird angle."

Jill gave a huge sigh. "All right...whatever!" She said as she went to grab her jacket. The whole group went back to the books: One down, two to go.

An hour later was when Taylor spoke up from the silence. "I don't know about you lot, but I need a pint. Anyone else?"

Jasmine spoke up in her Eastern European accent "Just one...No time to get more." The rest of the girls followed suit.

Roland was about to say something, but Harris stopped him. "Go on, then…We'll catch up."

The girls and Taylor gathered their belongings and headed out the door while Harris and Roland stayed behind for a tic before doing the same.

"Roland!" Harris said in an urgent whisper as to not attract the attention of others in the library. "Look, I appreciate what you did, but I can't have a light show go off here in public!"

"What you mean, mate?" Roland asked in confusion. "That was an accident!"

"Oh…OK," Harris said. "I thought you tripped her so I could catch her."

"Oh, I see," Roland said. "But if it weren't for the lights, that would be a good idea." Harris couldn't argue with that. Was there a way to do this without so much attention?

The Draughtsman was pretty much empty. Perfect for having a pint to take the edge off and getting back to it. Caroline was already at the bar to order a pint when she invited Harris over to join her. Harris went over to her hesitantly but just stayed polite as they exchanged more opinions on the upcoming examination. She was sensing his trepidation as they kept talking and getting more personal about their lives. It was the wrong time for any of this to happen as time was short before summer, and they both knew it. Caroline would go back to Yorkshire and join her parents at their Curiosity Shoppe. Harris had no clue what he would do during the summer holiday.

That was when Isla O'Keefe came in and took a seat alone at the end of the bar. Isla was a no-nonsense redhead from outside Belfast who studied here to escape the threat of machine-gun fire. She was rummaging through her handbag looking for jar money. Harris stayed in his conversation with Caroline while thinking of what scenario he could concoct to examine Isla. Maybe this wasn't even the time. Regardless, that was when Roland made his move.

He walked up to the redhead at the bar and spoke to her for a moment before he got her to dance a bit on the pub floor. She was waiting for her glass of Murphy's to settle anyways, so it was not so unusual. Roland then said for Isla to wait while he went over and asked to speak with Harris alone for a tic. "Pardon me a moment," Harris said to Carol.

He was led over to Isla when Roland said: "Here, dance with her a tic." And he ran over to the jacks.

Harris was left to dance half-heartedly with this girl whom he hadn't said more than two words to all term. "Uh, hi…" he said. While he had his hand on her back waiting to see if any light would show in a nearby reflection from the pub window. Nothing happened.

"So why exactly did Roland call me over?" Harris asked.

"He said you needed a dance partner. It looked like you were fine with Carol there." She replied.

Harris was about to respond when Roland came back to them and cut back in. "Thanks, Mate," Roland said. The two of them went back to dancing while Harris returned to the bar and his glass and a confused Carol. Harris feigned looking just as confused.

"What's that about?" Carol asked.

"I'm not sure," Harris said. "It's not like him to be afraid of someone walking off…You want to go for a walk?" Carol just nodded, and they went out the door with their bags of books on their shoulders. They walked down to Carol's block of dormitories on Banyan Place, and she turned to face him before they went in after talking the finer points of the exam's possibilities.

"Come on in." She said, waving him to enter the dorm room.

"I don't know if…" Harris began before she put two of her fingers over his mouth and breathed a "Shh…." She then kissed him gently on the lips and closed the door behind them.

Chapter 15 - A Useful Collection of Information

Harris woke up in Carol's bed, not sure of his next move. He wished he had taken the time to consult with Roland about matters such as these, but it just happened. Carol was on her side of the bed near the edge and Harris took the opportunity to slip out unnoticed. She appeared asleep while he dressed and made his way down the dorm hall and out the door, quietly.

He made his way home and ducked out of sight when his house door opened and there slipping out was Becky McGill. It was evident that she was in a similar situation as Harris and just made her way out into the cold May morning air not thinking anyone was coming in.

Harris went to his room and took a shower. Unusual, as he mostly did his cleaning up at night. Roland shook the doorknob to find it locked. "Be right out!" Harris said through the water as he finished up. He walked into his room and shouted, "All yours!" to Roland and got his clothes on for the day. There were no classes today, just preparation for the final exam. His rest break did make him feel better, but he didn't know how to handle seeing Carol again. He would ask "The Master" on their way to the library.

"OK, so here is what you need to know…" Roland explained to Harris after they got a roll and sausage at the corner café. "When you woke up, did you have your arms around her?"

"Nope," Harris responded.

"Did she have her arms around you?" Roland pressed on.

"Nope…she was laying on the other side of the bed," Harris said.

"OK, that's good," Roland said. "This meant she just wanted a hook-up. If you had your arms around each other, that means it was more than that."

Harris pondered this information for a second. "Is it always like that?" He asked.

"Nope…" Roland said, "But that's the answer you'll give if it becomes an issue."

The library was a crowded affair today with practically the whole campus huddled around the desks and tables in groups of 3 or more trying to remember what they forgot or learning new information if they weren't paying attention the first time.

"Mate, you never told me how it was," Roland whispered as Harris read the glossary of a pathology book.

"I was expecting more," Harris said quietly. "I was always told it was supposed to be a big, life-changing occurrence. I feel about the same as I did yesterday."

"It gets better over time," Roland said as he read a chapter about muscle atrophy. "I guess if you love the bird, it's supposed to be better than anything…Anyways, that's what I hear…can't tell ya, though, for sure."

It was then that they saw two females walk hand-in-hand into the library without a care in the world what anyone thought of them. Roland didn't know their names but recognised one of them as Jill's roommate.

"Lesbians get a pass," Roland said quietly to Harris out of the blue. "Let me try to enter public spaces with another guy like that, and I'd get me head stomped! Bloody double standard!" Harris thought it odd that Roland would make that observation. Anyway, it was time for the other issue.

The target of Harris's healing was clear now. How it was going to happen was a mystery as Harris had no classes with Rhona Haberl as she was in her 3rd year. How Roland hooked up with her in the first place was just a testament to his gift of gab. That would have to wait until the exam was over as she was probably in no hurry to hook up this close to years end, either.

That's when Harris ran into Caroline in the hall on the way to the loo. Neither one knew what to say to each other. They both stood frozen looking at each other for what seemed forever until Harris decided to say something to move the moment along: "I'm glad it happened." He then turned toward the loo and entered.

"I am too," Caroline said to the space vacated by Harris and made her way into her lavatory. It wasn't much, but it was enough for the two of them to be able to continue studying in peace.

Two more days of hovering over books and taking notes occurred until it was finally time to enter the examination room. Three hours of pencils and rubber erasers with no breaks for the WC would determine how much each person knew of the most mundane actions and illnesses of the human body. There were no speeches by a woman in a habit here. Grab a test, take a seat and fill out the little dots with a pencil was the rule here. Harris took his place at a single desk, said a quick "Our Father…" and got down to it.

Blood, Bile, heart, lungs, liver function…nine months of medical education squeezed into one place. He set aside thoughts of everything for these hours and hoped for a 70 or better. The weather turned to rain and thunder, which was the only other sound in the examination hall besides scribbling and erasing. No one said a word, but sighing was the communication along with an occasional cough or gastric event which reminded Harris of answer #27; B, not A.

He finished before Roland and just went home. His bed with squeaky springs was all he wanted for the next hour or three. Harris woke to the sound of the telly in the main room. Roland was watching a demonstration for Xenon rights that was broadcast by the British News Service. Roland saw Harris around the corner and motioned him to enter.

"It started an hour ago at Speaker's Corner," Roland said. "There was a quiet march through Hyde Park and then some wanker through a bottle at one of them."

The protests were violent, and the police were trying to separate the two factions.

"I guess the bottle never hit them. Instead, it reversed and hit the guy who threw it…after that, all hell broke loose." He then said sadly.

Harris said nothing but just looked on as people lunged at each other with sticks and broken bottles. The police were trying their best to keep them all separated along with Paragons, in their orange and black uniforms, using some rod that appeared to be some large cattle prod. They seemed to be doing a better job of keeping the peace. Harris just wondered if any "just plain" humans were among the Xenons or were this a strict species vs species skirmish? Finally, he had his limit.

"Enough! I'm going to the pub," He said. "The exam was bad enough."

"Hang on, I'll get me coat," Roland said as he tagged along like a faithful mutt.

Chapter 16 - The Gremlin

The Draughtsman was in full mode as the post-exam mentality took over. A couple of the rugby team members that Harris remembered from a while ago were drinking their fill and giving him a wide berth as Harris and Roland passed. They knew what Dermot did to him and didn't want any trouble. Harris just had a fizzy drink while Roland had a stout. Caroline was at the bar chatting with the two kissing-fish from the library, Jazzy was talking casually with Taylor while Becky was on Roland's left and acting as though she wanted to go for a "round two" in his bed. The big question of the evening was would Rhona Haberl make an appearance so he could end the threat she was carrying?

An hour went by, and Harris was getting bored. The alcohol was taking its effect on the room, but not for him. The rock music was playing in the corner from a local band called "Bank on it!" Roland was subdued tonight and avoiding his pick-up lines as he attempted to fulfil his part. The only problem was he was drinking to celebrate the end of Year One and was getting zozzled at the same time. He insisted as the night continued that he was up to the task.

Rhona Haberl finally did show up and had a sit down at the bar. She ordered a pint of Murphy's, which was a process as it took a minute to pour and two minutes to settle. That was the moment that Harris and Roland were waiting to happen. The plan was simple enough: Roland would ask Rhona to dance, Harris would cut in, and Roland would cover the "light show" by shining a torch at Harris's hands in a drunk bit of silliness. Harris stood by while Roland made his move. Unfortunately, Caroline was making a move as well toward Harris and was getting into his line of sight.

"Harris... Hi." She said.

"Oh, Hi Carol," Harris responded as he kept eyes on the two at the bar.

"Listen, I just wanted to say I enjoyed our time together..." She said. "I didn't know what to say when you left so I didn't want you to think of me..."

"SMASH!!!" The sound of a pint glass shattered on the bar disturbed the mood, and a bizarre battle was taking place on the pub floor.

"What the hell?" was out of both Harris and Carol's mouth at the same time as Rhona Haberl was on the ground, pummelling Jill John's lesbian roommate.

They both were pulling each other's hair and throwing punches while Roland was ducked under a table and covering his now bloody nose. The torch had skidded on the floor out of Roland's hand.

Even the beefy rugby players who were getting their drink on knew better than to try to break up a fight between these two hellcats. Harris took the torch and grabbed the unknown girl by the neck and threatened to bop the muffer with it when his healing light projected into her face. He quickly turned the torchlight on her face to cover his healing ability until she was sufficiently stunned.

"Like deer in the headlights," Harris said. He took a quick gaze and saw Rhona restrained by other patrons. No one caught Harris's "magic trick" as they were just enthralled by the fight. Harris got off the girl, and she promptly drank the first pint she could find to quench her thirst. To make things worse, it wasn't hers. "All right then!!!" Harris shouted to the entire pub. "Show's over…back to your knitting!"

The patrons went back to their pints and partying while Tom the barman pushed the two "less-than" gay girls out the door and shouted, "Out, both of ya!!!"

Harris grabbed Rhona and expected light from his own hands with the torch at the ready for a cover-up, but nothing happened. He had her in one grasp and picked up the messy Roland from the floor and dragged them to the exit. "I got these two, Tom!" Harris shouted as they left the pub. The barman just watched them go without knowing what Harris meant.

Harris placed Roland on the curb. "Sit…Stay!" Harris shouted at Roland like a dog. He even threw in a "Good Boy" as well. Roland just sat on the curb and gave a sarcastic "WOOF" while holding a rag over his face to soak up the blood he got from a well-hit punch from one of the women.

"And you lot…! Harris said to the birds who were standing around with their make-up and hair mangled. "Have a seat and keep the space!" They did what he said as Harris was still carrying the torch and had a look in his eyes that he might go off on them.

"OK, I talked Tom out of calling the Gardai…" Harris lied. He knew the barman wouldn't call the police and ruin the night.

"I got a friend with a bloody nose and you lot going off like the Friday Night Fights! What is going on?" The three then squawked like hens all at once.

"ENOUGH!!!" Harris shouted. "Rhona, you first…"

"Roland asked me to dance…" Rhona said, talking with her hands. "I just said no, and then Jenni came over and said she was willing. Miriam then came over and called her a Saturday night and said get over being a Gillette blade and to decide what she was."

Harris only caught some of that as he wasn't up on the lingo. "Could I have a translation, please? Harris asked.

Miriam chimed in. "I said she should stop being a bi-girl and choose one side or the other.

"OK, got it," Harris said with a nod. "…so why go and punch Roland, then?" He asked as Roland sat quietly on the curb, trying to deal with the pain.

"Uh, that was an accident," Miriam spoke up. "I was upset with Jenni after what she and Rhona did with Roland, and I wanted to take a strike at her…I missed."

"No, you didn't!" Roland said as he stumbled over to the discussion with a bloodied cloth in his hand. "And what do you mean BOTH of ya? He asked Rhona. "I only remember you and me in your room, then."

Jenni then covered her mouth in an embarrassment-type pose. She went scarlet.

"Jen!" Miriam spoke up. "I thought you were done playing gremlin."

Jenn turned her flushed red face to Miriam. "I couldn't help it. It just felt right. It was dark, he was there, she was there…"

Miriam just threw her hands up in disgust. "You had no right to do that!" She said. We were supposed to be exclusive!" "I need someone who'll be mine…and mine alone." With that, she walked over to Jenni and pulled off her own necklace of half a heart and threw it on the ground at her feet, she then turned and left. Jenni just watched Miriam walk off into the beginning of a drizzle of rain without saying a word. She tried to look at Rhona and Roland but couldn't look them in the eyes as she started to walk back to her flat, clutching her other half of the heart that now seemed to resemble a broken heart. Rhona turned and said, "Sorry, Roland." He just nodded as she walked home with Jenni to comfort the crying bird. Harris was still mystified as to what was going on.

"C' mon mate, let's go home," Harris said to Roland as they both raised their jackets high over their heads to keep the increasing strength of the rain out.

The two boys stopped at an all-night shop, and Harris had Roland wait outside under the awning while he got a bottle of cider and paid a Sikh cashier behind the counter a fiver, got his change and left. He came out and pulled Roland into an alley. "Right, hang on..." Harris said, and with a last look to make sure no one was about, projected the healing light into Roland's face. The left-over dried blood that wasn't washed away yet remained, but at least his nose was back in place, and the pain was gone.

"All right, then?" Harris asked. Roland just nodded and took a huge gulp of the bottled beverage.

They started home, walking quickly through the rain and Harris began asking questions.

"So, what did she mean by gremlin? He asked.

"I think while Rhona and I were shagging, she joined in," Roland answered as they made their way down the street with their jackets still over their heads. "I think it's a thing for her just sneak in on the action and make it a three-way like that."

"OK, that's just plain weird," Harris said. "One girl at a time seems hard enough to deal with."

"Yeah," Roland said. "My first three-way and I didn't even know it was on. Even in the dark, you'd think we would have known..."

He then paused to ask an essential matter. "Hey, did you take care of...?"

"Yeah, I got her," Harris said. "She won't infect anyone now." Not bothering to tell him it was Jenni, not Rhona treated for the malevolent infection. It made no difference either way as the problem was solved.

They got in, and Roland's renewed strength let him get on his own and have a shower. "I'm off, mate...later," Roland said as he closed the loo door. After his clean-up, he would be asleep in minutes.

Harris just sat in the sitting room, not bothering to turn the telly on. He just wanted silence for a bit and held his head in his hands as his light brown hair was wet and dripping on the floor. The house phone then rang with Harris picking up. "Hello?"

"Hey, Harris...it's Carol." She said quietly on the phone.

Chapter 17 – Home for the Holiday

Carol and Harris met for breakfast at O'Deer's Café over a cup a tea and a sausage and egg sandwich.

"So back to Yorkshire with you, then?" Harris asked.

"Ya," she said. "My parents will be asking a ton of questions about how things are and were. How I was getting along…the usual, I guess."

"Yeah, I'm still trying to figure what I'm doing," Harris said. "If I go home, my mum will want me to relax, and my Da will want to put me to work 24/7. There's just no in-between there."

"Ya, sounds familiar," Carol said. "Maybe there's a summer job you could get in on your own, then. It'll be work, but at least it'd be yours." Harris pondered that for a moment. He made a mental note to look over at the Academic office in job situations.

They shared a short kiss and Caroline headed home. Harris was still left, not knowing what to think. Was there something between them or just a quick fling and forgotten? Her behaviour suggested the latter.

He took a walk to the administrative office where there were a few secretaries left who stayed on through the 2-month holiday to prepare the next load of neophytes coming in to start their medical careers. He looked over the bulletin board of summer employment, but nothing outside the gates of the University. Even these were mundane tasks of cleaning the labs, on-campus dormitories and kitchens.

He decided to call his parents for help with his decision. They both told him that there was no shame in taking a mundane task to begin your career, no matter what. His father talked about how he delivered the papers and then kegs to pubs when he was in his upper teens. His mum spoke about working in dress shops in the city as a salesclerk. They both wanted him to take something on to keep himself busy. No matter what he did, they would support him. Harris did say he wanted to have his summer close to home in London, though. His parents were both delighted.

The next day he packed his items and got ready to say his goodbyes to Carol and Roland. He found out that Carol left the previous evening. It seemed a bit rushed to get out of Cork but figured their time together would be a pleasant memory, eventually.

He and Roland went to the airport together. When the loudspeaker announced the flight, Harris put out his hand to shake, but Roland gave him a hug, instead which took Harris by surprise along with a pat on the back.

"Same time in August, Mate?" Roland said.

"Same place, too," Harris said. He got on the walkway after waving him goodbye with a casual salute. Harris took his place in the window seat after throwing his carry-on bag above him. Next to him sat a young mother and a crying baby. "Oh, joy!" He thought as they took their seats. "Sorry sir, she's teething, then." The young mother said in her native brogue.

"Double joy!" Harris thought.

Well, he knew that the flight would take an hour, and this was a bit of torture he didn't want to bear. The young mother put her bag in the aisle to look for a bottle, so Harris touched the back of the baby's leg with two fingers, and the light shot out which he hid with the book he was reading. The infant went quiet and started to suck on his formulae for all it was worth when his mum presented it. By the time they touched down in Heathrow, the bottle was empty. He just hoped to get off the aeroplane before the infant's nappy was full.

His father was at work, and his mum didn't have a car, so after a long walk through the terminal, he grabbed his luggage from the carousel and took a cab home to Essex Street. He wondered if Gina was visiting her folks as well, but their house was still, and nothing seemed to be going on. He knocked on his home door, but no answer so he let himself in with his key. He dragged in his bag and suitcase. The place was quiet, and nothing seemed to have changed since Christmas. He then took his baggage to his old room which also appeared to have not changed since the holidays.

He then went outside and tried to play with Napoleon for a bit, but he had no interest in anything. One would think that hanging out in a doghouse would inspire him to chase a stick just to chase away the doldrums. There was nothing to do but go inside. Harris sat for a while, just bored. Mum must have been out with the other red hats. He watched Countdown on the telly which settled him for a half-hour and then decided to take a walk down Essex Street and have a look at the neighbourhood.

Around the corner, at Lancaster Court, he saw new businesses had opened. One of them was a gym with weightlifters in the windows working out. He was quite surprised to see the name on the sign:

HEART OF LONDON GYM

OWNER, V. RAVALLI

Harris entered and saw Vincent in a crimson tracksuit on a stationary bicycle. "Mr Ravalli? Is that you?" Harris said, and Vincent slowed the spinning wheels to a stop.

"Harris, my boy!" He said as he got off the bike and gave him a firm handshake. "Hey, good to see you! How are you?"

"Doing fine, sir," Harris said. "Looks like you are as well."

"Yes, I just opened last month," Vincent said with a dramatic wave. "Welcome to my dream job!"

Indeed, the place had old and new exercise equipment of the most basic variety along with some things that looked like they belonged in a torture chamber.

"I didn't know you were opening a gym," Harris said. "I've been a bit busy, myself."

"Yes, of course, you have," Vincent said. "What you see here is my retirement."

"Retirement, sir?" Harris said, surprised. "I didn't think you were…" Harris was careful in what he said next… "Anywhere near retirement age."

"Now you're flattering me a bit too much, boy." Vincent said, "…but you're smart to do so." He said with a big smile as he made his way to the water cooler. Harris followed. "Yes, I had some investments that came to fruition, so I decided to cut my hours down and open this place." He then wiped his face with a towel. "So, what are you up to this summer, then?" Vincent asked.

"I'm not sure," Harris said. "I'd like to do more than just sit in front of the telly for hours."

"Understood. That's what I used to do." Vincent replied.

"You know, if you want, I might be able to have you assist our activities doctor for the neighbourhood youth. I know they need someone to take care of the first aid stuff that goes along with sports." Harris pondered this as a possibility.

"Well, what kind of sport? Harris asked.

Vincent took a piece of paper off the nearby desk that displayed a full schedule of different activities: Cricket, football, boxing…many others over at Rickets Gate were happening on the weekend.

"You could get some experience working there with the other doctors," Vincent said. "Well, what do you think?"

"Where do I sign up?" Harris asked.

Chapter 18 – Family FYI

"Mum, I'm home!" Harris said as he let himself into his home.

"Allo, Doll!" Jean said as she gave him a peck on the cheek and a hug. "How was your flight."

"Quiet, actually," Harris said. "So, what's new around here then?"

"Well, not much..." Jean said. "You get to look around, then?"

"I did," Harris responded. "Some new businesses opened up…I saw that Mr Ravalli opened a gym down the way."

"That he did." She said. "Did you see him…or want to? I didn't know how you felt about him without Gina around."

"Well, he's not her," Harris said. "And if we see each other, we see each other, and that's that then."

"It sounds like you plan to be around there a bit," Jean said. "Did you join up?"

"Better…" He said excitedly. "He gave me a job!"

That news came as a surprise to Jean.

"Really? Doing what?" She asked.

"Assisting with first aid for the youth teams," He said. "I'll be under other doctors, of course, but I believe the experience will be good for me. Besides, I don't want to mope around here all the time. I need to keep my skills sharp."

Harris went to the fridge for a drink. "I can't wait to tell Da. This job will be just what he wants for me."

"OK, then." She said. "Then you go out and be the best you can be."

Harris then had a curiosity that didn't come to mind until now.

"Mum, how did you and Da meet?" Harris asked as he sat at the table after pouring his drink.

Jean had to think back about that. They married over twenty years ago, and their meeting for the first time was a distant memory. "Ah, yes. We met at Alton Towers on summer holiday." She said. "I was 17 then. We were both in the queue for a new roller coaster.

He was alone, and the operator insisted on filling the cars with two each. My mates at the time practically threw me toward him to keep the queue going. I was nervous as I had never ridden a coaster like this, and I ended up holding his hand for the whole ride. When it was over, I was still holding his hand. I took it away, and he said that he wouldn't mind holding on to it a bit longer. We spent the rest of the day together."

His mum had a smile on her face Harris had not seen before. She continued...

"We got ice cream and just talked about our plans after school. How he would become a doctor and how I wanted to become a bookkeeper. After that day, he would take the choo to see me every Saturday from Bromley to Watford. My parents thought he was mental for riding all that distance to see me, but they let us be."

Harris was almost afraid to ask... "Mum, do any of your family know that Da and I are Xenons?"

She looked down at her feet, almost in shame. "They don't." She said. "It's not something anyone would benefit from knowing anyhow, son."

"I understand," Harris said. "Not everyone can deal with it. I saw the protests in Hyde Park on the telly. It's the common belief we're more a threat, I guess. You must have been surprised when he told you that he was."

There was a long pause by his Mum here. She appeared deep in thought over that bit of knowledge.

"Yeah, it was not the best of times, then..." She replied. "I was afraid of him until he showed me what he could do. He took me to hospital where he was a house officer, and we sneaked into a girl's room with a venomous spider bite who came in an hour before. She was unconscious, and the staff was afraid of losing her as they didn't know which anti-venom to use. He sneaked me in as the doctor stepped out to go fetch her parents."

Harris listened attentively to every detail.

Jean continued: "He put his hand on her ankle, and his hands glowed. The girl woke up just as we left and shouted for her mum. He told me that she was released the next day with no symptoms and smiling on her way out."

Harris saw his Da in a new light after this. He was always kind of stodgy after coming home and didn't want to be disturbed. He would read his London Times and go to bed after watching the news programmes.

"Now really," Harris spoke. "How could anybody in your family have a problem with him after that?"

"I think the bigger problem back then was that he was Catholic, and I was protestant," Jean said. "He and I only had a problem in that I didn't want to have more than one child. I hope you don't feel denied that we didn't have a larger family, son.

"You did all right by me, mum." He said. "I know I wasn't the best at times. I got in the scruffs with the bullies and messed up along the way, but you did all right. I'll tell ya that, now." He hugged her as she sat in her chair. "I'll be down for dinner, then." as he went upstairs. Harris entered the bedroom, where it felt both familiar and unfamiliar at the same time. He just laid on the single bed that had no squeak but was smaller than the double size in his student flat and gave himself the "sour grapes" mentality. Gina didn't want him then he could find someone who did. "No big loss then… Hope she's happy elsewhere…."

"So then, why do I keep thinking of her?" He thought.

Chapter 19 – Additional Methods

POW!!! CLINK!!! BAM!!! These were not from a Batman TV show repeat, but what Harris always heard while working for Mr Ravalli at his gym. He was there at 9 in the morning and stayed until about 3 with a few actual doctors coming through to monitor a few of the older clientele. Mostly, it was to take their blood pressure and offer advice on nutrition. If there were problems, he would be there alongside the attending to get a first-hand view of how to deal with the public. The injuries were minor in terms of strained muscles and a facial cut from an errant blow to the head from a couple of boxers in the ring. Harris figured that he had better keep his abilities in check as these were minor injuries and nothing that needed his medical attention.

One day on his lunch break, Harris could have sworn that he saw Gina enter a nearby shop. He rushed into The Spell Binder Book Shoppe with a mad dash, but she was no place to be found. Since he needed to occupy his mind a bit, he stayed and looked about a bit.

He then found a section on natural healing methods. There were books on acupuncture, massage, herbal medicines and something that seemed familiar to him called "reiki."

He racked his brain as to where he saw reiki before as the book cover had a hand hovering over a bare leg that glowed. Naturally, that got his attention. He remembered the film, "The Karate Kid" where Daniel-San had an injured leg, and Mr Miyagi healed him by rubbing his hands together and holding them over the injured area.

He bought the book along with some natural herb guides and viewed them at home. It seemed useless on the surface, but maybe he could use it as an excuse when he had nothing else to say. After all, he heard that many medicines came from places like South America, where plants grew that helped the natives in their health pursuits and Asia where many centuries ago, they invented acupuncture.

On the weekends he would go with the teams to Rickett's gate and witness the sports teams and their games. Many times, these younger players were very aggressive toward each other. Even the cricket players were using all their strength toward their opponents. Harris had no clue what sport would be best for him. He knew Roland could be great as a cricket bowler as he managed to hit Dermot right in the eye last winter with a loose bit of rock.

Harris's frame was tall and thin, so rugby was not his strong suit, and he would rather watch football than play. He was also more isolated than most, so something that would cause him to focus on himself would be better. Golf, perhaps? There was nothing like that offered by the gym, so Harris figured it was time to get some strength going. With that, Harris started working out. He didn't want to become some gym rat but wanted to get some muscle tone started. After all, why should he ignore his health when concentrating on everyone else's?

Vincent allowed Harris free access to the equipment from the beginning as he was only paying him a pittance for the work. Harris knew the experience was worth a tonnage more to him, anyway. At first, he was concerned that there would be no effect as his own body acted differently than others, but he showed improvement over a couple of weeks that he pushed himself. The aches and strains that affected others didn't affect him, which allowed him to tackle the equipment a lot more than most would. After a few weeks, he looked far better than he did when he went in.

At home, he read over the supposed effects of different roots and plants. Some of them he found were just "suggestible" while he could see the value in some others. After all, if he were stuck with an answer to why a disease cleared up, he could fall back on these. The reputation of Reiki and herbs were nothing compared to the positive words he had heard about acupuncture. The thing was that those who practised this art did so over many years, more than his medical training required.

It could have been his history of bullying or just the thrill of it in that he decided to try his hand at boxing. The trainer, called Sam Brubaker, was a former bobby who was stabbed by a robber who was high on cocaine and was forced to take a clerical position. He taught Harris about keeping his head up and keeping his attention focused on the opponent and what they are about to do. Harris started out getting the cheese beaten out of him at first but improved over his short time. Of course, he showed no signs of facial or body trauma, which worried Harris that a former constable would take as a sign of being a Xenon. Sam, however, seemed to take no notice of his lack of bruising. Harris became faster in a short time and sharper in his mind as well. "Why didn't I do this years ago?" He thought. Vincent asked Harris to give a tour of the gym to a new client. Harris finally asked where Gina was and said that he didn't want to intrude as she had made up her mind.

"I was wondering when you would ask me," Vincent said. "Gina is working and staying with Eduardo and his family in Milan. She's working at his restaurant."

Harris felt it odd that he thought he just saw her at the book shop. Harris just nodded, and they got back to the business of the new client.

"Harris" Vincent began as the new client entered in a jacket, shorts and a t-shirt. "This is…"

"Dr Guiteau!" Harris said as he shook the hand of his mentor.

"Good to see you, Harris!" Julius said. "If I knew you were here, I would have joined aeons ago."

Vincent just smiled. "Well, since you two are alright…" and left them to it.

"So how is academia treating you?" Julius asked.

"I'm doing well," Harris responded. I just received my marks, and I'm in the top ten for the first-year lot!"

"Excellent!" Julius said. "All that hard work paid off for ya."

"Well, I have you and Da to thank for it…and Gina as well." Harris gave credit where it was due.

"You two still together?" Julius asked.

"Nah, she cut the cord 'round Christmas…though she never said why," Harris said without the sadness that went with it.

"Well, don't let that get you down then." He said. "You got a long life ahead of ya... So, this is it then."

Harris remembered what he was to be doing right now. "Oh yeah, well let me show you about." He said.

"OK, lemme hang this up," Julius said. He removed his jacket and revealed a body that looked like he had already spent years in a gym. It was the first time that Harris saw Julius in this kind of outfit as he always seemed to have on his business attire and noticed for the first time his muscular physique!

"Damn, Julius!" Harris said, surprised at his physique. "I remember you said you were in the army, but I didn't know you kept the guns!" referring to the fact that Julius had arm muscles that look like they could snap trees along with shoulders in two districts!"

"Yeah, I kept my regimen up until my gym shut. That's why I came here. Your father recommended it."

"Good on ya, Da!" Harris thought. "…OK, lemme show you around." Harris said as he gave him the gym tour.

Harris talked about how he began boxing as he showed the ring to Julius to which his former mentor to suggest going into the martial arts when he gets a chance. Perhaps it would help with his healing abilities. Harris did read about the chi, and how the mind and body's energy flowed along with these connections. Maybe there is more to all this than he thought?

Too bad all he had was a short time to learn this aspect as he only had until next week before he went back to Ireland.

Chapter 20 – Sport injuries

That Saturday, Jean had fixed Harris a full breakfast. No doubt wanting to spoil him before he had to return to Ireland. His father was at the table as well as reading the paper. "So, son…" Jean asked. "What you up to, today then?"

"I have one more football game to attend to before I finish," Harris replied. "I'm going to miss this job when it's over. How about you lot?" He asked over his eggs and toast.

"I'm going to market today," Jean said. "It'll be a bit sad to buy less food."

"Oh, sorry to put a strain on your kitchen," Harris said, referring to the fact he ate more because he exercised more.

"Now you don't give that a second thought, son," Jean said. "I have been taking care of you for these two decades. I never complained and never shall." She said as she kissed him on his head. His Da just smiled from behind his paper, not saying anything.

"Da…Can I ask you something?" Harris asked.

His Da acknowledged him with a short "Hmm?"

"When you heal people, do they get massively thirsty?" Harris meant to ask him long ago already.

Helmut collected his thoughts for a second. "Oh yeah…I forgot all about that." He said. "When I was younger, that was always the case. Now my patients are hooked up to saline lines, so that's not an issue now."

"Well, you know Da, Dr Guiteau is working out at my gym now," Harris said.

"I believe he told me that, yes," Helmut said. "It looks like you both have been working out."

"I have," Harris said. "I should have done this years ago."

"Well, just put yourself where you want to be," Helmut said. "I know I should be exercising as well, but I'm tired. Forgive me if I say that I am looking forward to the house to myself today just to sleep…it's been a long week, especially on Thursday.

His Da referred to a bombing that happened downtown. The investigation was ongoing as to whether Xenons, IRA or some other group was responsible. No side seemed to be claiming responsibility. Despite being saved, the patients of that incident had to stay in hospital for a bit. Harris took a quick look at this watch. "Well, that starts now. I'll see you both tonight." And he took his leave out the door to the bus shelter down the street near his old faith school.

This particular Saturday, he grabbed a bag of sundries for the day and took the bus to Rickett's Gate for a football game and this one was for a coveted divisional position. Harris would not be there to watch the final game but was excited for this penultimate match as the local Chelsea boys and girls were taking on their number one rivals of Kensington. This game was a bit of a nail-biter as the winner here would face Knightsbridge or Hammersmith, depending who fared better in that game. Parents and players alike crowded along the side-lines as the ball rolled this way and that on the feet of the red and green-uniformed teams. At the 4-3 mark, Kensington gave a sharp run-up to the goal and kicked the ball to an active line right past the goalie's head. It looked like a cannonball landed in the net with such a strong force that looked like it would take the goal net with it. Jessica "Jesse' James delivered that strong kick that tied the game.

Harris then spotted the Kensington team coach say something to one of the players and the boy appeared to object, but the coach yelled at him until he relented. So, another set up with Chelsea in control. The boy who had words with the coach charged Oliver Hatch and gave a powerful shin kick to the star forward for Chelsea, who fell to the ground in extreme pain. The referee gave the boy, Trevor Hahn, a red card for excessive force and dismissed him from the game. Harris ran out along with the attending physician, Dr Cole Greene.

Dr Greene and Harris carried off Oliver with his arms over each shoulder of the attending physicians as they took him into the brick building that held the equipment room. They laid him on the table, and Doctor Greene, who was a house officer at Saville Hospital, looked at the bruise and got an ice pack for the boy. The ice was doing its job of keeping down the swelling, but slowly. Oliver was still biting his lip in pain.

"Harris, can you stay with him for a bit? I need to keep eyes on the rest of the field." Dr Greene asked.

"Yeah, go on," Harris said. It wasn't odd to be left alone with a player to attend to his or her injuries, so Harris decided to try something else today after Dr Greene's absence. "Oliver…" He asked the player still in pain. "Have you ever seen The Karate Kid?"

Five minutes later, Oliver went back to the side-line after his respite and a near-empty bottle of water in his hand. Chelsea coach Stephan Robeson and Dr Greene were standing together watching the action and, naturally, surprised by the fact that the boy who was in such pain a short time ago was standing and ready to play again.

"Boy, you sure you up to it?" Coach Robeson asked.

"I feel great!" Oliver said. "Here, look…" and the boy hopped on the leg and gave a spin as well.

Coach turned to Cole Greene: "Well, Doc…what of it?"

Doctor Cole was surprised but impressed enough to let the boy back in. "If you think you're up to it…" He said.

"OK, hold on for the next time-out…" Coach Robeson said. "Let them get their confidence together." With that, they instructed Oliver to sit and stay out of sight for the time being. Oliver tossed his empty bottle into the rubbish bin while hiding prone behind the team bench. Well, they didn't too wait long. Kensington scored again, and they lead by a point. Coach Robeson sent Oliver back on the field to everyone's surprise. They all knew it wasn't a flop as they could both hear and see the hit that Trevor Hahn delivered.

Oliver led a rush to the net with his fancy footwork and fed it off two more forwards, back to him and delivered the goal, tying the score. "Jesse" James had the ball for a long time and was about to strike the Chelsea goal again when Oliver got his head in the way, and it bounced off the side of his skull, stunning him but sending the ball sailing to his defenders. Harris wondered if he was going to need to give more assistance to the boy, but Oliver was on his feet again and chasing the ball to Kensington's goal behind the other forwards.

Kensington's goalie caught the ball and kicked it back midfield where Jesse stopped it dead on the ground and ran it back toward Chelsea. Once again taking the kick that the goalie stopped on this side of the field and the teen boy picked it up and kicked it back into play.

Back down the field with Oliver and scant seconds to go and he passed the defenders with ease and took his shot that bounced toward his teammate, Chas Bocca lining up a shot that bounced three sides of the goal until it went in. Chelsea won ten seconds later when the whistle blew, and victory was theirs! The Chelsea crowd erupted in applause while Harris just calmly clapped as he watched the players congratulate each other.

Doctor Greene went to Harris and asked what he did to get Oliver back on the field. Harris just said that he held his hands over the injury like in The Karate Kid film and let his mind fill in the rest of the recovery. "I honestly didn't expect it to work. It was just a last-ditch effort to get him out of pain. I guess it would be called a placebo effect...unless you do indeed believe in that reiki sort-of thing."

With that, Oliver came over with a large bruise on the side of his head. "Any way you can fix this?" He asked Harris as his head started to turn a scarlet colour. "I best leave the rest of your mend to Dr Greene," Harris said. "That looks like a more experienced man need look at that."

Dr Greene was in complete agreement as he led Oliver over to the team bench and gave him a quick look-over. The teen was starting to stammer, and his eyes were getting glassy. "Harris, C' mon! We got to get him to hospital." They then put the boy in Dr Greene's car and sped off to Hospital. The A&E Department wasn't full, but it was busy with patients treated for everything imaginable. Harris knew he could clear this place out with an hour of uninterrupted healing if he were left to it but knew what attention he would gain as well. It was frustrating what people believed of Xenons: Abominations, monsters, daemons...ugh!

There was no way for Harris to pass himself off as an experienced medical professional here, so he left the so-called experts to do their work. He also felt a bit guilty for what course of action he put into motion. Maybe if Oliver were left to just lay in the equipment room in his painful state, he would not be in this fix. He sat in the waiting area for what seemed an eternity until Dr Greene got on the phone in the lobby. When he got off, Harris went over to him and asked how Oliver was.

"Oh...Harris," Dr Greene said. "I'm sorry I didn't know you were still here. Oliver is stable. We have experts coming over for his sake. You need a lift home?"

Harris shook his head. "I'll take the bus home."

Cole returned to the A&E department as Harris made his way down the hall to exit the hospital when he saw a man on a gurney laying by himself.

"Hello!" He shouted in a Scotch accent. "Hello, is anyone there?" He had been bandaged from some incident and was laid to wait for someone to show but was obviously in pain. Harris saw that his shoulder was at an odd angle. There seemed to be no one there to assist yet. Harris knew that he shouldn't be interfering in a place like this but found he could not leave him like this.

"I can probably help, sir!" He said to the man lying there. "Now, where does it hurt?"

"My shoulder, mate!" He said as he winced in horrible pain. "I fell off scaffolding over at the Cloisters!" He looked him over and found his short medical education allowed him to identify that he had a dislocated shoulder.

"OK, sir," Harris said as he placed his hand near his neck. "I'll take care of this!" and with that, he covered his eyes with a nearby cloth. "' Ere, you'll not want to see this coming sir." He was in pain way too much to argue. His hands started their glowing as he took a quick look down the hall to make sure it was all clear.

"Here we go then…One…two…" His eyes were covered, and Harris pushed his shoulder as the repairing light dissipated." The patient gasped, and Harris pulled the cloth off his eyes as the man laid with a smile of relief.

"All right then, sir?" Harris asked.

"Aye, much better lad. Thank you." He said as he looked in amazement just how young this "doctor" was before him.

"Lad, you're so young to be a doctor!" The Scotsman said.

Harris then leaned down closer to his ear. "Actually sir, I'm a chiropractor…I'm not to be practising here so I'd appreciate it if you didn't say about my doing anything."

"Aye, done," The Scotsman said and nodded.

Harris then patted him on the shoulder and headed out the door to catch his bus while the Scotsman, no doubt, got up to find relief for his inevitable thirst. The double-decker had him home in 15 minutes, and Harris thought again to the young boy and his brain problem despite being assured that Oliver was stable.

Jean was sitting in her favourite chair, watching the news when he got in. His father was not there, which was unusual for a Saturday.

"Mum, where's Da?" Harris asked.

"He had to go in for an emergency. Someone got injured during a football match." She responded.

"What?... I just came from there!" Harris said. Super...Not only did Oliver get injured, seriously during the game, but now Da had to be interrupted during his rest time. Harris just decided to go to his room with his meal and listen to music rather than watch EastEnders or whatever else came on the box. Harris also contemplated his actions. How would he know Oliver would be so severely injured? Maybe some other Xenons could see the future, but not him. He fell asleep, not knowing when his Da returned home.

Chapter 21 – Back to School Time

Harris packed his suitcase once again with clean clothes and books ready to return to Ireland. He was also anxious to hear how Oliver was. His father never spoke of his patients, of course, but Oliver was Harris's patient first, and an inquiry of his condition was in order. He went down to breakfast with his father reading the times and his mother fixing bangers on the cooker. "Good morning, all," Harris said. His Mum and Da returned the greeting as Harris took his place at the table. His father was quiet as he finished an article about British soldiers killed by an IRA bombing near Belfast.

"Da," Harris said. "How is that boy you were treating for football injuries yesterday?"

"Hang on, Son…," Helmut said as he finished the article. That allowed Harris time to cut into his eggs and sausages.

"Jean…" Helmut said. "Would you excuse us a moment, please?" With that, Harris's Mum wiped her hands and turned on the morning news in the living room.

Helmut set down his paper about to look like he was going to say something serious. "He's fine, son. I don't know if you know this, but I have never lost a patient." He said with great pride.

"Is his mental state all right as well?" Harris asked. "He seemed a bit out of sorts when I last saw him."

"Yes, he recovered after the hour he saw me. That must have been quite a blow he took to the head to scramble him like that."

"Aye, that it was," Harris said. "I had been treating ankle injuries for the most part, but that was the worst I had seen," Harris said.

"Of course, son, you had yourself out in public where your work was on display," Helmut said. "You have to make sure ALL your bases are covered if you are going to do that."

"Yes, Da," Harris said. "But I did all that when I…"

With that, Harris his head with his palm. "Oh, cock!" He said. "The leg! I didn't bandage the leg after the match!"

"Oliver's coach informed us…me, about the leg injury he took earlier before we went into surgery," Helmut said. "I put a plaster cast on his leg and told his coach it was probably adrenalin that kept him moving and that he was lucky he didn't make further mischief to himself."

Harris looked down dejectedly. "I messed this one up, majorly." He said.

"Son, this is part of the learning process," Helmut said. "You do, indeed, need to be careful, but it's more to the point that the stakes are so high. We are still off the radar of the authorities since they are looking for Xenons that may cause damage more than we who cause restoration. That doesn't mean we are to be any less careful."

"Yes, Da," Harris said. It was a stunning lesson that Harris needed to learn.

He collected his final wages from Mr Ravalli and shook his hand along with wishes for good luck and an invite to come work for him again if the fates allow. He also gave his goodbyes to Julius and said he would attempt to keep in touch this year. Julius said for him to "keep doing what you're doing." Both his parents saw him off that morning to the airport. Flying was becoming easier for Harris as he had taken this ride twice before. He read his copy of The Guardian and about the new daughter of Prince Andrew and an upcoming postal strike. The flight was mostly empty this morning as they touched down in Cork. He took his bags and caught a bus to The Royal University of Medicine, preparing his mind for whatever that lay ahead.

THE END OF PART ONE

Act Two

Chapter 22 - Start again

The same flat as the semester before was made available to Harris. Roland already said that he would take up his old room as well. Harris wondered what Roland was up to in the past two months. He went to the town centre and had a large lunch at The Burger Rocket. The muscle mass gained in London now required eating more. With that, he went on campus and signed up at the gymnasium for students. It was small, but it filled his needs. There was even promise of a new swimming pool to be built later in the year. The weights and stationary bikes were all he needed for now. He promised himself he would purchase a proper bicycle then.

He returned to the flat and saw Roland's jacket hanging in the hall. He expected the sound of the bedsprings to be singing from his room, but no such sound emerged. "Roland?" Harris knocked and entered his room. No one was there. He did see a few books on his desk about genealogy and another called "You Can Find Anyone." He exited and went back to his own room to unpack. The same items he brought before, and a few new ones had their place for the year. One box he didn't even bother to touch had the same things from a couple of months ago, including Gina's picture. He put that back in the drawer where it was before and forgot about it.

There was a fresh coat of paint in the living room along with brighter curtains and a new telly. Maybe the purchase of a VCR for his time there was in order as the nation seemed to be swept up in the desire for films on video. Movies would be a change as all he seemed to watch was Wheel of Fortune, Celebrity Squares and Mastermind. Harris loved quiz shows and always had a soft place in his heart for the different games of the past. Perhaps it was time for a change.

While he was in his room arranging his clothes, the sound of the front door opened. Roland walked in with a notebook and several other texts for the year. "Hello, stranger!" Harris said to Roland. The brown-haired lad set his books down on the sitting room chair and gave him a big handshake.

"Hey, boy!" Roland said. "Back for more punishment, eh?"

"Well, it's our lot in life, isn't it?" Harris responded. They both forgot that in Harris's case, it was more a ruse than an education.

"Well, sorry I missed you coming in…I was just at the library downtown." Roland said, pointing at the stack of books on the chair.

"Downtown?" Harris said inquisitively. "Have they a medical selection?"

"No, but they have something else I am interested in…" Roland said as he held up yet another book. "Genealogy. I'm trying to find my dad."

Up to now, Harris didn't inquire about Roland's family situation too much. He knew he had two brothers and a sister, but all from another father. Roland was the eldest and talked about how he seemed to get the brunt of his mum's verbal abuse.

"The last I heard, he was in Belfast. I just found out, but classes are on soon. I might visit there sometime this year." He said.

"OK, then," Harris said. "Well, I hope you can. At least you can go there without problems. I would probably be shot on sight if I went there." Alluding to the fact that Northern Ireland was no place for Brits at that time.

"Right then," Roland said, looking for anything to change the subject, and one look at Harris provided it.

"Hang on!" Roland said excitedly. "When did this start?"

"Eh?" Harris responded, not knowing what he was on about.

"You been working out, eh?" Roland said, looking at his now stronger frame. Harris didn't think he looked that different, but perhaps he did. He then told Roland about the gym, the football match and also about the books he found in London.

"Well, I guess we both have extra studies to look over... You settled in yet?" Roland asked.

"Yeah, pretty much." Harris said, knowing full well what he had in mind: "Pub?"

"Well, since you suggested it…" Roland said slyly. "Perhaps I can find a bird in her right mind this time."

Chapter 23 – The Old and the New

Of course, The Draughtsman was in full swing as students were all getting ready to return to the grind of books and papers to turn in daily. Some of the familiar faces returned, some were missing, and some new ones were present as well. Harris and Roland tried to make a point of at least saying hello to everyone they could. Jasmine Rubajinski was sitting with Taylor Carpenter in a corner seat. They looked like they missed each other a lot. They would leave the pub together before the night's end.

Jill Johns was at the bar drinking a Depth Charge with an unfamiliar and much older-looking guy. Miriam Knight was at the bar chatting up a new bird over stouts. They all heard Jenni transferred to a university in Dublin. Rhona Haberl was drinking alone at a table reading The Road Less Travelled. Becky McGill was chatting with Todd Hunter who went back home to the USA for the summer and missed Ireland as the people were far easier to get along. Caroline Patterson was getting friendly with a Russian student Harris did not catch the name of as it was complicated and heavily accented, and a very dark South African couple sat in the corner chatting with each other. Their names were also challenging to the ear. Harris had no clue how he would remember them all but recalled he only knew half of them at a time anyway.

There was also talk throughout the pub that computers would be employed throughout the campus shortly, so they would have to learn that skill as well. There was excitement and trepidation in that there was a new way to make learning easier and fear as that meant yet another skill to learn.

Roland brought two lagers and a notebook to the table and proceeded to tell Harris what he had been up to this past summer. "Right…" He began. "My mum showed me a snap of me dad and her from years back. He was a good looker, and I guess a bit of a himbo. Me mum gave him the glad eye for a while and then she got plugged with me, and he ran for the long grass. I'd not see him ever. All I have is this snap I found of him."

With that, Roland showed Harris a picture of his brown-haired mom and a red-haired male. The picture showed both of them were around Roland and Harris's age at the time.

"Mum's afraid I might end up like him," Roland said.

"Might?" Harris said with raised eyebrows.

"OK, if I ended up plugging someone here, I wouldn't end up leaving her in the lurch!" Roland said with the passion of an MP.

"OK, good…" Harris said. "Because as many times you've gone home with company…"

"I know…it's always been a concern with me, too," Roland responded. "Don't think I'm not thinking about that. I'm rubbering up every time now, even if they say they're using chemicals."

"Ok, well, back to this, then…" Harris reoriented their conversation. "Did you find out anything yet?

"His lot came from Northern Ireland. I traced the family back to when they lived in Castlerock and then moved to Belfast. That's it so far.

"All right then," Harris said. "Between that for you and the gym for me, we're going to be busy this year." Harris finished his pint the same time Roland finished his. "Here, I got the next one, mate." He said. Roland nodded as he gave him his glass and Harris went to the bar for two more of the same. It was then that he felt eyes on him like he was getting a lot of attention. It usually wasn't a good feeling for Harris. Back in intermediate school, a sense like this meant someone was about to slam him into a wall, but it was the females from whom he was attracting attention. He couldn't figure it at the time.

He took two pints back to the table and mentioned the feeling to his friend.

"Well mate, what you expect?" Roland said. "Last year, you were a face in the crowd apart from your drinking prowess, now you come in here built like a brick chicken house!"

Oh yeah! His new build. Harris had forgotten that change in him. He continued to feel like himself, no matter how he appeared.

"Looks like you got the option of taking someone home with ya, old boy!" Roland said with a sly smile.

It was a good feeling being a "Cock on the walk", but he didn't know if he wanted it. Just the feeling of having his choice seemed enough. Roland, though, seemed to feel otherwise as he tried to persuade Jill Johns to go home with Harris until she whispered something to him just as the older guy, she was with returned from the Jacks.

Roland quickly grabbed Harris and said "C' mon, we're off!" He said it with such urgency that Harris was not about to argue with him. They exited the pub with half their drinks left on the table and got halfway down the block before he asked Roland why the hasty retreat?

"That guy she was with was her father…" Roland said with an embarrassed tone. "…and on top of that, he's administration!"

Harris was relieved that they left when they did. It wasn't a significant loss that they went so suddenly. He enjoyed the pleasures he had shared with Caroline sometime back but was not really in the mood for it tonight.

"Sorry I had to drag you out of there so fast, then," Roland said in a tone of apology.

"Here, don't give it a second thought" Harris responded. "I'm not up for a bird keeping me up all night right now. I got to finish getting my books together for tomorrow."

Roland couldn't deny that. They got out the schedules for this year, and it was far more intense than the last term, as it should be. Last year, most of the action took place in the classrooms at the college. This year, they were to be dispatched to actual hospitals in the area and work with doctors on real cases along with medical mannequins and people posing as patients in the labs. The hospital thing was a concern as Harris knew the temptation of curing everyone he met. He knew from his experience with the injured Scotsman that it would require the utmost restraint to keep from letting loose the full extent of his abilities on a hospital ward of suffering individuals.

Then, there was a knock at the door. Who could it be at this hour? It was near ten, and they were both about to crash. Roland said he'd get it but kept an old golf club nearby in case someone less than desirable came to the door. Harris looked down the hall in his dressing-gown as Roland opened the door wearing his.

It was Jill Johns. Roland was hoping she wasn't going to go off on what happened earlier, but she had anything but trouble in mind as she threw her arms around his neck and gave him a huge kiss. He returned the kiss and practically dragged her into his room.

Harris knew what this meant. He got out his Walkman and played a Pet Shop Boys cassette at top volume as the bedsprings and screams of joy erupted from next door. As the band sang "Always on my Mind," he tried to make sense of what he just saw. First, an attempt to push Jill on him, then she came over and went right for Roland. Harris was well aware he didn't know much about relationships apart from his own experiences, but this wasn't normal...was it?

Chapter 24 – Why We're Here...

After their regular morning toilette, Harris and Roland grabbed a sandwich at O'Deer's café and then went on their way across campus to the first class. It was an introduction to the medical mannequins.

There were some suppressed giggles in the lab when first introduced. These were much like the resuscitation dolls when one learns CPR, but these were also able to have a heartbeat in different rates, breathe in different patterns and have various levels of body temperature. The feeling was if you can handle a doll and keep a straight face, you will be reliable and real with an actual human.

A short lunch break brought Taylor and Jasmine to the long table that Roland and Harris shared. Jill came over, and she and Roland were civil to each other but nowhere near the lovers they purported to be last night. The two South African students asked to join in as well, and they took a seat with the lot of them. They had some interesting stories to tell about Apartheid and the chance they had to get out of Johannesburg. It was apparent they wanted to prove themselves to everyone that they could and would make the grade.

Harris felt lucky that his own minority wasn't evident to the bigots of the world but felt angry toward the oppressors Nelson and Siboh Nghegdela had to face before they escaped their previous lives for the possibilities that Europe offered. What was an actual offence was the fact that they couldn't go home again due to their people being too proud to take anything from the whites, no matter who or where they were and what they got from them.

The exams, practicals and papers they had to turn in was an avalanche of page after page of medical exploration and explanation. This all built on the base of what they learned in the first term, so there was no learning it and forgetting about it like back in St. Joseph's.

In the meanwhile, Roland was doing his research looking for traces of his father and family's history. He even went back as far back as Scotland. Harris meanwhile took bike rides around campus and town to clear his head.

He also grabbed iron at the campus gym, maintaining what he built up over the summer. He was at the level that he wanted now. Perhaps more Sean Connery than Arnold Schwarzenegger in their younger days but it was what worked for him. He even began a karate class to understand further what the Asian practitioners had in mind when creating their systems of fighting and healing.

Roland spent just as much time with his nose in the book while making phone calls to faraway places. He did join Harris in Karate and also lifted weights twice a week to try to keep fit. He couldn't outlast Harris, though...nobody could.

Roland excelled in something else, though and that was the sheer amount of birds he was pulling on the weekends. What Harris was struck by was that none of these women were harbouring any ill, nor loving feelings toward Roland afterwards. There was a woman on Friday who was different than the one on Saturday, and they differed week after week. At least he wasn't plugging any of them as that would be the death of both him and the unlucky mother-to-be.

Occasionally, there would be visits to a local hospital for witnessing the work of doctors and surgeons caring for their patients. There were occasions where the surgeons would choose two or three potential doctors from the group and ordered them to "scrub in" and get a closer look at the operation in question. "The human body was more elaborate than any machine on Earth and doctors were the repairmen." Dr Cyrus Greenwald said. Harris realised that when he got this close to people when they were at their most vulnerable, that this was where he needed and had to be. It was one of the most sobering moments of his life.

Not to say there weren't fun times, too. The pub was always there, and his bike rides were relaxing rather than a workout. It was also a time when he wasn't thinking of anything but what a beautiful day it was. He rode by a pitch at the park and watched a group play a sport called hurling which he only heard of but never saw until now. It was one of the most violent and insane games he ever saw. A combination of lacrosse, hockey and rugby. Harris read the rules in a pamphlet he found in the gym…

A dozen or so players ran this way and that after a small ball (sliotar) that they couldn't pick up with their hands but rather scoop up with a long stick that had a flat end (camogie.) They would run a long distance with the ball balanced on the end of this blunt halberd or throw the ball in the air and whack it with the end of the stick hoping to hit between a pair of upright posts or into a net past a goaltender. The uprights scored one point and past the goaltender scored three.

Harris watched their scramble continue on the field and saw many were playing without helmets. All he could think was "Wow! I'll see you lot later in the A&E Department!"

Harris entered his flat and sat his bike in the hall. He grabbed the mail on the hall stand and entered the sitting room while Roland was talking on the phone and making a contentious argument about how he had the right to know his father's last place of work. It seemed the person on the phone was not willing to say anything useful. Roland called her some names he'd no doubt have to confess to later on and hung up on her with such force, Harris thought the phone would snap in half.

Roland looked up and saw that Harris entered. He continued to fume more than a chimney fire. "The nerve of that woman! Telling me anyone could call and claim he was family. Who is this guy? Prime Minister?" Roland said as he slumped on the couch in the sitting room. He just sat quietly for a moment to collect his thoughts. "I need another path here. I wonder if he went to church?"

Harris listened as he scanned through the mail. "From what I hear, computers will make it easy in the future."

"Ya, I don't doubt that. Roland said. "I just don't want to wait 50 years until that happens."

Harris remembered that when he broke up with Gina last year, Roland said they should go out to the pub and defuse. It was with that idea that Harris saw the postcard in the stack of letters he had.

"Sound like you need a break as well, mate," Harris said as he showed the invitation to his best friend:

Attention Groovy Ghoulies!!!

Halloween night soirée on 29 October at 8:00

At the opulent residence of Caroline and Jasmine

110 Banyan Avenue, No. 2

Find your favourite skin or fancy dress and make an appearance!

On the other side of the postcard was a photograph of Frankenstein's monster and his bride posing like a wedding picture. Where did they find that?

"Well, mate…" Harris said. "Looks like it's time to find your Superman mask.

Chapter 25 - Just say NO to drugs

So, the Halloween party would be at the flat of Caroline and Jasmine where Harris hadn't been since last year for a night. Roland put on white make-up, a white & jewelled jumpsuit, sideburns glued on with a black wig and lots of gold jewellery. He went as the ghost of Elvis!

Harris went as a heavy-metal rock star with a long black wig, studded leather wristbands, a sleeveless shirt with the band *Lightning* on it and leather pants. All this while carrying a ukulele strapped around his neck! The stringed instrument as a goofy touch.

They walked across campus dressed this way, but not looking so weird as most other students dressed up in various forms of skins, costumes and fancy dress heading to other parties.

Harris and Roland continued to Caroline's door, and they let themselves in with conversations and music blasting all over the place. Harris surprised himself as a gathering like this used to have sent him running into the night.

Roland was chatting up yet another bird, this time it was Marla O'Holton, a fourth-year girl who was a full foot taller than him. Everyone knew he was doing it, and the other girls he had been with paid him no mind about it. Harris still couldn't help but feel it strange that this was the accepted behaviour. This feeling continued as they vanished together into a broom cupboard for a few minutes.

There was something else going on that he did not see before, and that was drug use. The odd smell of marijuana filled the air. He had no clue what it was at first until he saw Taylor and Jasmine in a room way down the hall after he used the loo.

They were in a storage room on an old blanket and staring at a lava-lamp as if it was the most interesting and exciting lifeform they ever encountered. Taylor even gently waved Harris in and told him to take a seat on the blanket around the lamp.

"Do you smoke at all, friend?" He asked. Harris shook his head. Harris tried smoking in his younger days but didn't stick with it as he got nothing from it. Jasmine took a large toke off the jay and blew the smoke into Harris's face.

Harris expected nothing to happen as alcohol did nothing to him but what followed was different. His head buzzed, and he zonked out. He then started seeing cartoon animals in place of Jasmine and Taylor. The experience got even more unpleasant as they began to shag, despite his presence.

Harris felt he better leave the room and entered the sitting room where a costumed Bugs Bunny, who had a voice of Caroline was asking if he was all right while she actually, was dressed as a witch.

Harris just nodded and got a bottle of lager out of a large bucket in the kitchen while watching Donald Duck talk to a Womble about how expensive college was in the US. This experience was not working out well.

Harris walked out to the back porch and watched Winnie the Pooh and Paddington Bear discuss holding a human heart during the surgical visit and felt how strong it would beat as the patient laid on the table, his chest opened and exposed. Daffy Duck came over and asked if they had a chance to watch Dr Greenwald perform open-heart surgery this past week? Harris just sat on the back stoop watching the clouds form letters. They were random and spelt nothing. Acronyms, maybe?

A large eye then looked down on him from the sky, detached from any giant face that would harbour it. No fear, nor emotion went with it. He could only finish taking this ride as the world passed in slow motion.

After what seemed like hours or so, the effects faded off and Roland's voice, him no longer looking like Danger Mouse, sat with Harris for a few minutes, and the world went back to being inhabited by humans again. "Hey, mate." He said. "You OK?"

Harris just nodded. "Alcohol doesn't work on me, but cannabis does," He said. "What's up with that?" Roland just shrugged.

"Guys, we got a problem!" the voice of Duckula spoke from behind them.

Harris shrunk back from the figure. "Oh, man, I'm…" Harris began to speak until Miriam took her mask off and Harris breathed a sigh of relief.

"What?" Miriam asked with her fanged duck mask in her hand.

"Never mind…what's up? Harris asked.

"Rhona Haberl is knackered on something. She's threatening everyone with a hurling stick!" Miriam said as they heard and saw the window smashed.

They all rushed in and saw Rhona dressed in hurling gear trying to keep everyone at bay by swinging the long pole. A pint glass lay shattered on the floor.

"You're not stealing my vagina!" Rhona shouted. There was some snickering about that from the party-goers.

No one wanted to get close to her. She looked as if she were ready to use anyone's head as a sliotar and knock it into the nearest net.

"Should we call Gardai? Jasmine asked in her accent.

"...and let them find the Turkish delight here? Miriam responded. "I should coco!"

"Everyone! Get back!" Harris hollered. When she was on the upswing, Harris pushed her full body into a room and locked the door behind them. He ended up on top of her, and she started crying and mumbling about something, but he couldn't hear what it was.

He got off her and pushed the long camogie under the bed to get it out of her hands. He wasn't sure whose bedroom he was in, it didn't matter. She just laid on the floor, not moving, but just breathing heavy. Harris opened the door slightly, and Roland was at the door.

"What am I dealing with here?" Harris asked while she just laid with her fists digging into the carpet, trying not to fall off the planet.

"It's LSD, mate," Roland said. "Looks like she took some acid before she came over. I swore to secrecy about who..."

"Never mind." Harris interrupted. "Just get me a glass of water."

Roland did what Harris asked and was back in less than a minute with a glass from the sink.

"Right friend..." Harris said. "I'll be here a bit...just cover for me."

Roland nodded and went to talk to the hosts. They all went back to the party, leaving Harris to take care of Rhona. She was now staring at the ceiling, acting like she was having a conversation.

Harris then spotted the phone on the side of the bed. He made a call to London.

The phone was answered by Dr Guiteau, who was sitting in his chair reading the paper. "Hello...7439," the voice said as he answered the call with the last four phone digits.

"Dr Guiteau… Harris here." He said.

"Harris? What…?"

"Listen, I have an emergency here…I'm at a party, and this girl just went into a panic mode. She started taking swings at everyone with a hurling stick. Someone said it was acid.

"Bad trip…OK, we can deal with this." Julius said calmly. "Antidepressants will short-circuit an acid trip. Have you got any?"

"Not yet," Harris said. "That's all I need, though…thanks." He then gave another thought. "Hey Julius…don't tell my Da about this. The less he knows, the better."

"OK then, good luck," Julius said as he hung up the phone.

Meanwhile, Rhona was trying to crawl into a hole in the floor. It was going to be an undertaking as the gap was just an inch wide. "I want to go home!" She said, thinking that was the way out.

Harris knew he would have to make up a story about antidepressants if anyone asked. With that, Harris put his hand on the back of her head and tried to let the light from his hand heal the distressed girl, but nothing happened.

"Damn it!" Harris thought. His Da's words drifted back to him "We can only heal the physical." Harris knew he would now have to find real antidepressants. He went back to the door and called to Roland.

"Mate, I need antidepressants. Harris said. "See if anyone got any," Roland said he knew where he could get them. Harris stayed with Rhona and turned on the telly for her. The news came on, and she just stared at the ordinary newsreader as he spoke of the usual terror actions of the IRA, Sein-Fein and, of course, Xenons.

She cocked her head and asked "Why is his head floating over there? Is there a camera problem?" She then looked and pointed at a painting of a waterfall and asked how they got the water to flow and fall on the picture?

Roland was back and panting in 20 minutes with a handful of antidepressants. He knocked on the door and Harris opened just a crack. "Here you go, mate." He said while breathing heavily. "How many you need?"

Harris had no idea, so he took 7, a lucky number. He told Roland not to have anyone worry, and he would take care of everything. When he turned to Rhona, she started beating him with her hands.

"What do you mean Mum never loved me?" She yelled, not knowing where she was. He pushed her off him. Now the point was how he was going to get her actually to take the pills? He took a 6-sided glass paperweight with Jasmine's family photograph (he assumed) and crushed the medicine into a powder and dumped the mixture into the water glass.

But Rhona was still on the warpath and looking for anything to defend herself against Harris. "Rhona, please…" he begged, but she was taking swings at him with a large textbook. He ducked her continued attacks until she tripped and fell on the desktop and started bleeding as she hit the floor. Harris felt horrible about it as she laid down and cried in pain. Harris fixed it as the light projected out of his hands into her head and restored her physical health while confident she would remember nothing.

Naturally, she was thirstier than she ever was and drank the water without resistance. Harris then went to the door and had Todd get him a refill on the glass of water. He said that if anyone asked, he would be in there for another hour until she burned out the drug. Harris took off his shirt and dipped it in the water to clean the blood off her face. She came back to the real world about a half-hour later.

"What happened?" Rhona asked.

"You took some bad formulae," Harris said. "How you feel?"

"I feel great." She said. "But why are we here?" She noticed his shirt was off. "Were we gonna…?"

"No," Harris said. "You needed to be away from the crowd a bit, so I brought you in here, then."

It was then that Rhona remembered what she did. She hugged Harris and cried. Harris just let her get it all out.

"What are they all gonna think of me now?" Rhona asked.

"They're all going to know to avoid acid in the future," Harris said. "Anyway, don't worry about it. Let's wait a moment before we leave."

"OK." She said as she held him, first, as scared and concerned and then as emotionally connected as she held him tighter.

But Harris had to pose one question to Rhona while they were sitting there...

"Rhona, as a female..." Harris tried to be delicate here. "What is it about Roland that makes all the birds here want to shag him?"

Rhona just looked puzzled at Harris. "What do you mean?" She asked.

Just then, Jasmine came in.

"Hey, you two oks? Jazzy asked.

"Yeah we're good," Rhona said as she continued to hold Harris.

"OK...I just wanted to know if you two were shagging in here." Jazzy said.

Harris couldn't believe she just came out and said that.

"Jazz, gimme some credit!" Harris barked. "If we were going to do that..."

Jasmine just responded quietly. "OK, All I wanted to say was if you were, just keep duvet on bed." And she left pushing the knob button to lock the door, satisfied that everything was all right.

"Can you believe she said that? Harris said.

Rhona looked into his eyes and responded with a deep kiss. "Sounds like an idea." She said as she pulled him down on the floor with her.

Chapter 26 - Seek and ye shall find...

The party hook-up was just a bonus as they were both out the door before the night was out. They shared one more kiss and went on their way. She also made mention that she would be on the hurling pitch tomorrow afternoon. He should come to watch. He said he would try to get out there. Rhona was great, but Harris didn't feel totally into her. He surmised sex doesn't do that alone. He would see what her attitude was the next day and go from there.

Harris slept in that Sunday and just laid in bed until noon. Earlier, the painful groaning from next door indicated that Roland had a hangover that shook his senses. He would have offered to cure him of it, but his friend was out the door before he had the chance. Where was he going? The library was shut today. He microwaved some porridge in their kitchen, which they rarely used and bicycled over to the pitch at the park and enjoyed a sunny, albeit cooler day watching the two teams square off. Rhona did a terrific job of running the length of the field. There were a couple of times when he thought she would get a stick in the eye, but she held her own. Some of the players were wearing helmets. She wasn't one of them. Her team lost by 3. Afterwards, he headed for the gym and lifted iron for an hour or so.

Roland was still a no-show when he went over to the dining hall to grab dinner. He had finished another practical on phlebology before heading over. He encountered the Nghegdela brother and sister and started collecting their thoughts on brain neurofunction for Dr Saugeen's class on Tuesday. Jill and Carol then came over to join them for lunch, followed by Jasmine and Taylor. After they all had lunch, they got the books out and continued studying for Tuesday.

Rhona, sheepishly, came over without lunch but a large notebook and three texts hoping she wasn't going to be shunned for her behaviour last night. "Hi everyone!" She said. "Listen, I'm sorry I caused so much trouble last night..."

"Girl, don't give it a second thought," Carol said. "Now get those books open. We got a lot to do!" Rhona happily took her seat next to Harris. She was relaxed as she got out her notes.

"By the way, Rhona," Harris said. "I saw you play earlier. You guys were stellar!"

Rhona smiled and said "Thanks." as she reached for her pencils. "Hey, where's Roland? I thought he would be at your side like a faithful hound."

"No idea," Harris said. "He was out the door when I got up."

"It's noble he wants to find his dad," Taylor said. "Especially after all these years."

"I wouldn't mind knowing my family's history," Caroline said. "Maybe after all this."

"I know my Da has his lined out," Harris said. "I've seen it maybe once." ...and they all continued with studying. Harris was wondering to himself where his best mate was. His grades were perfect, like Harris's, so he knew he should get there to keep it up.

Harris walked home after Rhona excused herself to tend to her muscle cramps from the game earlier. There was no question that Harris could have fixed that in a way that didn't only involve his Xenon ability, but he felt he had to keep working so he then bicycled home with his pack on his back full of textbooks and parked his bike in the hall. Harris then walked into his room and dropped off his backpack in his bedroom before stopping at the fridge for a bottle of anything. That was where he saw Roland sitting on the chair with his head in his hands.

"Roland?" Harris called his best friend. "All right then?" Roland looked up, and it was evident that he was crying.

"Mate...what's up?" Harris asked.

Roland got his composure. "Found him...I found my dad." He said as he pulled out a handwritten piece of paper with the name Bruce Bartleby. A former member of The Church of the 7 Sorrows. Current residence in Clancy's Caravan Park in Holywell, Northern Ireland.

"The priest I talked to wasn't seeming to be a friendly type to him, but he was willing to help point him out," Roland said. "He was forced to leave the church."

"Forced to leave?" Harris was surprised to hear that. "Why?"

Roland hung his head in shame for him after a deep sigh, "My dad has AIDS."

That was unexpected. AIDS was hard enough to accept but now to find your kin has it, even if you haven't seen him, ever.

"I don't know what to do," Roland said through bloodshot eyes. "Should I go see him? Should I leave him be?

"Well, you remember how you were when you discovered that I was a Xenon?" Harris reminded him. "You came to accept me for what I was after I healed you. This guy is your Dad. You are going to have to see what you feel for him even for all his faults."

Roland remembered how he was after Harris told him about his abilities. It wasn't his proudest moment. "My dad, a hetty...who 'd be believing that?"

"Like a wise man once said to me..." Harris recalled his Da's words. "Without forgiveness, there is only death."

"That's profound, mate," Roland said, and then he remembered what Harris was and what he could do...or could he? "Hey, you think you could cure him?"

Harris thought of his past pathological studies. He cured Roland's herpes, and that was a viral disease, as was AIDS...but that wasn't his primary concern.

"Probably could..." Harris said. "The only thing that concerns me is that it's in Northern Ireland. That's not exactly first on my list to visit as I'd have a bullseye on me, throughout." There was a definite pall of disappointment on his friend's face, but he recognised his fear of this world. He, himself, never strayed into the northern border that separated the two Irelands although his growing up in Enniscrone was closer than Harris was to that part of the world.

"I know you think it's a risk, mate..." as Roland plead his case. "But you wouldn't be standing out, I don't think. Besides, you are on a medical mission, so that's got to carry some weight.

Harris geared himself up. He couldn't let his best friend's dad suffer. "Right, get transport arranged. We need to do this on Friday, and we got tests to take until then. "Oh yeah!" Roland said suddenly realising he needed to get cracking on his books. He went off to his room, smiling. That left him with another question. How did Roland's dad feel about Xenons?

Chapter 27 – Road Trip

After the test on Tuesday, a practical on bone density due Wednesday and three more papers on parts of the extremities a day later, the two mates took their small travel bags of belongings on a bus to travel up north. They would get as far as Blacklion on the Northern Ireland border and find another way to Holywell, even if it meant walking all the way. All the time, Harris was a bit nervous as he was about to head into what could be called "enemy territory." A war he had nothing to do with, nor would want to fight.

They took the ride on a half-loaded bus to the north across the green countryside of this part of the world stopping at several similar bus stops on the way. Holywell was 200 miles from Cork, so the ride was going to be a long one. Harris thought about bringing the book Dante's Inferno with him but found after glancing at it for a moment in the library that he couldn't read it without a team of experts to translate it, so he brought his trusty Walkman, a college text on pathology and that day's copy of The Sun along.

Anyway, Roland may want to talk on the way as he was a nervous passenger what with him having no idea how to speak to his dad. The bus pulled out at 5 am from the station on their way to their northern destination. Maybe some conversation about other things would relax him a bit. Even though they shared a flat for three semesters, there were still a bunch of things that they knew nothing about each other. "Go ahead, mate. Ask me anything." Roland said. "Maybe a few questions off-topic would be for the best."

"OK, you got the antidepressants rather quick the other night." Harris had the feeling he shouldn't have asked it when his words hit the air and felt sheepish about it afterwards. "You don't have to tell me…" He said, trying to walk it back.

"It's ok…they're mine," Roland said, looking down. "I always had a problem with keeping positive, so I started them last year."

"Really?" Harris said. "You always seem so upbeat."

"Of course, I do…" Roland said. "They're working, eh?"

Harris felt dumb saying that, but Roland carried on.

"You should've seen me before, then…But they do have a side effect that I hate. I can't…"

Here, Roland was having problems with his words, especially being in public on a bus with about 20 other people.

"I can't...complete." He said quietly. Harris just looked at him questioningly.

"With a bird...I can't finish the job." Roland whispered. It took a moment to get the gist of his meaning but finally caught on.

"Oh...you can't come!" Harris said louder than he should and got a couple of stares his way, so covered it as quickly as possible.

"...To the party next week. Don't worry yourself over it." Harris said hoping that was enough to cover up his public faux pas. The other passengers went back to their business.

"Nice one, mate," Roland said, rolling his eyes.

Harris then thought for a bit about the other thing he wanted to know. "So that's why you haven't plugged anyone. I figured you would have a family of dozens by now." He said quietly.

"It's painful, I'll tell you," Roland said just as quietly. "Now that I gotta use the Johnnies as well so I don't get manky again, that doesn't help. A lot of times, the birds leave thinking it's their fault. I try to tell 'em about the tablets, but they think they're the one to change everything."

Harris now felt sorry for his friend. "Why do you keep going through it, then?" Harris asked.

"I don't know," Roland said. "They keep throwing themselves at me, so it's hard to say no." The last part still mystified Harris. Roland was a good-looking lad, but he didn't have cinema celebrity looks or status.

The rest of the time, Harris let Roland use his Walkman to pass the time while he read his paper. Roland then let Harris listen to his tunes that he brought along. Harris was more top of the pops like Michael Jackson and Morrissey while Roland was more a Bronze and Motorhead type.

They got into Blacklion in the late evening, and Roland decided it was too late to even start with seeing his dad at this hour, so they got a room at a motel and would go first thing in the morning. The owner turned an eye up seeing two young men with just a small bag each with them and had to say, "Keep the noise down if you go doin' anything!" Leaving Roland and Harris that to interpret.

All they wanted to do was get a shower after spending all day on the bus and sack out. The two beds were worse than their dorm mattresses, and that was saying something! The next morning about 8, Harris had a small breakfast, and Roland seemed to be stalling as he had ordered a large breakfast, made two trips to the jacks and just sat pondering, nervously after they paid their cheque. "Roland...C'mon," Harris said. "Time to do this." He nodded, and they both exited the motel café.

They walked across the bridge, which became Northern Ireland, to the village of Belcoo. That stroll took about 30 minutes. Roland had the phone number and called his dad from a phone box on the corner. He had a nursemaid called Tamar who visited during the day. She did the favour of fetching the two travelling medical students in her car about 20 minutes later and taking them to Clancy's Caravan Park. The place looked dilapidated. It was as if they pushed Roland's dad into some leper colony with plumbing...they hoped. Tamar said she would be back in a bit as she had to visit the chemist and shop for Bruce and the other residents.

Roland knocked and entered the caravan as Harris stayed outside for the time being at a small metal table with a chair to match. It was probably a sweet little dining area at one time, but weeds grew high around it as attention to detail waned. The structure was old and rusty, where his friend's dad resided. There were several others just like it as well. The smell of the area also started creeping up. It wasn't a sewer, but more like a dead animal. What kind of place was this for people to live? The property was bordered on one side by a large lake with no beachhead. The road behind each side of the encampment was bordered by meadows and forest. It would be a beautiful place to live if not for the run-down structures that littered the area.

After he went through both sides of a Whitney Houston cassette, Roland said to enter. He had a good cry as he wiped his bloodshot eyes. Roland made the introduction.

"Harris Gibraltar, this is Bruce Bartleby. The man laid on the bed covered in welts and bruises that looked like he had been in a fight along with some jungle rot-type of sickness. Harris shook his hand with full respect.

"It's nice to meet you, sir," Harris said. "I know Roland went to great lengths to find you."

"I'm glad he got here to see me off," Bruce said in a gravelly voice. "I wish I was deserving of you, son. Your mom did well with ya."

"Thanks, Dad," Roland said with the tears starting up again. "But that leads to the other reason we're here." And with that, Roland let Harris get to brass tacks. "Go on, mate."

Harris walked over to the patient. "Bruce…sir." Harris was hesitant as to what reaction he was about to receive. "I can help you, but you have to know where it's coming from…I'm what the world has deemed…a Xenon."

Bruce looked at Harris in shock and bewilderment.

"With your consent, sir…" Harris continued. "I can attempt to heal you of your condition. Your son can attest to my abilities. But it's only fair to ask you for your approval before I try. Bruce sat motionless for a moment and then lunged with all his strength at the young Harris. "Figures…" Harris thought until Bruce spoke again.

"YES!!!" Bruce shouted. "YES, Please!!! Do what you need to, I'm ready!" He roared like he was about the be awarded a check from the pools. He then smiled with the gum-boils and mouth-cankers hanging off his lips. They didn't need to see that but no matter.

"Well, all right!" Harris said, and Roland just smiled. One more detail needed to be fulfilled. "Roland, a glass of water or something for your father!"

"Right, hang on! Don't start without me!" Roland said and went to the fridge and looked for something to drink. He pulled out a bottle of plain water and brought it over to hand to his father when he finished receiving his treatment. Harris then instructed Bruce to lay back on the pillow until he finished.

"Right, this is new for me so let's hope for the best," Harris said as he rubbed his hands together and let the blast of white light hit Bruce on his upper arm and his sores went from sickening welts to healthy skin. He had his greying hair turn back to mild red, and his mouth ulcers reduced to nothing.

He jumped out of bed and went to the loo to a full-length mirror and was about to check himself out when the thirst took him. Roland gave him the water, and he drank it down in one go. After he finished his water, he continued his look-see to his satisfaction. Bruce then returned to the bedroom and hugged his son.

He then gave a big bear hug to Harris that made him feel like he broke one of his ribs. The pain didn't last, and he was there smiling with the two travellers.

"Thank you so much, friend! I feel I could run a mile!" Bruce said and then realised he was just in a gown and no Y-fronts! "I think I'll get dressed, then," Bruce said. Harris remembered curing his friend's herpes last year and letting his manly bits out in the wind. "Like father, like son." He thought.

The boys then went into the small sitting room with sparse furniture. A dirty sofa and a folding chair were all there was, and neither looked comfortable. They smiled and said nothing. They just listened to Bruce singing himself an old Irish tune of some sort.

"How could anyone live like this?" Roland said. "My dad deserves better than this. Everyone deserves better than this!"

"Agreed," Harris said. "I wouldn't be surprised if he wanted me to do the same for all these men."

"Could you?" Roland asked. No time to answer as Bruce re-entered the room.

He came out in clothes that were a few years out of date. "I guess it's time to hit the shops again." He said with a big smile.

"I'm sure I can help you there, dad," Roland said. That was the first time he emphatically called him "dad."

"I'm just glad you were accepting of my help, sir," Harris said. "People would tend to shy away when I tell them I'm a Xenon." Harris quickly looked at Roland when he said that. Roland just shrugged as it was in the past.

"Well, it's fine with me," Bruce said. "After all...I'm a Xenon myself!"

Chapter 28 – You Are What You Is...

Tamar O'Connell knew her place in the world. She couldn't wait to go to college and become a nurse. Educated in Limerick at the same University where her father went to become a thoracic surgeon, he welcomed her wanting to follow in his big shoes. The only thing that concerned her family of 8 brothers and sisters (her being the eldest) was the fact that she worked a job with those who had HIV.

Some of her family made the ignorant comment that it was God's will that those who were so unclean with themselves were deserving of this slow death. They were also concerned that HIV was catching and that she would contract the same sickness as well. Her father and she both knew that it was difficult to become infected with this disease through casual contact. Her father always encouraged the young nurse to do whatever she needed to for the sake of her charges. She remembered his words looking in the long mirror at herself in her white blouse and black skirt before beginning her first job at Clancy's Caravan Park. The men she would take care of were a write-off as far as the medical community was concerned.

"You look wonderful, my dear." Her father said as he looked at her through her open room door. "I'm so proud of you to take up this job."

"Thank you, Dad." She said. "We seem to be the only ones who think that, though.

"Now don't you go worrying over that." Her father said as he faced her in his business attire and greying hair. He was of average height, and weight and the lines in his face suggested he was overworked.

"Remember that they are human, too and need caring and love like anyone else." He said. "There seems to be a short supply of that where they are. They will depend on you now for that attention, so make sure that they know there is someone who cares about them. The medical community could learn a lot from you in that respect..."

It was also unusual to work alone and with no supervision. No one dared to enter and to show her the ropes inside the confines of the camp. Their relatives just left them off in the caravans, paid the rent and ran away. Nicholas Clancy opened his dilapidated park to this lot, knowing the turnover would be quick. He was desperate for the cash and figured he could make a tidy living off the dole cheques that would be rolling in every month.

They were not going to be spending much of it on anything but food, beer and smokes. At times it was a depressing job as more than once she came to a caravan finding one of the unfortunate sick lying lifeless in bed or the one who had taken his own life by ending his mortality in the large lake behind the encampment. She was especially well-liked by these living patients of the dumping ground for the infected. Friendly and loving faces were in short supply here, so she provided the angelic alternative to their suffering. She would pick up their groceries at market and medicines at the chemist's and would talk at times if they wanted to unload their emotions. For that, they all came to love her.

She was in her button-up white blouse and black skirt about to enter Bruce Bartleby's caravan with a sack of medicine bottles in hand when the door flew open and a visually upset young man ran through the door toward the lake followed by the other young man shouting "Wait! Wait!" that she ferried there in her car not more than an hour or so ago. She couldn't hear what he was upset about, only that the other lad was trying to comfort him.

"Mr Bartleby!" She shouted, not seeing him at first as she entered his home. "Are you all right?"

Her main concern was with Bruce, though and she continued to step in to find him walking out of his kitchen in better shape than she ever saw him. Her mouth was agape as she dropped the sack of medicine and looked up and down at the gentleman whom she had been treating, like the others, for the past month, standing upright and disease-free.

"Mr Bartleby!!!" She exclaimed. "What on earth happened here?" Bruce was calm and happy as he stood there in a red and black madras shirt and corduroy pants. He smiled, free of any ailment and put his hand around her shoulder and led her to the living room. "Come, my dear." He said. "Let me try to explain all this…"

Meanwhile, Roland came to a stop on his knees and sobbed on the rotting lake dock.

"How?" He cried. "How can this happen?" Harris just let him have his meltdown until it passed and made sure his friend didn't do himself a mischief. He remembered his own revelation as Gina's father laid sickly on the dining room floor and the healing light that brought him back from the edge of death.

He was no less panicked at the time as he hid in a doghouse also afraid he would be led away in chains like a rabid animal.

Roland's father was no less sympathetic in the caravan as he explained to his son a few minutes ago about his own ability to attract men for their company so quickly and easily and how he was twice-over an outcast as a gay man and a Xenon. Two facts he hid from the Catholic church and his kin. He often wondered how revolted his family would take the fact that he was a Xenon as well. The AIDS condition was bad enough as he couldn't hide his sexual alignment. To compound that with Xenon status would have eliminated what little sympathy they had left for him.

Roland calmed down and was able to raise his head to face his friend. Part of the embarrassment came as he was far less than sympathetic to Harris when he found out what he was. Now Roland was living what he feared encountering when growing up. "What the hell am I going to do now?" He asked his friend. Harris was far calmer than his best friend as he knelt beside him on the rotting boards of the old dock. "Mate, you don't need to change what or who you are. You are what you have always been, and now a bit more. You have your friends, and now your family grew a bit more. You've no reason to feel you are any less a person than what you have been." He patted his shoulder in sympathy.

"You are going to be a great doctor and marry some bird who will spend every pound you earn and live happily ever after. Nothing will change that as long as you keep doing what you're doing. Be proud of that." Harris smiled at his friend as Roland backed off his panic. The newly discovered Xenon stared at his face in the lake. He looked no different and felt no different than he had, physically, for all these years. He remembered saying to Harris his plan of finding the girl who would be his one and only. Whatever needed to happen to stop his behaviour of taking every girl on campus to bed was what would need to happen when that time came. They now both got the answer of how Roland so easily and quickly got action whether he wanted it or not. It was easy to see how hard it would have been to turn it down. Harris was in no hurry to turn down his opportunities, after all.

Talking of birds, the only one in the area approached Harris with more important things on her mind. She emerged from Bruce's caravan after a lengthy discussion of what he and his son were along with the man who could end the plight of this colony of human suffering.

"I gotta talk to my dad a bit more," Roland said as he walked back to Bruce's caravan passing the young nurse on her way out.

"Doctor, may I have a word?" She asked in a thick brogue. "It's not "Doctor" yet, luv," Harris said, smiling. "But what may I do for you?" Harris already knew the question but would let her ask, nonetheless. She motioned for him to enter one of the caravans. It was her own that was touched up better than the others and looked like it was undergoing some remodelling. Her quarters had a decent bed and furniture as well.

"Bruce explained everything to me. He said that not all Xenons are bad and some are downright miraculous in what they can do." She said. "There are a lot of sick men here who could use that same level of help."

"Of course, dear." He said. "I took one look and was disgusted by the conditions here. I'm impressed that you stayed on for their sake. Few would."

"Well, these men need someone. They have no one else, so I was more than willing to take up the mantle." She said with pride.

"OK, this would be my first mass-order, as it were. I hope I have the strength to heal the entire lot of them. So, to do this, I will need something from you." Harris said. Tamar had the wrong end of the stick as she looked down at her sensible running shoes.

"Yes, of course." She said a bit disappointed but thought that the cost of helping these men would be well worth it. She started to walk into her bedroom and began to unbutton her top. Harris talked of other things as he looked out the living room window but did not appear to take notice of what she was doing.

"I need to cover up what I am because there are so many who don't want Xenons in the world. I wouldn't be surprised if some of these men felt the same way."

He stated without looking her direction. "With that, I'll have an envelope for you in a few days that you'll give to any authority that comes to investigate why several of these men walked out of here on their own volition."

"Oh." She said and stopped to rebutton her top in that she realised that he had more professional ideas presented to her. She faced him properly dressed again.

"What do you need from me, for now?" She asked.

"I'll need you to come with me when these men fall asleep," Harris said. "I'll go in and take care of them tonight, if possible." Tamar was quietly giddy at this prospect.

"Is there a phone around here?" Harris asked. "I need to call someone in Cork."

"There's an office across the way with one," Tamar said. "It's Clancy's, but he's not around today."

"Right, gimme the rest of the day and, hopefully, we'll be ready to start getting this lot back on their feet by this evening," Harris said as he pointed to her uniform top. "…and my dear, you jumped a button on your blouse." He grinned and walked out the door to check on his friend at the lakeside. Tamar came over angry and embarrassed at herself as she fixed her top. Harris knew what was up. Maybe it was from being with his friend for so long. It was time to bring the father and son up to speed as well…

Chapter 29– The Sacrifice of Donovan Price"

"OK, wait a minute..." Taylor said on the phone as he spoke to Harris from his flat in Cork. "A disease that mimics the symptoms of HIV and AIDS?"

"That's right," Harris said. "I can't give any details on it as..." Here Harris had to cover up. He hated lying but could only speak the truth of what was going on to a select few. The last thing he wanted was to make enemies of his good friends.

"...These are men who need to stay out of the limelight." Harris made up all this on the fly. "The medical reports all say HIV/AIDS, but something doesn't add up here. The white cell counts are all too high, while the symptoms aren't related to HIV... It looks as if something went afoul with the testing."

Taylor cleaned his glasses and said he would get back to him in an hour or so. Roland was doing the same with some of the girls he was in class with (and more.) Miriam and Jasmine were enlisted to help, but Roland instructed the girls to avoid saying anything to Caroline as her father was an administrator there and he could scuttle the whole deal by claiming them all inexperienced and let the work to those who knew what they were doing, supposedly.

Harris paced in Clancy's office for a couple of hours waiting for the call-back. The plan was to heal everyone that night while they slept and keep them unknowing what was going on. If anyone were to back out due to Xenon prejudice, it could ruin everything they were trying to set up. For now, they needed an alibi — a diagnosis of something other than AIDS. Anything else would probably work. "Ring!" Harris shouted at the phone in Clancy's office...A moment later it did.

"Hello?"

"Harris, it Jasmine." She said in her Estonian accent. "I have your diagnosis..."

"Yes, luv... What is it?" A moment of silence went by as Roland entered while Harris on the phone. Harris then came over with a look of disbelief.

"Are you sure?" Harris was astounded as it was the only answer they could come up with at the college. There was no better answer. "Thank you, Jazzy," Harris said. "I'll see you in class on Tuesday." And he hung up the phone. "Roland get your Dad and Tamar in here!"

They all gathered in Clancy's office and heard the diagnosis that was presented by some of the most brilliant minds The Royal College of Medicine had to offer...and still couldn't fathom it!

"Malaria?" "Seriously?" Roland exclaimed.

"OK, look..." Harris said to the stunned party of 3. "It only takes one person to spread a virus like that. We need just one straw man to take the brunt of exposure to all this. They all came in at the same time, so that works." He then turned his attention to the young nurse.

"Tamar, you know these men the best. Was anyone here in different regions recently?" She just shook her head.

"OK..." Harris went on. "Was anyone here lonely coming in?"

"They are all lonely coming in." She said. "Their families all gave them the toss, so they don't end up infecting them, they think."

Harris was deep in thought but didn't want to waste any more time than he had too. "The man who threw himself in the lake...Can you tell me about him?" He asked.

"He was called Donovan Price." She said. "He was a local for many years. No one knew anything about him aside from that he worked construction." Then she had a thought...

"Hang on, then," Tamar said. "He did sort of a foreign country thing. He helped build a football stadium in Italy. He said he loved that part of the world."

"Did he say where in Italy?" Harris asked.

"Yeah, Palermo," Tamar replied.

"Those guys would be bringing in cheap labour from Africa. Many from Tunisia." Bruce said. "Some of those people would sooner kill hetties than look at 'em!"

"What of his family?" Harris asked.

"They disowned him aeons ago," Tamar responded.

Harris collected his thoughts and felt this was the line they'll use.

"Right then," Harris said. "Our man is going to do well with his sacrifice. He got Malaria, the test centre thought it was AIDS, and the rest will all play out. "

Harris then took a sip of his tea sitting next to Tamar's table lamp and grabbed his Walkman. "So, Tamar, we'll start at nightfall," He said. She gave both a nod and a smile.

"What do we all do until then?" Roland asked.

"Act natural," Harris said, "...and pray." with a shrug and a smile as he put on his Walkman headpiece and went outside to the metal table. They had three hours before bedtime, so Harris sat there and studied his pathology homework by the porchlight of the run-down caravan. Bruce stayed out of sight as he watched television in his place while Tamar and Roland got acquainted in a more modest fashion than the randy lad usually did.

Now that he found out that his bedding birds were an ability rather than by a woman's desire, he felt it was not a direction he wanted to take anymore. Tamar was different. She was a woman who cared in a way Roland had not seen. The women in college all seemed to want to become doctors for their own benefit, and the patients were the fortunate recipients of their accomplishments. Tamar's motives seemed selfless and always for the benefits of her clientele. She didn't mention the sacrifice she was willing to make for them at the hands of Harris. She was also thankful that she didn't have to relinquish her virtue to him for their sake.

The plan was simple. Tamar would enter each caravan at about eight o'clock and administer a mild sedative with their nightly shot of whiskey. What the boys called "Happy Hour." She would often sit with them for a few minutes as they told their stories of youth and life to her. There were many to hear of:

Bill Kelpfish was an ex-army officer who retired 12 years ago from the IRA, Mills O'Keefe was a civil servant who was outed by his fellow Gardai and dismissed by the constabulary. Herman Hall was a defrocked priest, and Michael Paladin, who was the youngest patient here divorced his wife of less than a year after not being able to lead a "straight" life.

There were others, of course. All had stories of a tragic circumstance to end up here in this dumping ground of degradation. All of them agreed. If they had it to do all over again, they would_____...

The blanks were full of the different ways they would take new approaches to life. None of them suspecting that their second chance was at hand.

Ten o'clock, and it was time to begin. Tamar had the keys or the means to let Harris through the doors of the wood and metal caravans to where her patients slept. The instruction was a simple one. After Harris took care of each man, a bottle of water would be set beside them. He never tried to heal anyone while they slept, so he didn't know how much time would go by until the thirst kicked in. Maybe they would go all the way until morning, perhaps it was immediate.

Herman was first. A shot of healing light and a hasty exit by the two of them to continue to the next caravan. Tamar would look in on them each in ten-minute intervals. If found, she would make some excuse up to be there. She always had a reason to be there whether it would be to check on strange noises or the smell of smoke.

Mills was next with a fast in and out to his bedside. Clark DeWitt, however, was watching telly and fell asleep in his chair. He already had a bottle of lager next to him with one taste taken so no need to leave him anything.

After they took care of Michael, Harris had to stop for a two-hour nap. He didn't realise that all this healing would take such a toll on him. After the respite on Tamar's couch, she woke him to continue. He got to Edward Cook's flat and gave him the same treatment. He then stirred in bed afterwards leading them both to a quick exit.

It was then on to Stephan Lowe's bed where they were lucky to catch him when they did. He was in more dire shape than anyone there. He would probably awake thinking that his soul was being called to God as the pain would be gone allowing him to feel better than he did in all his 48 years of being alive.

Ten men in six hours and Harris finished with Bill as he stood at his bedside. They scared each other as Bill woke and found Harris looking down at him and the light finishing its effect. Harris just put a finger over his lips, and he slowly exited as Bill took a long swig of precious water. His doctor was out the door and gone when the bottle went empty, and he fell back to sleep, not knowing what or if something just happened. To further cover the tracks, Tamar collected all the empty, glass water bottles next to the beds. They all drank them immediately and fell back to sleep.

Harris needed to sleep after all this healing. He stumbled into the caravan of patient zero and fell into the bed that belonged to the former Donovan Price. His lights went out as soon as his head hit the unkept pillow.

A dust cloud formed briefly over him about a meter or so. He could care less as sleep engulfed him before the particles fell back to earth.

Tamar went and crawled into her bed while Roland threw an old duvet on the floor with an extra pillow placed under his head by his dad as he made his way to bed. The couch felt too lumpy for the lad to crash on.

The morning would be a brand-new world for everyone there.

Chapter 30 – We Will Not Forget You...

They emerged from their tombs to find the sun shining down on this November Sunday in Holywell. Not quite dead, not quite tombs and not at all saints. Men in dressing gowns and night clothes stepped out onto their respective porches and wondered what happened that night. They went to bed immersed in pain and suffering lesions and ulcers to wake up feeling joyful and ready. They didn't know what for, but they would be there jumping to it whatever it may be.

To them, Bruce looked like another healed face in this crowd. No one knew what to say or do. All they could do is approach Tamar, and she gave the presentation that Harris had presented to her. The testing centre was wrong in their HIV assessment, and Donovan Price took his own life rather than suffering what he thought was a double threat to his existence. The main thought that flowed through Clancy's Caravan Park was "Now what?"

That was one of two amazing things that happened overnight in this part of Northern Ireland. The other being that Roland didn't try to sleep with Tamar. He probably could have talked her out of her self-imposed innocence, but he didn't attempt it this time even though she was game. Harris took it all in as morning continued. The young nurse found some eggs, tea and toast in Clancy's kitchen that she whipped up for herself and the boys in on the healing. Bruce and the recovered patients then went into town for the first time in ages hoping to find something opened this early on a Sunday.

They spoke that morning about what would follow. These men would have to find new means of support. There were some people in the gay pride brigade but not around here. Tamar said she could get a few men to come up and help from Limerick and Dublin to assist getting their lives in order. Belfast officials would have nothing to offer. After all, they were the ones who put these men in a "leper colony" situation, anyway. It would be interesting to see how they handled this mess.

Many of them would also be curious about the "mistake" that the testing centre made. There would be talk and scuttlebutt about who didn't do what and how it does not occur again in the future. Out of this chaos, though would come new starts for new lives.

Roland then came over and talked to his best friend and colleague. "Mate, listen…" Roland said to Harris. "I'm gonna stay for another day and help get me dad situated. "I don't want you to feel I'm abandoning you though, eh?"

"Don't worry about it, man," Harris replied. "Your dad needs ya right now. Just don't forget to come back." Harris said with a smile.

The bus would leave Blacklion that day at noon. Tamar gave them a lift to where the bus would pick Harris up, just outside a chemist shop on Mill Road. Roland gave a quick man-hug to his friend, and Tamar gave him an even more passionate hug for what he did.

"I'm afraid I left you without a job, dear," Harris said to the young nurse.

"Not a worry then." She said. "There will always be sick people in the world. They'll have to be glad there are people like us."

Harris rode away on the bus with a pathology textbook in hand and his Walkman pumping out The Clash as he studied on his way back home. He remembered that his Da showed him The Gibraltar family history book when he first found out that he was a Xenon healer. Christmas was coming up, and he would be heading back to London to spend holiday with his family. It made him want to take a better look into his family's past. He wondered how his predecessors dealt with this ability.

The bus was empty when he left that morning and gradually filled up on its way to Cork with each small town, they stopped in. He would also have to explain to his fellow medical students the mix-up and how the symptoms cleared up. Part of it would be psychological on the side of the men there, and part of it was a medical error. He felt that Northern Ireland was nothing to be afraid of. Well, at least in that part of the country. He was sure that he would have been safe there if he had hung around. "Best not to risk it, though." He thought as they passed through the countryside on their way home.

For the most part, it was a smooth trip until the loud pop emerged from the front of the bus, and the steam rose in a small, then massive cloud in front of the driver. There was nothing to be done about it. The bus pulled into North Limerick to the awaiting passengers ready to travel south towards Ireland's second-largest city with Harris on board awaiting to return there himself.

He and the other passengers were forced off the bus as the driver entered a small shop and asked to borrow their phone.

The radiator was steaming like a geyser going sideways as Harris and the others awaited the verdict of their wheelman. That was when the driver emerged 15 minutes later stating that a bus from Shannon would be picking up the lot of them but that it would be at least 2 hours before it would show. Nothing to do but wait in this part of the city. What to do?

Not far from the shop where the bus was parked was the sound of a choir singing. Harris had a couple of hours to kill, so he walked to the next block toward the sound until he happened on the source of the music. Today was Remembrance Day here in Ireland, and several people were gathered near a cenotaph to pay tribute and commemorate the fallen men of the armies of past wars.

One older woman gave Harris a poppy to wear on his black jumper as a few of the other women from a nearby church were serving tea to the audience of about 50 or so. Most were older people with old soldiers wearing their dress uniforms and medals while the rest seemed to have just exited their respective churches.

The protestant vicar gave a prayer while a town official read a poem called "In Flanders's fields." A teen boy read another poem called "We shall keep the faith." After which, a few in attendance placed wreaths at the edge of the stone memorial. It was then a young girl in a white dress then took the stage called Orla Moore. A blonde lass of no more than 14 who had an angelic voice. Harris sipped his tea from a foam cup as the lovely lass sang, acapella and with perfect pitch, a song called "I vow to thee, my country, all earthly things above." Harris and the rest of the audience were enamoured by her fantastic singing voice:

I vow to thee, my country, all earthly things above,
Entire and whole and perfect, the service of my love;
The love that asks no question, the love that stands the test,
That lays upon the altar, the dearest and the…

Unfortunately, she never uttered another word as the time bomb planted next to the cenotaph went off!

Chapter 31 – Casualties of war

Widespread panic ensued as debris fell on the participants. Orla Moore was killed instantly. Her angelic voice would join the chorus in Heaven above. An older man, maybe her grandfather, cradled what was left of her in his arms sobbing uncontrollably and screaming toward the sky.

Harris picked himself up from the ground where the blast knocked him down. There was blood on his shirt and his face but no scars, nor scratches. He would have changed places with any of the dead or wounded as he could have easily survived a blast handed down like that, he thought. There were people in pain with dead and near-dead all around. Time to go to work!

The panic assured Harris that he probably would not have anyone's attention. He put his hands under the wounded to keep the bright light from being seen. A woman with a severe burn to her face, a man with a large wound on top of his skull, another man, a choir member, who had a severe abdominal injury and a young girl was lying face down keeping whatever injuries were hers hidden away. They were all healed with no one the wiser of how it happened. Then the teen boy, he who read the poem during the service, was lying face-down with a large piece of metal debris lodged in his back. It was buried well into his spine so Harris pulled it out gently, the best he could and tossed the metal and concrete scrap aside. The boy was unconscious and felt nothing.

His hands glowed brightly on the teen's back as the restoration took a bit longer. Perhaps reconstruction of his spine had to take place. He left the teen lying on his stomach and ran to the next patient. The teen jumped up and ran to the tea stand begging for anything liquid along with six others that Harris had healed.

He then went over to Orla while the older man had his back turned talking to the Gardai and put his hand over her ankle that peeked out from under the sheet that covered her body. Nothing happened…dead was dead. He ran away when he felt they were going to look at him oddly. Harris went to an officer and gave his statement and said he was visiting a friend…in Blacklion. He was on his way back when the bus broke down and was forced to wait for the next one, so he came over after hearing the choir…and so on. He was instructed to go to the emergency vans and be checked out.

He was going to walk by the crowd of medics treating the other injured when a slightly muscular, female paramedic grabbed him by the arm and sat him down on a rock.

"Hang on…you'll be all right." The rather burly woman in uniform said to him. Harris protested. "Thanks…I'm fine already, though." She was insistent and lifted his shirt, which had blood, rips and tears but was excellent under it. She was left mystified at how Harris could have all these rips on his shirt and no wounds, not even a scratch. "It was make-up for a skit!" He said as he shook her off and ran back to town.

He then hid behind a church and slipped on a clean shirt while shoving the old one back into his travel bag. The ragged shirt with some bloodstains did look like he should have suffered more. He would dispose of it when he returned home.

Meanwhile, the residents were all out of their homes trying to see what they could of the chaos. The crowd was thick in front of the now-destroyed memorial. No one was blaming this on Xenons. Only the IRA or Sein Fein…maybe both. Harris didn't even know what this war was about and who the targets were. Indeed, a teen girl with her whole life ahead of her was not their most important priority. The bus was averted for 5 hours until the madness cleared out. Harris fell asleep behind a large dustbin for a bit, regaining his strength from the healing until he and his fellow travellers got back aboard and could continue.

He couldn't study. All he could do is see the faces of those he helped and the ones he couldn't. He wasn't prepared to step into a battle zone like this. He had to keep reminding himself that a few more people would be going home alive and that a teen boy would be walking instead of spending his remaining years in a pushchair.

His thoughts kept going back to that poor girl killed so senselessly, and he wept in his seat, quietly, on the way home. He did sleep a bit more on the bus. All that healing sapped every bit of energy out of him, even with the brief nap.

The bus stopped outside of the off-licence in Cork, finally, and he walked to Savage Street in the cold twilight and made his way into his flat. He walked in and threw his pack into the corner of his bedroom, nearly knocking over the floor lamp. Harris just laid in his bed and stared at the ceiling until sleep set in. He noticed the lights for the answering machine were blinking and alerting him of messages. He let it go for now.

It was a wild weekend, and he needed to recover. He would tell his professors that he was sick and would be out for tomorrow.

He would also need to call on his friends for class notes…just not Jasmine as she wrote all hers in Cyrillic or whatever language they used in Estonia. He hated to do it as when he tried to play catch-up, something was always missing. It felt like the story of his life. He was always missing something.

…Like the church's video camera that was filming the Remembrance Day event.

Chapter 32 – Roland Takes the Pledge

Roland returned the next day with far less drama than Harris had gone through. He said the men at the encampment formed an offshoot of the Dublin University Gay Society who were celebrating a Supreme Court win, not more than a month ago. They would garner support for their cause and be able to find work with less discrimination. They would be all right, eventually.

Roland had come a long way as a man who hated certain groups to becoming a sympathiser for those who needed it. Of course, when you find out you are one of these few, you tend to gravitate that way. Harris and Roland both studied the class notes that were lent to them by Caroline and Taylor. The end of the semester was approaching, and everyone was looking forward to heading home for a bit.

The footage from the blast was all over the evening news. Newspapers, radio and, of course, the telly were all ablaze with this shameless act of war and cowardice by the IRA. The sympathy for their cause began to lose support and people's anger set in toward their terroristic actions. Before, their bombs were set off by remote detonation. The time bomb was indiscriminate as it killed Orla Moore instantly and with no remorse. The video camera footage displayed all of that. Her grandfather holding her and sobbing at the sky was the new picture of this war, and it was all over the place. It was a still taken from that footage that gave pause to the nation and awards for Best Image of the Year in Vision magazine.

Harris got his balance back after all this and just hoped his own horror story of passing the rest of the semester was something he could live through. He held off on Christmas shopping until he finished the testing. The groups that he studied with were now breaking off into separate study groups and were led by whoever was best at that subject.

Harris stepped up with his knowledge of Pathology, Roland took bone structure, Todd Hunter joined in with brain structure, and Jasmine took blood and phlebology. It was refreshing having different accents leading these groups. They invited Nelson and Siboh over then to join in. The pressure was building as there was about a month to go before this semester was in the past.

While Harris got up and headed to the jacks at the library, he heard a voice behind him. Rhona ran up and hugged him with her backpack still on her shoulder that swung around her neck and hit him square in the face. "Oh god, Hun. You ok?"

She asked as he rubbed his nose after getting pummelled with the weight of her textbooks. She didn't take notice that her backpack hit him. She was just joyful at the sight of him still alive.

"I'm all right, hon." He said. "It was nasty, but I got through it... Are you going to join us?"

"Yeah, sorry I'm late." She said. "I had to take a call from my dad. He's working with the Gardai."

"Really?" Harris was curious. "Doing what?"

"He used to work in forensics before he retired." She said. "The boredom got to him, so he's coming here to start teaching hepatology."

"Yeah, I saw that on my new schedule," Harris responded. "I guess I'll have to brush up on my liver skills...Uh, I've got to get in there. See you over there." He then rushed into the jacks just in time while Rhona took her place in Roland's group.

The latter part of the day was like all the others except with the attitude of Dr McCurdy, who came in with the Irish Independent under her arm. Her speciality was medical ethics.

"Good afternoon, all." She said to the class. A somewhat stodgy woman with the poise of Prime Minister Thatcher...and similar mannerisms to match.

"Today, I want you all to put your textbooks aside as we won't be needing them... I was reading the paper earlier when I came across this headline:"

"Medical testing centre under scrutiny for catastrophic mistakes."

...And the dateline was in Holywell, Northern Ireland. Harris felt a bit ill. Dr McCurdy continued in her slow speech pattern:

"Today, we shall be discussing the impact that this will have on the patients who fell victim to this error and the consequences on the medical testing facility as well..."

After class, Harris and Roland found themselves back at The Draughtsman with a lager each in front of them. Other students meandered around the pub discussing their lives, and whatever was most important to them that day.

"Well, that was a bloody palaver!" Roland said. "Two hours of calling the testers a bunch of dossers!"

"Yeah, I know," Harris said. "I don't want to see anyone lose their jobs over this, though. Mistakes are part of the game."

With that, Harris took a swig of the ale in front of him. "I need to get a file going of replacement diagnosis for times like these. Malaria won't work again."

Roland knew what he meant. They both also thought about how Harris had been doing all that healing out in the open. They discussed that as well. Meanwhile, there were a fair number of girls in the pub tonight. It was as if they were waiting for something. Harris took another sip of his lager with his friend. "So how are things with you and that nurse?"

"Tamar, then?" Roland said. "I'll tell ya, I never wanted to be with someone like her before. She is completely different. She wasn't stripping off when we were alone. She was willing, but when I said I just wanted to take our time, she was fine with that. She said other guys in her town were jumping on her like hyped-up puppy dogs and she had to fight them off. It was good just talking to someone real." This change of Roland's attitude caught Harris by surprise. He never really gave any thought to bedding birds before he cared about them. It was kind of refreshing.

"So, you're done being the rooster to this chicken house?" Harris asked slyly.

"Not the way I'd state it, but I think I am, then," Roland said. To Harris, it sounded like Roland was on the lash too long and about to take the pledge. If you go to AA to stop being a drunk, who would he go to, then? FA?"

"All I can say is good luck, Mate," Harris said. "The female population here may come over disappointed."

Roland just smiled and shrugged as he finished his pint. They went home and slept in a silent house.

There was no noise from either bedroom aside from some last-minute note-taking from Harris's pen.

After all, end of semester assignments, practicals and tests were still due before the month was out and Christmas holiday would give him a well-deserved break.

Chapter 33– A Visit with an Old Friend

Last practical written, last test taken; the final report filed. Johnny-boy, the nickname for one of the medical mannequins came through his hepatitis and could feel free to stare at the ceiling in comfort until the next classes began. The new computers were finished being installed in a lab so that would also be part of Harris's immense semester schedule in January.

For now, he packed his bag for a fortnight and purchased his ticket to fly back to London. Roland was off to Limerick to visit his new exclusive girlfriend and his own family later on. Harris wondered if his friend would stay true to his word to keep her untouched. "Well, it's their business, anyway." He thought.

Harris just wanted the break. He spent most of his time with his nose in a book and not bothering with much else. For his time off, that ratio would change so the respite could be fully appreciated. He did take a copy of a book on the brain and cranial matters as he could pick his Da's brain (so to speak) on some of the finer points he lacked in.

Roland said his so-longs as Harris continued to pack for his flight. He took a walk to the Artemis Café, downtown where the bus would drop him off to where his girlfriend was now taking care of patients in a veteran's hospital in the southern part of Limerick in Dooradoyle. He would also meet her lot for the first time. At least two others in her family would be taking their preliminary testing to carry on the family trade.

Before leaving, Harris found a wrapped package next to the telephone. The tag read "Happy Birthday!!! Keep coming back alive!" Harris didn't remember telling Roland about his birthday, but it was indeed on 28 December. That unusual zone where you feel cheated as a child that Christmas and one's birthday were so close. He did know that Roland's was 2 August so neither one was close for the other to celebrate with them.

He opened the package to reveal something odd…a disguise kit from the magic shop downtown: Fake moustaches, a pair of round glasses with just clear glass and a hat. The package also contained a small book on the basics of disguise. Harris felt it was odd that he would give him that.

Anyway, he packed that lot up with the rest of his items to go across the St. George's Channel and got on the local bus to the airport.

The flight was smooth going with no crying babies, no fear of flying in his stomach and no problem stowing his bag. Only a man who was snoring three seats back and loud enough to be noticed by all the other passengers caused the only distraction. The young medical student put on his headphones and listened to some jazz music to alleviate that noise for the hour flight to Heathrow.

Harris was getting to love air travel…at least these trips that took him home in such a short time. He touched down in London in what felt like record time and grabbed a bus to take him to Essex Street. Now he knew in advance that his parents wouldn't be there. His mum said she would be with the Red Hats at their tea and Da would be at work. They said he should go in and make himself comfortable.

The snow had fallen for an hour, but it was just a dusting as he walked down to where his childhood home sat near the end of the street in an anorak with a large knife hole in it covered with 6 cm of duct tape on the inside. A subtle reminder of who and what he was. He also wore a black jumper, Yankee blue jeans and half-boots. It wasn't a long walk but was glad the significant snowfall held off. He walked by the Ravalli's home carrying only his trip bag-all he needed for the fortnight when he saw Magdalena Ravalli sweeping the snow off the walkway out front of her home.

"Hey! Hi, Mrs Ravalli!" Harris said hoping that he would get a favourable response back.

"Harris!" She said with a big smile and gave him a big hug and a kiss on the cheek. "So good to see you!" Then she looked around quickly like she was about to share a secret. "Have you a moment? I need to ask something of you." She said in her Italian accent.

"Of course." He said. "What can I do for you?"

In the course of a few minutes, they were both in her flat. Harris had his hands hovering over Magdalena's back with beams of light shooting out while she sat at the dining room table with a glass of water awaiting the massive thirst to come. The early stage of breast cancer that she had yet to tell anyone about would be banished, and her health would be pristine.

"Thank you for that, Harris." She said, grateful to the young Xenon.

"Always happy to help," He said and took a seat at the table as well. "So how have things been here?"

"Well, our Vinny still has the gym, Victor is in line to make Father Superior at his parish. Eduardo and his lot are doing well... Harris could tell that Magdalena was avoiding the elephant in the room.

"...and Gina?" He asked.

"She works very hard at her studies, but otherwise, I couldn't tell you." She said. "I honestly am not sure. She hasn't told me a thing about her personal life in Bristol...I swear on all the saints."

"Well, it's all right," Harris said. "We knew it couldn't last with all this distance between us. I thought that I saw her last summer out the gym window."

"Well, she did visit before she went off to Turin for the summer. She was working at Eduardo's Restaurant." Magdalena said. "Maybe she too scared to see you then?"

Harris thought for a moment. "Yeah, maybe." He said. "She did cut out rather fast last year. I'm not sure why, though."

Just then, a ding from a kitchen timer went off.

"OK, if you think you are going to leave here without being fed..." She said.

She then stood up from her chair to take the lasagne out of the oven. "Gina will be coming home next week. If you have the chance, try talking to her again. My guess is she will listen next time." She said with a gentle smile and leaving Harris wondering what that meant as he set up his tableware. There was no way he was going to miss out on Magdalena's cooking.

Chapter 34 – Digging in the Dirt

Harris heard it said (or maybe read) that digging through family secrets was like excavating onboard a ship at sea. …You don't want to dig too deep!

After a very filling dinner, thanks to Mrs Ravalli, he made his way home to #2 Essex Street and the place he called home for so many years. He went upstairs and flopped his carry bag on the bed. The room that was once his and reconfigured after he left had not changed since he was there over the past summer. Even a biro he used to take notes that had a light built into its pointe was laying on the desk. It still worked, surprisingly.

Well, his choices were that he could flop down and read, listen to music or watch a programme on telly but all that he could do back at his flat.

Harris had something else in mind. The book labelled "Gibraltar Family History." He had mentioned to his Da about reading it to get a sense of his past. The sizeable leather-bound book was in a box on the dining room table. It appeared very old and it seemed someone restored the large book around the turn of the century. A table lamp set next to the tome's container as if the whole setting was beckoning Harris to read it. He then poured a cup of tea and sat down to understand how his family's history came to be and how the legacy survived for so long.

The first entry was short. It was only an old painting on a cloth the size of a tea cosy. The name seemed to be James - something. - The Gibraltar name probably came later. Sure enough, a few females were born into the batch. One burned as a witch.

"…And I thought being caught by The Paragons was bad!" Harris thought.

The family had changed names through marriage several times as he read the book through. The Gibraltar name had not emerged as of yet. Some females remained unmarried. Maybe they were real crones? Altogether, there were about 100 or so entries in the book with a few brothers and sisters added in as well. Harris began to wonder why he didn't have siblings.

Finally, familiarity! …And it was Unger Gilderbrund, in 1908 where there was no connection with the past at all. Harris could understand a male taking the name of his wife if there were some family strife. That wasn't the case here.

Grandfather Unger married his bride in 1945 in Zurich, Switzerland. Paula Winterhooven was his grandmother's name. Harris had never met his grandmother as he was born at the time of her funeral. He continued his research through the large book to find a photograph of Unger and Helmut with Harris being held by his grandfather as an infant. He never saw this picture until now.

Harris wanted to know more about his grandfather, but two pages from the massive book were ripped out. Only the leftover bits in the binding were all that remained. Well, this was a disappointment as he continued to read on about his father and it was all the things he...well, he thought he knew:

Name: Helmut Nicklaus Gibraltar

Birthplace: Vorarlberg, Switzerland

Birthdate   14 October 1946

Parents: Paula and Unger Gibraltar

Married: Jean Addams in 1967

Along with this, a couple of notes about his professional schooling and career. His past work as House Officer in Barbican Hospital, His current placement as head of neurosurgery and his partnership with Dr Julius Guiteau, the current chief of Psychiatry, both working at Saville Hospital, Bloomsbury, Central London

The family name materialised out of no place. The answers were ripped out from the family's history. Why? Was this on his grandfather's request? Did Da want to hide something? Harris's entry sat in the book fresh with a graduation photo of him that he sat for soon after he healed Sister Fyre of her stroke. There was space to write in after the entry that said "Attended Royal College of Medicine, Cork, IR. And it awaited details after his medical schooling took place.

Harris continued to peruse through the large book and took notice of similarities to himself. Every one of his ancestors was born in Europe. Some as far north as Norway, as eastward as Poland or as far south as Greece. The names were a mix of all these, but the thing above all else was that every relative in the book that carried this gene of healing finally died over the age of 100 except for a couple who met their end at the guillotine. If one kept their head, it seemed they would keep their life.

Just then, his mum walked in with a turkey in hand, and she set it down on the kitchen counter with an exclamation of happiness.

"Harris, love!" She went over and hugged her son along with a kiss on the cheek. "Here, lemme look at you." She gave him a visual observation and was satisfied with him. "I see you still have the Adonis figure. You been eating well?"

"Of course, Mum," Harris said. "But nothing beats the food here." He put that in a way that she wouldn't know Mrs. Ravalli had his mum's kitchen expertise beaten by a mile. Jean then noticed that Harris had the book out and the lamp lit. "You learn anything new, then?" She asked.

"Nothing really except grandfather's section is in tatters," Harris said. "That was a bit of a surprise. That and the family name wasn't as old as I thought."

"I see," Jean said. "Well, I'm afraid that everything in there is a mystery to me as well. Your father just showed me the details of his father when his wife died. I know the entry was short.

"Yes, I was wondering about that, Mum," Harris said. "Do you know why pages are missing from his section?" Jean just shrugged not knowing.

"You'll have to ask your Da when he comes in tonight…Do please let me know. I'm curious, myself." Jean said.

Harris then helped his mum in the kitchen with the Christmas dinner to be had later that week. Her relatives would be arriving in a couple of days. He chopped onions until he could smell them no more and had a steady trail of tears from the vegetable's gaseous emissions to prove it.

Helmut Gibraltar arrived home at about half-past eight. He saw Harris and greeted him with a very short hug and handshake. It was much like when he saw Roland coming and going.

"Well, Da…" Harris said. "I appreciate the book being here. There's a lot that I didn't know about the family, including how our surname jumped about."

"Well, that happens with females," Helmut replied. "You should be glad it did change, or the name might be unpronounceable."

"Yeah, I believe that was one of the names." Harris joked. "But I was wondering about grandfather. I noticed some of his pages were torn out. Why is that?"

"Well, son…." Helmut began. "You have to realise that the most senior member of the family who can still think on his feet becomes the caretaker of this book.

Your grandfather took up that mantle before I did and felt that his entry would not inspire the next in line. I'm not sure what to think about that myself. No one can be entirely proud of what they did in the past. That is just life."

Harris was surprised. What could a stiff and proper man like grandfather have done to feel that way?

"Any idea what it could have been?" Harris asked. Helmut just shook his head.

"The book came to me like this from Bern. I believed it was bad form to do so, but I received no response about it." Helmut said.

Harris closed the large grimoire with a feeling of wanting more. "You can put it away... It looks like I'm done here." He said, and his father accepted it with a knowing nod. He put it back into the box and set it on the shelf to await the next entry or perusal. Jean was watching Wheel of Fortune when the males of the Gibraltar family joined her. She then told Harris that Uncle Thomas would be flying into Heathrow Wednesday afternoon from the states and that they might need to pick up some brandy at the shop before then. Harris also wanted to say hi to his first human patient tomorrow at his gymnasium as well.

After they went to bed, Harris went down to the kitchen at 2 am for a cuppa and a copy of something to read to help him sleep. Perhaps medical ethics? He always felt like dropping off in McCurdy's class, anyway. He scanned the books on the shelf, taking care to move the box containing the family history book. The copy of Brain Matters by Matt Bathgate was his desired reading choice that night. A footstool that was in front of the shelf went unnoticed by Harris until he tripped over it and sent the box and the family book over on its side.

"Oops!" Harris said quietly of his faux pas and proceeded to pick up the box, and its contents slid out the container by accident.

"Sodder!" Harris expressed a bit louder and then covered his mouth in an expression of speaking too loudly. He picked up the book and was about to put it back into the box when he noticed the bottom of the box was false. It concealed a couple of note pages and a small tobacco box that looked old and metallic. He took the item out of the false bottom and set it aside and then quickly read the discovered pages that were ripped out the book. His eyes widened at the notations.

He tried to take the lid off the metallic box with a great deal of effort as it stayed shut for many years. It was as if it was begging to keep its contents hidden.

He took a butter knife from the kitchen, and the box finally gave up its secrets despite his hoping not to see what was in the container. The horrific find was there, nonetheless for him to witness.

The pages stating Adolf, himself was tended to by Dr Unger Gilderbrund!

The waters from the metaphoric ship flooded in wildly as Harris stared at the tin box containing the swastika armband.

Chapter 35 – History Revision

The feeling of sickness and anger flowed through his soul. "This is not me!" Harris wanted to shout at the top of his lungs as he put the box and the torn pages on top of the tome waiting for Harris to show his Da. Did he already know? If he did, Helmut did not show it.

He tried going back to bed but continued to feel the pain in his stomach wretch through him. How could he? How could he be a part of a bloodline that would do such a thing? If he could, he would drain every bit of family blood out of himself! Then he thought "Well, he's dead...Dead as Caesar. So why should it bother him? His mind wandered all of this until sleep finally took him over.

At 8:00 in the morning, Helmut knocked on Harris's door. In the old days, he would barge in, but he gave him respect now that he was of age. Harris said, "Just a tic!" and slipped on a dressing gown to answer the door.

"Where...did you find these?" Helmut asked breathlessly. Harris grabbed his father by the arm and dragged him into his old room and closed the door behind the two of them.

"The book box had a false bottom. I only found it after accidentally knocking the works over last night." Harris answered. Helmut collected his composure for a moment and sat on the bed next to Harris with his head in his hands. His Da was more human he had ever seen him.

"Son, I had no idea those items were in the box. If I did..."

"I know, Da," Harris said. "It was just disturbing to find."

Again, Helmut thought for a moment about what to do. To be discovered as a Xenon was bad enough but to be seen as a Nazi as well... "I...have to make a phone call," Helmut said as he left the room. Harris just sat for a moment thinking about what he should do next. He jumped in the shower and tried to make himself presentable to the world at large. He got dressed and headed down the stairs to the living room. He felt that maybe he should not have made this bit of knowledge apparent. Perhaps hiding it from everyone would have been a better option?

He heard his father in the other room speaking, in German, to whoever was on the phone. Harris slowly returned upstairs to his desk. The heated argument continued with Harris understanding just a little of what he overheard as he left.

He did hear a couple of German swear words exchanged which were the first ones Harris learned. (Boys will be boys.) Harris then fetched the actual book he was looking for during the night.

The verbal confrontation attracted Jean's attention as well. She came down in her dressing gown, wondering what was going on. Helmut hung up and went to Jean. "Jean, luv…listen…" Helmut said. "It looks like Harris found that missing piece of the puzzle I told you about from the book last night."

"Mother-of-god, no!" She cried.

"Gilliam will be here tomorrow, but I'm going to meet him at my office. I don't want him to know where we live." Helmut replied. Jean just shook her head in sad agreement.

Helmut went upstairs to Harris's room where he was looking over the book on brain maladies. He didn't want his father to know that he listened to as much as he did. Helmut knocked on his door, waiting for Harris to invite him in.

"Son, you and I are going to my office tomorrow. Hopefully, we'll get some answers then." Helmut said. "You would be best served to keep this out of your mind until then."

"Yes, Da," Harris said.

There was no mention of what happened or what was discovered by them for the rest of the day. They went back to the usual trappings of Christmas like putting up the Christmas tree and decorating their flat. They went to church on Sunday morning with Father Ponsonby Derry leading the mass. Jean's family would be showing up Tuesday for the holiday celebration, so Helmut wanted to get down to what needed doing as quickly as possible.

After lunch, he told Harris to come with him to his office. They took a cab to Saville Hospital with hardly an eye looking their way. It was Sunday, and there was a skeleton crew in hospital today taking care of patients. They went into his office and Harris grabbed a magazine that was over a year old. He made a mental note to bring in more current reading material for his patients.

"Da, what are we doing here?" Harris finally asked.

Helmut sat at his desk chair after fixing two cups of tea for his son and himself while an empty cup sat on the desk, awaiting someone else.

"Son, the man we are about to meet is an author who began working with your grandfather a few years ago on his memoirs. From what he told me, my father had first-hand knowledge of how the Nazi's operated. Even though the 3rd Reich fell out of power in 1945, there are still sympathisers to the cause. I didn't want him to come to our home, so I felt it was safer to meet him here in a more public setting, as it were."

There was a knock on the door. "Come!" Helmut said.

A stout, short, gentleman, who was nearly bald, walked in wearing a dark three-piece suit like he just left church and thick glasses with black frames. "Allo, Mein Herr." He said in a thick German accent. Helmut returned the greeting, but they did not shake hands.

"Harris, this is Gilliam Swanger." The man did not make any move to shake hands with Harris, either. He just nodded to him in acknowledgement.

"Hello, sir," Harris said.

"Gilliam, please, let's stick to English as I want my son to hear this as well," Helmut said. Gilliam nodded in agreement.

"Son…" Helmut began. "Herr Swanger here has been helping your grandfather compile his memoirs for several months. I believe he can help us in understanding your grandfather's intentions many years ago."

"Wait, wait… Months?" Harris asked. "Grandfather Unger is alive?"

"In matter of speaking, he is." Herr Swanger said in a stilted accent suggesting English was not his first language. "Your grandfather vas struck with debilitating dementia."

"I see," Harris said, crestfallen. "I'm sorry. I thought he died already."

"My father hired Gilliam here to record his thoughts before his mind went all together," Helmut said. "He is here to finish the puzzle you found, as it were."

Harris just nodded. "Go on, then." They let Gilliam begin…

"I am unsure you both know of something called "Operation Valkyrie" That happens many years into second vorld var."

"I have heard of something like that," Harris said. "Wasn't that a plot to assassinate Hitler?"

"Ja," Gilliam said. "Your grandfather vas present at time of this attempt. Several so-called, heroes of Deutschland vanted nothing more than his elimination as they feared his continued leadership vould collapse Der Reich und take der country with it…that is vere your Unger came in."

"What did my father have to do with all this?" Helmut asked.

"Please realise your father vas no admirer of Der Fuhrer. Vith that said, der men plotting to overtake him vere hated by Unger even more as they believed to have a key to take over more efficiently than Hitler ever could."

With that, Gilliam poured a cup of tea from the pot before he returned to continue the story.

"There vas a meeting that vas called to order of der Reich officers that vas supposed to be at Der Fuhrer's bunker called Der Volf's Lair on 20 July 1944. A bomb in a briefcase vas set under table. It vent off und killed several. The public contention vas that der officers vanted to assassinate Hitler und surrender to allies. …That is part your father contradicted."

Helmut was taken aback by this information. "What do you mean?"

Herr Swanger leaned forward on Helmut's desk "Your father knew that if Der Fuhrer vas took out, der men who vould replace him vould not surrender, but step up attacks on der allies und stretch out der var effort to overtake rest of Europe …. und der Allies."

Herr Swanger was ready to take the abuse of his next words. "That is vy your father saved him."

Helmut was angry. Harris was as well. "My father saved Hitler…?" Helmut asked, gruffly.

"I assume you know your father's…abilities?" Herr Swanger said.

"I have heard of them, yes." Not letting on that he and Harris had the same gifts as Unger.

"Der Fuhrer, as fan of all occult things, believed your father a gift from der hand of Mephistopheles, his-self. That he vas conjured to serve him, und him alone.

He applied these gifts to Der Fuhrer, und that same day, he met vith Il Duchy. Mean vile, your father made his escape to Svitzerland." Gilliam said.

"I not entirely sure how he managed that, though. His mind vas going as he told me this, so…"

Helmut and Harris sat quietly as this information was mulled over by them both.

"I vish I had better vords for you both." Herr Swanger said. "It is rotten situation."

"It's not your fault, Gilliam," Helmut sighed. I suppose my son and I should be thankful things turned out as they did. Otherwise, we wouldn't be here." Harris somehow took no comfort in that thought.

"Where is my grandfather now?" Harris asked.

He in Guttannen, Svitzerland living vith my sister. She is nurse by trade. Ve kept him there for 2 years ven ve pulled him out of Bern. It vas for his own safety.

"Safety?" Harris asked. "What do you mean?"

"Your grandfather's gifts ver extraordinary! Gilliam said. "Der Fuhrer turn over every rock looking for him in der hopes of breeding him like thoroughbred. His escape to Svitzerland stayed a mystery to der Reich…und continues to stay one today."

Gilliam finished his tea with one final gulp. "I am afraid that is all I can offer."

The three of them walked out of the office to the front of the hospital. Gilliam couldn't take any more time as he had to catch a flight to Berlin. Now that the wall had fallen, some secrets and those harbouring them had finally come out of hiding.

His cab arrived, and Herr Swanger was about to leave when he touched Helmut's arm and told him "Wir sprechen uns bald, Herr Gibraltar." Helmut nodded in agreement to his "speak to you later" interpretation and exited the building only to have the cab speed off without him in it and another black car race up to him and unloaded a volley of machine-gun fire from an old "grease-gun" rifle.

The bullets hit the outside of the hospital entrance shattering the door glass and bystanders ran for their lives. The two Gibraltar men hit the floor when they heard the shots and heard screams of panic in the background. The black car raced off without a trace.

Helmut and Harris were on the ground, surrounded by broken glass. Harris slowly got to his feet and made his way over to where Gilliam stood a moment ago.

His clothes were there, his briefcase and glasses laid on the ground, but he was no place to be found.

A stray bullet grazed Helmut's cheek, but the evidence came and went fast except for a small trickle of blood. Helmut ran over and grabbed the briefcase and glasses.

"Harris, grab the clothes!" He quietly, but urgently, told his son.

Harris did what his Da said, and he followed him into the single men's loo. The crowd of visitors were still making their way to the exit in a collective panic. Helmut took the clothes and laid them out flat and face-up like a body were in it. He instructed Harris to guard the door. Meanwhile, Harris was wondering if his Da was going crazy.

"All clear, Gilliam!" Helmut said as a black, gaseous form streamed in from under the loo door and then hovered over the clothes. The cloud entered the laid-out clothes through the neck of the wardrobe. He reformed into the abandoned clothes until he was laying on the floor before the two of them.

"Ve should take der back door," Swanger said as he put on his thick glasses. Harris just sat there slack-jawed as the Xenons made their way to a service entrance. Helmut quickly arranged a private car for the German gentleman.

They then ran through an empty hall and saw a trail of blood on the floor. A middle-aged man in a dark blue suit laid on the floor with a large bleeding wound in his leg. It was Administrator Artemis Clark. The same man who negotiated Helmut's position at Saville Hospital.

"Harris, you and Gilliam keep walking, I'll be along." Harris nodded as the two made their way down the empty hall. Helmut projected a bright light from his left hand while standing behind him out of the field of vision and covered his eyes with his right. Artemis then dashed for a nearby water fountain and started drinking for a solid minute while Helmut hoped for his silence at their next salary negotiation meeting.

Helmut then walked toward the large double doors to join his son and the targeted biographer while shaking off the exhaustion. The scene reminded the elder Xenon why he didn't heal on the fly as his youthful son did.

Ten minutes later, Gilliam was on his way to the airport with Dr Guiteau behind the wheel of his late-model Peugeot.

Harris wished he had the time to talk to his former mentor but could only shake his hand while they arranged the escape of the biographer out of the area. The police were beginning the investigation while the father and son caught an eyeful of the damage. A few people were being treated for minor injuries from the broken glass. They would have to settle for the standard medical care offered by Saville Hospital.

Helmut and Harris took a cab home after they walked around for a bit looking dumbfounded like everyone else. They said nothing about the incident until they returned home. "I'm not as young as I used to be," Helmut thought. It was not what he wanted for Harris as he tried to avoid this war, himself.

Chapter 36 – Transportation Has Been Arranged

Harris couldn't wait to get home and discuss what just happened with his Da. Who was that mad prick with the gun? Why was Swanger in their crosshairs? They got to the Gibraltar residence and went into their home. Jean came out after washing her blonde hair in the bathroom sink.

"How did it go?" She asked Helmut.

"I learned a lot…and then he was shot at on the street!" He said.

"Is he all right?" She asked with grave concern.

"He is," Helmut responded. "Julius picked him up at hospital. He pulled his usual trick to avoid getting filled with lead."

"Just how much did mum know about all this?" Harris thought.

"Excuse me, Da," Harris spoke up. "I know I am going to regret asking this but what's going on? Just then, the phone rang.

"Hello?" Jean answered.

"All in due time, son," Helmut said, leaving Harris feeling impatient.

"Hang on." She then handed the phone receiver to Helmut.

"Yes?" a moment went by. "I…" "But…" Helmut rubbed his brow with his hand in exasperation. "OK, but I'm not going alone." There was a long pause as he looked at Harris. "How did you find…never mind." Helmut looked at his son. He put a finger in the air in a "Just a moment" pose. "Tell her the Tube station at Hounslow West… How fast can she get there? …Yes, dumb question…See you there in 2 hours." Helmut hung up the phone.

"C' mon son, you're about to meet your grandfather," Helmut said. Harris couldn't believe it…He couldn't wait! Helmut was less than enthused.

"How are we getting there?" He asked. "Train? Aeroplane? Bus?"

"We have to meet Julius and Gilliam at Hounslow Station," Helmut said. "I'll fill you in more when we get there." After which he turned to his wife of 20 years.

"Luv, go to the mattresses." He said. Jean nodded and gave and a huge kiss to her husband. Whatever "go to the mattresses" meant, she knew what to do.

"We'll be back then," Helmut said.

"You better!" She said as she wiped the blood off the now non-existent scratch from his face using a few drops of water from her wet hair. "Thank you, luv." He said to her.

Helmut then turned to his son. "Time to ride, son…And bring your travel bag, too." Helmut added. "We may be there for a bit."

Harris raced upstairs and grabbed his clothes not yet worn and stuffed them in the bag. He began to wonder why they were about to visit the elder Gibraltar now. Especially in his limited capacity. He put on his anorak and followed his Da, who was already out the door. They walked to the new bus shelter in front of the Ravalli's home and boarded a double-decker that arrived a few minutes later. His Da and mum didn't drive. He began to feel that perhaps they should…He thought for sure that he should learn.

After a quiet bus ride and two tube transfers, they got to the Hounslow West tube station and took a seat on a bench that was under a large red and white sign that said "Underground." Just a mile away was Heathrow Airport, so a flight was possible. Harris didn't have a passport, though. He wondered how they would deal with that.

He got bored waiting for whatever needed to happen, so he reached into his bag for his Walkman. Instead, he found the disguise kit that Roland gave him for his birthday. He also found a small booklet within the packet that talked about the basics of disguise so he began scanning the tiny pages where it explained how one should blend into the background by copying the activities of those around you and observe how they walked, their accents and even the way they held their cigarettes and copy these movements. He felt he never took notice of how people were so subtly different across Europe. The little guide also mentioned how a small change in appearances, such as wearing a hat or glasses, can throw people off, especially if they are in a hurry. There was also mention of camouflage and hiding in plain sight from hiding behind a newspaper to entire duck suits that snipers used in fields to tunnels in the battlefields of south-eastern Asia.

Another half-hour passed, and Helmut mentioned that they were about to leave with the appearance of Gilliam and Julius along with a woman Harris had not seen before in a long black coat and purple beret. The men spoke in quiet voices even though there seemed to be no one else about.

"Julius…" Helmut asked his trusted associate "What going on?"

"There's a group called The Sons of Berlin," Julius said. "They want to attempt to take Germany back now that the wall came down and figured with German unification now accomplished, they can take the entirety of Deutschland and lead it back to the Nazis. They also figured they could use Xenons to do it. What would be a better way to repopulate and then overrun the country?"

"Sounds like their logic," Helmut said.

"Ya, und der vey Xenons have been treated, some of them may vant to be part of this new scheme." Gilliam chimed in.

"Uh, excuse me…" Harris interrupted. "I thought you lot were heading to Switzerland."

"Well, we would…" Julius said. "But the airport is being patrolled with Paragons and police who don't have a clue what's going on. That's why we brought her." He pointed to the woman who had taken a seat at a station bench. Julius called to her and waved her over to join the group. He introduced the woman with long black and grey-hair of around 60 years to Harris.

"Ruth Alexander, this is Harris Gibraltar, Helmut's son," Julius said.

"Nice to meet you." She said in a French accent. "You are spitting image of your father."

"Thank you…" Harris said. "I hope that's a compliment." He then said with a smile. She just stared back, not knowing what to say. "So, what's the plan?" Harris asked.

"We have to get my father away from those S.O.B.'s," Helmut answered. "We weren't about to do anything until you found those missing pages yesterday & Gilliam told me what was happening. Now we have to get him hidden away."

"…And how's that done, then?" Harris asked.

"Ve must move him," Gilliam said. "He must be moved off der continent avay from their arm's length und avay from their little bit of power, for now. If they get vat, they vant, they could take a foothold und to start their rebuild of Der Reich."

Harris thought about the whole matter. Grandfather's condition could make him an easy target. "OK, but where can he go?" He asked quietly.

"Australia," Helmut said.

"He'll be out of sight and out of mind there…. but we're wasting time. Let's get going." He finished.

"Oui," Ruth said. "We must do this quickly." Here, Harris was confused. How fast can you get to Switzerland, let alone Australia, quickly with the airlines compromised?

"So, how will we deal with airport security?" Harris asked wondering if the boxing and martial arts he had been learning was going to be needed.

"We don't," Julius said and then gave a nod to Ruth as she stepped a few feet away from the group and made a large circle in the air followed by a few smaller ones and produced a tunnel-type light where one could see The Alps in the distance.

"Let's go!" she said as Gilliam stepped through the tunnel and vanished. Julius then went in and did the same.

Helmut and Harris looked at each other and Harris said, "I hope you lot know what you're doing!" and jumped in the ring. The trip was instantaneous as he stood in the backyard of a Swiss wooden chalet. He felt a hand grab his arm, pulling him backwards. It was Julius pulling him out of the way as Helmut emerged out of thin air. Ruth then appeared, and the whole group was left standing in the cold of Switzerland after a trip of less than a minute that would have taken a minimum of 4 hours by air. The port closed behind them with the presence of Ruth.

"Right, let's go then!" Gilliam said as he waved the pack of Xenons and the human, Julius to the Swiss chalet at the top of a hill. Harris looked around and saw green under his feet and was captivated by the sight of snow-capped mountains in the distance.

"Switzerland…I used to live here." Da said. "Nothing much changed." As he took in the view but was less impressed as he had seen most of it before as a child here. They entered the back door to a warm house mixed with the pleasant smell of bread baking that soon became overpowered by the stench of a human under nursing care. Gilliam was the first up the stairs to the living area. A dumpy, older woman with her hair in a tight bun was standing nervously in the middle of the room.

"Helga…vat is it?" Gilliam asked.

From behind her emerged a tall, older man in a long wool coat covering a brown shirt with short white hair and an eye patch over his right eye… He was also holding a gun on her!

Chapter 37 – Going South...

"Allo," Said the man with the gun. "I am..."

"Ve knows voo you are...Herr Richter!" Gilliam said as if everyone in the room knew who he was. Harris was not clued in on his identity.

"Gut," Richter said. "Introductions are not needed then, Herr Svanger." He kept the gun aimed at the Xenons and humans in the room. "I must thank you for leading me here to Herr Gilderbrund...or Gibraltar, vutever he uses now. He vill be most necessary in our plan to reunite Der Fatherland." Unger just laid in bed with a long white beard and staring into space with his mouth half-open.

"I vould not assist the likes of you or your slime!" Gilliam said emphatically.

"Of course, you vouldn't, Herr Svanger," Richter said. "Not directly, anyvey. You vere easy to track, though."

Harris knew someone had to stop him, so he made his move. "Herr Richter!" Harris spoke up to the surprise of everyone there. "What do you want an old, broken down figure like Unger here? Why don't you take a younger guy, like me?"

"Aww, how sveet!" Richter said sarcastically. "No, thanks! He then shot Harris in the stomach. Richter would have shot him more than once, but the luger jammed in his hand.

"Damn pistol!" He said, shaking the handgun trying to eject the used cartridge.

Harris fell forward on his knees immediately. The pain in his midsection felt like his guts had split apart. Blood went all around the front of him on his clothes and the floor. Helmut and Ruth were about to race to his side when Harris held his hand up to stop them. The bullet was hot and burned inside him and then dissipated to Harris's healing ability leaving all amazed, especially Richter as the spent shell fell quietly on the floor in front of him.

Harris stood up with the searing pain faded and his body sealing up the wounds. He was actually surprised that he could recover so quickly from the shot. Harris just looked at Richter with a gargoyle-like smile on his face while a stunned Richter tried in vain to eject the magazine from the German handgun. "OK, that woke me up!" Harris thought. He inspected his bloody shirt. "Well, that's not coming out!" Harris said, sarcastically as he spoke to the amazed Ex-Nazi.

Harris then approached the amazed Nazi while smiling and seething with anger at the same time. "See what I mean? I can deal with whatever injuries come to me." He said, trying to sound as evil as the man who just shot him. "I can also be very helpful to your cause…" And with that, Harris stood nose-to-longer, miss-shaped nose with the Nazi with one eye and poured his healing light into him. Richter didn't notice the beam until he finished and was a bit worried at first at what Harris had just done to him. Then he felt his one eye that was under the patch was twitching with feeling. Richter removed the eyepatch in utter amazement.

"Mein eye!" He shouted. "I had no vision for 30 years out of it!" He then turned to Harris. "Very vell!" He said to Harris. "You vill be the leader of the new order just as soon as I take care of this…this…" That was when the thirst hit, and Richter were on all-fours clutching his mouth and throat. Just what Harris had in mind.

"Just a side-effect, sir…easily remedied." Harris went to the small kitchen while passing Ruth with a whispered "Get ready." Richter did not hear it as he was suffering from his lack of fluids. Ruth sneaked her way to the back of the suffering Richter, ready to do her part.

Harris noticed on the kitchen counter several bottles of lager with a 20 or-so letter name on the label. He took one and walked it over to the ailing gunman. "Here you go, Richter…just what the doctor ordered…Catch!!!"

Richter was on his feet ready to make the catch as Harris tossed him the bottle high in the air while at the same time pushed him into the awaiting vortex, compliments of Ruth, that she formed into the floor. The nasty senior vanished without a trace.

"I thought he'd never leave!" Harris then said in his best Groucho voice and smiled. He was suddenly surrounded by everyone patting him on the back and saying, "Great job!" with a massive sigh of relief going through the chalet.

"Vell, you had me fooled a moment there." Herr Swanger said.

"Yeah, sorry for that," Harris said. "Where's your loo? Swanger pointed down the hall to the first door on the left.

Harris excused himself and took a moment to go into the small room and clean the blood off, quickly and changed his shirt. He hoped to get some new clothes for Christmas as moments like these were eating into his wardrobe.

"Are you all right?" Ruth asked to which Harris just waved dismissively.

"Ruth, where did you send him?" Helmut asked as Harris re-joined them.

"South for the winter." She said in her French accent. "Antarctica."

"Well, at least he'll be able to see it," Harris said. This time, Ruth suppressed a small laugh.

"There may be others," Gilliam said, bringing everyone back to reality. "Ve best be getting on…The last detail is yours, gentlemen." He said, aiming his words at Helmut who replied with a nod.

"Right, so, how are we to do this? Harris inquired. "Do we need that pushchair?" pointing to one setting in the corner.

Helmut walked over to Harris and put his hands on his shoulders. "Son, today, your grandfather leaves under his own volition." Harris was left confused. He looked at his grandfather who only stared into space for the whole time he was there, including his grandson getting shot. He also knew that they couldn't heal him as his incapacitation was due to his mind and not his body.

"But how, Da?" Harris asked as he turned back to his father. "We can only heal the physical, right?"

"Correct, son," Helmut responded. "…But we aren't alone, are we?"

And with that, Julius walked over to the senior Doctor Gibraltar and put his hand over his eyes with his hand glowing golden light. Instantly, Unger sat up in bed a bit confused but feeling a new man.

"Danka, Mein Herr." He said to Julius. Harris was in utter shock and amazement as he had no idea that his mentor was one of his own. "Boy, you think you know a guy," Harris said quietly.

Ten minutes or so later, Unger was dressed in decent clothes and stood before the awaiting crew of Xenons and Helga who was the only human there, apparently. Harris was through making assumptions, though.

"Son…Ve have things to discuss." Unger said to his son, Helmut.

"I quite agree, father." Helmut responded "But not here. We best be off." He then turned his attention to Ruth to make the next vortex to take them out of the country.

Once again, she made a spiral with her hand, and a black hole appeared with a small office on the other side.

"Abracadabra!" Gilliam said with a smile as he jumped into the awaiting circle. Julius followed, and then Harris shouted, "Like this, grandfather!" Harris vanished into the vortex along with Unger who acted like he did this before. Helmut was about to jump when he noticed Helga out the side of his eye. He grabbed her by the shoulder and said she was coming along. She resisted with a few "Nein! Nein!" until he gave her a gentle persuasion. In other words, he kicked her in the shin and shoved her through the vortex with Helmut following. Ruth rolled her eyes and said, "Oy Vey!" under her breath. She followed with the gate vanishing behind her.

Helga continued to protest in German in the words that Harris first learned as a boy and a few others that put Helmut in a tizzy. "Frau Helga!" Helmut shouted at the hysterical nursemaid something in German that calmed her down enough to join the others, peacefully in this new locale. She still kicked Helmut in the shin, though and shouted "Schweinhund!" at him. He took it as though he deserved it as he rubbed his leg in pain.

Harris took a long look at this new location. It could have been anyplace in the world. There was just a simple desk, chair, file cabinet and a shelf of books in French. It had the feeling of a feminine touch with lace curtains and flowers growing in an old cook pot.

"OK, so, where are we?" Harris asked.

"This is my home," Ruth said, tiredly. "I found this to be the safest place to hide…in plain sight…pardon, S'il Vous Plait.

With that, she exhaustedly walked down a narrow hall while propping herself against the wall into a room off to the side. It reminded Harris of when he healed the AIDS patients in Northern Ireland last month and how tired he became after repeated healing. "These abilities come with a price." He thought.

Harris then looked outside the window with the lace curtain.

There was no sound of people except themselves and only streetlights as it was the middle of the night here. The homes and stores made it look like any other city.

Helmut walked up behind him and took a view out the window as well. "Son, welcome to Australia."

Chapter 38 – War story

Harris had more questions than answers. "Da, who are all these people?"

"Just some friends and allies I made along the way, son." He said. "Ruth and your grandfather go a long way back…to the war, actually. As I said before, Herr Swanger and I met when my father was trying to write his memoirs.

"…And how about Julius?" Harris asked. "I only met him when I got this ability to cure."

"Julius and I go way back as well," Helmut replied. "We did our time as house officers together at Barbican Hospital. We discovered we shared abilities quite by accident." Helmut waxed nostalgic over their time together as the Gibraltar father and son took seats at the small kitchen table.

"We got along all right but didn't know a lot about each other, at first. Then he caught me attempting to fix the fractured skull of a builder who was hit by a large steel beam. I could heal his head of that injury, but his brain was, basically, mush when he came into the A&E. That's when Julius came in and saw me projecting light beams into his head. I had never been so nervous in all my existence."

Helmut grabbed a cuppa and retook his place at the small kitchen table meant for no more than two people.

"Instead of calling the bobbies and having me dragged out, he said, "You too, eh?" and healed the man's mind like he just did with your grandfather. They sent him to another hospital after we sedated him until he was out of our hands. That was over 25 years ago…Wow, has it been that long?" He asked himself.

Harris looked around the tiny flat. Gillam and Helga were on the sofa, engaging in some conversation that his limited German kept him away from. Julius was keeping a watch out the living area window, and Grandfather Unger was sitting in a reclining chair reading The Australian Free Press-the daily paper. Ruth was missing, though.

"Da, where's Ruth?" Harris asked.

"Asleep," Helmut said. "She's not as strong as she was in her youth, so four jumps in a row are a bit much for her. It must have been exhausting for her in her youth, I'm sure. I figure we'll give her a few hours and then head home as well."

Harris looked at the clock with a cat that had eyes that went left and right along with a tail that went to-and-fro. It was 4:00 in the morning.

Helmut said. "Maybe you should try to sleep a bit as well."

"After all that we been through today, who could sleep?" Harris asked. "Let me use the loo though. I'm still crisp with my own blood."

Harris was still too wide-awake and excited to wind down, even after the hot shower. The water pressure was horrible, and it felt more like fog than water for the 10 minutes he stayed there.

Harris then put on the last of his clothes which were suited more for the middle of a London winter than the weather here. Julius, Unger and the Swanger siblings were no place to be seen when he left the small water cupboard. His Da was also among the missing. Perhaps they went to bed.

He listened to his Walkman for 5 minutes, but that didn't content him. He walked to the front door, wondering if he should explore the outside world. He started to open the door and, at that moment, wondered if the door was alarmed. There was no sound and no alarm, so he continued to walk through — nothing too remarkable, just a light and a sky-blue hallway that could have been anywhere.

He reached the end of the hall to a door that seemed to lead outside. He was just about to open it when a hand slapped him on the shoulder that caused Harris to yelp in surprise.

"Shhhh…!" It was Unger Gibraltar. He was no longer a weak figure in a bed but an upright gentleman that looked at his grandson with a mild grin.

"Grandad…Bligh Mie, you gave me a start!" Harris said.

"…Und you nearly gave us all finish!" Unger replied in a German accent as he pointed to the alarm wires next to the front door. "You don't live like us without some level of paranoia, me boy".

"I'm sorry," Harris said, hanging his head. "I was just curious where we were."

"Never mind," Unger said. "Come on back in. Let me get to know you." They walked down the hall while Harris made an inquiry.

"How did you know the door was alarmed?" Harris asked.

"I lived here until I left to return to Svitzerland. This flat is Xenon safe house." Unger said. "Ruth set it up for those she rescued from Paragons and such.... und by the vey it looks, she still does." They went back into the small kitchen and took a seat. Unger took two bottles of beer out of the cabinet along with two mugs and gave one each to Harris.

"Right…this is the first-time ve got to sit down like this," Unger said. "This lot certainly have turned themselves inside-out for my sake."

"Da said you were a great doctor... but not much else," Harris said.

Unger sighed. "The less that vas said about me, the better I suppose," Unger replied sadly. "I never vanted the position vat I vas given by that madman but it vas that or have my head removed. I thought if I kept my enemy closer, I could remove him. Ven the chance to set the bomb came close, I vas ready to assist any vey I could."

Unger continued over his fresh pour of Australian beer.

"Like everyone else, I vas told that surrender vould occur after Der Furhur's death. That is until I overheard their real intention. Remove Der Fuhrer und take controls of Der Reich's Var machine and vipe der allies off the map." Unger took a slug out of the bottle that wouldn't fit in the mug. "Der sad part vas I almost vent along vith it…until I met Ruth."

"Yes, Da said you both go way back?" Harris asked.

Unger drank from the mug a bit of the lager. "Ya…She was 15 ven she vas brought into camp at Treblinka. The longer her internment lasted, the more other prisoners tended to disappear around her. You saw vat she can do. She vas a true hero of her peoples. Of course, as a Xenon, she could not possibly exist." He continued sipping his mug with Harris hanging on to his words…

"Your father said you carry our family's gift?" Unger asked. Harris only nodded.

"A guard savagely beat her for his bemusement while I tended to the interred to keep disease at minimum. Ven I saw vat he vas doing to her, I stab him with scalpel in back of neck. I treated her from edge of death. She then realised vat I vas und she got rid of the body by sending him into abyss. They never found any trace of him."

"Good," Harris said, quietly.

"She continued to make her peoples vanish to various safe locations around der vorld. Mostly to America. Ven der assassination attempt vent badly, she helps me escape to Svitzerland. I begged her to come vith me, but she knew she had to stay und help her peoples. From vat I understand, ven it vas her turn in der gas chambers und der soldiers opened the doors, no vun be there."

Unger smiled and finished his mug

"So how did you both find each other again?" Harris asked.

"Its vas just a matter of time until she found der best doctor in Svitzerland. She knew it vould be me. I vish ve could have stayed together then, but the vorld vouldn't have it. She married a lawyer in Nice und raised a family there. I, of course, married your grandmother."

Harris took it all in. "So, what happens now?" He asked.

"Not sure," Unger said with a shrug. "All I know is life could go in a thousand different directions. That goes for you, too. Vich ever path you choose, you make the best of it...und then you go further." With that, Unger stood up from the table. "Your father is very proud of you." He said with his hand on his shoulder. "I am very proud of you. Vat ever vey you go, you be der best...und then some." He then left his empty mug on the table and walked down the hall.

Harris finished his drink and then opened the door that his grandfather entered. There were a dozen cots set up along the walls along with one regular double bed where Ruth slept. Each sleeping cot had a travelling companion along with Unger taking the one closest to Ruth. A small table lamp provided the only light in this chamber.

Harris took the cot nearest the door. He took off his boots, slipped them under the chosen bed and fell asleep under an old quilt.

Chapter 39 – A Day Well Spent

Harris woke to his Da, giving him a small shake. "Oy, Harris…I thought maybe you would want to take a short stroll before we head back home?"

He wiped his eyes and remembered where he was…wherever it was. At least he was in good company. "Sure, Da…where are we, though…specifically?"

"Brisbane," Helmut said. "Ruth and my Dad should be safe here."

Harris just had a shock go through him. "Hey, I didn't go Christmas shopping yet. You think I can get a few things here?"

"I'm sure it would be OK. We can't take a long time to do it, though." Helmut said. "Here, you can go put these on…" With that, he handed Harris a pair of summer shorts and a polo top. "It's also summer here."

It wasn't the best of outfits with the shirt the colour of bright red and a size too large, but it would do for now. Oddly enough, the shorts fit perfectly. He then also took the fake glasses and the hat along. He decided not to bother with the false moustaches as they looked just that…false! The air today was dusty and dry, and the temperature about 35C (95F) as Harris walked with his Da and Julius from the small house to the large, modern-looking building that housed dozens of shops. He wanted to keep things simple, so he looked around for a half-hour at a tourist shop with the usual tchotchkes that fit the casual traveller's image of this part of the world, namely boomerangs, stuffed kangaroos and koalas.

Further down the indoor area, there was also a bottle shop and a chemist on one end with the rest being clothing shops that would take too long to decide as he knew no one's clothing size but his own. It allowed him to grab a proper shirt that had "Australia- God's favourite summer destination." printed on it with a picture of an old "man" fishing. There was also a grocery store that didn't fill the bill, either. He kept hearing a song lyric about something called a "Vegemite Sandwich." The song made it sound appealing, but he passed.

He decided on the bottle shop and bought a carton of various wines from the area and a bottle of brandy for his Uncle Thomas. He remembered his Mum saying they needed to fetch that for him, anyway. He also bought a couple of boomerangs since no trip down under would be complete without them.

Julius and Helmut offered to take the items to the flat as they were heading back. Helmut took a moment to stop at the chemist's shop to look at…something.

They both thought he might have had some idea in mind for a gift, so they let him go and gave him an hour. "Remember #10 Jacob Street." His Da said. The house was three doors down from The Petrol Shop, so it would be easy to find.

Earlier, he found a journal for his Da with a picture of a mastiff on the front cover. It would be perfect for him to keep a figure of Napoleon nearby. He also picked up a cribbage board for Julius. He remembered his mentor saying to him, "Don't forget to have some fun as well." He then paid for the items with Australian dollars he had exchanged at the bank on the other side of the shopping centre and was about to leave when he decided to take a look at the bottles of vitamins and herbal medicines on a large rack. He had never seen so many of these items in one place. "That's a lot!" He thought. It inspired him to use the natural healing scheme again when needed.

Just then, he felt he weren't alone. A young girl stood behind him with nearly no hair. "G'day, sir." She said. Harris returned the "G'day' as well.

"Oy, I'm confused," She said, respectfully. "Why are there so many bottles of vitamins 'ere?"

Harris answered. "Well, there are so many because every one of them does a different job, you see." He pulled a bottle of St. Jon's Wort off the rack and showed her. "If your depressed, you take this one…" Then he pulled a bottle of Melatonin down. "…and this if you can't sleep. There's all sorts for a lot of things."

"Aye, I see." She said. "Well, 'fraid none of that would help me, then."

"Eh? What you got, luv?" Harris inquired.

"Leukaemia." She said matter-of-factually but with little sadness.

Harris felt sympathy for this young Sheila. No more than 12 and stuck with this sickness. "I see…" he said sadly. "What do you take for it, eh?"

"They give me pills of some sort, but they don't do jack. And the radiation treatments make me sicker than the leukaemia does."

"Yeah…" Harris said seriously. "Just the power of prayer, I guess."

"God doesn't answer my prayers," She said, looking down.

"Well, he answers all prayers. Sometimes the answer is no." Harris said. "Not sure why that would be, but our parents don't always say yes, do they?"

"Yeah, that's true." She said.

Harris knew what he had to do here. "What's your name, girl?"

"Lisa," She said. "Lisa Muldoon."

"Lisa, I'm…John Lloyd." Harris said not wishing to reveal his real name.

Harris stayed on his one knee. He took his hat from the disguise kit in one hand and held it over his left hand while he blessed himself with his right and aimed it on her back where he was sure no one would see. "I'll pray with you now."

She bowed her head as Harris spoke. "Dear God, it may be too much to ask for you to cure Lisa but do please help her in this trying time for her sake…Amen." With that, he stood upright again after shooting his light into her back.

"You are blessed, Lisa…Always remember that."

She looked up at him and said, "Thank you." With that, she held her mouth and felt a terrible thirst. "Pardon me!" and ran for the back of the store where the large transparent fridges kept juices and fizzy drinks. She went for the first bottle she could find which was a bottle of Catawba grape juice and drank it all in one go. Her mum was in the queue for something and called her over.

"Lisa! Whatever are you doing, girl?"

"Sorry, Mum…I just came over with the worst thirst ever!" Lisa responded, holding the now empty bottle. Her mum, wide-eyed, took the empty bottle to add to their shopping items. Lisa then pointed to the currently vacant space near the vitamins. "See, I was praying with that man over there at the…Where'd he go?"

Harris was well out the door with his hat and fake glasses on and a shopping sack in his hand as he disappeared into a thick crowd of Christmas shoppers as he exited the shopping centre and made his way back toward The Petrol Shop which would lead him to the small home his companions occupied. He was about to turn the corner when he heard a couple of loud blasts.

Two men ran out of the shop with one holding a shotgun and the other with a sack shouting "Go, go, go!!!"

They jumped in a Ford Falcon and sped off while Harris hid behind a large dustbin. He ran into the shop to hear the gasp of someone behind the counter. He ran up to find blood everywhere, and a clerk was bleeding from a shotgun wound, suffering in agony. Another customer came in, not knowing what was happening.

"A man was shot here! Call 999!" Harris shouted at him. The man nodded and ran out to a public phone on one side of the building. Harris went behind the counter and held the man by his back and healed him with no regard to hiding the light as the counter obscured their view from the rest of the store. The man was recovered in 20 seconds or so, his breathing back to normal and his pain subsided.

"You all right then?" Harris asked. The man in his 20's just nodded in bewilderment and stood up looking horrified at the tell-tale blood on his shirt. He stood up and then ran to the fridge for a bottle of some liquid refreshment. Harris slipped out the door where the other customer was making a call to emergency services on the phone close to the shop wall.

Harris walked quickly toward Jacob Street with his shopping bag in hand where his fellow Xenons were hiding. Gilliam and Helga were out front, both smoking with their hands in an odd, underhanded angle like the disguise book mentioned and saw Harris head their way. He didn't bother to take notice that the bag he carried was covered in blood, nor that the two men were following him from the petrol station.

"Hey!!! Wait!!!" The clerk shouted with his shirt covered in blood and ripped to shreds.

"Hey, who are you?" The customer said as he dropped his phone a moment ago to join the chase.

This time it was Helga who drew back her hand and formed a ball of lightning with it in front of Harris that caused him to stop in fear.

She threw two glowing balls at the men, and they exploded in bright light and loud pop sounds. They then looked around as if they had no idea what they were doing there. After Gilliam motioned for Harris to enter, the three Xenons went into the tiny house and shut the door leaving the pair of humans unsure what just happened. The humans walked back to the store while police vehicles and an ambulance were parking at The Petrol Shop ready to serve, as it were.

"How'd you get blood on ya, mate?" The now-confused customer asked the clerk.

The clerk looked down at his destroyed shirt and went "Ack!" and felt a bit ill even though he now had no physical injuries.

Harris went up to Helga before they joined the others in their group and tapped her on the shoulder. "Danke, Frauline." She patted him on the cheek, "Wilkommen." She said.

The group of Xenons were in the small living area getting ready for their exit. Harris went and had one more discussion with his grandfather.

"Grandfather, what will you do now?" Harris asked.

"I vil not be standing idly by vile der vorld passes, mein boy," Unger answered. "There vill alvays be something for me to do. Mein Ruth here has it in her head she owes me for rescuing her so long ago. Vee vere in a place ve didn't vant to be und the more vee stays together, the better off vee be. Maybe she right about that."

"Harris, you got everything?" Helmut asked.

"Yeah, I'm coming." He said.

"Just be good and be true to yourself, Harris," Unger said. "Vee are all proud of you." Unger finished as he patted his shoulder and smiled.

Harris then went over to Gilliam and Helga. "Good luck, young Harris. You vill do vell in life...I do know it, for fact." Gilliam said.

"Thank you...Danke...both of you." Harris said.

Ruth and Helmut had hashed out where to land, and Helmut said his goodbyes to his father. Mainly, he was relieved he would be alive and well here and to keep in contact as much as possible. Ruth went to Helmut and kissed him on both sides of the cheek. "Merci...Thank you for everything." She went to Harris and did the same. "Merci, Harris...you will make the fine doctor."

"Thank you," Harris said as he picked up his bag with his carry pack and the carton of wine bottles that he bought...minus three vessels for his fellow travellers.

Ruth made a large and then small circle in the air producing a vortex to appear in mid-air that showed a bus shelter in a dark London street. The father and son stepped into the portal and went from sunny and hot Brisbane, Australia at 2 pm to a cold London suburb at 4 am. It was then that Harris realised he was still in short pants!

He quickly opened his bag and slipped on his blue jeans and jumper in a dark bus shelter while Helmut, similarly dressed, borrowed his anorak. At least they didn't have far to go as they were on Essex Street and practically home. Harris took the occasion to look at the Ravalli's house which, of course, was dark and inactive at this time of night. They went into the house after Harris dug out his key. Helmut, shivering, told Harris that they would fetch mum tomorrow and that she was safe. Harris just went up to his bedroom to read, rather than sleep.

So, let's see…Harris thought. "In the past 24 hours, we had travelled well over 20,000 miles, been shot and recovered, disposed of a Nazi, saved a little girl from leukaemia and restored the relationship between a father and son (and grandfather and grandson.) All that and even had time to go Christmas shopping.

Indeed, A day well spent.

Chapter 40 – Christmas at home

Harris was still getting acclimated to what time of day it was. He had already slept enough, so he wrapped a couple of Christmas gifts from the blood-covered shopping bag. It was about 8 in the morning when he heard Mum return to the house.

"Mum, hi!" Harris said and greeted her with a short hug.

"Glad to see you both." She said as Da walked in behind her. "Everything all right, then?"

"It was interesting, to say the least," Harris replied.

"Well, you can tell me all about it later." She said. "Now that the panic is over, I can get back to planning dinner for my family. Your Uncle Thomas will arrive Wednesday, and I still have to get a bottle of brandy for him."

"Oh, I took care of that," Harris said and went over to the carton of wine bottles and picked out the bottle of Australian Brandy he picked up yesterday.

"Well done, son." She said as she looked at the label. "Product of Australia, eh? …Well, that should be different." She said as she happily went to the kitchen with the bottle.

"Da, you got a minute?" Harris asked.

"Of course, son…" Helmut said, "Let's talk upstairs.

They went into Harris's room where Helmut sat on the desk chair while Harris sat on the edge of the bed. "So, you probably want to ask about Richter, right?" Helmut asked.

"Well, I was going to ask where Mum was," Harris replied. "But since you brought him up…"

"Well, Karl Richter tried to rebuild his power on two other, separate occasions," Helmut said as he crossed his leg and played, nervously, with his shoe. "Now that the Wall fell in Berlin, he had it in his head that the east would be willing to attempt to corrupt the west again, and the use of Xenons would be an easy means to the end."

"Da, our kind are not easily liked or trusted…" Harris said. "What made him think he could gain control of them?"

"He is very good at influencing people," Helmut said.

"Well, don't you mean "was" good at it? After all, he probably wouldn't last in Antarctica." Harris stated.

"I am hoping that is the case, son," Helmut responded. "We don't need him making anything or anyone do his bidding…again!"

"Da, you make him sound like he's a…" Harris stopped with a gasp. "Do you happen to know any humans?" He asked sarcastically.

"It's as you said, son…he's probably on ice." Helmut said.

Helmut felt it essential to change the subject right then and there…

"So, your Mum…yeah," Helmut said. "I sent her to hide in plain sight…she was at the Ravalli's."

"…And what abilities do they have?" Harris asked exasperated. "Can they fly or turn invisible?"

"Son, please!" Helmut spoke up. "I sent her there just in case we got followed home. I hired a taxi to drive to Birmingham and back again and made a huge spectacle of making it seem she was in the car. The Ravalli's owed our family a debt of gratitude for Vincent and for something else Magdalena wouldn't divulge… I gather, you know?"

Harris just nodded.

"I just told them to take care of her until we got back, and I left it at that," Helmut said. "No one was in danger here. Not your Mum, nor those two."

"What about Gina?" Harris asked.

"She's not there yet," Helmut said. "She'll be in tomorrow night."

"Good…OK." Was all Harris would say.

"Anyway, they were very receptive to allowing her company," Helmut said. "Everything worked out fine, and that's that."

There was a moment of silence between them to take it all in.

"It was quite an adventure." Harris then said.

"Aye, that it was," Helmut said. "Let's go see what your mum is up to."

Time passed as it always did with the arrival of the relatives. Aunt Minnie came in from Portsmouth along with Rick, her young, 5-year-old nephew, bringing with him a few toys he just received and played with underfoot that included building blocks and a hand-held video game from his Dad. Jane and Wendy also visited from Watford along with their husbands who brought small token gifts along with them. Mark, who was Jane's husband, even gave Harris a gift as well. It was a reflex hammer that looked expensive. Arthur and Wendy got him a new shirt which was something that he needed right now.

Harris excused himself for a bit to see what Gina looked like now. He put on his hat and glasses that had served him well in Oz and hung out at the new bus shelter, that was built just recently, with a newspaper for a half-hour in the cold weather to see a cab pull up to the door and saw his high school beloved walk into her childhood home…along with a man that she kissed, romantically. They went into the house with a few pieces of luggage.

It was gut-wrenching at first, but it became all right as time went on. Gina had moved on and appeared happy. She took no notice of Harris as he sat behind a newspaper as his camouflage, as subtle as it was. Harris felt it was time to move on with his life just as she moved on with hers. After they were out of sight, he returned to #2 Essex Street and joined his lot for Christmas. The young doctor then handed out the bottles of wine, save one for his best college mate and one for the Ravalli's. Rick received a boomerang from Harris that he purchased very recently.

Harris himself received a gift from his Da in the form of an old, albeit unused Doctor's bag to go along with Unger's stethoscope he received the year previous. Helmut had to show Harris how to open it as it had a trick lock. The young doctor in training looked at his lot and counted his blessings. He was just where he needed to be right now and lucky to have whom he had in his family.

Chapter 41 – Meanwhile...

New adventures would be upcoming as the New Year countdown rolled to the end of 1989. Harris never wanted to join the revellers at Big Ben when the clock struck midnight on New Year's Eve. Not only because of the crowds being so frightening to him but that he now had no one to kiss on the stroke of 12, so he stayed up and watched the telly with his parents. All the excitement and none of the worry about getting back home.

There was a news programme that came on that reviewed the significant events that happened that year, including the bombing he was privy to in North Limerick. He was out of sight of the camera as it was all pointed to the grandfather, called Luke O'Keane weeping and screaming at the sky while holding in his arms his dead granddaughter. The older adult, in question, was quoted saying that "He wanted to see no reprisal, personally, for the bombing. There will be no peace if we continue this path of blowing each other to bits." The man took "Without forgiveness, there is only death" to the maximum! Harris didn't believe he could feel the same way if he were in his boots. The price of being human...or himself.

The year in review continued with the usual recap of football and cricket tournaments and news of the Royal Family. All the things that many people cared about more than him. In America, Times Square would be lit up with rock music and a giant diamond that dropped on Broadway. He toasted with his Mom and Da, "Here's to better days!" and, basically, headed off to bed. The Americans had another 5 hours of waiting for their Happy New Year. The only reason that came to mind was that his Uncle Thomas said that he would be in that New York City crowd now that he was back home in the states.

Elsewhere in the world, a man watched the same year in review programme in his home in Ireland. The man was called Edmond Haberl, who would now be a professor at the Royal College of Medicine in Cork, IR. His daughter, Rhona, attended classes there as well two years ahead of Harris. His time as a former forensics' detective were, sometimes, still requested by the Gardai in Limerick and elsewhere. He had been charged to find any further clues that had to do with the bombing on Remembrance Day and to present his findings as to the perpetrators of this murderous action.

Sadly, there was nothing to note after investigations took place, and it became an act of war that claimed several civilian lives in the horrible attack.

Rhona was out with friends at a New Year's Eve party while his misses, Marie Haberl, was content to sleep in her favourite chair. She was one to feel it was just another night. Edmund watched the broadcast and the brief clip of the attack at the cenotaph. It was then he noticed something odd. Something they all missed, previously…

During the video of the poor grandfather O'Keane clutching the lifeless body of his kin in his arms, he noticed a pair of legs lying behind the man and granddaughter. In the span of a few moments, the legs jumped up and ran off the screen. It was the most fantastic thing Edmund had seen. To jump up after that bomb went off was curious to the former officer. He then remembered that he had a copy of the original video lying in his office. To make sure he missed nothing, he fired up the untouched tape of the massacre there on the video he had set up exclusively for times like these.

The grandfather was well out of sight while Orla Moore sang her hymn to the small crowd gathered there. The bomb went off, killing her with blunt force trauma to the head. (The Gardai and the medical examiner confirmed this report later in the week.) The boy who read the poem earlier was standing close to the stage as Orla sang, so he took a large piece of the damage as well. He was on the ground laying on his stomach as a man, who appeared just a bit older, stood over him and proceeded to rip large pieces of debris out of his back.

This part stunned Edmund as he couldn't see anyone standing again after something like that, let alone surviving. The extraction of foreign objects was followed by what seemed to be a trick of the light. A beam from his hands that looked like it came from a torch shined on the boy. The man ran out of frame from the camera shot, and the injured boy stood up a moment later. Not only did he exit the scene but ran as he was doing it. Quite surprising for someone who had just suffered an obviously, massive spinal injury!

Edmund rewound and replayed this scene repeatedly even as the clock went past midnight and the world was celebrating the passage of time and the entry into a new decade. His wife stayed asleep through the celebrations as he tried to comprehend the scene before him on the video screen. Unfortunately, the face of the man delivering the lifegiving beam had his facial features obscured by the poor quality of the video. He could make out just enough to put together a basic profile. He was Caucasian, brown-haired and quite young. Maybe between late teens to his early '20s?

He finally put the tape to rest after several viewings and went back to the world of the current. There was no crime on the part of the mysterious man. It was just fascinating to watch someone that severely injured snap back to health under those conditions. Edmund would not forget the activities of this life-giver standing over the boy, whoever he was.

Was he an angel? An alien? ...A Xenon? The latter seeming to be the least likely. After all, Xenons were terrible creatures who wanted only to bring destruction. More than likely, they would have planted the bomb in the first place. Maybe even working with the IRA. The responsibility for the bombing, it was announced, was claimed by Sein Fiene. They had set a time bomb to go off when a parade of British soldiers was to pass. However, it was mistakenly set to go off an hour later than it should have.

Harris was unaware of all this as he was at his own childhood home to pay a visit to his family for a holiday and to visit his former boss and patient, Vincent Ravalli at his gym. Harris stayed friends with the father of his former girlfriend and even had a standing invitation to work for him again. He also presented Vincent, along with a bottle of Australian red wine, his thoughts toward his daughter. He harboured no disrespect toward her and wished her the best. Vincent offered no opinion to Gina's new boyfriend. Whatever made her happy was her own business.

All good things had to end as Harris said his goodbyes to his Mum and Da as they saw him off from their door as Harris took the cab back to Heathrow Airport.

Chapter 42 – Lonely Boy

An hour at Heathrow, an hour in the air and only ten minutes at the airport in Cork when Harris caught the bus home. Everything was well-timed and ready to go as classes would start on 8 January and run until 18 May. He opened the door and saw an anorak in the hall that belonged to Roland. He also heard subtle snoring in his room, so he let him go and put on the telly to an episode of Countdown as he grabbed a beer and a mug out of the kitchen cabinet. Harris thought Roland would do well on that show as he was a master with words from doing the crosswords out of The Guardian as a hobby.

Roland came stumbling out of his room at 4 pm in pyjama pants and a Tipperary Hurling Team shirt. He grabbed a bottle of the lager from the cabinet while Harris held up his bottle and shouted "Hey mate! Happy new year." Roland just put his finger to his lips and said "Shh!" He did wave "Hi" with the bottle of Aries Brew and went back to his room. Harris assumed he was still hungover. New Year's Day was a couple of days ago, so he wondered how much of the cider he got into?

Harris got lucky with the Telly. The Kilkenny vs Cork Hurling Match kept his mind occupied for the next couple of hours until Roland got awake but still retained the headache. The game was finishing when Harris held out his hand without speaking, and Roland just walked into it to receive the light of healing to end his hangover.

He then walked to the kitchen and just waited for the thirst to kick in. It did a few seconds later, and Roland had a glass of water to finish the pain off with leaving his head bright and alert. He brought another glass of water into the room with him.

"Hey, thanks for the disguise kit," Harris said. "It came in handy over the holiday."

Roland just gave him an acknowledging wave.

"So, mate," Harris said. "How'd your holiday go?"

Roland took his place in the reclining, comfy chair and seemed frustrated that he missed the match.

"I just had the most bizarre fortnight ever!" Roland said. Harris thought in the back of his mind; "Mate, you have no idea what bizarre is…" but let him go on…

"I was to stay at Tamar's place and to room with her bratty little brothers. That's all right…I had two myself. Her sisters were friendly at first, and then even more so as time went on. I started to get really uncomfortable."

"How many sisters does she have?" Harris asked.

"Five, then…two of them were very young, so they were more interested in their dolls than me, but the other three got close…I mean personal space close. One tried to pull me into her room and another into a broom press…and that one was just 13!"

Roland took another large gulp of water.

"I was figurin' I got lucky her Mum didn't see that. Her Dad was at hospital until late. I told Tamar what was going on, but she couldn't believe it…then while me girl wasn't looking, her Mum made a play for me!" Roland said with panic and disbelief in his voice.

"Wow!" Was all Harris could say.

"I couldn't go on…I just stayed at the hotel down the road from them." Roland then said, sadly. "It was so frustrating. All I wanted was to celebrate Christmas with my new girlfriend and not have all this happen. She came over, and we just celebrated together. I just said I was more comfortable there."

Harris was stunned. "So…what did you two do, together?" was all he asked.

"Well, we just watched telly and exchanged gifts," Roland said. "She went back to her lot, and I said I was going to visit my family, then. They all wondered where I was. I told her to say I had a family emergency and had to be off."

"What did you do?" Harris asked.

"I just went home," Roland said. "My mum is still a bit cross that I found my Dad again, but that wasn't the big thing. It turned out I couldn't stay there, either."

"Why not?" Harris asked.

"My sister, Alice. She made me very uncomfortable being there…Did I tell you she was adopted?"

Harris realised that Roland told him very little of his family…only that he had one.

"You didn't tell me…Hang on!" Harris said. "Your sister and you…"

"Yeah…" Roland said. "I woke up, and she was in bed with me…In the nip!!! Wearing only socks!!! I packed up and left before mum found us together."

Roland continued. "I met up with me Dad for a bit in Magherafelt. That didn't go any better what with all his friends being…Well, I was getting the eye there as well. I didn't stay, or someone might have tried something. I don't know if it was paranoia, but figured it was best not to risk it."

Harris was now getting depressed for his friend. "So, what did you do for the rest of the time?"

"What else could I do?" He asked. "I went to the only place left I could go and be safe…here!"

That would figure as everyone was out for the holidays. Roland would be lonely here, though.

"Does anyone else know you're here already? Harris asked.

"I don't think so," Roland said. "Otherwise, I might have had people try to get close here." He then asked his best friend; "Harris, why you think this is happening to me?"

Harris had just one explanation to offer; "Mate, I think I know…first, did you handle Tamar at all since you both got together? Just, out with it then!"

"Well, we snogged a bit, here and there. That's all so far, though. Tamar's just so great without having to…"

"Does she know you're here?" Harris interrupted.

"I haven't talked to her since I took off over Christmas. I said that I would be better off at home away from everyone else."

"Mate, listen…You need to call her and get her here…And shag her!" Harris blurted out. Roland was surprised at that comment from his friend.

"I can't just do that!" Roland said.

"Mate, look!" Harris said. "Every female since you stopped having them has been giving you the "glad-eye!" It's probably just building up with you, whatever it is, that's getting these birds wanting you! You need to either take Tamar or be taken by someone else…It's just getting to that point, now!"

Roland didn't realise all the birds were looking at him like that since he went celibate. Roland got up and went to the phone. "This is not going to be easy to explain!" he shouted from the hall where the phone sat on the table. Harris went to his room to give him privacy. He was hoping this would all be sorted before tomorrow when everyone came home from the Christmas holiday.

Chapter 43 – Day of the Living

Tamar couldn't get to Cork until the next morning. She was wondering where Roland had got to after she left the hotel. The tricky thing was that Roland felt explaining this to her would mean she would toss him.

The nearest locals were several homes down, so they started wondering if anyone else was going to try to get close to Roland. He even began putting on manky aftershave in a futile attempt to keep the birds away. The other students were just beginning to return to their dorms and housing.

Many factors were going through their heads right now. How far would Roland's "appeal" go and how many would be coming for a "visit." There were over 8,000 students enrolled here and Roland and Harris only knew a couple dozen or so, but that might not stop others from showing up. Would Roland have trouble from men, like those of his father's persuasion?

Tamar came over at about 10 am or so and visited Roland at his flat. They greeted each other with a chaste kiss and went into his room to talk. Harris just read in the living room. For a while, the only noise in the flat was Harris eating crisps. There were, then, sounds of growing anger coming from Roland's bedroom. Apparently, he did not make his case well enough, and Tamar was about ready to storm out. Harris caught her before she left.

"Roland, what are you playing at?" She asked. "If you want me, you can have me. You don't have to spin tales making me look like a cheap tart!"

"Dear, that's the last thing I would want to do!" He said. "I just wanted to be truthful and give you what you wanted...You said you wanted to be pure for your wedding night. You mean more to me than anyone, and I want to be true to you!"

Tamar heard all of this and couldn't believe any of it. Roland wasn't ugly but all this discussion of women throwing themselves at his feet...

"Seriously..." She said as she was walking out the door "I know Harris has his extraordinary abilities but all of this..." She stopped speaking after she stepped out the door and noticed the incoming horde of women...and a couple of men were walking down Brown Way ready to turn toward Savage Street. One of them being Todd Hunter!

Harris just thought, quickly "Todd? I would never have guessed!"

Tamar stepped back inside their flat. "What is this?"

Harris rushed her back into their flat and let his theory out on the two of them. "Listen...Roland hasn't touched another woman since we all met." He said with all sincerity. "I think that whatever he has in him is building up and getting into people's psyche. Harris continued as Tamar was absorbing all of it. "Roland has his choice of every woman out there. He wants you and you alone. He wants nothing more than to please you." Roland could only stand there and nod.

The crowd was getting closer, causing Harris to push the chair from the living room into the front of the door. Tamar looked out the window. It looked like a scene from Night of the Living Dead out there with better-looking zombies, some in make-up, some in club wear and a few in lingerie...Gutsy move as it was still January!

Tamar grabbed Roland by the arm and dragged him into his room and slammed the door behind them. Harris took his place to guard the house. First, he secured the backyard door by pushing the fridge in front of it and defended the windows with the golf club kept by the door for self-defence. A window shattered causing Harris to push Carol Patterson back through the window. How was he going to explain away all this to the landlords? "Sorry, Carol!" He said knowing she would probably forget it all, anyway.

From Roland's bedroom, there was screaming of delight. "Great, it's noisy enough here! Now that!" He thought.

Harris even thought about calling out the Gardai but had no idea how to explain this ridiculous situation! The chair was beginning to buckle as it served its duty wedged under the doorknob and pushed to the floor with the banging on the door and window.

Suddenly, Roland screamed as well, and every noise from inside the bedroom and outside the doors and windows of the flat went silent. Harris just enjoyed the sound of silence for a moment that fell over the flat. He then went to the front door and pulled the chair away that was his only defence a moment ago from the onslaught. He slowly opened the door to many confused women who were there for no apparent reason. Harris had to think of something quickly to avoid any further problems...

"I'm sorry, everyone. It looks like the weather in New York had forced him to cancel his flight. He apologised and said, "perhaps another time."

The women were all still confused. "Who apologised?" A female student asked whom Harris didn't know.

"David Bowie, of course." He just threw it out as a go-to that would attract everyone there… "That is why you are all here, right?"

No one really knew why they were there. The women and men all turned and headed back up Brown Way off of Savage Street. After replacing the chair and fridge, Harris decided it would only be right to leave these two behind as it sounded like they were gearing up for round two. He grabbed his anorak and walked to the O'Deer's café for lunch.

He then thought about all this over his chips and eggs and how Tamar would be a regular part of his mate's life now. No doubt she would be there more often to keep the peace. Harris even felt a bit of jealousy for the two of them. Roland found what he wanted and chose the nurse from Limerick to be his "one and only," even after being spoiled for choice.

Harris's head drifted back to Gina, and he felt like stabbing his hand with a fork for thinking it. "You weak-minded fool!" He said to himself. "She moved on! You saw her coming out of the cab with her new guy…get over yourself!" He paid his chit and went to the library to continue to do what had served him so well in the past; Fully throwing himself into his work. His studies turned to the physiology of the liver — the class to be taught by Rhona Haberl's father, Edmund.

"Rhona…" He thought. "She wasn't the best bird in the cage, but she would be willing to go have fun with him…probably as long as she knew he wasn't a Xenon."

Her father, Edmund, was now in his office getting his lectures and lesson plans ready. In the back of his mind, he still wondered who it was that healed the young boy during the Remembrance Day bombing?

Chapter 44 – Time management

"OK, mate…we gotta stay calm." Harris said.

"I know…" Roland said. "There isn't a lot of time, though."

"Right…" Harris responded, "But we are men of medicine. We are far more intelligent than most."

"Yeah," Roland said. "This should not be a difficult challenge for us."

"Agreed," Harris said. "Tell me again what the book says, and we'll give it another go…. What time is it?"

"About ten minutes to five," Roland said.

"OK, I know we can do this…go on, then," Harris said, ready to take direction for this all-important task…

"The wire from the wall goes into the machine where it is marked "IN", and then the short wire is attached to the machine where it is marked "OUT," Roland said as he continued to read the video machine guide. "Black on black lettering where it says in and out…There's a genius at work, then!" Harris thought he attached the wire from the wall to the video machine.

"OK, where does this end go, then?" Harris asked. "… and don't tell me again to stuff it up my…"

…And with that, Tamar walked in.

"Hello, you two." She said as she greeted Roland with a passionate kiss. "What you both up to, then?"

"Just trying to hook up the video before we start studying," Harris said. "We get this done, and then we can be free to study and catch the game tonight."

"OK, good thinking" Tamar said, smiling. "By the way, the end you're holding goes into the telly. Harris didn't think he was standing there with a wire in his hand. He screwed the end into the set, and the game was set to begin.

"All right!" Harris said as he saw the two teams take the field. He put in the cassette and pushed the record button. "I hope that's right." He said. He turned the telly off and told his friend "OK, Roland…let's get down to it…"

But Roland and Tamar were not there. They were in Roland's room, making sure a repeat of what happened earlier that month didn't occur. Harris went into his dorm room and opened his new book about the functions of the liver and lower GI tract. Then there was a sound of screaming by Tamar and Roland pleasuring each other in the most intimate of ways. Harris put on his ever-faithful Walkman and turned the volume way up with a Depeche Mode cassette playing. He thought the next time that he should go to the library. At least there was nothing due yet as classes didn't start until the next day.

It was the first day back, and he was off to new classes for a new term. GI and Liver, Reproductive Health and Endocrine courses were in the mix in this term along with computer usage classes. Harris thought that with what he could do, how much of this did he need to know? He already knew what would be his Da's answer; "All of it!"

Dr Edmund Haberl took his place for the first time as a professor, so no one was sure what to expect from him. It would probably be a surprise to him as well. Roland and Harris took a seat with the rest of his colleagues. The women who were encroaching on their flat some time ago seemed to have no memory of what transpired that day.

"Cock," Harris said to his friend. "I got to hit the Jacks, like now!" Harris ran out knowing he should have skipped that last extra cup of tea that morning. "Don't take too long!" Roland said as his friend left the lecture hall. In the meantime, Dr Haberl entered the lecture hall and said, "Good Morning, Doctors!" A feeble "Good Morning" returned to him. It was early in the day, and many were not quite awake yet, especially after the long holiday.

Dr Haberl then took roll call with the last names shouted out and a loud "Present!" coming back at him. 30 students were role-called, 29 of them responded until Harris arrived. "Gibraltar, sir! Present!" He said to Dr Haberl and then took his seat. Dr Haberl was writing on the chalkboard when Harris came in, and he took his place next to Roland. They kept their seats together as their surnames were close: Fitzsimmons, Gibraltar...

It wasn't until halfway through the class that Dr Haberl got a good look at the face of the healing Xenon behind his desk. He felt it was familiar, somehow.

"Gibraltar, is it?" The man with the black and grey, kind of curled hair asked his pupil.

"Yes sir…. that be me," Harris said with all seriousness.

"Lad, have we met? Dr Haberl asked.

"I…don't believe so, sir," Harris answered, leaving Dr Haberl to shrug and continue with his basics of the liver lecture.

Well, nothing was new except the classes themselves. A ton of homework was assigned every week with practicals and reports due in a very narrow time frame. It seemed reproductive health would be uncomplicated, but the endocrine system and hepatology had more detail to go into, and most diseases and problems regarding these areas weren't easy to see on the surface.

Now there was also an additional class to go along with the medical work; that being computer classes. There were words bounded about like the Information Superhighway, The Web, Email, Chat rooms…It was easy to follow, but the computer was time-consuming in how long it took to get some information. The words would appear pretty quickly, but pictures would take a couple of minutes to come across. Someone was getting rich off all this as well. A few names from America were bounded about like Gates and Jobs.

Back at their flat, they would put the game on in the background, but Harris found it distracting. He went to his room and hovered over his desk with the music on. Now he could watch it whenever he had free time thanks to the magic of the videotape at home. Harris continued for the next hour until he felt he needed a break. He got up and went out to the living area for a score update and was cautious about side-stepping any indication about who won earlier that day. Roland had the same idea and was on the sofa with a bottle of ale in hand. Harris was about to take his place on the reclining chair when he suddenly remembered something.

"Oh yeah!" Harris said excitedly. "I forgot to give you your Christmas gift!" Roland remained on his seat while Harris got a bottle of cabernet sauvignon out of his room that he bought for his friend while briefly abroad.

"Oh, savage, mate! Thanks!" Roland responded and saw the receipt stuck to the bottle. He read it with disbelief.

"Australia?" Roland exclaimed. "When you go there?"

"Just before Christmas," Harris said. "I went to visit my grandfather."

"Nice," Roland said. "How long you stay?"

"About 6 hours," Harris said with Roland just looking, oddly. "It was just a whirlwind trip."

"I guess," Roland said. "Well, thanks for it, then. I guess I'll split it with Tamar next time."

Up to now, everything seemed tolerable. Tamar only came over on the weekends as she had her job during the week. They would go out during these evenings for a nice dinner. Harris wasn't in any hurry to pull any bird with all the studying he felt he needed to finish. There was a significant difference in him now and in his days as a young, punk teen. He then got to thinking "Did I always have this in me and just didn't care?" Something just felt amiss about the whole deal the more he thought about it. For now, he shrugged it off and got back to bile function and breakdown.

"HEY HARRIS!!!" Roland yelled from the living area. Harris ran into the room with Roland just still sitting there in his seat.

"Yasir?" He asked, "What's up?"

Roland rewound the end of the tape past the game but now into the News Night programme.

"I figured you best see this," Roland said and pushed play on the remote unit. The unemotional newsreader, Colin MacAfee, gave the report:

"Authorities are still flummoxed over the strange robbery that occurred just before Christmas in a Brisbane, Australia borough. New security video released this footage of a man who was gunned down behind the counter in a robbery that amassed only about £200...But the bizarre part of this story occurred just after the bandits left, and a man entered and administered some aid to the cashier that not only saved his life but was reported to have cured deafness in one ear that the cashier, reportedly, had suffered with for many years."

The video showed "The mystery man" running behind the counter on to the floor and out of sight of the cameras, a bright light appearing although the cashier and the man in question were too low to be seen. The store cameras did not catch the man in his hat and glasses. Those items looked precisely like the ones that Roland bought for him as a Christmas gift.

"Sodder!" Harris explained and fell into the recliner and covered his mouth with both hands.

"The unknown man who administered the aid remains at large. He is not wanted for arrest, of course, but police wish his assistance with their inquiries. The two men were…" With that, Roland stopped the tape.

A long silence passed before Harris said anything. Even then, he could only think to say, "I need more disguises."

Chapter 45- The Face in the Photograph

Harris kept up his usual routine. Studying, going to the gym, go to classes and then too tired to go on. He couldn't even watch the football matches until the weekends. Even then, he would have to fight to make time for it. Every minute of the day seemed to be taken up by his studies. Also, when Harris was working out, or biking on the cold Irish spring afternoons, he was concentrating on studying. Definitions and functions were always going through his head. What the endocrine system did, and all its features kept his brain busy. The possibility of becoming a pathologist crossed his mind several times. His father selected neuroscience, but Harris had other interests in terms of medical research. The new computers had access to all forms of information from medical libraries across Europe, America and other places. They still needed to be learned and memorised, though.

He would have also loved to hang out with Rhona Haberl more, but she was ahead of him in her fourth year while he was in his second. He could see her on some weekends. They went to the cinema every so often or even just made out in either of their rooms. Her workout for physical strength came on the hurling pitch. Harris didn't know how to feel. He did like her and all…but love? That wasn't coming to either of them, enough. Their company with each other would do for now.

Meanwhile, Edmund made it his business to find out who this mystery healer was. The positive identity, he felt, would be a longshot and perhaps this curiosity of alien biology was suitable enough to pursue, if not for law purposes, certainly for the scientific component. Edmund then reached out to his past Gardai brothers for help. He sent them a still shot of the video in the hopes of clearing up the face of the angel of mercy through a process called depixelisation. It was new science and not perfect, but Edmund took what help he could get. The photograph was sent to Dublin and Edmund was told to be patient as it would probably take a bit of time.

Rhona could pick up that Harris was not entirely into her, but they would stay close, regardless. He found her a fun bird to hang out with, and she felt about the same way about him. If they didn't last, they would, more than likely, part the best of friends.

A month later and the mail came for Edmund at his Limerick home containing what the Gardai in Dublin had retrieved from the video still of the mystery man. They were quite pleased with their results and believed Edmund would feel the same.

It was a Saturday in late March when the photo arrived by post. He had just removed the folder containing the photograph in question while in the foyer when the door opened, and Rhona entered to her mum and dad's surprise.

"Allo, dear! What brings you by?" Edmund asked his daughter with a hug.

"I'm afraid I got to get mom to help me with some clean clothes," Rhona said and with that, brought into the room a large bag of laundry. "I'm all out!"

"All right, dear," Marie said to her daughter. "I'll deal with these." With that, Edmund left the folder on the table in the foyer to enjoy the company of his daughter. Although they were on the same campus during the week, Rhona was off at local hospitals or far across campus in other sections of her studies. She was also up to her eyeballs in notes and meeting patients. Rhona stayed for dinner with her folks and her two brothers after they set an extra place at their dinner table. She then spoke of how difficult the classes were in her fourth year and how she met more and more actual people in the Cork hospitals. They both knew the school always did an excellent job of putting students together with graduate doctors and patients. After all, it was their job that they would be assisting with after graduation. Edmund knew all this as he went through the same training as Rhona many moons ago.

The early teen boys, Peter and Neil, went to their room to play video games. Marie went to watch telly in the living room and put on the programme, Glenroe. Rhona was returning from the loo to join her mom in front of the set when she knocked down the folder containing the photograph on the foyer table. She picked it up and looked at the face and was shocked by who she saw.

Her father had to run out to the off-licence to buy a few bottles for the evening's match later. He returned home to find his ordinarily happy daughter seething with anger as he entered his house. He took one look at her and thought "Uh-oh!"

"Um…What's on your mind, dear?" He asked, wondering why she was scowling.

"Dad, look…" She said, restraining her anger as best she could. "You want to know whom I'm going out with you just come and ask me! You don't need to put one of your men on 'em like a suspect! I'm a big girl now and don't need a follow!"

Edmund had no idea what she meant.

"What are you on about, Rhona?" He said as calmly as he could. He always kept his civility when interviewing the accused in his Gardai days. He did his best here as well to keep himself in check. That was when she threw the photograph in the folder at her father and said, "Tell your cronies to mind their own fecking' store!!!" She then stormed to her room which remained hers while she was studying in Cork. The sound of a door slammed shut followed her exit.

Edmund was flummoxed. He didn't know what she was speaking of until he picked up the particular photograph from the floor and out from the envelope. The familiar face of one of his students was clear and concise as Edmund continued to stare at the picture.

"Bloody hell!" He exclaimed, quietly as he ran into his office. He just wanted to get a better image of the man in the photograph. He didn't expect an identity reveal like this! Then another thought crossed him. "My daughter is dating him!" Edmund knew that saying anything to Rhona right now would be like throwing petrol on a car fire, so he let it go for now with her. What was he to do now? There was no crime apparent, but he was still a...Xenon, was it?

He then felt duty-bound to say something but how to explain all this? So, he called and left a message on the answering machine at the college for Monday: "Beep!"

"Chancellor Rosewood, this is Professor Edmund Haberl. I need to speak to you first thing, Monday. You may consider this important..."

Meanwhile, Harris was unaware of all this as he was at a dorm party at Nelson Nghegdela's flat as they celebrated the freeing of Nelson Mandela. It was the South African's namesake, after all. He stayed to raise a glass to the freedom fighter after nearly 30 years of his incarceration. Harris was home within two hours of hanging out with his fellow students with no idea of what he had waiting in store for him the next week.

Chapter 46 – How Do You Solve a Problem Like Harris?

Somehow, Edmund Haberl didn't feel right about unmasking the activities of Harris Gibraltar. Again, there was no crime here. Just the fact that a Xenon dared to educate himself here in Cork was something he felt needed the attention of the College Chancellor. Perhaps it was that he felt protective of his daughter?

He brought the videotape to Chancellor Rosewood. As they viewed the unedited portions of the scene, Edmund pointed out the man pulling debris out of the teen boy's back. How, with a trick of the light, the young boy was able to not only stand again but run away from the scene of the blast. With that, he also showed the photograph of Harris Gibraltar at the area where the terrorist bombing occurred. He also gave a quick explanation of how depixelisation worked. Nothing too technical as he didn't fully understand the process, himself.

"I know this boy!" Ian said, excitedly. "I spoke to him last year after nearly being killed by a local goon!"

Chancellor Rosewood then did what all men in his position would do…He called an emergency meeting.

A clandestine gathering of twenty-or-so professors converged around the meeting table late on a Tuesday night. At first, this bothered the professors as they had their own work to do to keep their classes running smooth. They sat at the boardroom table in a large semi-circle and viewed the same video presentation shown to the Chancellor, earlier on a massive telly set up for the members. Edmund continued to stress that no crime had been committed here…only that the lad was believed to be a Xenon.

"Ladies and gentlemen…" Ian Rosewood said to his medical colleagues. "Our position here is murky, at best. This apparent Xenon has come to us as no more a student in the medical arts. He appears to have no agenda that would suggest he was dangerous. He has also not used this special "gift" that he possesses on anyone for any purpose while here, good or bad, as far as we know."

There was a murmur in the ranks of the gathered doctors…

"How are his marks?" Doctor Murray Simmons of the paediatrics medicine section asked.

"Impressive." Chancellor Rosewood answered. "In fact, Extraordinary. His errors have been few and far between. He has shown that he has dedicated himself to his studies fully."

"What about his parents?" Dr Robert Alton of the Oncology Department asked. "These things tend to be generational."

Ian quickly looked through the notes of Helmut Gibraltar that Edmund collected via a couple of phone calls. "Over 20 years of service with Saville Hospital in London…Currently, he's the chief neurosurgeon there with a spotless, remarkable record…nothing special there, though, for his father. His mother is the same way as she worked for a few charities and churches in the Central London area."

"Why do you believe he's here if he could already accomplish this?" Doctor April Cole, Harris's reproductive medicines professor asked.

"If I were a betting man, I would say it was to be able to access patients without restriction," Rosewood responded. "He could have taken any other path to get near the sick and unfortunate. He could have been a medic, a nurse…even a custodian. He wants this and is prepared to take the high ground to get there."

"Doctors, can we please get on to the main point here?" Dr Gail Turner of the Obstetrics studies department and another one of Harris's leading professors chimed in… "This is, after all, a Xenon! No good can come of this!"

"Dr Turner, I will admit unfavourable news about Xenons in the world inundates us, often." Chancellor Rosewood said. "But we can't fault every single Xenon for all the evils outside these walls."

"No, but they have certainly contributed to it." Doctor Rick Tremper of the Neurology department said. "Not to mention that if this got out, imagine what it would do to future enrolment!"

Murmurs of discussion went flying in between each professor's comments. It made the meeting sound more like a session of Parliament than a college meeting. Next came Shanna Avis who was not a doctor but the teacher of computer sciences: "Look… He has contributed no evil intention to anything or anyone thus far. Why are we so bent to believe that he would do so? The feelings of this lot are ones of paranoia, more than logic. As men and women of science, we should hold ourselves better than this."

"Oh, come now, Shanna!" Dr McCurdie said in her own slow and self-righteous demeanour. "It's how they build your confidence and then when you don't have your eye on them, these foxes rob your hen-house…and everything therein."

"All right then! Enough of this conjecture!" Ian Rosewood said, trying to bring order to this mob. "We are, indeed, men and women of science." He then took a sip from his water glass. "We don't go and interrupt a student's education with "What if's?" We owe a certain level of awe and admiration to this young man."

Dr Rosewood considered the looks he was getting from his fellow professors. "Let us put a possible solution on the table…If anyone can offer one up?" The table fell silent until Dr McCurdy offered one:

"The answer is simple: We simply accuse him of cheating and load his files with possible moments of such."

The 20 or so doctors at the table gasped in shock as they expressed their anger to such a foul solution. Not only because of its purely evil context but for being proposed by the college's ethics instructor!

"I'll pretend I have not heard that, Edna!" Ian said. "Not only because of the source but because of the past occurrence of the cheating scandal at this college in '72. That occurrence resulted in thirty-eight expulsions and five discharges of past professors. It also installed me as the present chancellor here!"

Chancellor Rosewood thought for a moment. If Harris Gibraltar showed them that he was only there for education and the betterment of everyone, and Harris would be a success that they could look upon as a testament to their prowess as educators. He then related this thought to the gathered men and women of medicine and science. Again, a murmur from the table of professors suggesting most agreed…

"Ian, If I may make a suggestion…" Prof. Haberl finally spoke. "I believe you are correct, although I would suggest that we test him ourselves before we send him out with just the proof of this one video."

Reality then set back into Chancellor Rosewood. "I cannot argue with that logic Edmund," Ian said with a sigh. "I want to believe the hype that we have set to this young man. It would take another spectacular act to accomplish this. One that we all could see occur and one that would hold testament to his abilities." They all sat agreeing with a hushed mumble.

"Now, what kind of act?" Ian asked. "Do we all sit around waiting for a disaster to occur?" Again, silence from the gathered professors.

"Aye, that's the rub." Chancellor Rosewood said as he took a file on his desk that contained Harris Gibraltar's records and notes, closed it and tapped it on the table to straighten its contents. "It isn't like a solution will just fall into our laps."

His tapping of the file was too close to the edge of the table, and all the papers fell over him onto the floor.

"Oh, Bugger!" He exclaimed as he put the papers back into the file folder. He then found an article that he intended to talk about regarding upcoming mission trips, and an idea occurred to him as he quickly read the article…that fell into his lap!

"Well, I'll be damned!" He said.

Chapter 47 – At the Bequest of the College...

Harris, of course, was unapprised of the meeting in his "honour." He was busy with studying and trying to keep up with his avalanche of practicals and reports. He, finally, just put aside trying even to watch sports as he had barely enough time to take care of his own physique. He could hardly take the time to watch Rhona on the weekends on the hurling pitch, either. That one hurt the most.

Roland was as much in the same boat with barely enough time to meet with his girlfriend. Tamar did her best to understand as she was in his position when she studied to become a nurse in Limerick.

At the beginning of April, Harris received a note on his door requesting him to join Tamar and Roland for dinner in town at Bartell's Bistro on South Mall Street near The River Lee. They wanted Harris along with them for dinner that weekend.

"Sure, why not?" He thought.

They were not the only ones requesting Harris's company. The office of the Chancellor called and left a message on the phone answering machine that asked for his attendance that Friday afternoon right after his reproductive science class at about 4:30. Harris's schedule included two hours of each class with an hour break in between. Harris believed that it had something to do with his grades being high. Were they questioning his intelligence?

Harris showed up at Dr Rosewood's office not even thinking he was to meet with Chancellor Rosewood, himself. He had only met him one-time last year after Harris's stabbing incident to ask if he were of the mind to continue after such a vicious attack. Harris, of course, did continue and stayed at the top of the game as he came up to the end of his second year of studies.

Harris was then invited into the Chancellor's office by Dr Rosewood, himself. Harris was still unaware of why he was there. Ian then took Harris's file and reviewed it with Harris:

"Right... Harris Unger Nicklaus Gibraltar. You were born in 1968 in Bern, Switzerland to Helmut and Jean Gibraltar. You resided in Chelsea for most of your days and attended St. Joseph's Academy until you attended here."

"Yes, sir, correct," Harris responded.

"Your father, Helmut Gibraltar, has been the head of the Neurology department for the past decade at Saville Hospital, London." The Chancellor said.

"Also correct, sir," Harris responded.

Chancellor Rosewood then asked with all sincerity. "Tell me, Harris…What made you decide to become a doctor?"

Harris wasn't about to tell the total truth here. "It's in our family tree, sir." He said. "My father is a doctor; my grandfather was one as well. It was in the legacy of the family that I should join the ranks of serving in the medical field."

"I see," Ian said. With that, Ian played on a television screen near his desk the news report of the bombing in Limerick and Orla Moore's killing.

"Have you seen this report?" Ian asked.

Harris was starting to get an ill feeling inside. "I have sir…I believe most of the UK has by now."

Ian then changed the tape and played the view that was unedited and encompassed the full picture of him pulling debris out of the back of a teenage boy. The trick of the light, Harris's face obscured by low video resolution and the young boy running off the screen. Harris leaned a bit toward the video screen.

"Chancellor, I have not seen this video before," Harris said.

"Few have." He said to Harris with a concerned look on his face. "The low video appearance made identifying the man who cured this boy nearly impossible to identify."

"Nearly?" Harris thought as he got an even worse feeling inside.

"Other techniques were employed," Ian said and with that, presented Harris with the photograph obtained by the Gardai of Dublin his face from the video in more than enough detail to show that Harris was the miracle worker of the area. Harris slumped in the chair across from Chancellor Rosewood and sighed as he put his head in his hands.

"Well, that's that then." He said with contempt to the Chancellor. "So where are the Gardai or am I to have a running start?"

"Harris, no one is calling anyone right now," Ian said which kind of surprised Harris. "To send you out would be killing a golden goose…to turn a phrase."

That gave some relief to Harris, but what was to come?

"So…what of it, then?" Harris asked. "Expulsion? My test grades are stellar and always have been!"

"Yes, I am well aware of that." The Chancellor said. "You can handle taking care of a patient's physical injuries. What else can you do?"

Harris then spoke with pride as he seemed to have nothing to lose. "I can cure heart attacks, strokes, cancers…venereal and viral diseases… I know I can, I've seen me do it!"

"Do others here know what you are capable of?" Ian asked.

"A couple of people do," Harris answered. "I am not at liberty to name them, however!"

"No need," Ian answered… "Which brings me to what I wanted to offer you…"

With that, Chancellor Rosewood handed Harris a folder that said "The Kupuko and their endangerment."

"Harris, let me give you the shortened version…" Ian said. "Last year, there was a contingent of eight missionaries who went into the rain forests of central Brasil to make contact with a tribe that had stayed isolated and out of reach from the modern man living there. The tribe was called the Kupuko."

Harris scanned the file folder handed him, quickly.

"They were brought out of their shell, so to speak, with the gifts of farm tools and modern-day items of assisting them in their lives. It was peaceful and calm for about six months or so, and then I am afraid things soon went to hell in a bucket."

"How?" Harris asked.

"One of the missionaries developed a rhinovirus. It wasn't anything for the lad to get over, but it soon spread to the entire tribe and not one of them had any defence against the infection. The tribe lost ninety members in a couple of months."

Harris could see it happening but was astounded, nonetheless. "Ninety? You are telling me a tribe incurred such huge losses...due to a common cold?"

Ian just nodded.

"I have heard about that happening…In War of the Worlds, perhaps!" Harris said. "To have it happen in real life, though…it seems impossible."

"I wish it were, Harris." Chancellor Rosewood said." If this lot doesn't get looked after soon, their numbers will vanish altogether."

Harris just looked over the file from a group called The Unity League. A group similar to the Peace-Corps but with shorter missions. He had heard of them but was unsure of what they did. He was half-studying the file and half wondering what he was going to tell his Da?

The devil would no doubt, be in these details.

Chapter 48 – Everything changes…

Harris then had to explain this mission trip to all his friends and family. Roland and Tamar would know why. His Da and Mum also knew about why he was representing the college in this endeavour. To add insult to this injury, the Wallach Amendment went through in the UK and other parts of Europe that would restrict travel for known Xenons on aircraft. Harris would have to keep his abilities under the table, or he would end up walking to South America and back again.

First, he called his Mum and Da. The selection by the Chancellor was a disappointment to his Da as it meant failure to stay hidden. "Son, how in the name of God himself, could you let this happen?" Helmut asked.

"I know Da," Harris answered. "They have video monitoring all over the place now. Even the church was recording the goings-on at The Remembrance Day in Limerick."

"Son, who else knows your ability?" Helmut asked. "…Beside that roommate of yours?"

"The Chancellor has sworn to secrecy the staff here who are in the know, Da." He answered. "They know to stay quiet or have to deal with him. They don't want to do that."

Helmut was quiet for a bit and put Jean on the phone. "Harris…"

"Yes, Mum?"

"So how long will you be gone?" She asked.

"This tour is supposed to be until just before Christmas," Harris answered. "I leave after finals, take care of business across the pond and come home. For that, I receive my accreditation and then…well, I'll figure it out then."

"Son, this is so far away," Jean said. "We want you safe. You know that."

"I know, Mum" Harris answered. "I also know I am stronger than I know. I have faced dangerous situations before far from home. I need to get gone and back before I think about it too long."

Helmut took the phone back. "We will see you before you leave, won't we?"

"Of course, Da," Harris answered. "Whatever happens, I need to keep going. I have come too far to stop."

Now it was time to tell the other most influential people in his life…Harris said to Roland that he would be there to join him and his lady for dinner and asked what news they had.

"I'm sworn to secrecy, mate," Roland said. "It will be worth it, though." Harris was guessing what it was. His news, however, would be just as big a surprise to the two of them.

Harris looked up Bartell's and found it was a rather posh place, so he went to town and bought a Navy-blue blazer, Khaki chinos and an oxford shirt over desert boots. The shops were beginning to fill with grunge-type clothing as opposed to the 1970's era resurgence that was hanging on what felt like a bit too long.

Bartell's Bistro was a gentlemanly place with the smell of massive cuts of beef travelling from the kitchen to tables on sizzling plates along with the aroma of wine and cigars filling the air. Some places began to ban smoking indoors but not here. Roland had on a similar outfit to Harris. Tamar was looking lovely in a blue gown and her long hair up. They drove from the boys' flat to the restaurant in Tamar's Toyota Corolla. Roland knew how to operate the Vauxhall sedan that was at his family farm for many years. His mom taught him how to drive, but he did not need to get behind the wheel in years. Harris never learned how to drive but vowed to do so, someday.

They took their table, and the two men ordered some small chops while Tamar went with the chicken. They also ordered some wine and sat down to the reason for such a grand place…

"Well, mate…We wanted you to know first, before anyone." Roland said. "Tamar and I are getting married!"

It was one of two scenarios that Harris expected as he gave a big smile to them both.

"Congratulations, you two!" Harris said with a sincere smile. "You are both deserving of all the happiness of the world!"

"Thanks mate!" Roland said.

With that, Harris poured a glass of the Rose' Chateau Beauchamp '84 and toasted the happy couple. He let them have their happy news in public while his announcement would have to wait until they were in a more, private setting.

After an elegant dinner that could not be topped, Harris told them he had to deliver his news to them both over a drink at the flat of these two medical students. They wondered why Harris would have chosen to provide his pronouncement over a bottle of blackberry brandy at home.

His news then answered that question…And then they both threw back the brandy, quickly!

"Dear God, mate!" Roland said. "…and they let you go without a hassle?"

Harris then filled in his friends with the story of the bombing tape, the Kupuko Tribe, The Unity League and the Chancellor's offer of secrecy.

"Let's face it, friends," Harris said. "This is a hell of a lot of information to come down the pike in one week."

"Yeah, I know," Roland said. "…But South America? That is a lot to ask of someone."

"As far as they know, I am the only one who can do it," Harris said.

"Are they even going to let you do it?" Roland asked. "From what that tribe has been through, I'll bet they don't want to accept help from the civilised world."

"Yeah, I thought of that, too," Harris said, sadly. "But they need help and if I am the only one who can do it then so be it. I'll go there and come back before Christmas."

They both sat silently.

"Have you both set a date yet?" Harris asked.

"Not yet," Tamar answered. "It probably won't be until summer. A June wedding is what we're going for."

"And I want you there as the best man!" Roland said, pointing. "So, you better come back in one piece."

"Consider it done," Harris said, happily.

There was a bit of sadness, as well. Things were to change so dramatically, and these two were to have their place in the world as a couple come next year. Maybe Harris would find some bird to settle with when he came back? Even if the best one got away, there were millions of others out there.

Chapter 49 - Longer Good-Byes

There was one more opinion that Harris wanted to get about his upcoming travels, and that was from his mentor. He talked to Julius Guiteau for a solid half-hour on the phone, getting a long list of what he needed to know while in foreign lands. He told Harris of his travels across the Australian Outback, the jungles of Africa and in the steppes of Chile. Unfortunately, Harris would be nowhere near there so nothing familiar could be said.

"Be wary of the natives since you are strange to them and vice-versa. Julius said, "It would also help to stock up on fly spray and a good knife. Whatever you do, don't go cheap with either since you'll be in the thick of it and you'll want the best."

Harris continued to finish his work up to the final weeks of studies. He also had to tell Rhona of his upcoming trip as a missionary and that he would be taking some time off from his studies to work with the natives. He also said that he would be back past Christmas break and not to worry about waiting on him until he got back. For a break-up, it was as subtle as you could be. Rhona continued to wonder if her dad had something to do with his absence next semester. In a way, he did. Of course, Rhona couldn't stay silent about this and, before long, all of Harris's inner circle knew about his trip far away. His friends all wanting to give him a fitting send-off, so they had a party in his honour at The Draughtsman. It was, mostly, a tropical island affair with many of the girls dressing in bright dresses and the guys in Hawaiian shirts. All of which missed the mark of the area, but he wasn't about to say anything as everyone was getting their drink on and their company close. He figured with finals in a fortnight, it was an excellent pressure-release.

He also thought, with all this, that it felt like he was stealing all of Tamar and Roland's thunder. They said not to worry over it, and they would get their own attention later on.

Everyone got together for one more study session before the finals for years-end. The girls were not letting Roland get to them or vice-versa. It wouldn't matter now as he was committed. Harris wasn't thinking of anything but finals right now.

He then met with the Chancellor again on Monday after his finals took place and Harris setting a fantastic example with all his studies. Ian wanted to make sure he had all the details of what he needed. This time, he received his flight itinerary:

He would fly from London City Airport to Atlanta, then to Miami and then he would be flown to the airport in Rio De Janeiro and then finally to a small airport in Central Brasil and be driven the rest of the way. He would also have the support of several members of The Unity League who didn't know what he was. Despite being far away from the Paragons and other authorities, he wanted to keep it that way until necessary. To that end, he would work as the assistant to Doctor Dennis Dunedin, an Australian expatriate who was familiar with the terrain. The others would be mostly American and Canadian volunteers.

He didn't know what to say to his favourite mate. He said his goodbyes to his friends, already. Jasmine and Taylor, Caroline and Miriam, The Nghegdela siblings, Jill and Rhona…

Roland and Tamar Accompanied Harris to the airport in Cork. He hugged his best friend's girl and then him for about the same length of time.

"Remember, you gotta come back!" Roland said as he entered the jetway. Harris just waved as he boarded the aeroplane to London. The flight was fast and easy to Heathrow. He wished he flew into the London City Airport as he would be leaving that way in another day. His parents met him at his gate and took him to their home.

His Mum was more loving toward Harris than usual, He father sat near him with a look of grave concern. They both wanted him to have the best, to be proud and stand tall. They just wished he could do all that closer to home.

"Son, I just want the best for you," Helmut said. "This Unity League thing is not going to be a walk in the park, you know."

"Yeah, Da. I know." Harris responded. "I couldn't see the value of camping when I was younger like in the scouts. The idea of tent camping makes me cringe. Still, lives are on the line, and I must be there. You know how it is."

"I do, son," Helmut said. "I know you'll do well…just come back quickly."

"It's going to be a mess there," Jean said. "Do you have what you need?"

"I'll get some supplies when I get there," Harris said to her. "Dr Guiteau said not to go cheap with it."

"It's going to be hell there with the snakes and spiders, and God knows what else." His Mum continued. "I wish there was something we could do for you."

"Just be here when I get back, Mum." He said. "I just want someone to come home to."

He then went to visit the Ravalli's at their home. Magdalena was talking to Vincent on the front step when Harris came up and said "Hello?"

"Harris, dear!" Magdalena said and hugged Harris. Vincent shook his hand and said he was glad to see him.

That is when Harris explained that he was off to South America this summer and autumn. Vincent was a little disappointed as he hoped to have Harris work for him again but understood the importance of his work once Harris explained the details.

"Well, we'll miss you this year. We added hurling this year to the youth line-up."

"Vinnie, honey..." Magdalena interrupted. "This is a big step for our Harris. A little hurling is nice but come now!" Vincent relented and wished him well.

"Would you please tell Gina about me?" Harris asked. "Just that everything is fine, and I wished I got to see her again."

"She is supposed to be home in a couple of days," Vincent said. "You have to go so fast?"

"I'm afraid I do," Harris said. "I'm on a schedule to get there and meet with the rest of the group."

"We'll tell her then," Magdalena said. "You say you are coming back for Christmas. Maybe we can all have dinner together then."

"I like the sound of that," Harris said.

His parents came with him in the cab to London Airport early so he could get his bearings. Traffic was horrible, as usual. He was thinking with all the cars flooding the roads that he would miss his flight anyway. He made it and in better time than he thought. Perhaps he was just anxious. The gate was a long walk from the terminal entrance and Harris would be there for a few hours, so he didn't miss his flight. He hugged his parents, and they wished him well and hoped the time would fly by.

They headed out as Helmut had patients to attend to leaving Harris at the gate for 2 hours waiting for his flight in jogging pants and a loose shirt. He didn't like looking this dishevelled in public but figured it was comfortable for the long trip.

He got on the aluminium tube, loaded up his carry-on bag on the overhead and took a long look out the window of the aeroplane at the skyline of his home city in the distance, the tall buildings and the other airliners waiting for their passengers...

He also saw some lunatic running on the tarmac shouting at the aeroplanes. He couldn't hear what he said but was acting as he wanted on board. He had a scraggly beard and looked like a homeless man that seemed to be all over London these days. Harris wasn't too concerned until he started shooting lightning pulses out of his hands the same way he shot healing light out of his, except at longer distances. One of the pulses hit his aeroplane, and all the lights went out along with the usual sound of engines priming running down. "Oh, good!" He thought sarcastically as other passengers were panicking in the dark.

The lunatic Xenon did the same with two other aeroplanes, apparently and then was surrounded by police that feared for their own lives until the Paragons appeared in strange suits made of rubber with their trademark black and orange striped patterns. They seemed to be well trained in dealing with Xenons who went this course of loony.

The man was taken down in a pile-on and then restrained by irons around his wrists and a collar around his neck. He noticed one of the officers shooting a hypodermic needle in the man's neck and the renegade Xenon fell to the ground in a heap. They carried him off the tarmac to an awaiting wagon while his feet dragged on the pavement.

Harris was sad to see one of his kind going bonkers and then restrained like an animal, but he also was mad at him as that was the appearance that Xenons had been presenting themselves as of late. He and fellow passengers had to leave the aeroplane, with their carry-on luggage in hand meaning they would not be boarding that flight any time soon.

The next flight was at 3 pm the day after tomorrow as they also had to recheck all the aeroplanes for further damage leaving him stuck in Central London for the time being.

Now what?

Chapter 50 – The Appreciation For What You Miss

Harris walked through London Airport and fetched his things from the baggage carousel and walked out to the front of the terminal. Somewhere in the distance, the song "Learning to Fly" was playing on a car radio. He wished he could. The thought of dragging himself back through London traffic with a full load wasn't appealing. He went to a phone box and made a call to his parents and explained what happened…

"Well, that's the government for you…" Helmut said. "If it's not broken, they aren't doing their jobs!"

"I couldn't agree more, Da," Harris said. "Listen, I don't want to deal with traffic again. I am going to get a room someplace for the night and wait until tomorrow."

"Harris, dear…" Jean said. "If you go to The King George Hotel, I will make sure you have a room there. They owe me a favour, but I never took them up on it, yet. Just think of it as a going-away gift from us."

"OK, Mum…but isn't that place a bit…you know…fancy?" Harris asked.

"Yes, it is, dear." She responded. "And for you, it better be the best. You will probably not be having it so great in the jungle. Go and spoil yourself tonight."

"OK, Mum, I'm off," Harris said. "I'll let you both know when I get there."

Harris hired a cab and headed for Cadogan Street and The King George Hotel. He felt he looked a fright walking through the lobby as he was in his most comfortable togs for a long flight. Harris announced his name and immediately, he was besieged by several bellmen and attendants to take his bags to his room. He suspected either his Mum or Da showed some kindness here at one time as he spent his time there treated like royalty.

He got to the foyer of his room and offered a £5 note to the hotel workers, but they disappeared before he could give it to them. He was always taught to tip as excellent service was deserving of such, but they didn't hang about. Harris just entered the room and thought there had to have been a mistake. It looked like a meeting room with a large sofa and a television large enough to make a company presentation. It was when he spotted the bed that he knew this was his for the night.

The bath looked like marble brick on the outside, the shower with a large head that looked like it put out gallons at a time, and the bed was the most comfortable he had ever laid on. He heard no sound when he crawled on the large mattress that felt as big as a football pitch. It all felt like a colossal error was made, and they would soon be around to shove him off to a smaller room. In this place, it wouldn't seem to make much of a difference if they did. He did call his parents and told them about the luxurious quarters. They didn't seem surprised.

"Da, did you offer some help to someone here? This place looks like the Queen herself should be here, not me!"

"Good!" He said. "I might have had a hand in it, but your Mum is the one to thank for this."

"Thank you, Mum!" He said with all sincerity.

"Your welcome, dear." She said. "I know you like exercising. If you ask, they will get you something to wear to swim or workout in."

After he ended his phone call, he did, indeed examine the workout room and saw a pool there big enough for the Olympics and a gym twice the size of Vincent's. He put himself through his paces for a good two hours and swam to cool off. Afterwards, he ordered a meal via room service of a prime rib and some desserts that would have belonged in Buckingham Palace.

He then got in bed and tried to sleep and realised that he just couldn't. "Well, of course not!" He thought. "It was only 8 pm! Who could shut down now with all this?" He then put on his one dress outfit of chinos, Oxford shirt and sport coat that he brought along in case he ended up someplace nice. He made his way to the pub downstairs, which seemed rather sedate. It was mostly young men like himself and a few women were conversing and reading the papers at small tables around the edge of the walls. He made his way to the bar where the barman was standing and waiting for something to do.

"Hello, sir." He said, smiling. He also seemed glad to see someone who didn't look they were of the aristocracy.

"Hi," Harris said. "What's the favourite drink around here, then?"

"Mostly high-priced wine for this lot." He said in a voice not to disturb the rest of the clientele. "We got National Brew on tap, though."

"Sure, that sounds good," Harris said.

The barman, whose nameplate said "Albert" served him up a mug of some cheap lager that Harris preferred over some drinks he came across.

"So, Albert or what do they call you here?" Harris asked.

"Al's fine." He said. "Most of the time they just say "Oy, over here!" He said, smiling.

"Harris is the name here." He said and shook his hand. "Is it usually this quiet?"

"Well, it's preferred. The night goes on, and they turn up the volume, loudly" Al said. "You here, then for the wedding?"

"Huh?" Harris looked over across the hall and saw a sign that said:

Anderson/Hunter wedding.

"Nah," Harris replied. "I'm just here when my flight got cancelled due to... reasons."

"That nutter on the runway, then?" Al asked.

"Yeah..." Harris said. "I overheard that he just wanted to go home. You would think they would let him go to get him out of their hair."

"That's the government for you," Al said. "They love to fix the unbroken."

That sounded very familiar to Harris.

"So, where you bound?" Al inquired. "If I may ask..."

"Brasil," Harris said. "Kind of a Unity-League mission."

"Mate, that is a trip and a half," Al said. "You go for long?"

"Yeah," Harris answered. "Six months and I'll be back for Christmas."

"Well..." Al then said as he wiped the bar down with a rag. "The nice thing is when you go a long time away from those you love, you appreciate them more when you get back," Al said with a smile.

It was then the quiet ended with the sound of a group of women near his age singing the song "Darling Nickie" by Prince.

A song that was still banned by the BBC. "Uh-Oh…Hen party." Al said. "Good luck, mate." He then headed over to serve drinks to the group of rich, beautiful women on a drunken tear. Harris just raised his mug to Al as he went to serve drinks to the demimonde. It was not their first stop on the pub crawl…that was obvious. They wore t-shirts that said "Bridesmaid, Maid of Honour and left plenty of room for the "Bride-to-Be" to enter. She was a lovely bride. Young and blonde, no more than 23 or so. Harris could see how she could get her talons into some guy.

They then got the record machine fired up with a handful of coins with a song called "I Knew the Bride When She Used to Rock and Roll" and went to get some of the men reading their papers to get up and dance. The girls' caterwauling was getting to Harris. He took a seat at a table by the side of the wall for a while, but the noise was still getting to him. He thought about going back to his top-floor room and watching some of that gigantic telly when he looked at the bar and noticed a woman not dancing.

She was, without doubt, the most beautiful woman Harris had ever seen, and he wasn't about to let this moment slip away. He picked up his mug with the beermat and walked toward the woman at the bar. She was drinking something bright blue with a paper umbrella in it. She knew someone was approaching her but couldn't see the face as the mirror behind the bar was obscured with an extensive line of liquor bottles on the shelf. She didn't turn toward him but figured she would just let him down easy…

"If you want to dance, you'd do better with the other girls here." She said. "I'm not for it tonight."

He then said the words that shocked her to attention:

"Hello, Gina."

Chapter 51 – Reunited

She turned with a start and was nearly breathless. "Harris! Uh…Hi!" was all she could get out while Harris took a seat next to her at the bar.

"It's nice to see you again." He said. "I didn't know you were in town. I just saw your parents yesterday."

"Yeah, they don't know I'm here, yet. I'm just here for the wedding." Gina said as she pointed to the same wedding sign.

"Friends of yours?" Harris asked.

"My friend's sister is a bride's maid." She said. "I don't mix well around the upper-class, so I'm here with my glass of courage." She pointed to her drink.

"Agreed," Harris said, holding up a mug which really did nothing for him.

They caught up on their lives for a good hour or so. Gina talked about her experiences at Veterinary school and her love of animals. She wanted to live on a farm even more than when she started college. She also spoke of her recent boyfriend, Alex. He went on to cheat on her a month or two ago, though she felt oddly indifferent about it.

Harris told her only a bit about what he was through in the past two years as he wanted to tell her everything but keep her attention so they could stay together as long as possible. The AIDS men, The bombing, the trip to Australia, minus the details about the Nazis.

Their parting over the first Christmas break, however, bought up a question that Harris wanted answering. "Gina, I believe this to be true but confirm it for me, if you please?" Harris asked, and Gina nodded that she would.

"It was your brother who pretty much broke us up over Christmas before last, now wasn't it?" He asked with all the knowledge that it was true.

"Yeah, he did." She answered with a sigh.

"Yep, that's what I thought," Harris said as he slammed his hand down on the bar which was solid oak and could take the abuse.

"…and here I took the effort of healing his leg even after he practically kicked me out of the confessional…Anyway, I thought he wasn't supposed to say anything about what goes on between us there…"

"Oh no, Harris!" Gina interrupted. "You got it all wrong!" With that, Harris just looked at her mystified.

"Eh? … What do you mean?" He asked.

"It wasn't Victor who said we needed to break up. It was my other brother… Eduardo."

Now Harris was perplexed.

"Eduardo?" He exclaimed. "What I ever do to him?"

"Nothing," Gina said. "He heard that Dad was saved by you during his heart attack and understood that…but when he heard about Victor's leg …Well, he figured it was your… "abilities." Gina said while making sure no one else was listening.

"OK, so his leg got better…so what of it?" Harris asked, still confused.

"Harris, that leg was supposed to be amputated the next month!" Gina exclaimed. "My Victor even stood up for you against Eduardo, but he didn't feel that Xenon blood should mix with ours, so he told me to break it off, or he would make sure the Paragons did!"

Harris came to a sad realisation…

"It was my fault we broke up. If I didn't do anything, we could have still been together." Harris said as he laid his head in his hand, exasperated, with Gina comforting him.

"No wonder your brother was happy to see me that Christmas. I thought he was a snake and here, he really was happy I fixed his leg."

"Well…" Gina then added quietly. "He was even happier that you cured his diabetes."

"Oh, gawd!!!" He said as he returned his head to the bar with Gina patting his back for comfort.

Al the Barman came up and asked: "Is he alright?"

Harris just waved him off, and Gina just nodded that everything was fine. Al just shrugged it off and went about his business.

Harris just regained his composure and relaxed. "I didn't know how powerful…" He continued. "I'm all right. It's just the shock of seeing you, and now I have to go away, again."

"Aren't you working at my Dad's gym again?" Gina asked.

"No, and I wish I were," Harris said and then told her how he was off to South America tomorrow, his mission to save the tribe and how he ended up at a hotel far past his station in life.

"I see." She said, disappointed. "That's too bad you won't be around, then."

"Yeah, especially meeting you here" Harris added. "You know, I never really got over you. I missed you all this time." He said to her, looking straight into her lovely eyes. "and I know you have missed me too."

"Oh yeah?" She said quietly

"Yeah, I know it for a fact." He responded calmly.

"…and how do you know that?" She asked.

"Because you have been holding my hand for the past five minutes." He said.

She looked down and found their hands clasped together.

"Oh," She gasped and was about to let go…

"You don't have to let go." He said. "Not now…Not again."

"Well, it was bound to happen that we parted." She said, trying to sound matter-of-factly.

"Yeah." He said.

"We were hundreds of miles from each other and leading our own lives." She added.

"True." He said.

"And now you are off to parts of the world even further away…" She said as they got closer to each other at the bar. His hand was on her back, her hand was on his neck. The kiss that followed was long and deep.

They left the bar together, unnoticed, for his room upstairs. They didn't stop kissing, even in the lift, heading for his top-floor hotel room.

There was no stopping them tonight. They took out two years of frustration of being away from each other on every inch of their being. Gina saw Harris with his shirt off for the first time since they went swimming a few summers ago and just rubbed her hands over his new physique and his hands travelled over hers as they were not this intimate for a long time.

In the throes of their passion for each other, he could have sworn there was pounding on the walls and doors even though there were only two other rooms on this floor. When they went quiet, there wasn't a noise except their heavy breathing and the beating of their hearts. Harris swore that he left a couple of love bites on her neck but didn't see them a few minutes later. His hands didn't glow, making him wonder if he just imagined the vampiric bites.

They both stopped for water a couple of times as they worked themselves into a thirst. Harris didn't stop to realise that the knocking was in his imagination. They were together now. Who cares? The last thing that either of them wanted right now was to be away from each other. They slept close in the middle of that enormous bed that night holding each other close after the most intense and intimate sexual experience either of them ever had.

Time would bring reality back to them and crash their party in the morning.

Chapter 52 – Aftermath…

Harris remembered Roland once telling him that if you woke up and were holding (or being held by) the woman you slept with, that she probably had feelings for you and vice-versa. Well, the two of them woke up twisted like a pretzel holding each other in every sort of way. Gina was only getting up to use the loo. They were lost in each other so much last night that nothing mattered to them, …and what should have been an issue started creeping into Harris's thoughts …like birth control!

He saw blood on the sheets and figured she must have been cycling. At least that was some level of protection. She called for Harris to come in and join her in the shower. His hands were all over her with a bar of soap in one hand and a flannel in the other. He couldn't stop kissing her all over, and she didn't stop him. They would have to talk about the future but just not yet.

They ordered a light breakfast and crawled back into bed to stay warm wearing robes left by the Hotel in the wardrobe.

"I don't want this time to end," He said to her as they tenderly held each other.

"I don't, either," Gina said. "It's such bad luck of timing we have to…"

"I love you!" Harris said interrupting. "I could kick myself for not saying it earlier."

"I love you, too." She said, and they kissed again with the same passion as they entered.

"I don't want to leave!" He said. "Now that I have you here, it's worse than death having to go again."

"I know." She said. "But you are needed, or that lot is going to perish without you. I know that you couldn't live with yourself if that happened."

He had a thought while she kept bringing unwelcome reality into their conversation…

"…And I know that if I kept you away from…" She said with Harris interrupting again.

"Will you marry me?" Harris asked with all sincerity and Gina was amused more than anything.

"Harris, honey..." She tried to say.

"No, really!" He said. "We could find a priest or a judge...or some street vicar who got his ministry licence through the post!"

She just giggled at that idea. "Hon, you are a nutter!" She said.

"No, I just don't want to lose you again!" Harris said with all sincerity of a man clinging to life.

She leaned on one elbow and looked into his eyes and saw how much he felt for her. She saw the same in him as she smiled and stroked his face with her hand.

"Hon, I'll tell you what..." She said, making the deal. "You are gone until Christmas, right?"

Harris nodded.

"You come back and tell me you feel the same way...and you can put a ring on this finger!" She said, holding out her left hand.

He kissed her again, deeply. "I will hold you to that!" He said as he kissed her again.

She looked at the clock, and it said 11:00.

"What time do you have to be at the airport?" She asked.

"We have an hour," Harris said.

Gina began to get up. "Oh, well, you better get..."

"No, no..." Harris said. "WE have an hour!" and with that, he covered them up again and they fell back into each other's arms for a bit longer extending the happiness they felt.

London Airport was back to normal with people everywhere at once heading for their gates. Extra security was employed at the terminal with a few Paragon forces in riot gear keeping watch after the horse ran out of the barn, as it were.

Harris was only away from Gina for a moment as he called his parents and told them he was off, for sure this time.

"Did you enjoy the hotel? Jean asked.

"More than you could know, mum," Harris said. "I did get lost once and had to take a cab back to the front door." They just had a gentle laugh and let it go at that as Gina asked him not to tell them they spent the night together. Her brother would still be on her about wanting to marry a Xenon. She'd have to smooth things over with him first or else she would tell him to "Sot off," if needed.

They shared one more passionate kiss before he got on the aeroplane. He was indifferent, yesterday about leaving for parts unknown. Now all he could do was bide his time until he returned. He felt depressed as he took his seat and to be transported to the other side of the world...again!

She re-joined the wedding party the next day for rehearsals and took notes of ideas for her own nuptials. Cake, flowers, location, the bridal party... She knew Victor would conduct the ceremony. If Eduardo could be convinced, the catering as well. Gina also wondered what it would be like to be married to Harris. She was sure that he would be the perfect husband. He would be there for her and allow her to have the career she wanted, the animals for pets and to take care of their children...

"Children..." She thought.

END OF PART 2

Act Three

Chapter 53 - Bienvenu de South America!

Flying from Ireland to the UK mainland only took an hour or so. Here, Harris was spending hours in the air trying to keep himself occupied. At least he was in first class by taking a bit of his extra cash to bump himself up to the better rows of seats. It was more comfortable and felt that it was owed to him as his original flight plans got cancelled due to the outrage of one of his fellow Xenons. He thought it was indignant to capture the poor sot but knew he had no way to change it. Perhaps this corner of the world could see the possibility of people like him.

On the other hand, the poor guy's outburst assured his seeing of his former girlfriend and making her his potential fiancé. It was hard to be angry over that outcome. It was less than an hour into the flight, and he was already missing Gina. He knew he shouldn't have slept. He did manage a nap, read a bit of the mission paperwork Chancellor Rosewood gave him, studied his Portuguese-English dictionary while he listened to music piped in from the aeroplane's sound system through a bought pair of headphones.

His connection would take him from Atlanta, GA to Miami, FL and then further south. His first visit to America and it would be short as he would only go as far as the airport. There was also something that he had not felt before, and that was turbulence! No one else on the aeroplane was screaming in panic, so he assumed that it was business as usual here. The pilot then came over the intercom and apologised for the fright, nonetheless.

It was a long walk when they touched down in the airport in Atlanta, Georgia. There was also no guide to where he needed to be aside from his manifest. His next gate took about a half-hour walk. The airport was immense with shops offering small items and magazines to enjoy en route, so he got a tea and made his way along the long, long walkways and "slidewalks" which resembled flat escalators that sped up his pace,

He finally came to his gate after what seemed to be a marathon of walking. The aeroplane was slightly smaller than the one that flew him to Miami airport. He stepped outside for just a moment from the air-conditioned shelter of the airport and was immediately hit in the face by a blast of hot, humid air.

He retreated back after a second or so. Manufactured coolness was more desirable than to venture any further. He didn't have long to wait, and his gate was closer than the last stroll through the glass and concrete structure.

The next flight took him to Panama, where the amount of language that he could understand went from the southern United States English to nothing. He realised he knew very little Spanish. If he needed help, he would have to struggle to find assistance. The airport was small, and they were using numbers more than words here. He was on his way in short order.

Finally, he touched down in Rio De Janeiro, where it was a bit warmer than he thought. It was winter in this part of the world, but it stayed temperate at 25C (77F). He was supposed to meet his representative from the Unity League at 4:30 that evening, but his ride was late to show up. He then ate at the airport restaurant where apparently food came to die. He also exchanged £100 that he was carrying for 500 Brazilian Reals at the international desk.

He wasn't the only British tourist in the area. There were many others from Europe and the USA, but no one seemed to be in a talking mood. Most of them were there for the beaches, the food and, of course, marijuana. His only experience with the weed did not make an enticing case to attract him back to it. He even started looking around for someone to heal just for the fun of it.

Finally, a burly man with an accent and a thick moustache wearing a white shirt stained with about everything he came in contact with approached and asked him his name.

"Harris Gibraltar, sir…er, senior." He said with all politeness.

The man waved his arm and Harris followed with his bags carried and rolling along behind. The driver made no move to assist him with his luggage. He drove him in a noisy, broken-down taxi to the Hotel De Playa and told him the plan:

"You here tonight, me here tomorrow at 9." He said. Harris handed him five reals to the driver who seemed to be happy enough with the tip.

He had a room that was just "good enough." Of course, he felt spoiled from the last hotel room he stayed in two nights ago and anything would be better than an aircraft seat, 1st class or not. He got a good night's sleep and cleaned up with a lot of soap while careful not to drink the water.

It would have made no difference with his physiology, but it smelled like there was an underlying odour of rust and dead animal.

He got the same cab driver, and this time the driver did help him in with his bags. Harris gave him 5R and added two more, and the driver was off. Harris ended up in an office building in another part of town. He took his bags himself with him to visit a man called Juan Montoya in his office.

"Buenos Dias, Doctor Gibraltar," Senior Montoya said as he shook the hand of the young Xenon. Senior Montoya was in a classic grey business suit with thinning hair and browned skin, not from the sun but a lifetime of nicotine. Harris responded with his own "Buenos Dias" as they took a seat at Senior Montoya's desk. The official lit up a cigarette from a table lighter and got down to business.

"You come highly recommended by your school, doctor." Senior Montoya said as he looked over a file on Harris. "They said you could do something to assist with Kupuko Tribe?"

"That is correct, senior." He responded.

"The Dr Rosewood tells me you are…different?" Senior Montoya asked as if someone were listening in on them both. Harris played along.

"That is correct, sir." He answered. "My skills are not what you would call "routine procedure." I do have the ability, I feel, to assist this lot in their time of need."

"I don't mind telling you that this whole situation dealt black eye to Unity League and its management." Senior Montoya admitted, sadly. "We have been proud, independent organisation for years. To have situation like this where we have caused downfall of people is most depressing. It also casts shadow over every other peacekeeping mission that wants to contribute to the fellow man."

"I am ready to assist, Senior," Harris said. "So, tell me the game plan, as it were."

Senior Montoya pulled out a file labelled "CONFIDENTIAL" containing several maps and a few papers. The first map showed an area depicting a road into the mountainous regions, then a route to get to the compound of the present volunteers. Another showed the paths to the village of the Kupuko. There was also a river map and a general overview of South America.

"Now then…" Montoya continued. "You will go in as league volunteer and, as far as anybody knows, take the guise of physician assistant to Dr Dunedin. You will have to improvise from there."

"Yes, I understand," Harris said as he examined the maps.

"You will spend one more night here and then flies to Moura Airfield at 10 am tomorrow," Montoya said. "A jeep will take you to compound then, and you can then set up what you need to do."

"Bueno…Ok, then." Harris said.

That was where trepidation set in by Montoya…

"Uh, by the way…" Montoya threw in. "You cure anything, right?"

Harris just nodded.

"I had a little spot of… something from one of locals here…If you could, possibly, uh, give me an assist…."

"Got any water?" Harris asked with a subtle grin.

Chapter 54 - Into the Mountains...

The hotel life was getting Harris spoiled. He was going to miss room service and sleeping in climate-controlled rooms. The room was nothing like the previous ones with thin walls where he could hear a telly on one side broadcasting a football game and a prostitute in another room applying her trade to lonely men, one right after the other in half-hour sessions until about 2 am. Harris just took the noisy time to study the maps given to him by Senior Montoya. The Unity League official was even generous enough to present him with 50R and insisted Harris take it. He figured that he could use it for supplies tomorrow.

He looked at the areas to be resided in for the next six months and then realised that he never went camping in his younger days. He loathed most social interaction with his younger ilk back then and wondered why people would pay money to live like they were transients? He also knew, though, the most astute of doctors travelled to and lived in the thick of run-down and squalid conditions to study their subjects; Albert Sweitzer, Richard Attenborough, and his own mentor, Dr Guiteau.

He slept in that old hotel room with the door forced shut and a chair wedged under the doorknob. Harris's entire world was in two pieces of luggage and a doctor's bag where he had his notebooks, Walkman and several bottles of water. He also had acupuncture needles to match the books on the subject and the files on the Kupuko Tribe that listed the encounters that took place from the missionaries that dealt with them until their exile.

The first encounters were promising and their conversion to Christianity over their long-standing praise of He-Who-Controls-The Forest, whoever that was, created in them a placement for their prayers. It seemed the praise for this Christian God is what they deemed to cause their own Deity's anger and struck them down with an illness. He just needed a few to show he was there for their kind and not for some power-play of souls. He was there as a doctor, after all, and not as a religious figure.

The jeep pulled up for him at 10:15 outside his hotel. Nobody seemed to be in a rush here. He did his best to deal with the driver as he didn't appear to speak English. Harris threw his bags into the back of the jeep and said "Let's go" and pointed forward. The driver chattered about this and that in Portuguese. Harris had no clue what he was talking about but just nodded, politely.

He looked for the word "Stop!" in the Portuguese-English dictionary outside of a small shop. He was glad the driver knew that much as he put his hand up and said "Uno memento" and hoped the driver knew not to drive off. Harris remembered that he needed supplies and went in to buy a knife that looked serviceable and fly spray that he hoped would do the job.

He also bought a compass and a canteen. Water was so crucial to his type of healing that it would be ridiculous not to have a container nearby. He got back into the jeep after dropping 70R, and they sped off to the airfield.

The aeroplane was just a little cub big enough for him and the pilot who spoke English but had a very thick accent. "Allo, Senor! Mi Nombre es Raul Gomez" He said happier than most people he met. "Hola, senior!" Harris said.

"You are ready for flying?" He asked.

"Si senior," Harris said. "As soon as I get these in here." Harris then pushed his luggage into the back of the aeroplane. Afterwards, Senior Gomez handed an envelope to Harris:

"I tell to give this to you…" Gomez said. There was no time to read it as the small aeroplane taxied the runway and took off quickly. Harris was a bit nervous as he never flew anything this little before. Senior Gomez handled everything well for the 90 minutes that took them to Moura Airfield. He felt every bump of that landing as they touched down in a small airfield. It was nothing like the big cities where he spent most of his life. The buildings seemed to make up the airport and not much else as there was only a small building for passengers and a couple of hangers. He went to the reception building, and it was empty of anyone. Raul was then off to the aeroplane hangar to do whatever pilots did after their flights.

About 30 minutes had passed, and an old jeep showed up as he was reading a Sky Mall magazine that he had lifted from one of the flights while sitting on the bench outside the airport office. It was hot here but felt he should get used to that. A young woman with curled brown hair in a t-shirt and green shorts drove up to him. "Are you the new P.A.?" She asked in an American accent.

"Yeah." He said. "Harris Gibraltar is the name." He wiped the sweat off his hand. "Sarah Hartley." She said as she shook his hand. "Get your bags, and we'll get on with it." The Shirt she wore had a baseball diamond emblem on it that said "1988 Little League World Series."

Harris threw his items into the jeep, and they started up a steep mountain pass with a ton of hairpin switchbacks, taking them high into the mountains over the river basin. She drove quickly up the hill without a care in the world which scared Harris, but he did his best to hide that fact. While they climbed into the mountains, Sarah chatted with Harris about her story:

"I came here to study the psychology of the natives. They all had different takes on the world as they do back home. You know how Americans are split up?"

"I know they were during the war between the states!" Harris shouted as they were in an open-top jeep going over bumpy, so-called roads.

"Yeah, it all still exists in a way!" Sarah shouted but casually over the din of engine noise and rough passage. "The northerners are cold and stodgy. The southerners are friendlier and more laid back. You go out west, and people act wilder depending where you go. Texans keep the cowboy mentality, New Mexico is artsy, Arizonians are all business and California is everything else."

They slid for a moment on some slippery rocks near the summit that caused the jeep to slip near the edge of the precipice, but Sarah was unafraid and just continued like it was a routine drive on the M1. It took about a half-hour or so to get to the encampment which consisted of two small buildings in the middle, about a half-dozen tents on pallets, a wooden shed on the right with a large tent and a quasit hut off to the left. On the far right was a running river with a calm current that flowed out of site.

"Well, home sweet home!" Sarah said. It was about what Harris expected. A lot of green trees, hot weather and very little else. "Thanks for the lift," Harris said. "Where's the Doctor? I got to introduce myself."

Sarah pointed at the quasit hut. "He might be asleep." She said. "I'm sure he's there, though. Everyone else is probably still working. Go and present yourself to him, …and if he doesn't get up when you ring the bell, throw it at him." She smiled and then drove to the back of the encampment, apparently to park.

"Throw the bell at him?" Harris thought. "Well, this should be fun!"

Chapter 55 – Welcome to the Jungle

Harris took his luggage and dragged it to the doorway. He stepped into a room with a few wooden, folding tables and steel chairs. It had some notes laying on each making it look like an office. He put his luggage and doctors' bag next to the wall and went behind an open wall with an arrow and a large red cross above it.

"Doctor Dunedin?" Harris called out to no answer, but he heard snoring coming from behind a counter. A man, aged 50 years or so, with a scraggly salt and pepper beard, laid behind the desk in a bedroll. Next to him was a jug that looked like a moonshiner would use. There was a bell on the counter that Harris rang and the Doctor rose from his nap. Harris had felt like throwing the desk bell at him to get him moving but restrained himself.

"Oy! It's still daylight!" The doctor said and stood up in a plaid shirt and khaki shorts as he hid his eyes from the light and saw the young medical student in front of him waiting to speak.

"Slow day, Doctor?" Harris asked.

Doctor Dunedin stumbled in his bedroll as he tried to stand and was not in the best of moods.

"Who the hell are you?" Doctor Dunedin barked.

"I am, the hell, Harris Gibraltar, sir…Your new assistant." Harris said calmly.

"Oh yeah, right…right" Doctor Dunedin said. "'ang on a tic…" he said in a thick Australian accent and went to the loo. Harris saw a folding chair and sat down for about 10 minutes until Doctor Dunedin came out a new man.

"Right, now then…" He said. "Welcome to the jungle, mate. I don't get why they sent for you from so far away, but you'll get on well, I'm sure."

"Whatever this guy is taking, I want in on it!" Harris thought.

"So, who have you talked to so far, here?" The doctor asked, "…and call me Dennis, everyone else does."

"Right, Dennis," Harris responded. "I only talked to Sarah. She drove me up here."

"Right, OK then," Dennis said. "You'll want to put your stuff in that room back there. There's a cot and a couple of crates. You can use them 'owever you like."

Harris got his baggage and dragged the bags to his makeshift home. The cot was just thin material in a frame, and there were three crates each piled on one another, making it look like shelves. The whole room was the size of a walk-in closet, but it was all he needed. There was a window in the back which was closed and made the air stifling.

"Oh yeah!" Dennis shouted from down the hall. "Be sure to keep the windows closed during the day or the thieves can get in!"

"Thieves?" Harris shouted back. "What thieves?"

Dennis came to his doorway. "Monkeys." He said. "They love to get in and run off with your stuff. Anything shiny or looks like food, they'll steal it."

"Great," Harris said. "Anything else I should worry over?"

"Oh yeah! Plenty!" Dennis said with a smile, and with that, a voice came in from the counter.

"Yo, Dennis!" The voice said as Harris looked out the window to a drop of 20 feet. All he could see were trees, otherwise. Dennis then motioned to follow him. When Harris left his room, a woman a bit shorter than himself had appeared. She was of Asian descent in a plain white shirt and khaki shorts.

"So, this is the new sawbones!" she said in perfect American English.

"That's right, Hye Euan Lee, this is Harris...Gibraltar, is it?"

"That's right...Hello Miss Lee." He shook her hand.

"Nice to meet you, doctor...and just Lee is fine...So, is Dennis helping you out?"

"Yeah, no problem," Harris said.

"Ok, well finish up and then come eat. Then you can come out to the bonfire in an hour or so. You can meet the rest of the crazies here." Lee said and left.

"Crazies?" Harris asked with a tilt in his eye.

"Well, you gotta be a bit loony to be 'ere, mate," Dennis said. "Go on and finish unpacking then. I'll give ya the grand tour when you're ready." And with that, Harris walked out of the office and into his new room for the time being.

He then put the rest of his things away while also finding a crate filled with garbage that he emptied into the trash bin in the office and used that as a bed stand.

He put his Walkman and his picture of Gina on it along with a can of fly spray and a few books he brought on natural healing methods and pathology. The insects weren't nasty yet. Maybe they were out of season? He would ask about that and a lot of other things as time went on. Harris left the office making sure his room window was closed, per his instruction. Dennis was unloading the jeep of some crates of oranges and other fruits that Sarah had driven up with him.

"OY, Harris!" Dennis said. "Over 'ere!" and put the crate of fruits in his hands and said to follow him as they made their way to a large tent which was the mess hall with one long table and several steel folding chairs set up around it.

"We set up two meals a day, mate," Dennis said. "One's at eight in the morn, the other at five. We got a dinner bell for both when they're ready. He pointed to a large triangle made of iron and a similar stick for ringing it hanging nearby on a rope. He went on...

"You pack a lunch for the afternoons. We got selections for that as well in the supply room." In the back of the mess tent was a loud, mechanical roar.

"That loud machine you're hearing is the generator," Dennis said. "We got a fridge and a deep freeze for anything we are lucky to get delivered."

"Can we get mail?" Harris asked.

"You betcha!" Dennis said. "But it only comes once a week, so if you want to order anything or talk to anybody by post, you better get your letters in before Sarah takes off on Monday mornings. The mail is slow, though…That's the only thing."

Another man, a short, strong-looking Hispanic man came out in a white apron covered in what looked like the morning's breakfast. He has a wisp of black hair hidden under a white cap.

"Harris that is Tomas Feliciano and he is our cook here…and don't bother trying to talk to him, he has no grasp of English. Just tell him "La Comida estuvo muy Buena." That means…"

"The meal was very good." Harris jumped in. "I read a few useful phrases on the aeroplane."

"Muy Bueno," Dennis said. "Let's go over here…" Leaving Tomas to grunt and sneer as the two doctors went on with the tour.

With that, they walked across to another tent that had chainsaws, hand tools and a shortwave radio with a microphone.

"That whole setup with the radio is Arliss's thing. He can fix anything and get a call through to anyplace." Dennis said.

"OK, good," Harris said. "The only thing I have that's electronic is my Walkman, though…and why all the chainsaws? Do you go through that much firewood?"

"You'll hear about that as time goes on," Dennis said. "No one has come to be missing a limb yet…Thank Christ."

Dennis continued his tour with the latrine and a warning to check for snakes before taking a seat. "Also, you might want to take a loo roll, or you might get stuck there until you get an assist!" Dennis said with a smirk. He also pointed out the tents of the other members. Each one was the size of Harris's room and on wooden pallets off the ground. "Lee and me, we've been here about a month, the rest about a forte night. We were surprised to 'ave you come along then."

They went back to the medical office, and he showed where the supplies were. Not much to worry over as there were only cuts and bruises so far and the more important stuff, like plaster and surgical tools were still in plastic wrap in the hopes they would never be needed.

"The showers are over 'ere," Dennis said, pointing to a tent on the other side of the quasit hut. "There is a spring for clean water that goes in the holding tank, and we take some for the shower tank and maintain a fire under it that we check every morning and sundown. That way the water is warm enough for at least a decent shower."

"So, the drinking water…" Harris began.

…" Is what you carry in your canteen. Dennis jumped in. "The tap for that is on the side of the building, and you can wash up in those sinks over there," Dennis said pointing to a couple of makeshift sinks with plastic buckets as basins.

"Oh yeah, one more thing…" Dennis said. "Be sure to shake your boots in the morning out to make sure there's nothing in there. There are some snakes and insects that would love to make a home of your boots at night. Your foot becomes an invading force that they would love to attack," Dennis added. Harris just cringed and wondered what kind of world he just entered.

They stepped into the main room of the quasit hut. One door also said "Hye Euan Lee – League Leader" to the office and another door said "Private." Harris guessed that must have been her room.

"Well, that's it then, all of it. All we need now is for you to meet the rest of the lot." Just then, Lee came in.

"Ready to meet the inmates, then?' Lee asked jokingly.

"Bring 'em on!" Harris said.

"Hey, Lee!" Dennis called and got her attention….

"Una uso wa nguruwe yenye rutuba," He said in his sweetest voice.

"Na uume wako ni ukubwa wa mrengo wa nzi" She responded with a smile and walked out.

"Damn!" Dennis said. "How did she know that?"

Harris was confused. "What was that?" He asked.

"I told her she had the face of a rutting pig…in Swahili! She then told me something incorrect about my anatomy…"

Harris was still confused.

"Never mind, come on," Dennis said. "Let's go and meet the gang…"

Chapter 56 –Words Around the Campfire

The fire circle was just an ash circle in the middle of the camp the size of a child's paddling pool. Several logs were stacked nearby to keep the fire lit when it was going. Several pieces of the more massive logs were stacked around the fire pit as makeshift seats. A bunch of people then appeared out of various locations as the sun began to wane.

A large, caramel-coloured man carried over another giant stack of logs that he set with the others. While he did that, an older woman with long greying hair was walking out from the trees toward them with some strange beast in her arms. Then a guy came out of the woods with a notebook and a pair of wire-rimmed round glasses. He took a seat on one of the log stumps and wrote something in his journal. Another guy, kind of heavy-set, came out of the latrine with a magazine that he threw into a tent. He took a stump near the firepit as well.

A woman, his age with curly black hair, went over to see the creature that the older woman was holding and was fascinated with the furry fellow that looked like a giant guinea pig. She was Hispanic-looking and wearing a white t-shirt that said "Frankie says Relax" on it as well as a pair of oversized round sunglasses. They, then all walked over to the strange creature asking questions about it to the woman who was carrying it.

"OK, everyone!" Lee shouted. "Take a seat for a minute!" No one was making a move as they were all enchanted by the strange creature. Harris, dutifully, took a seat by the fire and waited for Lee to bring order to the group.

"C'mon everyone, take a …" No one paid her any mind until she used two fingers in her mouth and blew an ear-piercing whistle that everyone heard and caused a flock of brightly coloured birds to take flight. Then everyone sat down.

"OK, now…" Lee said. "Let me get this out, and you can go back to that…What is that, Diane?"

"This is a capybara, and I've been studying its habits here." She said.

"Cool," Lee said. "Now then, I wanted you all to get a chance to meet your new teammate here. This here is Harris Gibraltar."

"Hi all," Harris said as he waved at the crowd. The returned the hello in a subtle murmur.

Lee then continued; "Harris, here, is from England and he's here to assist Dennis. So now we have two doctors for whatever you need. I just wanted to make the introductions since we all now know each other here."

And then Tomas rang the iron triangle despite Lee talking.

"Ok, we can all make the rest of our introductions after dinner, I guess," Lee said, and the lot of them made their way to the mess tent. They all grabbed trays of …something and took their place. Harris sat across from Sarah who came in late after another jeep run up the mountain.

"Hey, Doc." She said. "You getting on all right?"

"Yeah, I'm still the new guy, but I'll get the hang of it…By the way, do I want to know what this is?" He asked, quietly, pointing at the serving tray of green vegetables and the unidentified main dish in question.

"Probably not," She said, also quietly. "Accept it and smile, though…. The natives have far less than this every day." She grabbed a similar tray and took a seat with the rest of the group. It tasted all right, and it was filling enough. Harris then took the tray to the washer and left it with the others. He wasn't sure if he was going to be asked to do KP work or not, but he would accept it if needed. As they dropped off their trays, they all said the same thing to Tomas: "La Comida estuvo muy Buena, senior." He said the same thing with Tomas looking at him with what seemed to be scorn but nodded and grunted just the same in acknowledgement.

They were chatting quietly during dinner not letting conversation interfering with their chowing down so when they got to the fire pit and kicked it up to a high flame, they started conversing amongst themselves. The camp crew all took seats on the stumps around the fire.

"OK, let's do some introductions since this is everyone now," Lee said. "I know we all did it before, but Doc here is our newbie, and we want to be at least aware of each other.

"Then you start, Lee!" Sarah said.

"All right. My name is **Hye Euan Lee**, I'm born and raised in San Francisco and went to Berkeley. I have a masters in foreign languages and am working on my PhD. I can also speak 30 languages…and counting" She said beaming with pride.

All eyes turned to the Caramel-coloured man: "My name's **Theodis Greene**. Born in Mobile, Alabama, spent most of my life in Raleigh, North Carolina and went to Clemson." He then seemed depressed. "I went on a football scholarship but got injured, early on. Now I'm doin' a course in civil engineerin'."

"Sorry to hear that, man." A thin and very white college-age man said as he turned to the gathered group. "My name is **Arliss Collins**. I'm from Balzac, Alberta and taking a break from college right now from The University of Calgary in the new computer science field. All those computers are going to break at one point or another, and I want to be there to fix them."

The next one everyone knew her as she was the first one they all saw as she drove them to the camp. "Well I'm **Sarah Hartley,** and I'm from Williamsport, Pennsylvania and went to school at Penn State. My major is Psychology, and I'm working towards my master's degree when I get home."

"That's where they play the Little League world series, isn't it?" Bart Smiles and said. Sarah nodded. "I went there a few years ago with my brother. He had a great team…" He then turned his attention to the crowd.

"I'm **Bartholomew Smythe**, just call me Bart." He said with his New England accent and hoped that he got through to everyone that he seemed unhappy with his proper name. He had a button-up shirt, wore a hat that hid scraggly black hair and khaki cargo shorts. He was also more stout than the others.

"I was born and raised in North Attleboro, Massachusetts, and I go to Harvard. I'm studying Ecological Economics and hope to find new medicines and methods of protecting the rainforest from overdevelopment."

Harris was looking around, wondering where Dennis went?

"Great!" Diane said as she sat without an animal in her lap. "I'm **Diane Hamburg.** I'm from Lansing, Ohio, and my college is the University of Memphis where I studied Animal Science and Research. I want to study the animals for my school students, where I teach at Grover Cleveland Elementary School in London... Ohio." She hoped for a better reaction to the London reference due to the pair of Englishmen in the group. The crowd didn't bite, so Lee kept it all going…

"Very nice," Lee said. "Mara, go ahead."

Mara seemed bothered, more than anything, to have to speak to everyone as she stood up looking like she was about to fight someone.

"All right, I'm **Mara Garcia,** and I'm from The Bronx, New York. My school is Seton Hall, where I'm studying Political Science…and quickly sat down.

"Right," Lee said, shaking off Mara's lack of social graces. "Harris, take us home."

"Huh?" Harris said, losing his place as the next one to speak. "Oh yeah…OK, well, my name is **Harris Gibraltar** and I was born in Bern, Switzerland, raised in Chelsea in London and my school is the Royal University of Medicine in Cork, Ireland. I am hoping, eventually, to become a pathologist."

"Royal, man?" Mara said. "Seriously?"

"Yeah, everything is royal this, royal that back home," Harris said.

"Yeah, we got the same thing in Canada," Arliss said.

"Well, God bless America!" Mara said.

"Ok, chill," Lee said. "Let's finish up and have ourselves a welcome party, shall we?"

With that, Arliss got a boom box and played some Run D.M.C, Theodis threw some more wood on the fire, and Bart…he pulled out some "happy" cigarettes.

Harris was a bit nervous about lighting up as the last time didn't impress him. Still, he didn't want to seem rude, so he imbibed after seeing Diane enjoying the smoke and thought "Well, what's the worst that could happen?"

He took a long drag, and it caused him to cough for a full minute or so. He then became very thirsty as he watched Mara dance with Theodis, and both appeared to levitate. The others were faded out in a blur. He ran to the shower room and took a drink from the water coming from the spout. He sat on the floor for a moment cooling his head on the aluminium wall of the quasit hut.

"Man, I can't do this!" He thought as he closed his eyes on the shower floor mat.

The next thing he knew it was morning, and he woke with his head under a running shower.

<u>Chapter 57 – Rude Awakening</u>

"All right! I'm up!" Harris said to the old doctor with the now, soaked beard and looking at him with grave concern.

"Mate, you 'ad we all scared for a bit there," Dennis said.

Harris looked out the high window of the shower room and found it was daylight. "Just how long was I asleep?" He thought.

But the bigger question was "How bad did I embarrass myself?" he asked Dennis.

"Well, I'm 'fraid you're going to have a lot to apologise for, mate," Dennis said,

Harris was cringing at that. "Oh, Gawd…what?" He asked with fear of the answer…

"First off, you punched Arliss in the face, then called Theodis something that I won't repeat and then you tried to feel up Sarah's bum!" Dennis reported. "And then you tried to talk Lee and Bart into a shower together with ya. That was when Mara hit you from behind with a tree branch!"

"Oh, gawd!" Harris shouted with his head in his hand. "They're all going to hate me, and I was only here a day or so!"

"Listen up, they're all at breakfast. Dennis said. "My advice would be to get in front of this as quickly as possible. Go apologise, say that you're a lightweight and that it won't happen again!"

"Yeah!" Harris said. "I'll do that right now…I just hope they'll let me."

Harris got up and ambled to the mess tent like a condemned man to the gallows. He entered the mess tent with everyone laughing and smiling until he came in and everyone just looked at him, expressionless.

"Guys, I am so sorry how I behaved last night. He said, looking down at his feet. "I am not a usual smoker of weed. I shouldn't have tried it, and I just didn't know better…I hope you can forgive me for how horrible I was." He just waited for the next words to be shouted at him, but Mara just spoke up.

"Harris, What the hell you talking about?" She asked.

"Well, last night when I…" and then Harris heard suppressed giggles behind him from Dennis and Harris got that he was set up.

"You bastard!" He said to Dennis, and everyone laughed, and Dennis gave Harris a brief man-hug and rubbed his hair quickly. Harris just laughed along with everyone else.

"Now, boy..." Lee said sarcastically... "Go and get yourself some breakfast. We got fresh eggs today."

Harris got a sectioned platter, and Tomas filled him up for the morning with scrambled eggs and toast.

"Gracias, Tomas," Harris said. Tomas just grunted and got back to his work

Harris then took a seat next to Lee and Dennis. "So, what? Mara said. "You don't got pot at your school?"

Harris started toying with his scrambled eggs. "Yeah, but it was just weird when I did it last. Everyone there turned into cartoon animals, but they sounded like themselves. How would you like to see Daffy Duck talking about heart transplants?"

"Point taken," Mara said. "It's supposed to get better over time, though."

"Maybe," Harris said. "I'm just in no hurry to try again."

"So, Harris..." Bart said. "You in a relationship?"

"Well, I got someone to go home to," Harris said. "We went to the intermediate school when we were younger, and we just got hooked up before I left after being apart for two years. It looks good when I get back."

"Nice!" Diane said. "I hope she's in good health?"

Harris was puzzled why she would say that but answered. "Uh, yeah, she's in great shape."

"OK, good," Dianne said. "When they're gone, that's when it hurts. My David was great except for his smoking habit. I lost him about 12 years ago."

"Sorry to hear that," Harris said.

"Yeah, well I figured I better stay busy or I'll think about it too much." She said.

"How about you, Arliss? Theodis asked. "Any special woman in your life?"

"Not really, but I'm not looking." He said. "At least not yet...I'm just saving up for a good one." There was some suppressed smirking at the table.

"Mara? You got someone?" Harris asked, and Mara just sneered back at him.

"Hard pass." She said. Harris just put up his hand and went back to his breakfast.

"Well, I'll tell ya…" Dennis said. "Being married is fine until it goes wrong. I don't know how my Judy is now, and I could care less."

"You got a kid out of it, right?" Lee asked.

"Yeah, and I haven't seen him in years," Dennis said. "Right now, Brian's as old as you lot. I hope he's doing well, though. It'd be nice to see him again."

"Theodis, you must have had your share of women," Dennis said.

"Oh yeah!" He said. "I do all right, still. A lot of the girls want to take care of me and make sure I'm outta pain. Maybe I can at least come out of school with a good job and a home in the burbs…I'd play again if I could, though." He added as he rubbed his hip, which looked like it aggravated him just mentioning it.

Harris wanted to ask Sarah about her life, but time was fleeting…. So was she, it seemed as she headed out the door?

"OK, everyone! Remember to get your mail to me by tomorrow!" Sarah said.

"Yeah, it's 'bout time to get," Bart said.

"Yeah, go on," Lee said. "Harris, I need to talk to you about a few things." Harris just nodded.

They all grabbed notebooks and backpacks and headed into the forest behind the camp while Harris headed for Lee's office. He wondered how much of this mission was known by her…and the rest of them?

He went into her office, which was a simple set up in a room with a table instead of a desk and a set of drawers that looked like it came out of a jumble sale. Two folding chairs seemed delicate as they sat across from the table. Theodis probably had to stand when he talked to Lee here. He wasn't fat, but he was enormous and muscular.

Harris took a seat, and Lee came in and closed the door behind her.

"OK, I got one question for you…and give me an honest answer," Lee said.

Harris then nodded that he would.

"I read in your mission report that you need to go to the Kupuko tribe…Are you insane?"

"I…" was all Harris could get out.

"Because after what they went through, they are ready to slaughter anything in their path…Believe me, I know!" Lee said. Here, Harris was puzzled.

"You read what they went through last year?" Harris asked.

"Read about it…" Lee said. "And experienced it, first-hand! I was lucky to leave in one piece!!"

Chapter 58 – Perverted Thoughts!

Well, this was a surprise! Her familiarity with the Kupuko tribe would seem a bonus on the surface. Too bad that she didn't feel that way.

"OK, so what happened?" Harris asked.

Hye Euan Lee then began her experience as an interpreter and hired missionary:

"We were a group of about 10 of us. Many people were missionaries hoping to meet, greet and introduce God to the many that made up this tribe. They were interested in the items set out of tools and household goods. Items we took for granted were magic to this lot. Even the …concessions that we made to them seemed to be a minor point as we introduced ourselves and what we stood for. Everything was fine for six months and then…"

"Hell in a bucket?" Harris said reviving the words of his medical school chancellor.

"Exactly!" Lee said as she recounted her horrible experience. "I watched the tribesmen and women suffer with what we would get over in days killing the people I called friends. We had no idea that we were the cause of their downfall!"

"It's not your fault," Harris said. "No one knew or saw it coming."

"Yeah, well, I doubt they will take it with a grain of salt!" Lee said. "My exit out of their village required some sweet talking!" Harris could only speculate what that meant…

"Don't get dirty-minded, limy!" Lee said in a most unsubtle fashion. "They were too afraid of getting diseased off someone like me for anything else."

"So, how did you escape?" Harris asked point-blank.

"All I could do is promise a couple of the more sympathetic tribesmen to bring someone here who could restore the tribe." She said. "I had no idea what to say or ask for at the time, but we put out the call and hoped for the best."

Harris sat silent for a moment. Finally, he spoke; "You got it in me."

Lee still seemed apprehensive but just went along that it would be all right. With that, she handed Harris a blue notebook. "These are all my notes from when I first met the Kupuko until my…Exile." Lee said. "I would advise getting as familiar with them as possible." Harris said he would.

"I am also going to get someone recruited to go along. Lee said. "I am not ready to face them again without more back-up." Again, leading Harris to wonder how she escaped the first time.

"So, you study that and then set a time for our departure tomorrow." She said as she picked up a leather backpack. "I have to go make sure these guys don't die in the forest." She then left the room and was soon out the front door of the quasit hut.

Harris took the notebook given to him to his room. Dennis was out with the rest of the crew visiting another tribe in the mountain. He said that he wore a surgical mask when he talked to the members of the Garto Tribe. They dealt with the missionaries and the so-called "Civilized" people for quite a while, so they knew what to expect from them. He treated them with medicines while Bart continued his research of natural herbs that could be used to cure maladies back home.

Harris read the notes given to him and tried to develop an angle to visit the Kupuko Tribe. They were not going to be friendly after what they went through, but he had to make the point that he was not detrimental to them and that he had only their revival in mind. In the meantime, the young doctor wrote a letter to his parents about his trip into South America, his meeting with Juan Montoya and the lot working with him at the encampment. He also penned a letter to Gina and sent it to the veterinary college she was attending in Bristol and wondered if she sorted things out with Eduardo.

He didn't have any idea what the other campers did during the day. For the time being, Dennis was not ready to introduce someone else to the Garto Tribe. Harris was to "hold the fort" for the rest of the day. Only he, Arliss and Tomas were here, and he didn't want to bother either of them as they had their own work to do.

He read some more book including some notes that Dennis left behind that belonged to him and Bart. They came across some plants that looked promising. One of them was a heart medication that they wanted to take back to America to test. It also said something about "Side effect-temporary priapism."

There seemed to be a lot of the research going into heart medications and anti-depressants. While he looked over those, it began to rain. The sound of raindrops on the quasit hut made it sound like it was under attack by stones. Harris put the notebooks back into the cabinet and even put a bucket under a dripping hole in the ceiling that was beginning to invade the journal's hiding place.

He then walked into his room and found his cot being dripped on with water. He moved it to the side of the space where the water wasn't coming in. Did this area flood?

The rain soon stopped, and the air was muggy. There was a thermometer that said 95° nailed to the side of the hut. Harris thought "London was never this hot and humid!" the muggy air made him feel like was sweating to the point of dropping dead! He folded a piece of paper into a fan as he walked to the back of the camp. He didn't see the rest of the area yet as he was waiting for Dennis to give him the tour when his schedule allowed him to do so.

There was a strange apparatus behind the latrine that had a small fire under a brass tub of some sort along with a copper-coloured hose that wound from one large can to another. Harris remembered something like this from an old film he saw. It was used to make moonshine. It did indeed smell like burning corn as it steamed unnoticed by anyone. It left Harris to wonder what other law violations happened here.

The area was just forest with a path next to the river. The water was gentle here as well. "Was the river safe for swimming?" He thought. On a day like this, he would be tempted to share the water with piranhas if there be any. He heard splashing up ahead, so maybe it was…

He saw what looked like Arliss and Theodis hiding in a bush to one side of the water and took cover behind a tree to see what they were watching. They didn't see the young doctor hiding from the pair. It was Sarah and Diane having a dip…and it looked like they didn't bother dressing for the occasion. Well, why should they? No police here.

Harris just kept his distance, however, as he saw Lee approaching the two of them from the other side of the forest. He wondered how she was going to handle this? Beat them with a branch? Shout out her anger?

She grabbed them both by the shirt collars and dragged them back. It was then she saw Harris from his hiding place as he watched the whole scene go down and waved for him to approach them. She didn't do or say anything until he arrived on-scene. Lee had an idea of how to deal with these peeping Toms:

"Well, boys…" She said, quietly, to the two of them still on the ground. "It's good that nudity doesn't offend you. That will come in handy, shortly."

Lee then turned to Harris: "I guess, as of now, these are the extra muscle I referred to earlier. We are ready when you are, Doctor."

"Tomorrow morning," Harris said, also quietly. "Meet me at the office and have some food ready to take along for a few days....and bring lots of water, too. We'll need it."

Harris and Lee started walking back to camp with Theodis and Arliss still sitting on the ground wondering what they should do next.

"Shoo!" Lee said with a wave, and the two peeping toms ran off into the woods back to whatever their clipboards told them to do. Sarah and Diane continued their skinny-dip, unaware of the exchange on land.

Harris distracted Lee from her thoughts to inquire about the strange brass unit behind the latrine. "That's Dennis's thing." She said. "He doesn't do much with the ganja, so he makes his own party-fuel. At least there are no revenuers here."

Lee then turned her attention to the next day's mission and was still apprehensive about returning to the tribe that banished her, that was apparent as they walked back to camp. Harris held his tongue except to say to Lee that calling Arliss "extra muscle" was too kind as he was as thin and tall as Harris, himself, used to be before his muscle regimen. He also asked about his boss.

"Will Dennis be joining us tomorrow?" Harris asked.

"Not unless you need him." She said. "He already said that he and Bart were going to explore some areas to the northwest and see about a new type of medicinal herb. They are already buzzing about something they said they came across last week."

"Ok, good," Harris said. "I don't think Dennis will benefit from my way of doing things, anyway." He left it at that for Lee to interpret.

Harris was wondering just how much Lee knew about him and what he could do. He held his words as they all had dinner together that night. Tomorrow would be a trying day, and the night would not be comfortable. At least he would be sleeping on a soft cot tonight despite it being paper-thin. Even the single sheet he slept under was feeling like a ton of weight as he slept and sweated.

Chapter 59 – The Great Caucasian Hope

Harris dropped his letters into Sarah's mailbag. He just hoped to be able to get whatever answers his parents and Gina sent back in a timely fashion...meaning before he returned home. Theodis and Arliss seemed to have no clue what was going on. Harris had to admit to himself that he had no clue how to approach the Kupuko lot, either. All he knew was that he just needed the chance to put them on the right track again. The thing that made him nervous was Lee and how scared she was about going back to the source of her exile. Harris knew he would be all right. The key was keeping everyone else alive.

They showed up at the quasit hut at 8 am as ordered with a pack each in their hands and loaded them into the jeep along with two canoes strapped to the now-enclosed top. Lee then showed up as well in khaki shorts and a white A-shirt and Harris was ready with his pack and the doctor' bag his father presented to him for Christmas. Everyone seemed to dress similarly in cargo khaki shorts and whatever t-shirts suited them that day.

Sarah drove them to the bottom of the mountain, being careful as the roads were more treacherous coming down than going up due to recent rains. On top of that, they were carrying canoes on the old jeep roof. She drove them to a trailhead at the direction of Lee. Their league leader then took a can of spray paint out of the jeep and sprayed three large dots on a cliffside and said to Sarah to meet her there at sunrise in two days. Lee thought that Harris didn't know what he was talking about, but the doctor-in-training was adamant that he could have everything sorted in such a short amount of time.

Harris also wondered if their absence was going to cause concern in the rest of the camp. No doubt that Dennis will wonder about these four. The others would also be more in the dark about what was going on. There was no time to deal with any of that. People were dying and in need of help. All they needed was the opportunity to prove themselves. What was getting to Harris was his need to hide what he was. The tribe would be no problem but who knows what Lee and the boys would make of him after this if they found out?

They started to hike while carrying canoes on their shoulders through the thick brush into the unknown which soon turned to a forest with the odd sounds of life. They then came across the river and put in for the paddle up the Amazon. There was life all over the forest as animals like monkeys and beautiful looking birds that were observing them paddle the waters.

On occasion, they would pass what they believed a floating log that turned out to be a Cayman or a snake. They all kept eyes out for the rogues of these groups trying to make a play for visiting humans. On the shoreline were observers consisting of sloths and tapir who were going about their own business of eating and avoiding being eaten by jaguars.

They paddled for hours and then came to rest on the shore of what looked like an empty beach. They dragged the canoes further on to the river's shoreline to keep them hidden, and they all took a nap for a solid hour before starting their trek into the rainforest. The sun beating down on them was relaxing with the trees blocking some of the direct rays. They then put on their backpacks and followed Lee into the forest. She slowly walked down a forgotten path keeping her eyes and ears out for the sounds of the humans. That was no easy task as the hunters of this area were astute at adapting to the animal's mannerisms.

A long line of the green forest seemed to crawl along the ground. "Those are Leafcutter Ants," Lee said. "They are in the millions here. Just be careful as you step over them." They all stepped over the moving conveyor belt of cut leaves using a couple of handy rocks. The bugs in the air were getting less irritating as they tended to stay behind in pools of water. The rest of the hike became long and rocky. The lot of them rested a couple of times not saying much as Lee was continually listening for activity by humans rather than wildlife. The Jaguars were the main concern as they would want to challenge humans to their territory regardless of what their opponent's intentions were.

Suddenly and out of nowhere, the first appearance of humans appeared all carrying spears aimed at the four of them. A group of naked men wearing nothing but war paint. One of them spoke directly to Lee in their primal language and looked like he would kill her right then and there. Harris put his hands in a praying motion and got on his knees, showing he had no intention of harming anyone.

The boys also did the same after they also saw Lee strike the same pose.

The tribesmen bound their hands and led them into the village, which was an additional mile up the forest path. They attracted the attention of the villagers, male and female, young and old, wearing nothing but decorative headwear if even that. The tribal elder looked upon the westerners with scorn. He and Lee had a heated conversation with Lee pointing to Harris every so often. The elder being ready to strike Harris with his spear while the young Xenon stood proudly with no fear.

"Lee…" Harris said. "Tell him to take me to his sickest people, and I'll heal them."

Lee looked at him like he was crazy. She spoke his words to the village elder who didn't seem impressed. They were ready to spear Arliss when Harris stood in front of his dangerously sharp weapon with defiance. If he had to prove his self-healing ability here to save his new friend, then so be it. The elder looked at Harris and was impressed by his bravery. "Lee, tell him that I am his only chance to let his people live." Lee then translated the words to the village head. He then ordered the villagers to take the two boys and Lee and guard them with spears.

Harris took his medical bag and followed the elder to a hut that had a large skull out front on a stick. The elder would go no further than that as he pointed to a path around the stick building. Harris went to the back of the shelter and found the entrance covered with a woven mat. He went in and was immediately sickened and saddened by what he saw. Ten men and women of various ages were lying on the floor, along with some children. Human waste was all along the walls. No one cared about this lot as they were deemed ready to leave the planet. The smell was horrid as he took out a nose clamp to attempt to cut down on the noxious fumes.

There was no time to lose. Harris opened his bag which had in it nothing really medical-related inside. Several bottles of water, a notebook and several sharp acupuncture needles occupied the case. Of course, he never really used the needles but were a distraction for anyone who would try to spy in his luggage.

There was no privacy here among the sick — only a large room where they would throw the dead through the entrance when it came time. Hardly anyone paid any attention to Harris as he looked for the sickest of the lot. He came across an older looking woman with some grey in her black hair laying on her side and gasping for air clearly from fluid in the lungs.

"OK, let's dance." Harris thought.

He began his healing, and the bright light scared the rest of the sick inhabitants as they clustered against the far wall. The sounds of panic came through the thin hut walls, although no one would approach out of fear. When the older woman stood and smiled after drinking a bottle of water, the rest were satisfied that Harris was there for their greater good. They all awaited their administration of healing touch from the strange white man and accepted their reprieve from death with immense gratitude. He had to take a break between each three to rest for about 10 minutes.

Harris made shapes with his hands in the hope that they would recognise that he wanted them to wait until he healed everyone, and all would leave at once.

Two hours or so later, Harris went to the far wall of the hut when he healed the last of the lot. "Lee, can you hear me?" Harris shouted.

"Yes!" She shouted in return.

"Tell them to hold their ground!" He shouted back. "We're coming out!"

The villagers stood in disbelief as the now-healthy villagers emerged from the hut in a long line. Harris stood behind them looking exhausted but keeping his feet.

"Tell that chief guy to approach and stop at the skull!" Harris shouted exhaustedly. "Let him be satisfied that this...the crisis is over!" Lee then delivered the translation of what she heard.

The elder walked over to his, formerly, sickened peoples and looked them over to his satisfaction. He was mystified as to their sudden absence of sickness as was Harris's travelling companions. There was no reason to have them stay in the death hut any longer and had them join the other villagers in cheers and praise. The spears were no longer holding back the other westerners. They had no clue what to say to Harris but were thankful to witness this miracle. The tribal chieftain said he wanted to speak to Harris about something. For that, he needed Lee to come along, A significant taboo to the other tribe leaders but was allowed under these conditions. The head chieftain who was threatening Harris an hour ago invited him to stay with his men in the night hours for something that involved his future.

"The master said that you are to stay with them this evening and partake in a celebration that will reveal your path," Lee said.

"My path?" He asked.

"Your future," Lee said. "They claim to have ways of showing you what lays ahead." Of course, it all sounded like fortune-telling and new age scuttlebutt to Harris, but he saw what little they had, and they had time to kill until tomorrow. He consented to whatever they wanted to show him. The other three went to the fire circle and traded stories with Lee giving the translations of how she tried to hold her promise that she would protect the tribe. They all wanted to know who this man was who came to the camp and saved them all. She could only make things up as she didn't understand herself. Even saying he was something called a ...Xenon.

Chapter 60 – True or False

The Kupuko had no idea what a Xenon was, so it was easy to make things up about him. This assertion didn't sit well with Theodis or Arliss, but they let her speak her tale as it meant that they would leave alive and with the blessings of this group. Most of it, the two westerners didn't understand, anyway. They could only hear the word "Xenon" stand out. She was making all this up on the fly...but making positive things up about a creature they were all told from birth that was going to eat them while they slept if they didn't pay attention, do their homework and all those other things parents make up to get their kids in line. Well, that part was tricky.

That evening, while Lee spun the tale, Harris sat in a circle with the other elders of this group in an open-air hut. There were three of them mixing up a dusty mixture of leaves and dirt along with some strange liquids and plants. He had no clue what was going on with it as they chatted amongst themselves. He just sat patiently, waiting for whatever they had in mind and watched the smoke drift straight up into the sky.

When the mixture seemed to be ready, they put the mixture to simmer over a plate to heat up on the fire in the centre of the hut. Some of it even caught fire, but they paid it no heed as they brought a hollow pole over three feet long to the group and dumped the mixture in the tube after it cooled. One of the men spoke some odd words with his hands up to the ceiling. Harris had no clue what he was saying other than it seemed to be some religious invocation. The elder then took the tube of ash and leaves and held it up to his mouth. Harris had turned his head and coughed for a moment. When he turned back to the elder, he blew the mix into a cloud that Harris breathed in by surprise. It was rancid!

Harris coughed for a solid minute and even threw up. He panicked for a moment as he never threw up before. The feeling was terrible as his entire stomach churned in pain. He turned his angry face to the elders, but they were gone. Harris just had one thought go through his head at that time; "Uh-Oh!"

It was all peaceful at first with the fire burning and a tingling feeling going through his body. It was all quiet at first. Just a still sense while the fire was going and the smoke continuing to rise through the open roof. Then it all began to hit him!

The ground began to shake, and he was besieged by snakes that crawled to him as he panicked, and then they passed around and through him as if he weren't there.

The fire that was raging in the pit seemed to catch the roof on fire. Harris then ran out of the hut and away from the inferno that looked like nothing from the outside. He ran out into the village where no one was around. He was alone with just the other fire burning in the pit.

Then, there was a sound of animal footsteps fast approaching, first soft and then louder as they approached. It was a giant capybara with red eyes about 10 feet in height …and on its back was Diane riding it like a horse!

"Harris!" She called to him. "Follow me!"

…and he did through the forest where she went too fast and vanished on the back of the gigantic rodent. He was alone in the woods with branches above him…they attempted to reach down and grab him until he curled up into a ball and nothing touched him.

There was then a long stretch of void until he found a hut with a bright light coming from the doorway. He entered to see Dennis in a surgical gown, preparing to work. He just turned to Harris and said "Scrub in! We got work to do!" He washed his hands in a sink off to the side of the room and put on black rubber gloves. He then went to see Lee laying on the operating table. Next to her were monkeys in surgical gowns that seemed to be operating the anaesthesia and the machinery.

"Well, she needs her appendix out! Are you gonna save her or what?" Dennis said in an echoing voice. He nodded and took the scalpel offered him by the senior doctor and looked at her stomach, lying flat out for the operation. Harris only did this operation on a foam mannequin before but went on…

He made the incision, and a horde of ants and flying wasps emerged from the open slit! Harris could only recoil until this image vanished into the darkness.

He reopened his eyes and was then in a hall of coffins as far as could be seen. All the coffins contained bodies…and they were all people he knew! Diane and Dennis were in two across from each other. Lee and Mara in the next two, Arliss and Bart, Sarah and Theodis…they were followed by Roland and Tamar with Harris getting more and more depressed with each he looked in. Vincent and Magdalena, his Mom and Da… and finally, Gina! He started crying and falling to the floor of black. "Why?" He screamed until He stood up again, and all the coffins were then empty! He felt a massive sense of relief over the empty containers!

There was a pram at the end of the empty coffins where he heard the sounds of an infant. He looked in and saw a baby girl with no nappy. She was a cute little thing. "Hello, dear." He said with a happier heart. "Aren't you a lovely thing?" The baby just laid in the buggy with her little arms and legs flailing about. He wondered where her mum was until he spotted a python approaching and attempting to crawl into the stroller.

"Getaway, you!" He yelled. When he grabbed the snake, it turned to ash in his hands and dissipated in the wind. The baby was content as she fell asleep in the carriage.

It was then several dogs, wolves and coyotes approached. They stopped well short of Harris and the baby as they all just sat outside the pram in what seemed to be at attention and awaiting further orders. The young xenon anticipated for one of the animals to make an aggressive move, but none did. All the canines assembled there then looked upwards.

Harris turned to see what got their attention. The baby levitated into space with no worry and vanished from sight. The beasts all retreated back into the forest. Harris just wanted all this to end.

He then heard a voice in the distance. "Harris!" It was Gina. She called to him in a far-away sounding tone even though she seemed to be standing right in front of him. "Gina!" He said and tried to hold her, but his hand went right through her.

"Harris, come back to me!" She said in that far-away voice.

"I will, Luv!" He said. "I promise!" She then faded like a cloud of dust met a gust of wind while he felt the warmth on his face and his face alone.

Harris then felt cold and intense light in his eyes from the morning sun. He and an anteater laid nose to nose, causing him to wake with a start and the strange beast running off. He was awake on the outside rim of the village under a tree. The naked villagers were in his field of vision, eating with his crew. He stumbled over to the group and just stood silently while they looked at the young medico. It was apparent he had a rough night.

The tribe elder was there and muttered words in his native tongue. "Haso no co san oy cay ya nu." Which Lee translated and delivered to Harris:

"Take whatever you envisioned and let it be a guide on your path." All Harris could think was how he was supposed to interpret a jumble of hallucinations? He even felt a bit humiliated rather than fulfilled.

The crew, later, made their good-byes to the now-tolerant Kupuko Tribe and made their way back to the hiking trail. The men were hoping Lee knew her way back to camp.

Chapter 61 – Lost Weekend

The usually quiet Theodis was now chatting incessantly down the trail as they headed back to the river.

"I couldn't believe those guys, man! They had nothing!" He said.

"Yeah, well they had spears!" Arliss said. "That was about all I was looking at for a while there."

"That lot faces threats every day…" Lee chimed in. "…And now they have far more to worry over. I'm just glad the sickness isn't part of it."

Harris was quiet as he was still reeling from his psychedelic trip last night.

"What do you mean?" Arliss said.

"I mean the diseases from the outsiders was just the beginning of their worries," Lee said, sadly. "They always had to hunt for their food, gather their water, reinforce against the weather when it got rough. Now they have the farmers and loggers coming in and encroaching on the lands that they and their ancestors lived and hunted in for centuries." She said all this while a tapir ran by with its young and a grouping of capybaras scattered into the forest as the lot of them walked by.

"They even stopped having children!" She continued.

"Stopped having kids?" Theodis said in disbelief.

"They felt it was their time to fade into the after world…until Doc, here showed up!" Lee said. She couldn't help but see he said nothing up to now. Harris was listening to all of it but still trying to make sense of what he saw.

"Harris, you OK?" She said to the young Xenon. Harris just nodded.

"So, did anyone tell the authorities here?" Arliss said. "Someone has to have said something."

"Yeah, but like anything else with government, they are slow to do anything," Lee responded. "I hope they do something soon or all this will be gone."

Their walk continued down the trail to the side of the river heading to where their canoes lay in wait to take them back to the put-in site. Lee had marked the area with several branches when they pulled in. It was just a matter of finding them.

The dry season has started to take place, which was reducing the level of the river and caused the water to recede and create what looked like more ground to appear. They continued to walk through the long grass along the river.

"Man, why do we have to keep walkin' through this grass?" Theodis asked. "It's cuttin' up my legs!"

"The trail is the safest way there," Lee said. "We just gotta deal with it."

"That ground along the river is all cleared out now." Theodis counter. "Why don't we just walk on that?" Before Lee could tell him Theodis found out. The deceptively dry sand gave way under him, and he was thigh-deep in the muck and still sinking.

"That's why!" Lee said, angrily, as she slammed her pack on the dry ground looking through her backpack.

"Hey, get me outta here! I'm sinking!" Theodis yelled as struggling in the soft ground the river was hiding a day ago that revealed the quicksand now visible from the retreated waters.

"Stop struggling, or you'll sink even more, dumbass!" Lee shouted as she threw a lassoed rope at the large man, now helpless in the river marsh. He tried to stay calm, but it wasn't easy as he felt his body slowly slip further into the river bed.

"Theodis! Slide the loop under your arms!" She instructed the caramel-coloured man as she threw the rope to him. "Harris, tie this to that tree over there."

Harris tied the other end around the trunk of the Euterpe Precatoria, ensuring that the big guy wasn't going anyplace. Arliss and Lee grabbed the rope and pulled only a little at a time with Harris in the back pulling in a slow, similar pattern to the other two. It took them a half hour to get Theodis back on dry land, and they all fell on the ground in an exhausted heap once their man was back on solid ground.

"Sorry guys," Theodis said, lying in the sun. "I was just afraid I was gonna drown in that shit!"

"That's a myth," Lee said. "You would have stopped sinking at chest level. The worst that would have happened was you would drown by rising river waters or died of starvation…. maybe eaten by some animal."

"Viva la Difference!" He said as they continued to lay in the sun a bit longer.

After ten more minutes, they gathered themselves and kept hiking through the grass, not minding so much, anymore. It was still scratching them as they passed, but it beat the alternative. They got to where the canoes sat undisturbed on dry land, now a bit more drained from the receded waters. There were no fish nearby as all the ponds stood empty of life by those predators higher up the chain grabbing food from the puddles of standing water and assured they would not be in the middle of an animal buffet. Lee went and stood on the beach to satisfy the boys that the sand was safe to walk on.

"Boys, I don't know about you, but I need a swim first before we set off." She said. "Theodis, you need to get the rest of that sand off ya." The caramel man of colour couldn't deny that as his legs were chafing from the leftover grit. The boys wandered into the water and pulled off their shirts and shorts bathing in their underwear and still mindful of any wildlife in the area while Lee joined them in the water…also topless! That didn't strike Harris as much as he was much more accustomed to this fashion in Europe, but the other two just gawked as they didn't know what to make of it. She didn't have much to display, anyway.

"Oh, gimme a break, pervs!" Lee said. "How do you think I lived when I was in the village full time?" They just brushed it off and swam for a few minutes to get clean the best they could in the cloudy but warm river. Theodis got the rest of the muck off him to his relief, and they were on the water, rather than in it a few minutes later and travelling with the current so it took less energy.

"So, Lee…" Arliss asked. "What did you tell the tribe about Harris last night?"

"Um, I was just thinking on my feet, so I don't remember much." She replied. "Just that he was from the Xenon Tribe from far away and that he was a high chieftain where we came from." Harris just grinned hearing this.

"I hope you don't mind, Doc." Lee then said to him. "It was all I could come up with at the time."

"Don't give it a second thought" Harris responded as he continued paddling. "You do what you gotta do to stay alive…Besides, what do they know about Xenons?"

Harris was in a daze as Arliss did the steering in the back. He just kept trying to make sense of what he saw. It was all a hallucination, of course, but was there a deeper meaning to it all?

"Man, I'd be insulted if someone called me a Xenon!" Theodis said.

261

"All their robbing and killing! I wouldn't think twice about..." His next sentence was interrupted by a jaguar killing a lingering sloth.

They all responded by shutting up and rowing their boats faster. Harris couldn't wait to get back to camp. He was sure the others felt the same.

Chapter 62 – Cut to the Chase

They were at the place Lee spray-painted and waited for Sarah to show up when they heard another vehicle approaching in the distance. Lee shouted to everyone to take cover in the trees and keep low. The empty logging lorry drove by with no payload. The driver of the truck paid no heed to anyone as he passed by the explorers. They came out after his vehicle was out of sight.

"OK, why did we have to hide?" Arliss asked.

"That was a logger," Lee said. "Some of them have no tolerance for anyone but their fellow workers. Some even like to get out and fight just for the fun of it. We don't need that drama right now."

"Great…" Harris said. "Another group to take abuse from."

"That one was probably, OK," Lee said. "At least he used his truck rather than the river."

Harris was confused about all this. "Meaning?" He asked.

"Man, did you see all the chainsaws we had in the shed?" Theodis asked.

"Yeah." Harris returned. "What were they for?"

Just then, Sarah drove up in the jeep and smiled as she didn't have to wait to pick them up again. "When we get back, we'll show you," Lee said as Sarah drove up beside them.

"Hey, how'd it go?" She asked.

"It went well," Lee said. "We all survived…without incident." She was not about to tell anyone else about Theodis and his misstep. Let him do it himself if he wanted. They secured the canoes to the jeep and were on their way up the mountain. Harris forgot what a long drive it was as he rode in the seat behind the big ex-football player and Arliss holding the sides of the canoes in the back of the jeep. Lee rode shotgun. Again, it took them half an hour or so to get back to the top of the mountain and their camp. It looked like Doctor Dunedin was waiting for them and not happy.

"Oy, where were you lot?" He asked. "We thought we saw the last of ya!"

"No problem, Dennis," Lee said. "We just had to deal with the locals."

"What locals?" He asked.

Lee took a moment to deal with the others in her party. "Boys, go put the canoes away…and then fill in Harris about the saws."

"Yes, 'em!" Theodis said as Arliss and Harris nodded. They got to work putting the boats away while Lee and Dennis went to the quasit hut office to discuss her absence. Harris put his doctors' bag near the hut and helped the boys with the boats. They walked the canoes to the shed, and they set them on end so they would drain. Arliss then opened the door to his workshop and pointed the chainsaws out as he took one from off the table.

"OK, here's the deal…" Arliss said as the other three looked on. "We have more loggers than that trucker we saw earlier to worry over. There are also the clear-cutters that work up the river a couple of clicks. They cut the trees and send them floating down the river. They're supposed to be cutting them into pieces if they do. He kept speaking while he took a bottle of oil and mixed it with gasoline, carefully.

"They are also supposed to be giving the bigger logs over to the truckers we saw earlier and selling them that way." He continued.

"I guess they think sending them downriver is easier. The only problem with that is that the camp could flood if they get stuck here…along with the neighbouring villages."

"So, how do the chainsaws figure in?" Harris asked. "If the logs are in the river, do you chop them in the water?"

"We pull to the shore the ones that are doing the most obstruction and keep the flow going until they pass." Sarah then said as she entered. "Lee then informs the local leaders and they deal with the cutters."

"Yeah, it used to be a slap on the wrist," Theodis said. "It used to happen, like, a lot. It's only starting to slow down, now."

"Yeah, so we better get you trained on what to do, Doc," Arliss said. "They're like any other piece of machinery. You've got to respect them and do what they're meant to do. If you don't, you take a chance of losing something valuable."

"Well, Dennis said no one here lost a limb, yet," Harris said. "And I sure don't want to mess up that record. When do we start?"

Arliss picked up the chainsaw he was maintaining and carried it out the door of the machinery hut. "OK, follow me." He said.

While they were having the discussions of the mean machines, Lee and Dennis were discussing her absence over the past couple of days. Dennis was not subtle in his concern for the wayward bunch of explorers.

"Woman, what were you thinking?" Dennis asked the group leader. "You know what happened the last time you dealt with those savages! Are you suicidal?"

"I did what I had to do to keep my promise!" Lee said. "I said to them I would get help, and I did! That guy from Ireland said he could send someone on who could do the job and he came through!"

Lee talked to him before about her frustration with getting help with the Kupuko and what happened to her party. They also discussed a while ago about who and what she was going to receive from the UK. He was left to determine that there was no way that they could combat the ravages the Kupuko tribe went through. Now, this upstart shows up and makes everything perfect?

"How'd he do it?" Dennis asked. "How was it done?"

"I have no clue." She said. "All I know was that I had a huge-ass spear pointing at my head as well as the other two boys and Harris was led into a hut and said he could handle everything. The next thing I know, he did."

They heard the chainsaws running as they walked out and saw Arliss tutoring Harris on their use. He did well and kept the balance going as a few logs were split to firewood as the other boys applauded approvingly at his efforts.

"Keep an eye on this one, Lee," Dennis said. "And let's just be glad this Xenon is on our side!"

Lee could only nod. "Yeah, we best not tell anyone about him. The crew might have a field day with him if they knew the truth…especially Theodis!"

Chapter 63 – A Peek Behind the Curtain

The big iron bell rang with the signal that dinner was on. Harris was quite pleased with himself and the way he handled the dangerous beast of a machine. Somehow, it felt like taking Napoleon for a walk and his trying to keep the dog from misbehaving if he saw a small rogue animal, like a squirrel or a cat in the vicinity of Essex Street. The big dog took Harris for a walk until he grew up and could control the canine. Sarah even mentioned taking Harris to the airfield when she went down to drop off the mail and let him try to drive on the level roads in the area. She also requested that anyone who wanted stuff should tell her now so she could order it. Dennis placed orders for medical supplies and a large sack of yeast. Lee put it under Tomas's request so no one would be the wiser as it would end up in Dennis's still.

Meanwhile, the camp cook was ordering more food for the camp crew. Sarah tried to converse with the cook in her high school Portuguese to get his order. The frustration on both their parts called for Lee to come over and translate. Sarah also knew the deal with the yeast and to order a bag of dried corn, also written under Tomas's checklist. Everyone else asked for little personal things, and even Harris asked for more cassettes and batteries for his Walkman and some comic books he started reading again from when he was younger. They all then sat down to a dinner of hamburgers that Tomas cooked to make more room in the freezer. It was a welcome relief as they had a variety of different things that were very unfamiliar to them. They thanked Tomas and went their separate ways after dinner. Harris went with Sarah to the airfield since they had a lot of sunlight left that day. She figured after they got the plane loaded, they could start his driving lessons. It would be a bit tricky as the old jeep was a manual transmission.

After dinner, Bart started questioning Arliss about where they were for the past couple of days as he seemed to be the easiest to question. He visited him while he was soldering some radio equipment to improve the shortwave antennae.

"I don't know what I can tell you, Bart," Arliss said.

"I can tell you Harris had no fear as he stood in front of me when that one dude with a spear threatened to shish-kabob me. He did the same for all of us, eh? Lee was there sputtering over whatever language they spoke…"

"What about Theodis?" Bart asked.

"He was in the same boat as me, eh?" Arliss responded. "Harris had no problem standing and guarding him, too."

"So, Harris was led into that hut with a skull on a stick?" Bart asked.

"Yeah, that's right," Arliss said. "Not even that Chief guy would go too close to that hut. I don't know what happened in there, but he came out with a dozen or so of the tribe, and they were all looking fine."

"How long was he there?" Bart asked.

"Aboot an hour, I think," Arliss said. "Maybe two. I was too busy looking at some savage with a spear to check my watch."

The sick of the tribe cured in one hour? Bart remained clueless by the possibility of what Harris had in his bag of tricks. What was he carrying to make that type of miracle happen? Bart then went to Theodis who seemed more defensive about the questions...

"Hey, what Arliss tell ya, man?" The hulking man asked.

"All he said was that you guys were on the wrong end of a spear while Harris did whatever he did," Bart replied.

"Yeah, well, I don't know what he did," Theodis said. "All I know is that they were happy to put 'em down when all those guys came out the hut."

"Any idea what he did?" Bart then asked.

"No clue, man," Theodis said. "They stopped trying to kill us afterwards, and Doc Harris went all sorts of crazy that night."

"Crazy?" Bart asked. "What you mean?"

"I asked Lee, and she said they gave him some hallucinogen that's supposed to make you see your future." He said. "All I saw was him running around chasing and being chased by animals in his head. We were told just to let him be and not touch him. I have no clue what he saw, but you saw what a lightweight he was around the campfire. I can only guess..."

"Did he take anything into the hut with him?" Bart interrupted. Theodis didn't take kindly to that but went on... "Just his doctorin' bag," Theodis said as he opened the latrine door. "He was insistent on needin' that." With that, he closed the door and went about his business.

Lee was not available for Bart to question as she was on the short-wave with Arliss checking in with headquarters. Bart took the occasion to notice that Harris's bag was probably unguarded since he and Sarah were at the airfield. Bart didn't feel himself a thief, but the temptation was too great to pass up. Why come back with just one significant medicinal discovery when it could be two? He went into the young doc's room in the quasit hut. Dennis, it seemed, was not there, either. He quietly entered the small room empty of any life and noticed his quarry. The bag sat under Harris's cot with nothing to stop him from inspecting it. He took one more look down the hall to see nobody. There was only the faint sound of water running from the other side of the building. He tried to open the black leather bag, but it stayed shut. There was no keyhole and no latch, so how was this done?

Bart was then interrupted and startled by a voice behind him:

"Trying to sneak a look at how the magician did his trick?" Dennis said with his arms crossed and looking angry at the young intruder.

"Dennis…" Bart said with a sigh. "He's holding the cure to sickness. You can bet I wanna know how..."

"Why didn't you just ask him?" Dennis asked.

"I did," Bart said. "All he said was that only he could do it."

"…And you didn't believe it." Dennis responded as he approached Bart. "And that he wanted to come from Europe, risk his life and his education, instead of just sending it here."

Bart was at a loss. Why he didn't think that through had him looking flummoxed. Nonetheless, he shot back "I'll bet you are as curious. You can't convince me, otherwise."

"Yeah, I admit I'm curious." Dennis relented. "But I'm sure there's nothing in that bag that'll make any difference. Unlike you, I can keep me curiosity in check."

"I couldn't help it, I guess." He said. "I couldn't open the bag, anyway. There's some secret lock on it I don't get." He then showed the bag to the Australian doctor who then looked at it with a feeling of nostalgia.

"Wow, an old Adler bag." He said. "I 'aven't saw one of those in years!"

"Can you open it?" Bart asked.

Dennis just looked at him, disgusted. "I can…But why should I?" He asked.

"C'mon, Dennis…" Bart said. "You're as curious as I am about what's in there."

Dennis couldn't argue with that. It would also silence any arguments Bart had later…maybe. "One look…we disturb nothing, we take nothing, and we put it back exactly as found and take what we see to our graves!" Dennis said as if the Almighty himself said it.

"Done!" Bart said and passed the bag to Dennis to open.

"My grandpa used one of these bags back in the war," Dennis said. "They 'ad a secret lock on it to keep addicts out of the morphine." And with that, he worked a small lever that was well hidden on the bottom seam of the bag, and it opened like the cave of the forty thieves.

"Now don't go scatter things about!" Dennis said. "Whatever's in there 'as to go back as it came out." They laid the contents out on the floor next to Harris' cot and examined the contents which consisted of several empty water bottles, three Judge Dredd comic books and a book on acupuncture. There was also the bag of needles that Harris opened to look like they served their purpose and a notebook of what seemed to be Qi maps of the human body.

"There you are, then," Dennis said. "He's a savant when it comes to the art of acupuncture."

Bart nodded a bit down-trodden with this revelation, but his curiosity was satisfied. They carefully repacked the medical valise and placed back under Harris's cot. Bart left to go back to his tent. He would have to settle for just one fantastic breakthrough.

Dennis went to his desk and sat silently to write in his journal. He knew the acupuncture angle was a ruse but was also in the dark how this young magician made this cloud of death disappear.

Chapter 64 – Mail Call

Harris made regular trips now with Sarah as she got deliveries from the plane to continue with his drive lessons. It was hard to hit anything when they were near the airport. He could even drive faster when he developed more confidence behind the wheel and aircraft wasn't landing as he taxied down the runway at full speed. These excursions were in addition to his trips with Dennis and Lee as they visited the different villages and villagers. This lot was far easier to deal with than the Kupuko were when he first arrived. The tribes knew the difference between the good and evil that emerged from the outer edges of the rainforest. Slowly, the bad guys took their hunting lands and the trees to go with it.

It was also nerve-wracking, at times, to watch uncut logs float down the river by the camp. Harris took the occasion to follow the river and a log's journey which ended abruptly about a mile or so away over the large waterfall. He crawled along the precipice in an attempt to look over the cliff and see the bottom but could only see mist covering the landing zone for the logs. He wanted to take the next occasion of driving lessons to see where the final landing zone was for the travelling sticks of wood. However, that would involve a hike as well.

Finally, letters from home! He received his correspondence from his parents in one letter about a month after he got to his base camp. He wrote that he would get used to the conditions here, eventually. They wrote back that they hoped he was eating enough and that his mission was going well, too. Arliss even showed everyone how to set up a time and a place so that they could make a phone call back home using his wireless set-up.

Another week later and Harris got a handful of gold in the mail…at least it was worth that much to him as it was a letter from Gina! He treasured every word of what it said, even the bad parts:

Dear Harris,

I hope you are keeping yourself safe wherever you are.

The summer is going at a snail's pace here even though it's high tourist season. I'm working in the zoo here in Central London as part of an additional studies programme.

I am hoping that working on these massive beasts will help me further with the more tame lot.

My brother, Eduardo, came for a visit, and I told him that I would marry you no matter what he tries to say or do and if he has a problem with it, then hard cheese!

He tried to argue with me about it for the entire day until I explained through his wife, Francine, my feelings and his constant speeches of mixed blood and all that were a waste of time. She must have said something to him because he backed off, eventually. He might not do the catering, however.

I'm just glad he stopped, though. My stomach has been getting sick and upset every day. Wish you were here to stop it. Actually, I just wish you were here.

Come home quickly, I can't wait to see you, my love.

Yours forever

Gina

Now, all Harris wanted was to get home and get back to leading a regular life. Well, as close as he could come to one. At Dinner, others had received their family letters as well except for Diane and Dennis who seemed to be devoid of life outside the confines of the camp. For Diane, she was entirely into her studies. She did have a son in the American Marines, but he was deployed someplace where he couldn't correspond until September.

Dennis was a harder case. He hadn't heard from his son in a long time. Harris wondered if he even tried to contact him. Lee was reading a lot of items from all over the place. Most of it was official work: The office in Rio, Chancellor Rosewood at The Royal College of Medicine and her own family back in San Francisco. Her father was a college professor at UC Davis while her mother worked for the Department of Education in Sacramento. She also had a sister who started attending Berkley last year. She spoke with pride of being a member of a family of educators.

The others were quietly going over their letters from their colleges and loved ones. Mara was reading her letter and seemed to be getting madder as she read on. She ended up screaming and throwing her food tray into the tent wall. She stormed out, leaving her food stuck to the cloth shelter.

"You couldn't pay me enough to ask what that was about," Theodis said, breaking the silence after her departure. They nodded in agreement as they continued to eat and quietly read their letters. Harris was curious but, like the others, didn't want to bring up what just happened.

Dennis mentioned that they would also have to do an inventory of the medical room shortly. The supplies were mostly for the benefit of the natives. It was going to be a long and tedious process for a day or so — neither doctor was in any hurry to start.

The next day went regularly. Lee came along as well on these excursions to translate. This particular day, it was the Denka tribe that they were assisting by providing help with infections and small wounds. There was the sound of heavy machinery in the distance. The sounds of encroachment into their hunting grounds continued daily. If the government were to act, they then better do it soon. They returned as usual and found Diana with her notes awaiting Lee's return.

"Lee, have you seen Mara? Diana asked. "We were supposed to monitor a family of anteaters, but she never showed."

"I haven't seen her at all, today," Lee said. "I thought she was getting an early start since her tent was empty."

They started splitting up to find her. Lee checked the path to the villages. She couldn't go too far as it was getting late.

Diane checked the river path and Harris looked all through the camp. Sarah just drove up the road but hadn't seen her, either.

In the end, it was Harris who found her in the medical closet with the jug of homemade hooch beside her. She was blackout drunk with a moonshine jug next to her. Harris went over to make sure she still had a pulse. His hands produced no light, so there was no need for healing on her part. She did feel his fingers on her neck and took a drunken swipe at him in which she missed him and shattered the now-empty jug.

"Kip your filly hands eff me, ya perv!" Mara shouted and weaved her way out of the quasit hut, still gripping the leftover top of the jug in her hand. Harris hoped she would head for her tent and sleep off the effects of the hard cider. He then let Lee and the rest of them know she was found and to cut the search and rescue short. Lee was angry, and so were the rest of the volunteers. They knew not to bother disturbing her until tomorrow since she wouldn't remember being yelled at.

Everyone was of the mind to make sure she paid for causing a panic.

Chapter 65 – Too Much Monkey Business

Arliss rang the breakfast triangle as hard as he could in hopes of giving Mara more effect on her assured hangover. The rest of the lot went to grab their breakfast of eggs and what they called "sloth-sausage." No one knew what the meat was but just gambled that it was edible for humans. Mara stumbled to breakfast in her oversized dark glasses. There were more sounds of the slamming of glass ketchup bottles, tray-emptying and people talking more loudly than usual. Mara just sat with her head on the table while all this aural punishment went on around her.

"SO, HARRIS!" Dennis said in a cacophonous voice. "I GUESS I'll HAVE YOU START THAT COUNT OF THE INVENTORY TODAY!"

"OK, BOSS!" Harris shouted back. "IM ON IT!"

Diane told Mara to sit out, helping her with the anteaters and took Sarah, instead. Mara just stayed in her tent while everyone else went on their way. Harris, Tomas and Arliss were the only other people in the camp, and they each had their own tasks to complete. Mara had a tough time of it as the sun's rays struck her tent, directly at noon. When she threw closed the canvas tent flap, it became oven-hot inside, so she went to the showers to cool off.

While the humans were all busy doing their work, no one noticed the marauding band of thieves that got into the camp. A tribe sneaked in consisting of a dozen tamarin monkeys that looked over the encampment with mischievous curiosity. They got into boxes, rooms and tents looking to play with anything shiny or edible. Their filthy little paws made quick work of the whole camp.

Arliss couldn't find the wrench he set down as one of the thieving mammals liked dragging the shiny tool along the ground. Harris was in the medical closet while his precious Walkman was being stolen and the tents, which only had canvas coverings as doors were stripped of their contents. For some reason, a rogue tamarin decided Mara's clothes were worth taking and attempted to run off with them as she showered. Her towel was all that remained.

Harris was the first to discover the marauders.

"Hey!" He shouted at them and gave chase as they dropped most of the stolen loot and ran for the trees leaving their ill-gotten gains scattered all over the camp. He then began the task of sorting it all. Harris then went and gathered the stolen items as Arliss sorted them into piles.

He also found the stolen wrench and returned it to Arliss. "Thanks...I've been to lawn sales that looked worse than this, eh." He said as he helped Harris gather the scattered items and secure them behind the door in the quasit hut. The only safe place right now to store anything.

He held up Mara's clothes and folded them just as she came out of the shower in only a towel as she tried to find out what happened to her wardrobe. She saw Harris holding them and was ready to pound the young doctor. "What are you doing?" She yelled while causing her head to ring in pain. Harris just handed her the clothes and tried to tell her of the thieves that besieged them a moment ago, and she punched Harris hitting him near his eye. He remembered to roll with the blow of the saucy American who dropped her towel during the altercation.

If she did leave a mark on Harris's face, it would have vanished with his quick healing. She put her towel back on and ran into the shower room and got dressed as Harris regained his composure. When she came back out adequately covered, he again tried to tell her, in vain, of the monkey raid. "Don't give me that, you perv!" She screamed as she attempted another swing at Harris but missed. Arliss stepped in and tried to break up the fight with her trying to take another swing at the Brit and all of them arguing when Tomas came over.

"OY!" He shouted and threw two halves of a bloody and fresh-killed tamarin on the ground in front of them with a gold necklace around its neck. Tomas picked up a bloody machete after tossing the carcass to the ground.

"No, eat! Make gas!" Tomas shouted and went back to the kitchen, leaving the other three in stunned silence. Mara just went back to her tent with her towel and the necklace after she pulled it off the dead primate. Arliss went back to tuning up the jeep now that the recovered wrenches in his toolbox were in less danger of being lifted. Harris continued the recovery effort of the attempted robbery. He then went over the area twice making sure they found everything. His Walkman headphones were an unfortunate casualty to the raid as the wires, already cheap and old, were savaged. He would have to put an order in with Sarah when she made another run to the airfield. Maybe he could borrow a pair from Arliss?

The others returned about 4:30 and Harris had to gather everyone to the firepit and announce what happened that afternoon. He led them into the office and put the things on the desk, letting them take what was theirs.

While they did, he told them all about the tamarins and how Tomas took out one of the rogues in a most brutal fashion. He didn't bring up his fight, nor the punch that Mara took at him. She was still in her tent, seething. Lee went over and tried to talk to her, and she let out the problem she was having that sent her in a tizzy:

She showed Lee a letter she received from someone called Nate. He told her that there was no reason to go on now and that he hooked up with her sister, Cecelia. It was bad enough to get dumped by your boyfriend thousands of miles away but dropped due to your step-sister…well, it just set her off the deep end. Lee hugged her and said to take her time with it. Getting drunk and getting her new friends worried was not the way to go about it. Lee left and let Mara stew a bit longer. At least with the sun going down, she wouldn't stew too much more.

Later that evening, Harris was discussing the inventory situation with Dennis when Mara showed up and knocked on the wall:

"Hey, can I see you a sec, Doc?" Mara asked.

"Of course, dear," Dennis said. "What can I…"

"No, I mean the other doc." She said, pointing to Harris.

"Pardon me a sec." He said to Dennis and walked around the corner with her.

"Look, uh, I don't apologise too well, but I'm sorry I hit you." She said. "I got some bad news today, and I went off on everyone."

"It's all right," Harris said. "We all have bad days."

She looked at his face. "I thought I hit you harder." She said.

"I felt it…I guess I don't bruise easily." He said.

"OK, we're cool then?" Mara asked.

"Yeah, don't worry about it." He said.

She nodded and left. Harris went back to his discussion with Dennis. The camp then enjoyed the calm before the next storm.

Chapter 66 – Log Jammed

There was, always a lot of rain in the Amazon. Hence the term, rainforest. These downpours lasted from minutes to days at a time. The river got high on the banks of the camp but always fell back in time if left on their own. They were thinking of bunking in the quasit hut, but that meant it would quickly, get too crowded. Harris, Dennis and Lee all had their rooms there along with the doctor's exam room, showers and Lee's office. It would be a major rethink to put more people into such a small space. The mess tent would be a problem as it had no wooden foundation that was propped up like the tents were.

The phone calls that Arliss mentioned were finally ready. Everyone would take turns on a scheduled day to talk to their peoples back home. Arliss took the first one, of course. He spoke to his mom, dad and brother in his town north of Calgary. The conversations were always about the same: "You eating all right? Staying warm? When are you coming home?"

Diane talked to her ex-husband, Ray. They had stayed civil since their divorce five years ago…until he said he was getting married again to his fiancé who was in her early 20's. Diane cut it short.

Dennis was getting angrier for some reason as well. He was up all night for days on end and slept for long stretches. Harris covered for him whenever one of the natives came in for some medical attention like cuts or broken limbs. It was evident that this was taking a toll on the job they were sent to do.

Harris would bandage up the wounded even though they were completely healed before they left. A fact he was not ready to divulge to anybody — his curing the Kupuko that quickly was going to raise enough eyebrows. His lot didn't have much to worry over except for Bart getting the first stages of blackwater disease that Harris drove out of him proclaiming his condition a 24-hour bug. He was fine two days later.

Even Lee was having her fill with Dennis as he shouted her down a couple of times for the gigantic sin of her wanting him to help Sarah in with the food crates from a delivery. Harris stepped in once again to assist with the carrying in of that week's allotment. It was time to get prepared as there was another massive storm on the way. It always rained on and off here, but there was precipitation expected during the next day, or so that would be heavier than usual.

Lee had to leave that morning since she had a meeting with several top officials from the organisation. Her expertise in languages was needed as many Unity League leaders from various countries were coming in for their discussions on other missions offered by the organisation. They could hire an army of interpreters for more money or just pay one person to work the whole two-day event. The time away would do her well as she could visit more modern and civilised surroundings for a bit. She rode with Sarah with her overnight luggage to the airfield and took a flight that Friday morning.

Coming back, Sarah also brought back more deliveries from the airfield. Harris accepted the medical supplies and his new headphones. Now he could enjoy music again. Dennis received another letter that Harris left for him on his makeshift desk, which was a folding table that he could write on. The older doctor man went to make a call on Arliss's amateur radio setup. When he came back, he looked to be in tears and just sat in his room for the rest of the night.

Usually, the rains were just a steady pattern of on/off showers that came and went without too much to worry over. Now they had a full downpour, and it was causing the river level to rise. A couple of sticks and logs floating in the river were also getting bigger with each passing hour. Then, the oddest thing happened. The water level in the river dropped to a trickle near the camp. Fish were flopping around without their liquid habitat, and a large group of colourful birds swept in and feasted on the doomed creatures. Just rock and mud were all that remained along with some tidal pools allowing some of the water residents to survive until they were picked off by other wildlife.

It was Theodis that ran up the trail into the mess tent and shouted that flooding was backwashing into the local Denka village. Arliss, Bart and Mara all grabbed chainsaws and ran down the path. "C'mon, Doc!" Sarah shouted to Harris with a long pole in her hand that she handed off to Theodis. Harris ran into the shack and grabbed the gigantic "Widow-maker" chainsaw there as it was the only one left. "Man, this is heavy!" He thought as he caught up with the rest of the group — the heavy machine was weighing him down worse than the others.

There was, indeed, a log jam that looked like beavers had built it the size of the capybaras that Diane was riding in Harris's vision.

Sarah shouted the order out: "What we need to do is get the key logs out of the way!" as she pointed to the pile of logs that were bigger than the rest and seemed to hold back the water.

"Be sure to back up well before you get through the log. The force of the water will do the rest! You don't want to be anyplace around that water when it finally lets loose!" She finished.

They all took positions around the giant deluge of logs. Mara was quite adept with sawing along the edges while Theodis pulled on some of the pile with the large hook and pole. He pulled at a bunch of the logs trying to break them free or ending up pulling loose ones off the collection. He also had to stop several times as the pain in his hip was aggravating him.

Arliss and Bart sawed at the base of the pile trying to free one, especially, large log by breaking it into pieces. The chainsaw went all the way through the lumber but with no result. It was weighted down with the other sticks that they cut and pulled in succession.

Harris jumped on top of the logs and just pulled a bunch off the pile and tossing them to shore. He then encountered a collection of large branches and tree trunks that would not move near the far end of the pile that seemed to be trapping the rest of the branches. Harris took the monster saw and made quick work of the debris. He fought to keep his balance as he walked on the immense pile of sticks and held his hand away from the controls, so his body didn't end up like the logs in question. After what seemed like all day, the pile began to shift. Sarah shouted to everyone to get on the riverbank, and the whole heap broke through with the force of the water, and the river normally flowed, again. Cheering and sighs of relief rocked the group as they set the chainsaws down and shut off their machines. The whole group sat on the wet but solid ground of grass and soil to get their energy back.

Diane came running up and said that there were injuries of the local tribe members. Harris said "Let's go!" and followed the older woman to the village to see what they needed. Only he and Diane went to the settlement as the rest of the group were exhausted. Sarah tried running up behind but was in no way ready to tackle any other project.

"Sarah, it's all right. We got this." Harris said to her. "Tell the others to get some rest and see if you can get Dennis over here." Sarah nodded and took off to the rest of the group as they gathered the power tools to head back to camp so Arliss could maintain them.

They would all want a shower, something to eat and about a week's worth of sleep.

Chapter 67 – TKO

The injuries were made up mostly of cuts and bruises on the villagers made by running from the deluge, but there was something else in some of the men. It looked as though some of them were in fights. Harris asked Diane, but she didn't have the gift of gab to speak to the Denka villagers. Lee wouldn't be returning until at least tomorrow. Harris could only take care of the wounded by bandaging them and then applying his method of healing when no one was looking.

They finished late that night and just stayed with the villagers as travelling back in the dark was not an option. They slept in Hammocks which was a weird feeling to Harris. The material was as thick as his cot, but the swaying movement was not controllable despite how still he laid. Diane stayed in a similar sleeping situation with the elderly tribal women. They helped her get to know the creatures of the forest. Many times, they became dinner later, but Diane didn't stay around for that type of meal. They both left at first dawn down the two-mile trek through this part of the forest.

Harris had to check on Dennis and make sure he was still among the living. He was no place to be found, though when he got back to the quasit hut. There was also a crumpled-up letter in the trash that Harris was tempted to look at but figured that it was none of his business to scour through another person's refuse. There was also a note on his desk that said: "5 pm - radio."

Lee returned that morning and was filled in by Sarah on their fight with nature on the drive up the mountain. Lee was still in her suit top and skirt when she came across Harris just getting up.

"Everybody OK?" Lee asked the young physician.

"Yeah, it was an adventure." He said as he looked over Lee in her appearance of civilised attire.

"What?" She asked.

"It just makes me a bit homesick to see you in something not out of a Banana Junction clothing catalogue.' He said. "You look like a London Solicitor dressed like that."

Lee just smiled and asked, "So, where's Dennis?"

"Here I am!" He shouted as he hugged Lee with a bombastic welcome.

"Hon, you look amazing!" Dennis said as he gave her the once-over.

"Nice to see you're feeling better," Harris said.

"Mate, I feel fantastic!" Dennis shouted. "You guys did a smash-up job yesterday! Taking on a dam of logs like that and still had time to attend to the Danka's needs...I'd still be in bed!"

At that time, the bell for breakfast rang at the hands of Mara.

"Come along then! Let's get our Bum-Nuts and Adam's Ale on!" Dennis said while Harris just looked at Lee with a puzzled look.

"Bum-Nuts and Adams...what?" Harris asked.

"Eggs and a drink of water," Lee said. "But what's he taking?"

"No idea," Harris responded. "I've not seen him this chipper since I first arrived."

They grabbed their trays, and Tomas served up scrambled eggs and toast with their water while Dennis walked through like he was the life of the party. Everyone just looked at him like he was on something. Harris and Lee took their seats with her still in her official garb. She ate before she changed while being careful not to stain her office clothes with errant food.

After changing into more appropriate attire, Lee went with the two doctors to the Garto tribe village. Much like the Denka, the Garto tribe were used to interaction from the outside world. Also, like the Denka, they were feeling the encroachment of the land marauders. In their case, it was illegal mining. There was gold in the hills and lots of it. The problem was extracting it a little at a time. They also used mercury to speed up the process of cleaning the gold for sale, which had the tendency to poison anything organic, nearby.

Dennis went off for a moment but didn't bother to tell anyone where he was bound. He did make it very clear that he needed to return to the camp by 5 pm that afternoon. Lee and Harris treated the Garto for their minor injuries and illnesses. They were only on a tributary of the Amazon, so the flooding and damages that occurred upstream didn't affect them too much.

The invading outsiders attempting to mine for the rare metal also tended to clear out the forests to further their explorations. Their interference created pressure on the tribes as their food supply lived in those trees.

The threat of encroachment on their hunting grounds both by the outsiders and the neighbouring Denka were also causing the two tribes to start turning on each other.

Dennis returned from his covert mission and anxious to assist in anything needed. "Now, what can I help with?" He asked. He checked the eyes of a few villagers until he got bored with that. He then got to watch some of the men wrestle with each other. He taunted one of the contenders with a lot of rude commentaries that they couldn't understand, and Lee was not about to translate. He even peeled off his shirt and attempted to get one of the tribesmen to wrestle him. The Garto male just looked at him as if the older doctor were insane and just ignored him. That made Dennis angry with this rebuff and was about to charge the native when Harris noticed his crazed actions and stepped in.

"Dennis, Dennis! Get a grip, Doctor!" Harris shouted at him while grabbing his shoulders and pushing his back in an attempt to get him back in his head. "Besides, it's just past four. Didn't you say you needed to be back at camp by 5:00?"

Dennis checked his watch and snapped to "Blimey!" He shouted as he grabbed his shirt and just ran for camp, not even waiting for Lee or Harris. The other two finished up with the leftover Garto villagers, and the younger league members made their way back to camp just past five.

"What got Dennis so riled up?" Lee asked.

"Dunno." Harris could only answer. "He was rebuffed by one of the villagers for not wrestling him. Why he would want to is a puzzle, anyway."

They made their way back to camp just as Mara was ringing the large iron triangle bell. They all took their seats except for Arliss and Dennis. The conversation of the day was all about how the rain season was coming up in a bit and what preparations they would need. Sarah had a notepad making a list that she would pass off to Arliss to radio ahead of the more essential items that would take time to gather. That's when the radio savvy Canadian came into the mess tent with a bloody nose.

"Arliss, man! What happened?" Theodis asked while Harris went over to examine the young man. Arliss told them between biting pain bursts "I got Dennis on schedule to make a call to his son in Perth, but I had a problem with the signal. It kept dropping in and out, and it finally stopped altogether. Then Dennis got pissed and slammed the radio off the counter. I tried to stop him from doing any other damage, and then he hit me square in the nasal passages with it!"

"I'll get ice for that!" Harris said and went into the doctor's office to grab a special type of cold pack that just needed a slam on the counter to activate and ice down.

He continued to talk about how Dennis and his son were in some heated debate about their past and how Dennis was always on assignment, someplace. That's when the radio went wacko, and Dennis lost patience with it. Harris entered the mess tent as Tomas lent him a towel to get the blood-soaked up.

"I never saw him so angry!" Arliss said.

"C'mon, mate," Harris said to him. "Let's get that nose of yours adjusted and something for pain."

It was apparent that Bart wanted to see Harris work with the needles but went back to sitting as it would have given away that he was snooping through his bag.

Harris set Arliss's nose with a bandage and told him to cover his face with a wet cloth while he, supposedly, applied some topical treatment to his face to relieve the pain. A bright light of a few seconds later and Arliss was feeling worlds better. Harris then applied a bandage to the already-fixed nose that he was ordered to leave on for the rest of the week. Arliss then went back to his tent to salvage his equipment and make whatever adjustments needed to fix their link to the outside world.

Harris later found Dennis lying behind the counter with another jug of the homemade cider. The doctor was a dishevelled mess as he looked at Harris with anger and resentment-more so, at himself.

"You got kids, Harris?" Dennis asked. Harris just shook his head no.

"You're lucky." He said. "If you're not there for them every minute, they seem to remember that." He laid on the bedroll, putting the large jug aside. "I was a rotten father…I know that. Maybe he'll forgive me, someday." He slumped on to the roll and turned toward the wall away from his physician assistant and tried to sleep. "Leave me alone, then," Dennis said. "I'll apologise to Arliss tomorrow."

"Mind that you do!" Harris retorted. "Arliss didn't deserve that!"

Dennis then took another large drink from the jug as Harris left him to stew. He then went to his cot and read some comic book until sleep came over him as well.

Harris woke up in his cot to a dark room. His window looked out the back of the quasit hut but just into thick woods, so the sun didn't shine through the trees.

He was the first one up in the odd-shaped building and looked out the door after slipping on a pair of shorts. The rain finally took a break for a bit. It was a misty morning with the air full of the sounds of animal life. He then went back to his room and put on the rest of his clothes. Dennis would wake up shortly as well as Lee and the rest of the crew. He went over to the counter and saw Dennis laying in a bedroll with the jug sitting next to his head. He was very still.

"Hey, Dennis," Harris said. "It's time to get up. We gotta go over to the Denka Tribe today." There was no movement of Dennis's bedroll.

"C'mon man! We're burning daylight." Harris said a bit louder as he sat in the chair and tied his boots. There was still no response from the doctor. Harris went over to the counter and rang the bell. He was still not moving.

"Yo, Dennis! C'mon!" Harris shouted at him. Dennis made no move at all, so Harris took the bell and tossed it and intended to hit his back. Instead, it hit his head.

"Oops! Sorry! Harris apologised with no reaction coming from the bedroll. Harris finally went over and saw the eyes of the doctor staring at him with no life.

"Oh, cock!" Harris shouted as he threw Dennis on his back and tried his light, but there was none emerging from his hands. He put his fingers on his neck, and his skin was cold with no pulse. Harris then started old fashioned CPR for 10 minutes trying to get something out of him:

"C' mon Dennis!" He said in a panic. "Wake up!" There was no reaction from his lifeless eyes. Harris ran into the medical closet and pulled out an adrenalin shot and shoved it in his chest. The doctor remained inert on the ground. Harris continued the CPR effort trying to get anything out of him.

"C' mon, Dennis!" Harris shouted at the long-gone corpse of Doctor Dunedin. "C' mon!" He didn't give up for 30 minutes of continued chest compressions.

"C' mon, Doc! Gimme a heartbeat!" Harris yelled in desperation. "Just gimme something I can work with, here!" Lee then came in from her room in her t-shirt and panties and saw Harris sobbing, exhaustedly, over the loss of their friend. She just hugged him for a bit, and both cried together over the loss of their friend and colleague.

Chapter 68 – Dennis goes home

Despite his hip pain, Theodis was the one to assist Harris in carrying the body of Doctor Dunedin to the back of the jeep. He was tied in and given every respect as everyone at the camp looked on. They all gathered to say their final good-byes to their friend and colleague. There was not a dry eye amongst them. Even Tomas wept as they attached Dennis to the back of the jeep. Sarah drove while Lee rode shotgun and Harris was in the backseat portion with Dennis. His friend, colleague, boss, mentor…Just before they left, Harris remembered to give last rites to Dennis that he looked up in a bible he had brought with him. They, then, started down the mountain on what would be Dennis's last ride down the insane road.

Lee had to use the radio at the airfield since one of Dennis's last acts was to turn theirs into a jigsaw puzzle that Arliss continued to reassemble. They had to remain at the airport until the pilot arrived. He said he would come out, even though it was his day off. Lee went into the small tower set-up and used a separate radio they had set up so she could call Juan Montoya back in Rio to explain what happened. Harris didn't have the expertise to know precisely what happened, nor the equipment to find out.

Lee said it would take at least two hours to get Dennis sorted, so Harris started puttering around the airfield. On the wall, he saw a map of the river and where the river flowed past their camp. There was a huge waterfall that he wondered about before the water went over the edge. In Portuguese, the map spelt out the fall was a drop of about 150m (490 feet.)

Lee was on the radio waiting to hear back from someone in authority when Sarah said they would be back later. She said to Harris "Come with me." They got into the jeep and started down the road they travelled to get to the Kupuko Tribe. The route they travelled put them at a trailhead a few miles from the airfield. They got out, and Sarah said "This way."

They walked the trail for a mile or so seeing the usual monkeys hanging on branches and birds that flew from tree to tree. After a long walk, Harris finally heard a sound of what would be rushing water. A welcome noise for how hot it was. The sound became louder the further they walked up the trail. They were now next to the river and following the water becoming more agitated and swifter until they came to a waterfall.

"Here we are," Sarah said.

"All that water that passes the camp ends here." She then sat on a large, flat rock next to the pool of water that collected at the waterfall base and sat cross-legged. "My place is here." She said. "I just come here and communicate with nature. I find birth, death and everything in-between starts and ends here. She closed her eyes and took several deep breaths and just let all the terrors of the day fly away."

The bottom of the waterfall was clear of debris. Just a deep pool was all the cascade fell into as the water crashed into the bottom of the cliff. It was serene, despite the crashing sound of water nearby. Harris tuned out all the stress that was happening around him and just let the sound of the water relax him. He wondered about Dennis and what it felt like to be dead. Was the doctor up in heaven looking down on the two of them as well as the rest of the world? Did Dennis feel like he was just asleep? He was in no hurry to find out, but the curiosity was natural considering any living soul didn't know such things, and even if he did, it would be too late to do anything about it. After a while, the stress passed, leaving him to adjust to this new reality. Before all this, he was even going to ask Lee to let him leave before December since Dennis had everything well in hand, and his part of the mission was over. He figured they would need the extra help now.

"Well, no sense wasting a perfect day like this," Sarah said. She stood upon the rock and threw off all her clothes on the flat rock and stepped into the water. Sarah took the leap covering her body in the cold water of the base of the falls. At least she didn't seem to mind the cold.

"C'mon in, Doc...The water is excellent!" Sarah shouted as she swam toward the falls for a better look. Harris didn't know what to say or do but to strip off and jump in as well. The day was torturous on the young doctor, so any diversion felt welcome. They both frolicked in the water for a half-hour or so while keeping a respectful distance from each other. The two then got dressed and walked back to the jeep as if it were the most normal thing ever.

He jumped in the shotgun seat. "If I weren't committed to someone right now..." He began.

"Hold it, cowboy!" she jumped in. "I just wanted a swim. You aren't my type, nothing personal." She then started the jeep and headed back for the airfield. He just smiled and shrugged. He now knew what he suspected about Sarah but was just glad for the heaviness to be taken off his shoulders for a bit. Whatever Lee would say about Dennis would force him back into reality.

They entered the airport hangar office with Lee on the radio madly waving Harris toward the microphone. "I have him here now, sir!" She said. Lee then handed a set of headphones to Harris and said that the voice he would hear belonged to Juan Javier Avado, the Medical Examiner for the city of Rio De Janeiro. Lee would translate through a separate earpiece:

"What was the state of the body when you found it?" Lee asked while turning the words of the M.E. toward Harris.

"I found the body in bed. A safe assumption is that Dr Dunedin had died in his sleep". Harris said, and Lee translated all this into the M.E.'s native Portuguese.

"Any foul play suspected? Lee asked.

"Negative," Harris answered. "The patient had what seemed to be a few alcoholic beverages before he went to sleep, but nothing else that I know of." A few more foreign words followed spoken by Lee...

"Did you take any steps to revive the victim?" The M.E. asked through Lee.

"That's affirmative," Harris answered. "I gave CPR for a good 20 minutes and administered an adrenalin shot as well. I attempted CPR for another 30 minutes, but it seems he was too far gone to respond. That would be my hypothesis, so that would put the time of death between 9 pm and 6 am."

Harris thought Lee would have a problem translating some of these words, but she was on them like a pro. More foreign words followed... "A plane is en-route to this location." Lee then said. "If you come across anything significant that caused his death, please let us know."

"Si, senior." Harris finished. "I will." and stepped away from the microphone. Lee then finished up whatever she was saying to the M.E.

He went out to the airfield where nothing was happening. He sat on a bench waiting for the plane to arrive and just sat with his head in his hands, depressed for not being able to save his boss. Sarah came over and sat next to him.

"So, what was the cause of death?" She asked.

"Heart attack, I guess," Harris said. "He died in his sleep." Sarah nodded in acknowledgement. A long silence followed...

"Hey, I didn't want you to get the wrong impression, Doc," Sarah said.

"Don't worry about it." He said. "Besides, I don't want to make an enemy of Diane."

"How did you…" Sarah said, surprised.

"I saw you both swimming together a couple of months ago." He said. "I didn't want to say anything…why should I?"

The plane landed a minute later, and they spent a few minutes figuring out how to position Dennis inside while keeping him in a respectable position. He was going home for the last time. There was no telling how he was to be interred and treated when he returned to Australia. Harris and the pilot placed Dennis in the back section of the plane as respectfully as possible. Lee and Sarah gave their final send-off to their friend and then so did Harris.

"Vaya con Dios, Dennis," He said to the draped body of the doctor.

Chapter 69 – Pass the Salt

They rode back to the top of the hill with Sarah driving and Lee in the shotgun seat. Harris was alone in the back seat. All of this was a tall order for someone who only did two years of medical training. As long as no one needed anything significant from the camp, he could serve out his time here without incident. The first thing was to make the office his own. It wasn't anything he looked forward to, it was just a job that needed doing.

He put himself in charge of cleaning and packing up Dennis's personal effects to send back to Australia. Dennis had little here of his own. Just some clothes and ablutions. He also found his journal that he kept since he arrived. Harris was unsure about viewing it. Was he supposed to read it and then collect the information left? Should he send it to his son, unopened? He decided to look over it since it didn't mean much, anymore. He just touched on several of the more related entries:

His arrival at the camp, how Dennis and Lee set things up. How they welcomed the incoming volunteers…Some of the entries talked about his more private thoughts:

"Lee had to escape the clutches of the Kupuko Tribe by pledging she could get help…I wonder if that's all she did?"

"This kid from the UK doesn't impress me in what he knows. He's a very young guy and green as grass. Do they know what they are doing? More so, does he?"

Another entry describes the trick Dennis played on him after his lousy marijuana experience. He also went on to describe Bart, and he got into his medical bag after the whole Kupuko incident. Harris knew this as his comics were placed back in the bag out of order.

He also went on to describe someone called Devi who worked for Montoro's gang. He had to meet him outside Garto's Village. Who's Devi? Who's Montoro?

He got to the last entries which were the most poignant:

"I got a letter from my son after I touched base with him after so many years. He knows very well the problems I've had in the past and was more than ready to forget I even existed. I told him that I would call him on the radio and that I had to speak to him."

The entry continued;

"This is the last chance I have to bond with him after all those years where everything went wrong between his mum and me. My getting mixed up with BMP didn't help anyone. Now I am feeling that I am getting drawn back to it and if it doesn't go right this time, then there is no use in trying anymore."

That was the last entry. What happened with that final radio call to Dennis's son? Harris went to speak with Arliss who managed to get the radio pasted back together and still wearing the white bandage and medical tape over his nose.

"I think we are good to go here." Arliss said, "Do you need anything? I'm going to radio for supplies." "I'll need to check the office," Harris said. "I'll have to get back to you on that…" He then addressed something else in the same vein.

"Arliss, you were with Dennis when he spoke to his son…" Harris said. "What was their conversation like?" Arliss stopped working and had to think for a moment without making himself look bad.

"Well, he had the headphones on, so I wasn't privy to all of it, but I did hear him talk about he was sorry he wasn't there for him growing up and missing out when he didn't show for…something. I'm not sure what, though but it was important to his son, that was obvious." Arliss took a breath before continuing…

"He also said something about his problem, and he was dealing with it. I'm not sure what was meant by that. He started getting madder as they went on. Then the radio started cutting out from interference and the next thing I knew, he belted me with it before smashing it on the ground. It takes a lot for me to hold a grudge…but I had one going until this morning."

Harris gave him a nod and then returned to the office and the job of putting things back together in Dennis's footlocker to send in a separate post to his son. That was when Harris noticed a salt shaker with a piece of cello tape covering the top holes. Harris then thought "Why would he go through all the trouble… Hang on!" He took off the lid and rubbed a bit of the "salt" on his gums, and they numbed a bit. Like it or not, he had to take the shaker to Lee in her office. He then handed her the shaker, and she did the same test on her gums.

"Bolivian Marching Powder." She said, aggravated. "He probably did a line yesterday when we went to see the Garto. He was acting all happy but aggressive then."

"Yeah…" Harris said. "And then when he spoke to his son…And the alcohol on top of that. He was probably trying to straighten himself out before bed, and his heart couldn't take it."

"I wonder if his son knew he was on the stuff?" Lee asked.

"I'm not sure," Harris said, hiding the fact he read his journal. "He and his son had problems in the past, Arliss told me they were arguing before Dennis broke his nose."

"Well, kid…" Lee said with a level of sarcasm since they weren't that far apart in age. "Looks like you'll have to continue to deal with us for a while longer. Let's head for the mess tent. That triangle will ring soon."

He knew what she was talking about, but it was still something he didn't know if he were ready for. Like it or not, this responsibility was now thrust upon him. Everyone filed in for supper after Bart rang the triangle and Lee made the announcement before getting their allotment from Tomas;

"Look, I don't want to come off cold. We will all miss Dennis. He was a great man and a good friend. As you can guess, though. Harris Gibraltar here has now become the new doctor. If you have any health concerns, you are more than free to bring them to him." Harris just nodded next to her.

They all murmured they would, and they all had a silent and sad meal.

Chapter 70 – Game-changer

The next month produced nothing out of the ordinary. The season would soon go from wet to wetter. Everyone was into their jobs and keeping an even keel as the days went by. They still had a couple of months before they headed home. The affection Diane and Sarah had for each other was apparent although no one would mention it. Sarah gave the impression that this was a summer fling for a while, but they became even closer over time. Theodis and Mara were getting friendlier with each other as well. Sometimes, they would disappear into the forest for an hour or so.

It was Sarah and Mara, who both had a similar research project going. They were investigating the role of women in the tribes of the Denka and the Garto and how these two tribes existed, as they did, not far from each other but with their own cultures and customs and a woman's place in the tribe.

Theodis went along to talk to the men about how they constructed their huts. They figured out how to build large buildings without the help of modern man a long time ago. These structures worked well in the rainforests to keep out the weather and support the weight of hammocks where everyone slept. Theodis went to find something either they missed, or modern man overlooked.

Bart continued his hunt for other plants and vegetation not discovered yet or to extract properties overlooked before. He was very excited as he knew the plants that he found earlier there would be a gold mine back home. All he had to do was bide his time until the assignment finished.

Speaking of gold mining, Lee got on the radio to inform the interior ministry of the encroachment of the renegade gold miners that were creeping into the tribal lands. The hunting grounds and the rivers were suffering losses in vast amounts as these destroyers came through and didn't care what got wrecked, whether it was cutting down scores of trees or letting the mercury get into the waters.

Back home in the states and the UK, there were campaigns of "Save the Rainforest!" "The entire world would die without the rainforest creating oxygen for the entire world!" and "The earth had only 12 years left before it burnt to death and global warming would turn the entire planet to ash!"

Lee didn't buy any of the science since she was there and knew the general conditions that they all dealt with.

Nevertheless, she and the rest of the crew were content to let them stoke the fires if it meant helping these tribes as well as all the other forest life.

Diane was content to gather what real-life information she could about the inhabitants of this part of the world with either four legs or fins and Tomas never spoke to any of them unless it involved the kitchen and what was needed. He was a real mystery. All they knew was his home was in Sao Paulo and made a good living as a cook. He took this gig to get him out of the dirty city as it was going through a tough time. They would all gather around the table, eating the excellent food before them every night. The camp dwellers could have been made to cook for themselves without his assistance, so having Tomas around was a luxury.

Harris wondered what Arliss was doing here, though. He seemed to do nothing but work on all the machinery. It turned out that this was what he was hired for as his need was more for utility purposes. Harris knew that times were hard in the job markets, but there were far easier ways to make a quid.

"Well, I'm sure I could be slumming it in a coffee shop, someplace, to make some cash but this is far more exotic, and it's really a once in a lifetime experience to travel someplace this amazing and get paid for it. Dennis came here for that reason, got rest him." Arliss said to him as he gave the once-over to Theodis's boom box that needed some cassette-player work.

No one went to see Harris for anything unless it was a more than a minor cut or illness that he bandaged or cured with a literal wave of his hand. If it were an injury, a bandage was stuck on with no one was of the wiser it was already fixed. If it were sickness, they took their medicine and would be hunky-dory overnight. The same treatment presented to the tribal peoples of the villages. He gave stitches to a man who had an axe-wound and told him (through Lee) not to remove the bandage for a week. It was repaired, of course, the moment he touched him.

There were times Harris would even feed his patients mild laxatives to mask that their now-cured illnesses were on the mend but needed some time to pass. He felt ashamed to have to stoop to such tricks but thought it better than being found out and dealing with the discrimination. He even offered to take care of Theodis's hip injury, but the big football player passed, saying that he had no faith his cure would come at the end of several needles. Harris wanted to find a way to help him before they all left toward the end of the year.

Another early deluge of rain hit the area, causing concern in the villages and the camp. Harris laid in his cot, just hearing buckets of rain hit the roof of the quasit hut. He had to run to the latrine at daybreak when he stepped on the hut floor and found he was standing barefoot in ankle-deep floodwater. He jumped out of bed in a panic and hammered on the door marked "Private" in the main room of the hut. The door led to Lee's dorm room.

"Lee!" Harris shouted. "C'mon, we got flooding!" He threw on some shorts and a shirt along with his boots that he didn't take the time to lace up and ran to the iron triangle and rang it for all to hear.

"C'mon! Get the saws!" Harris shouted. "We got flooding here!"

Everyone got out of their tents and charged for the saws. Harris somehow got stuck with the large widow-maker saw which he didn't mind anymore since he would be in less danger if there were an accident.

This time they ran right down the path that started the other side of the camp. Harris only walked this area a couple of times just wanting to see the edge of the falls. They didn't have to walk too far to see a dam-up of trees and debris that slid off the other side of the mountain. The hope was that there wasn't a lot of debris that was stopping the water flow, which couldn't be persuaded to move. The eco-warriors started their saws and began chopping at the bottom of the piles.

"Someone could get hurt doing this!" Harris thought as he chipped away at the middle of the dam trying to make a channel to allow water to pass and hopefully, break the remaining collection of forest waste away as the force of the water flowed through. He felt well-equipped for the task with the largest of the saws in his hands chopping through the wood.

Theodis stood behind him back-to-back as they chopped down as far as they could while the others worked behind the pile getting a solid grip on the saws and careful footing to keep everyone moving through the dam-up. "How do we keep doing this without getting killed?" Harris continued to think.

After about an hour of cutting, there was a rumbling sound of wood. All the saws stopped at the same time, and Bart was the one who made the call. "Off! Off! Everyone off!" He shouted, and everyone jumped off the giant woodpile. Lee told them a long time ago;

"When the timbers start talking, it's time to start walking!"

So, they all took their saws and laid them on the ground as the sound of the dam creaked and groaned until water burst through the wood and the dam broke apart in a matter of seconds.

"Yay! Yeah!" Everyone shouted as the water flowed and the flooding subsided. They were all standing in calf-deep water one minute, and it drained down to tops of their foot level in a minute. "All right!" Lee shouted. "Great job! Let's get the saws and get back to camp. We'll probably have a lot of drying out to do!"

They gathered the saws, but Lee left hers by the riverside. She walked over and picked it up, not noticing a dead branch that was about to fall out of the standing tree by the water's edge. It then fell directly on her from the weight of a passing kinkajou. A couple of the tree branches pierced her body, causing her to release an ear-splitting scream.

Everyone heard it and went to her aid. Diane and Mara lifted one end off while Theodis with his fantastic strength fought off his pain and lifted the other end, which was far more cumbersome. Arliss and Sarah then dragged her out from under the branch. When they did, a couple of tree branches that had speared her body came out, and massive amounts of her blood followed. She gasped for air as the blood entered different parts of her system the wrong ways.

"Doc!" "Medic!" Harris ran over and surveyed the damage. The branch stabbed her in the ceratoid artery in her neck, and she was losing blood by the quart. Arliss plugged the wound with his shirt to little effect, and her eyes began to glaze over.

Harris ran over there after dropping his saw to see her other wound where the branch also got her in the chest, and the blood was gushing out there as well. Mara tried in vain to stop the bleeding with her bandana. Everyone was crying and panicking over losing another one of their friends. There was no choice in the matter...

"I AM NOT LOSING ANYONE ELSE ON THIS TRIP!!!" Harris shouted while knowing in a split second that this was going to alter the dynamic of his being here. With that, he then let his hands shoot out its life-giving beams with much more intensity than in the past and seal up the damage the errant branch caused his friend. They all just jumped back and watched in fear and amazement as the bright white light did its work.

The large gaping holes in her neck and chest were sealed, leaving only the blood that was already spilt covering her body.

Lee let out a scream as the light dissipated and leaving her breathing heavy while Harris sighed with relief while everyone looked on with shock and disbelief, especially by the hulking football player. "What the..." Theodis began to speak before Harris cut in.

"Wait! Hold that thought!" Harris shot back as he got up and grabbed a full canteen lying on the ground and then rushed it back to the very thirsty Lee who drank it like she went days without liquids. She finished the entire container and just sat silently while continuing to breathe heavy and slowly while staring off into space.

"Lee, you OK?" Diane said to which Lee just nodded and shivered in a state of shock and let the emptied canteen fall to her side. Everyone then turned their vision to Harris and just stared at him. Theodis seemed to be fuming while everyone else looked confused.

"Yeah...Xenon" Harris said exasperated and not knowing what to expect next.

There was a bit of silence before Arliss spoke up. "I'm cool with that."

"Me too," Sarah said with Diane nodding in agreement. Lee just sat and said nothing as she stared into space.

"Not all of you are," Harris sadly stated as they watched Theodis, Mara and Bart walk to the mess tent.

Diane and Sarah helped Lee to her room. Lee was still in a state of shock over what just happened. They all were. Arliss said nothing while he gathered the chainsaws and walked them back to the shed. They would all need attention for the workout they just had.

Harris walked into his room and just looked around. He then went into a rage, and he threw his bag across the floor and his nightstand into the wall shattering it into pieces. His kicked his cot over and his Walkman was slammed down on the ground cracking the housing in his fury.

After a minute of gathering his composure, he set his bed back up and just sat on the edge of the wet, ratty bed with his legs over the edge and his head in his hands. His secret was out. He had to reveal himself or lose Lee as well, and that was not an option. He just sat and clutched his shirt at his chest. All he could do was stare at the wall for what seemed to be hours. No sleep and no movement.

Chapter 71 – Wine and Conversation

Harris stayed in his room not daring to come out for the rest of the day. He missed dinner but didn't care. All there was to drink was water, which the tap was nearby to refill his canteen. Nobody showed up at his door, either. He was in front of Lee's door about to knock but felt he should let some more time pass. She would be in top shape, physically. Mentally, he was unsure of her condition.

The next day was about the same. He stayed in his room, not wanting to take any chances of meeting anyone right now. He heard a food tray set beside his door. Someone brought him breakfast: Eggs, toast, orange juice and some bacon. Harris ate quickly. He hadn't eaten since yesterday. He also wondered who delivered it. Sarah? Diane? Maybe even Lee but when he looked out the window, she was not in sight. The lot of them were all arranging their departures for the day. Some of the items still hanging on their tents to dry from the recent flood. Dinner also appeared for Harris, and he ate what was given and left the trays at the quasit hut front door. He had another month and a half before they went home.

Another day of this and he finally got a visitor. It was Bartholomew. "Hi, Bart." He said, but neither of them could find the right words past that. "Come on in, please."

They took seats at a small table that he and Dennis discussed their lives over.

"I haven't been here since…" Bart began. "It's been a while." Harris just nodded.

Harris opened a bottle of wine that he had handy and poured it into a couple of paper cups he used for distributing water to patients.

"I got this from Dennis soon after I got here," Harris said. "We never did get to enjoy it together."

They both took a sip of the Lizzy Blonde White that came from Australia with the late Doctor. It was a good year and not at all bitter. Then Bart reached into his shirt pocket and pulled out something. "Here, I want you to have this."

It was a business card:

Lantana Medical Research, Inc.
2 Pembroke Lane
Boston, MA 02108
Bartholomew J. Smythe
Research and Development

"Uh, what is this?" Harris asked.

"Give them a $100 when you get back home and forget about it for ten years or so… It's going to be worth it." Bart said and noticed the scepticism from Harris. "I know you probably heard things like this before, but …just trust me on this."

Harris just made a motion like "OK" with his hands and tucked it in the pocket of his khaki polo shirt.

"Bart…" Harris got into the real question he had. "What does Theodis have against Xenons? He seems to have a bigger grudge than most."

"Yeah, he would…" Bart said and filled in Harris on what Theodis told him…

"Theodis was faster and stronger than anyone on the football field at the time. He would work out constantly and outrun anybody. He had a plan that he would be in the pros by 1993 and play for the Dolphins. Well, he was out with friends at a bar in Greenville and just coming home when he saw a bunch of guys looking at a large box in front of the main campus building. He said that he shouted, "Hey, what are you doing?" One of them waved his hand and Theodis went flying by some invisible force across the lawn. They ran away, and a bomb went off. No one was known to be in the building at the time since it was the weekend. It was, probably, some campus radical-types."

Bart continued;

"Anyways, He landed hard on his hip, and it shattered his pelvis. Now he says he has severe pain and gout most of the time. It's too bad, too. He loved the game, and his engineering studies are just a day to day thing for him."

With that, Bart finished the cup.

"Here, has another," Harris said and refilled both their cups. Another quiet minute went by until Bart spoke again.

"So…you can't do acupuncture?" Bart asked.

"Well, I can." Harris smiled and responded. "I just don't need to." He then finished his cup.

"It sounded like someone was trying to get him out of the way before the bomb went off, and he had a rough landing." He said.

"I agree," Bart said as he rubbed his eyes. "But he's not about to take it well since he lost his ability to play…Could you fix him?"

"I'm sure I could…" Harris responded. "If he would let me." Harris then wanted to know what he missed in his day of solitary confinement.

"Have you spoken to Lee at all?" Harris asked.

"I haven't," Bart said. "She hasn't come out of her room, yet." Harris was a bit surprised by this.

"Physically, she is surely in top shape." Harris said, "I guess she's still a bit frazzled, mentally."

"You haven't spoken to her, either?" Bart asked.

"I haven't gone any further than that door out there," Harris said, pointing to the office door. "Except to use the latrine when everyone was out of the camp this afternoon. I haven't even spoken to Arliss or Diane. Not even Sarah…And I think she left me a food tray at my door…unless you did it." Bart just shook his head.

"Maybe another day and I'll come out," Harris said and sighed. "Let any bad emotion die down."

Bart stood up and shook Harris's hand. "Thanks for the wine…and don't forget that card I gave you. I'm probably going to give everyone else one here. After what we have all been through, we earned it." He then took his exit.

Harris, again went to Lee's door intending to knock on it, but just went back to his room. "If she wants to talk, I'll be here." He thought as he returned to his room and played a tape in his broken Walkman. He was glad the Japanese built these things tough. He fell asleep over his book on brain maladies.

Chapter 72 – From out of nowhere...

Harris found another tray of food the next morning. He wondered who brought it although he could now rule out Bart, Lee and Theodis, more than likely. Mara would also be against him, no doubt. He ate the cereal that was given to him and wondered what his next move would be. He waited until everyone was on their way until he made his way to the privy with his loo roll in hand. Who knows if any paper were in there? He also found a snake laying on the floor alongside the plastic commode which he ejected out the door. There were so many snakes in this area that they ceased to become a concern unless they were poisonous and those tended to be a lot more reclusive than the common ones that crawled underfoot, also trying to stay out of the path of humans.

His next move was to get up all the gall he had and go over to Lee's door and inquire about her health. When he got to her door, it was just a crack open. He peeked in and saw no one there.

"At least she was up and about...good." He thought. He would talk to her later.

He finally went out to the lawn and walked across the way, wondering if someone was going to approach him after three days of his confinement. Almost all of them were walking toward the mess tent when one of them came up from behind him.

Unfortunately, it was Theodis, and it wasn't a friendly welcome as he knocked Harris down with the full weight of his body that sent the Xenon flying forward, knocking the wind out of him. He got up and could only turn and dodge another body blow. "Theodis! Stop!" A voice shouted at the ex-football player as he was ready to fight Harris with fists up and ready to box. Harris had his fists up and tried to remember everything the ex-bobby taught him about boxing at Vincent's gym and what the sensei taught him in his karate class back in Ireland.

Theodis took several punches that hit only air. Harris didn't want to hit him but felt he might have to if he got too close. Luckily, He telegraphed his moves so Harris could duck them without much effort. Theodis then bum-rushed him and knocked him down.

Only Mara was cheering Theodis on while everyone else was shouting at the beast, trying to get him to stop. He was too big to stand up to as he acted like a monster and hit Harris several times on the ground while he covered his face from the attack. Harris made the only defensive move he could make as he slammed Theodis's hip with a right-handed punch that aggravated his pain and stunned him long enough where he could slip out from under him. Harris hadn't fought like this since his early teen years on the streets of London.

Again, Theodis bum-rushed the young doctor, and they both crashed into the pile of firewood logs as Theodis pushed his one knee down on Harris's stomach and pinned him to the stack of wood. He then grabbed Harris's hair and slammed his head several times on the pile of logs with Arliss approaching but Harris using his hands to signal him to not get near them. There was no reason for him to get in the middle of this. Harris was about to take another hip-shot at Theodis when he produced his large knife and was looking all too threatening while holding it up to Harris's eyes.

"Theo, No!!!" Mara shouted. He was too enraged to listen.

"That's gonna hurt!" Harris blurted out.

"Damn right, it is!" Theodis shouted back as he readied the blade to plunge through Harris's eye socket.

He didn't get the chance as Theodis got knocked down and the weight of the athlete left Harris's stomach as Lee took the place of dominance over the now-horizontal ex-football player with her own large hunting knife at his throat. "Greene!" She seethed and shouted as Theodis slowly dropped his blade and Lee grabbed his brown shirt with her knife pressed against his neck. "Get up!" She screamed. He did and kept his hands up while Lee dragged him over to a log stump at the fire pit while displaying her anger. She pushed him on to the log to get him to sit. Bart had collected Theodis's discarded knife in the meantime, and Diane was looking after Harris who was, surprisingly, in good shape. Just dirty from the mud on the firewood.

He stood up with no problem when Lee came over, and she was surprised that he was in such good shape, vertical and fully recovered. The only thing hurt was his pride as she looked him up and down. He didn't want this. He just wanted to be accepted for what he was. "You OK?" She asked as she was amazed by his lack of injuries. Harris just nodded and still felt a bit unsure about her feelings. She had to break up the onslaught that Theodis produced but what about the rest of it?

"What the hell is going on here?" Lee shouted. "...And what is your problem, Greene? Harris finally comes out of hiding, and you have to do this!"

"You saw what he did! That creep...He's a threat!" He shouted. "He's a Xenon, after all!" Lee just looked at him with scorn even though she remembered his life was ruined by Xenons, though Harris was thousands of miles away at the time.

"Yeah...He's a Xenon!" Lee said as she leaned into his face. "...And you're a spade!"

301

She turned and pointed toward Bart. ".... And he's a cracker!"

Then she turned toward Diane. "...And she's a dyke!"

She turned toward Mara. "...And she's a spic!"

With that, Mara shouted "Hey!" Angered with the racial moniker fired at her while Lee ignored her reaction and just turned back toward Theodis.

"...And I'm a gook!" She said, pointing at herself. "So what? We are all here, and we need each other to survive until next month! If you got a problem with that, you could start walking home!"

She then jumped up on a stump by the fire circle. She then turned toward everyone else there surrounding the scene. "That goes for all of you!" She shouted while pointing with her knife. "If you are going to have a problem with a Xenon here, then you answer to me! I'm the one who requested his company, and it's a decision I stand by!"

It came as a shock to everyone there.

"That's right!" She continued as she sheathed her large hunting knife. After my fellow travellers were killed or exiled for our mistake, I promised that if there were a way to put things right, then I would make it happen. It was a surprise to find out a guy like Harris, here even existed! I put aside my prejudices and sent for him in hopes he could save the Kupuko tribe...and he did!"

A moment later, she jumped down and went over to Harris and looked at him, sincerely, in the eyes. "You saved my butt as well!" She said to him as she stared into his eyes. "I know that's your job, but..."

She paused for a moment and grabbed his shirt and kissed him full on the mouth for what seemed to be minutes. Harris was dumbfounded with the kiss presented to him while everyone looked on in shock and surprise. She let go and just turned and walked away. Everyone just stood and didn't move as she went back to the quasit hut. Harris was in a state of shock like everyone else. No one moved as they didn't know what to do next.

Tomas then took it upon himself to break the stalemate. He came out and rang the large iron triangle that broke the hypnotic hold on the group as they entered the mess tent. Harris went in and grabbed a tray of food and took a seat at the head of the table. He didn't know what was for dinner. He didn't care. Diane sat on Harris's left and Arliss on his right, and they silently dug into what nourishment was in front of them. No one said anything as they took their places.

Theodis took a seat at the other end of the table with Mara on his left while Bart and Sarah filled the gaps. Everything was quiet until Tomas stood next to the table.

"I go to holiday next week." He said in his broken English. "You cook yourself until me get back." And then he returned to the kitchen. That bit of news got the conversation going.

"Does anyone here know how to cook?" Arliss asked and then felt a bit sheepish about breaking the silence at their table. A long pause followed.

"I can put something together, depending on what we got," Diane said. "I used to cook for my men when I was married."

"I can, too!" Mara said. "I had five brothers and sisters to deal with at home."

"I can get something together, too," Harris said. "I'll just need to make a call, later." He turned to Arliss. "Does the radio work? I need to call a friend in London."

"Yeah, I got you covered," Arliss said.

The next twenty minutes were full of getting food schedules ready for the next week. Theodis just sat and ate while the conversation went across the table. He wasn't shutting out the conversation. He was trying to remember his mom's western omelette recipe.

They all just went to bed after that and Harris was contemplating talking to Lee more. He just let it go and went to bed. Before he slept, he had one more thought before he turned out the light…" Gina is still a better kisser!"

Chapter 73 – Chef takes a Holiday

Now things were getting a bit back to normal except for the fact that the food schedule was still a bit up in the air. Harris called London to Magdalena who, happily, gave him a couple of her simple recipes. He would have to make some substitutions here and there, but it didn't deter him any.

Everyone took a stab at cooking for the camp. Mara made a bunch of tacos for everyone while Diane made a meatloaf that didn't look great, but the taste was terrific. Arliss just put together something simple. It was called poutine, and it was French fries topped with gravy. It was supposed to have cheese curds as well, but they had none. He made that along with some hamburgers.

Then Harris stepped in and made a lasagne that took all day to put together but was incredible thanks to Magdalena's recipe. Harris remembered it well as it was the first meal he had at the Ravalli's home. Theodis even chipped in with a western omelette meal that his mom made for him and his brothers when they were young.

The odd part came when it came time for Bart and Sarah to cook. They had no clue what to make, and both decided that they would go at it together on this next-to-last day until Tomas was scheduled to come home. They were shocked when they dug into the back of the deep freeze and found a bunch of frozen dinners still in boxes!

"Hang on!" Bart said to Sarah. "We could have been eating this all week instead of all that work and preparation?"

Sarah was equally mad. "Make those and let's finish it!"

They came to dinner when Sarah rang the triangle, and everyone was quite surprised to see meals laid out from boxes in sectional trays sitting in front of them.

"TV dinners?" Theodis asked gruffly. "Where was these?"

"In the back of the deep freeze," Sarah said. "Tomas didn't tell anyone he stocked up before he left."

"…Under my orders!" as Lee came into the mess tent leaning against the tent frame entrance and announced, prepared for this scenario. "What? You don't think I know what's in and out of this place every day?"

Theodis spoke up: "What's the deal Hye Euan? You trying to motivate us by starving us?"

Everyone was a bit angry about it but let the group leader make her case:

"Look, after what we have all been through, I wanted to make sure we could all still function as a group. There have been some terrible events that have happened in the past few months that threatened to rip us apart. You have all gotten through this week stronger and happier than you thought possible. No one starved and food was plentiful. How it was to be served and cooked was all a matter of you all stepping in and making it work. Be proud of yourselves. You all deserve it!"

Then Lee walked over and looked at the trays of microwaved dishes. The food seemed barely edible, and the portions were tiny.

"...and let's face it" Lee continued. "You all deserve better than this. However, this is what you all get today, so dive in." She left them to shrug and just eat what they had while chewing on her "food for thought." At least there were so many frozen dinners left that they all had two and left the rest for tomorrow.

Harris returned to his office and delved back into his books. It looked like he was soon going to go back to Cork, so it was time to get back into his studies. Going back meant taking his place like the other students and return to the facade. He was curious if The Chancellor would want to send him on another trip like this. Hopefully, not too soon.

He stayed up rather than sleep at his regular time and kept reading. He wondered how the others were doing back home. How was Roland holding up without him? Was he still enthralled with his new bride-to-be? What about Gina and her animals? He knew Mum and Da were doing all right since he spoke to them a bit ago when he talked to Magdalena about her recipes. They were doing fine, too. His mind drifted back to all his other mates as well: Rhona, Jasmine, Taylor...

His thoughts were interrupted by a knock on the counter. It was Mara.

'Allo Mara." Harris said. "What's up?"

She seemed to be both embarrassed by her past behaviour and by some other concern.

"Hey, Harris." She said. "Uh, I think I caught something in the jungle. My guts have been in turmoil, lately..."

Harris's hands were in his pockets and not vibrating when he removed them to lead her into the exam room.

He gave her the usual physical examination that a doctor would conduct but found nothing out of the ordinary.

"I think I know the problem, but we're going to need some confirmation."

With that, he gave her a small cup and told her to fill it in the latrine.

She came back a minute or so later with the yellow liquid in a cup with a cap on it. Harris already had his rubber gloves on and placed the special stick into it. Mara just sat on one of the chairs for a few minutes and was, obviously on edge as she chewed her fingernails.

Harris silently examined the test kit and said "Yup" to himself as he went out to talk to her. He just nodded. They both knew what the deal was. She was pregnant. She just looked down at the floor, depressed.

"You have a problem with abortions, Doc?" She said.

Harris did, but that wasn't the more significant issue. "That notwithstanding, I don't have the equipment for it."

She just nodded and was about to leave when Harris asked just out of curiosity.

"Are you going to tell Theodis?" He asked.

"Probably not...and I don't want you to tell him either!" She said sternly.

"I can't." He said. "I have a code of confidentiality with all my patients...and I wouldn't, anyway."

She nodded and was about to leave when she spoke up. "Doc?"

He turned, and she hugged him and felt she overstepped a line and then just left. He took no feeling from it. She was scared and needed a bit of contact. Mara always had the appearance of being tough and street-savvy, but she had the same concerns as anyone else. He then returned to his office and fell asleep while reading the chapter about nervous disorders for the third time.

He then woke up at about 8 am with his legs on his desk and sitting in his chair. Not at all more comfortable than his bed. He heard some excited stirring outside when the jeep horn honked. He then heard footsteps rushing into his office and a hand pounding on the hut wall.

"Doc! Front and centre!" Lee barked out the order as Harris got to his feet and ran out the door. Sarah was next to the jeep along with everyone else gathered around Tomas. The surprise came when Tomas was carrying a young girl in a blue dress with a vomit stain on it. She also seemed to be shivering with chills, and he could feel she had a fever when he put his hand over her head, quickly. It was then that he noticed that she had just one arm. Her left arm and hand were missing from the elbow down.

All were silent, and everyone's eyes were on Harris as they wondered if he could clear this up as he did with Lee. He didn't know about the arm, though. Granted, he once grew back an eye on a vicious Nazi. "OK, hold her," Harris said to Tomas through Lee's translation. He was curious if his ability would allow growing her arm back. His hands were vibrating like mad for the last couple of seconds as he let the light flow into her, and they all watched for the next minute her arm regrow.

"Look at that!" He heard a male voice say but unsure who it was.

First, an arm bone formed out of no place, then nerves covered it, a layer of muscle and then skin. The light faded, the girl stopped shivering and Harris felt her head. No fever. The blood started to pump into the new extremity, apparently as it moved without its host's knowledge.

"I didn't know I had that in me!" Harris said excitedly and a bit of a giggle. He turned to the crowd. "Somebody, bring her some water!" He then shouted as they all looked on in amazement. Mara then stood next to them, holding her canteen and held it as the girl downed it while holding it with her right hand. The container nearly dropped, and the little girl surprised herself by catching it with her restored hand. The reaction was a bit different than Harris expected as she screamed and gasped. She then gazed in amazement at the restored appendage until she calmed down. She went and hugged Tomas "Papa!" She shouted as she showed him her new appendage. Tomas just hugged her for all he was worth. Tomas then went and hugged Harris who wasn't used to all this admiration after what he went through, lately.

Tomas then spoke to Lee, and she translated: "I'll be back later tonight! I have to take my Marisol home." She said to the group. Tomas and his young daughter jumped into the jeep to return to the airport with Sarah behind the jeep wheel.

"Hey Mara," Sarah shouted. "Did you say you needed a lift?" Mara thought for a second and then just gave a dismissive wave. The three of them jumped into the jeep and sped off down the mountain.

Harris noticed Mara and Theodis talking while he was getting pats on the back of appreciation from Arliss, Bart and Diane. Mara then walked up to Harris with Theodis in hand after the crowd left. "Doc, can we borrow your office a minute?"

"Yeah, go on," Harris said as he went to find Arliss.

"Hey man, I need to make a call…" He said.

"Sure Doc, where to?" Arliss asked.

"Ireland," Harris answered. "I want to talk to someone…"

Chapter 74 -Revelation

"Hello?" The voice said over the headphones.

"Hello, stranger. It's me!" Harris said.

"Me? Me who?" The voice asked.

"It's me, Harris!" He said. "Is it that early over there?"

"Whoa!" Roland was now excited. "Harris, mate! Sorry, I didn't expect to hear from you."

"No worries," Harris said. "So how are things back home?"

"Well, I guess about the same." He said. "Tamar and I are getting on all right, but it gets hard to get together sometimes. I have been up to her house, and everyone is better now. No one made any more moves on me. In fact, I think her sister, Bridgette, doesn't like me too much, though…and she tried to get me to take her on their wash machine last Christmas!"

Roland kept talking, which was fine by Harris. All he wanted was to hear some familiar voices right now…

"Hey, talking of that I told our lot that I was getting hitched to Tamar, and now it looks like Taylor and Jazzy are planning to make it permanent!"

"Jazzy and Taylor?" Harris said. "Well, those two were always crazy on each other."

"Oh yeah and get this!" Roland said with a cheek. "McCurdy is out!"

Harris was indifferent as he had no clue what she wanted to do with him at the meeting regarding his fate after the video of his activities surfaced.

"Why?" Harris asked. "What happened?"

"I guess she found out you could do some shady things with the new computers. One of them was engineer bank fraud!" Roland said with his excitement of hot gossip.

"Oh, man!" He said. "Teaching ethics and then that? That's Hypocritical!"

"Yeah, at least!" Roland said. "They don't know how long to give her in the neck for it since it's all new!"

"Oh yeah," Harris said. "That reminds me…"

And with that, Harris told Roland about his hot stock tip that Bart passed on to him a fortnight ago. He already said to his Da to set up an account for him and himself if he wanted. Helmut had the paperwork in his name ready for Harris to sign to make the other account his own, then. Roland wasn't familiar with how to buy stock but promised to do so as his mate never steered him wrong before.

Bart was getting even more excited with whatever it was he found and promised that it was going to revolutionise the world of heart ailments. Harris was still a bit apprehensive but figured he would take the Bostonian at his word, and the most he would be out is £100.

Things were settling down. In less than a month, he would be home again. Gina would be talking about their wedding in between their continued studies. He knew there would be no way that she would give up her dream of becoming a veterinarian. There was no way that he would want her too. Harris also had his studies to masquerade his abilities. He made it clear that everyone there in the camp needed to keep his methods on the QT when they got back.

He took a cup of tea that Tomas made for him, especially and walked by the river. It was serene for a change, and everyone knew the high-water season would be coming soon. The Denka resided where the river, usually would not be a problem and the Garto were used to floods that have been occurring due to regular seasonal shifts. The tribes inhabited the rainforest long enough to understand the river's patterns and turns.

He sat cross-legged next to the flowing waters on a large, dry rock and just listened as Sarah taught him when they were at the bottom of the waterfall. The sound of the river prompted his relaxation enough to put his mind at ease. It wasn't easy to find places like this in Ireland or London.

The library was the closest place, and there wasn't a steady background noise like the sound of the river or the waterfalls. When it was winter, the sound of heat travelling through iron pipes caused knocking and rattling that was distracting to the doctors in training, himself included. His mind was at peace here as the noise of the flowing water sent any anxious feelings downstream.

Hye Euan Lee then approached, and he could feel her presence as she walked over to him due to the stillness and where his mind was. He did not move as she drew nearer to him.

"Harris?" She said. "Everything OK?"

"Yeah, I was just enjoying this place on a new level." He said. "Here, pull up some riverbank."

She sat next to him on the flat rock which seemed to be the only dry place here.

"You meditating?" She asked. He nodded.

"Yeah, I haven't had a moment just to relax, lately," Harris said. "Things are finally calming down. Less than a month, and it'll be back to the real world."

They just sat alone on the bank. Everyone else was passing a makeshift bong made of some leftover piping that Arliss put together. They handed it off to each other in an attempt to make their minds slow around the firepit. The still was not bothered with since Dennis left. No one took notice of the two by the water's edge.

"So, what happens when you go home?" She asked.

"Well, I'll probably go back to school in Ireland, become a doctor and marry my Gina." He said. "I'm amazed things turned out as they did…"

Then Harris filled her in about his flight out of London getting knackered before he came here. He also mentioned the hotel and coming across his former girlfriend by accident.

"So, you aren't engaged yet?" Lee asked.

"She said I could put a ring on her finger when I get home," Harris said. "That's just what I'm planning to do."

"Then you're still a free agent," Lee said as she sat closer to him.

"Well, yeah, I suppose I am for the moment." He said.

She then stood up behind him and wrapped her arms around his neck. Harris didn't react.

"You seem to be jumping at this, quickly," Lee said. "To get back together just like that…"

"Well, we knew each other for years, and we feel it's right." He replied.

"…and yet you broke up." She said.

Harris was about to answer her when she took her arms back.

"I guess it's just me and a bit of jealousy talking." She said. "I just think we Xenons should stick together." And with that, kissed him on the cheek and walked away. He then shrugged it off and went back to his meditations."

Harris wasn't about to join the others around the smoke as he knew how it affected him. He went back to his office and room. Lee making a play for him came as no surprise as they were so close all these months. He put on his short pyjama pants and was about to crawl into his cot with more reading on brain matters as he recounted his words that Lee said to him.

He didn't have a chance to tell her about the meddling of Gina's brother or how they were always crazy about each other despite breaking up and dating others. Harris felt solid in his commitments back home. There was no changing his mind even when Lee said…

Harris's eyes shot wide open, and he sat straight up in his bed, pushing himself out of the cot and didn't bother with his dressing gown as he ran to Lee's door marked "Private" and banged on it. She opened the door calmly with a Mona Lisa smile as he asked...

"What did you mean "WE" Xenons should stick together?"

Chapter 75 - The Last Temptation

She put her hand on his arm and dragged him into her room and took a peek out the door to make sure no one heard what he just said.

Harris only looked in here one other time, and that was after he healed her and a couple of days went by. The room was kind of like his in that it was sparse with only a laughing Buddha with its big belly about a foot tall or so. It was the only decoration with its gold colouring that gave a small bit of liveliness to the drab living space.

"You are the dumbest smart-person I ever met," Lee said with a smile.

"You talked your way out of the Kupuko tribe because you "could" talk to them when no one else…" Harris said as he thought for a moment. "So, truthfully how many languages can you speak?"

"All of them," Lee said with pride. "I was speaking to everyone when I was twelve or so because I could. If someone talked trash to me, I would call them out on it no matter what language they said it in. When I told my Dad about it, he told me what I was and how to deal with it."

That sounded familiar to Harris. He told her his beginnings and what happened with Vincent Ravalli's heart attack and what his father said to him.

She then told him how a group of French girls were laughing at her and calling her a "useless American" in French while she was visiting Paris with her family. She walked over while they were at the Louver giggling under the artwork when she spoke, in their language, how they had no future except as one of "these" models…and they were standing under the Picasso exhibit at the time.

She also described going to Thailand and translating letters and documents in Khmer because the vicious tyrant, Pol Pot killed most of the translators along with the rest of the population in his home country. Language and translations of communications no one else could understand was the family business when they weren't at college. It was a sad reality that no one ever wanted to deal with again.

"Well, let's not discuss that," she said. 'It's just too sad. You seem to have nothing but good things happen to you."

"Everyone has problems." He said as he filled her in about the bombing and the death of a young girl and the saving of a young boy that brought him to Brasil in the first place, due to the video.

"So, here we are then." She said.

"Yup, here we are." He then said.

A moment went by, and they kissed with passion. Harris withdrew with guilt.

"No, I shouldn't be doing this." He said.

"I have no problem with it," Lee said. "If you're worried about birth control..."

"No, I don't mean that!" He said. "It took so long to make things right at home, and I feel like I'm gonna screw it all up..."

She then put her arms around him and said. "No one knows...and no one will."

The embrace was tempting, and the kisses that followed were as well. The cot wasn't that strong. Would it break under their weight in the time that followed? Lee didn't scream or make any noise as they lay naked together while kissing all over themselves and crashing into each other with unrestrained passion. He didn't mind her staying quiet, just not dead!

It wasn't easy to lay side-by-side on the narrow frame after the activities and a shower. Everyone was sleeping off the effects of the weed that grew nearly everywhere in the camp.

They laid blissfully next to each sound asleep until a stray bit of sun hit Harris in the face at sunrise. His hand was tight around her as there was no place else to put it. Her head laid on his chest as she barely moved during the night. The only stirring was her feet jerking a bit during the night as they spooned together.

He sat up in the cot, and his eyes cleared in the unfamiliar room. Strange streaks of light were on the floor, reflecting the little bit of sun that came through the window. He didn't realise why the peculiar patterns appeared on the ground until he stood up from the cot and his feet plunged ankle-deep into cold water. It was everywhere!

"Lee!" He shook her in the cot they shared. "Lee! We got more flooding!" Her eyes shot open to the sight of her floor covered in water.

She got up and threw on some clothes from a box on a stand while Harris sloshed to his room and did the same. The waters even invaded the medical room where bandages and items that were not needed except to masquerade his abilities sat in cardboard containers that were now in the muck. He put on sandals while Lee ran to the iron triangle and sounded the alarm. Everyone was still asleep and unaware of the waters invading the camp until the sound of the big black metal triangle alerted everyone with its distinctive sound.

"Everyone up! Everyone up, we got flooding! Get the saws!" She ran for Arliss's tent where he slept in the back of the workshop, and he stirred when she ran in.

"Arliss!" He screamed. "Get the saws ready!" That got his attention as he jumped up and his feet his calf-deep water as the outbuilding was at a lower ground level. He jumped up and threw on shorts and sandals, and he grabbed his favourite chainsaw, ready to rock!

Everyone else did the same in their tents while Tomas, it seemed didn't return yet. They all piled into the workshop and grabbed power saws not even aware of what they were up against yet. Mara ran out to the middle of the muddy compound from her tent when she got a love-bite from a passing snake.

"OUCH!" She shouted as the marauding viper swam away in the flooded camp. She had no clue what got her other than it left two large puncture holes in her leg. Harris ran to her when he saw that she grabbed her leg in pain. Without a word, Harris blasted light into her left shoulder chest while her right arm. She was fine a few seconds later.

"Now, go and get some water!" Harris shouted. "You'll need it!" and patted her on the other shoulder. Mara thought about just going to the water's edge until her mouth began to feel like a dry sponge. She held on to the power saw and drank straight from the canteen-filling tap near the quasit hut. She re-joined the brigade at their target...and it was massive!

A large pile of logs formed at the same place where the last batch had bottlenecked and clogged the river, but it was different this time. Diane, with a pole and hook in hand, was the first to make the determination. "Those are cut logs! No roots!" The idiots in the mountains had decided to float whole logs down the river instead of trucking them out. If they went one tree at a time and sent down someone to guide them, then it may have worked.

However, there were too many here and going no place without an assist.

Harris, with the most massive chainsaw, charged the pile along with the others as they had done twice before. The risk factor increased as more logs were floating down the river behind the already engorged pile of logs. They all started sawing for all they were worth as the deluge continued. Harris's giant saw led the pack in progress as he cut for all he was worth down the line of lumber clogging the river.

Theodis dropped the pole, took a saw and started cutting along a large log as he was frustrated with the lack of progress shown by the rest. The familiar rattling started, and the rest of the crew got out of the path of logs about to give way except for Harris, who didn't hear the order to back off.

The pile broke away with him still standing on a large log, sawing away while they were shouting at him to move. The dam shifted with him on it, and he found out too late what happens when a river current backed up with tons of lumber gives way. He fell with a massive amount of wood passing above him. When the logs passed, he was still not in sight.

"Harris! Doc!" They all shouted but saw no sign of the young Brit. Theodis then surprised everyone when he grabbed a rope and jumped into the raging waters after the last large log passed. "Theo!" Mara shouted. "What are you doing?" He started kicking the deep water for any sign of life until he saw another batch of logs appear upriver ready to barrel down.

"Pull me in!" He shouted. The lot of them fought the current as he tried to hold the rope for dear life and kick his legs against the current with excruciating pain in both his arm and his bad hip. His focus then changed from trying to find the Doc to just avoiding the onslaught of logs approaching. A couple of dead branches were still stuck in the river bottom and allowed him to kick the pile and try to get back to his crew on dry land. He was losing the fight as the logs were fast approaching when a hand projected out of the river and grabbed Theodis when he accidentally dropped his grip of the rope. The doctor's head surfaced and gasped for air. At the same time, Harris had grabbed the burly baller by the arm, and his healing light kicked in at the same time.

Theodis took the occasion to take a few quick gulps of river water to quench his thirst as the crew tossed the rope again and then drew in the line and tried to pull in the pair. Theodis had a firm hand on the lifeline, but Harris's leg was caught underwater on a thick branch which kept him from moving. He let go of Theodis and shouted "Go!" to the lot pulling him to shore.

Harris attempted to loosen his leg underwater from the threatening branch. Theodis was back onshore and tied the other end of the rope around himself, making him the anchor. They all threw the line to Harris, and he caught it with one hand. He was still, however, snagged by the branch underwater. He began to hate trees!

While he was working out his leg, another grouping of logs came floating downriver. Harris's leg was finally free of the hidden branches, and the camp residents began the process of dragging him to shore. They were standing calf-deep in the river as the current tried to pull them into deeper waters with the logs quickly approaching. If he held on to the rope, his friends would be crushed by the approaching logs, themselves.

"Dammit!" He thought. He had no choice.

He released his grasp and floated down the river rapids to the fading screams of his friends as they ran back to shore to avoid the next onslaught of logs. The river current slammed Harris into rocks and debris on the way to the ultimate destination.

He then felt a moment of weightlessness when he went over the waterfall. The feeling ended way too early as he hit the water across where Sarah taught him meditation a couple of months before. The pressure of the water and the weight of all the logs that followed had plunged him deep into the depths at the bottom of the falls.

All went black.

Chapter 76 – Exit

A few of them jumped into the jeep and started down the mountain. Sarah couldn't go too fast, or she would end up killing her passengers, that being Lee, Theodis and Bart. Arliss was on the radio back at camp trying to raise a search party in the area.

Mara just felt useless sitting alone in the mess tent. Diane came in feeling about the same. She just sat with her on the other side of the table. Neither said anything. All they could do was sit and try to figure out what went wrong. Mara went over to the woman and held Diane as a daughter would cling to her mom. Both cried at the loss of their friend.

Arliss raised a search party from the constabulary. They would drag the river from down the Amazon to the falls. Sarah led them to the base of the falls where she and Harris meditated and swam after the loss of Dennis a couple of months ago. They walked down the path several times even yelling out "Harris! Where are you?" in a futile attempt to locate their lost colleague.

There was a large pile of logs at the base of the falls along with rocks and debris along the path but no sign of the young Xenon. The contention was that at the bottom of that massive pile of wreckage and sticks, Harris was buried under it all.

Lee had to go back to the airfield. When the pilot landed, he refuelled the Piper Cub and was sent back into the air to follow the path of the river in the hopes of finding some sign of life. Meanwhile, she radioed Rio and talked to Juan Montoya. His words to her were biting:

"Hye Euan Lee, am I to understand that you lost another doctor?"

She went on to explain what happened and that it wasn't her fault. The blame had to be placed on the scumbags that didn't take into account the river's tendency to flood when jammed up to save a buck. The foreman of the lumber company was later charged with…something. It made no difference. The damage was done.

The distress calls then followed the chain. Juan Montoya told Chancellor Ian Rosewood of what happened. He then explained it to the board at The Royal University of Medicine where Ian told Roland of Harris's demise, personally.

He broke down in tears for hours before leaving for Christmas break. It was equally heart-breaking for Tamar as well. They were close friends ever since they met.

Lee wrote the letter that no team leader ever wants to write for the second time that year:

Dear Dr and Mrs Gibraltar,

It is with sincere regret that I must inform you of your son, Harris has gone missing in the Brasilian

rainforest. Harris was helping clear logs during a flood when he was swept away by the river waters while

assisting another camp party member get back to shore.

We fear he was swept over a waterfall and went missing afterwards in the flood debris. There have been

extensive efforts to find him but no trace as of yet. I'm afraid we are left to fear the worst in this situation...

The news was gutting to the young Xenon's parents.

They had no actual body to return. Just personal effects. Harris's doctor bag, stethoscope, reflex hammer, broken Walkman and cassette tapes…All the things he had to keep him going in life as well as his notes and books.

The news also came as particularly awful to The Ravalli's household. Father Victor was in tears when he took the call by phone. Gina received the news at Queen Anne's College in Bristol. She took it extraordinarily hard and cried for days.

There was a memorial held at St. Peter's Cathedral that was Gibraltar's family church forever. The place was quiet and crowded as many from the College in Ireland made the trip including Roland and Tamar and even Bruce Bartleby who was now working as a reporter for The Belfast Telegraph.

Taylor and Jasmine also showed along with Rhona Haberl and her father, Edmund. Chancellor Rosewood also showed up in the audience of the mourners along with his wife, June. Vincent and Magdalena Ravalli, along with Victor. The one missing from all this was Gina. Helmut and Jean were a bit saddened that the one person that inspired Harris so much was not there.

Jane and Wendy showed up as well, and Harris's Uncle Thomas flew in from New York. Doctor Guiteau cut short his trip to Sydney, Australia where he was attending a psychiatric conference to make the occasion.

Hye Euan Lee was there as well but stayed in the last pew of the church. She didn't know how well-received her presence would be, so she kept to herself in the back of the church.

Oddly enough, two other people took a seat in the back, and they also sought anonymity. That being an older man with a German accent and his friend, a French woman with black and grey hair. The pair seemed to materialise out of nowhere. They started a short conversation in three different languages where the moniker, "Xenon" was spoken and mixed in the conversation.

Father Ponsonby Derry gave a heartfelt welcome to all who showed. The number of friends and family that Harris had was a testament to his all-too-short life. They swapped stories of his antics at the college, his early days in London and the friends he made on the way.

Roland gave an emotionally-jarring obituary to his best friend. "Being with him was life-changing. There are things that wouldn't have happened without his presence, and I couldn't thank him enough. He was there when I met my father, my fiancé'… I was there when he was almost killed. He just shook it off and kept going. He was amazing!"

He also said that there were some things he would not divulge, but he was appreciative of his "brother from another mother." He became too full of emotion near the end to continue. Tamar could barely speak and didn't try. They went and hugged Harris's parents which was the first time they met in the flesh. It was unfortunate that it had to be here.

Taylor went up and said that he was thankful for the help Harris gave in assisting with his homework and how he enjoyed his company. Jasmine did the same and gave a few words of a blessing in her home tongue. Only Lee knew the words she spoke. They moved her to tears in that back pew.

Chancellor Rosewood gave the only honour he could bestow on Harris right now. He gave him full accreditation and that he would be presented, posthumously, with the full title of "Doctor."

Vincent went up and thanked Harris profusely for allowing him to continue to live. He also said that if he could give his life for him, he would as Harris gave him his back. Magdalena gave similar praise and apologised for Gina's absence. Gina did send words that she was always in love with Harris and that her love for him would never die.

They concluded with a hymn, and those who wanted to visit his memorial marker could do so at Chelsea Garden Cemetery two streets down. Most started making the trek to the memorial garden that hosted several nameplates on marble blocks after they sang the last chorus.

Victor was not among those walking there as he ran to the memorial before the benediction and the final hymn. Without Harris's assistance, running or anything else on foot would have been uncomfortable, if not impossible. He entered the mausoleum and there, sitting by herself across from Harris's marker was Gina in a black dress with matching gloves and a black hat with a veil covering her tearful eyes.

Her brother went up to her and told her the crowd was heading there now and that he would fetch them a cab. She said she would be right along.

"I should have never let you go." She said softly to Harris's brass nameplate:

Dr Harris Unger Nickolas Gibraltar

B. 1968

D. 1990

"Without forgiveness, there is only death."

She kissed her hand covered with a black glove and laid it on the marker. The only kiss she could give.

"I'll always love you, dear," Gina said, sadly. "…And I will always have part of you with me." She then strolled down the mausoleum hall and out the door to join her brother in a taxi to return to their childhood home.

The odd gait she walked with would disappear in a couple of months.

Chapter 77 - New Beginnings

On 10 May 1991, the sounds of happy shouts came from the hut in a part of the Amazonian rainforest which only the Kupuko Tribe knew how to access. The yelling to be heard by all in this part of the forest was passed from tribesman to tribesman. Everyone working in the village, swimming in the river or walking the forest paths stopped what they were doing to go to the main hut and see a new attraction.

There was Likuko with her new-born baby suckling at his mom's breast while the two laid in a hammock. He was the first baby born in the village in over two years as the tribe figured they can have children again now that the plague had passed when the mysterious white man saved them from extinction.

Every member of the tribe went to the baby to touch it while giving a blessing of "Aw Ku Ta" when they felt the new-born boy's head.

The mother was the first to say to him "Aw Ku Ta." Then the father, Shu Nata, spoke: "Aw Ku Ta."

Every child in the village who survived the brutal plague came up to the new-born boy and put their hand on the child: "Aw Ku Ta." They said one at a time.

Every elder of the tribe spoke the blessing: "Aw Ku Ta." With their hands laid on the infant one after the other...

Every other woman in the tribe: "Aw Ku Ta."

Every other man in the tribe: "Aw Ku Ta."

The recovered patients from the edge of death in the quarantine hut gave their blessing of "Aw Ku Ta."

Finally, a Caucasian hand from an outsider touched the new-born:

"Aw Ku Ta." The outsider clothed only in paint and leaves said as his hand glowed and a bright white beam projected into the new-born baby's head.

The End of Book One...But this ain't over yet!

Made in the USA
Middletown, DE
10 January 2020

82948913R00194